Allie Burns grew up in Kent where she now lives with her husband, two energetic children and a couple of laidback tortoises. She has an MA in Professional Writing from Falmouth University. She is also the author of *The Lido Girls*.

Also by Allie Burns

The Lido Girls

The Land Girl

ALLIE BURNS

ONE PLACE. MANY STORIES

HQ
An imprint of HarperCollins*Publishers* Ltd
1 London Bridge Street
London SE1 9GF

This paperback edition 2018

First published in Great Britain by
HQ, an imprint of HarperCollins*Publishers* Ltd 2018

ISBN: 9780008310097

MIX
Paper from
responsible sources
FSC® C007454

This book is produced from independently certified FSC™ paper
to ensure responsible forest management.

For more information visit: www.harpercollins.co.uk/green

Printed by CPI Group (UK) Ltd, Croydon CR0 4YY

For Dylan and Evie

Chapter One

March 1915

Emily held her breath as she stood at the top of the stairs. When she was sure it was safe she tiptoed down, which was not that easy in her brother John's work boots, even with the gap in the toes stuffed with balled-up newspaper.

The muffled chatter from her mother's knitting party flooded the hallway. She quickened her pace to reach the safety of the door that led through to the kitchen, only to narrowly avoid colliding with Daisy – the housemaid – and a platter of crustless sandwiches. They greeted one another and before Emily could remind her, Daisy nodded and said, 'Don't worry, I haven't seen you.'

Emily opened the back door and the dazzling sunlight caressed her skin. She would have to make it up to Mother later because she couldn't sit in that stifling sitting room, knitting socks for the soldiers at the Front when the sun shone.

'By the way,' Emily called back to Daisy who was straightening out the sandwiches again. 'Did you leave this on my pillow?' She waved a newspaper cutting that she'd found on her bed in an envelope addressed to her.

Daisy shook her head. 'I found it on the doormat, hand delivered.'

Emily shrugged. She would thank whoever the sender was when they made themselves known.

Outside, she leant back against the scullery door, and admired the plump, carefree clouds, shifting their shapes and rushing onwards against the backdrop of the heavenly blue sky.

She held up the notice cut from the *Standard*, reading it slower this time to take it in. Her heart began to thump.

Women on the Land

Highly trained women of good birth and some country-bred women, hitherto working in service, or in trade, will make themselves useful in any way on a farm to gain experience.

May we make known that we wish to hear from farmers, market gardeners and others wanting the services of women for work on the land.

The notice went on to say that educated girls would act as a shining example to village and city girls – encourage them out in their numbers to do their bit for the war effort.

But whoever posted this through the door must know that she wasn't 'highly trained' in anything other than English literature, and that wasn't an easy situation to fix. She did spend far more time on the farm and outdoors than was usual for a girl like her, as Mother was always reminding her, but that didn't mean she could turn her hand to farming so easily; she'd need to be trained and the notice in the *Standard* said that took six weeks.

She couldn't in all good conscience leave her Mother to attend a course. Mother hardly slept and was afraid to be left alone since Father had died two years ago, and it was even worse now Emily's older brother, John, had received his officer commission, turning Mother a ghastly pale whenever the delivery boy came up the path.

2

At the tool shed, she lifted Mr Flitwick's hoe and carried it back to the kitchen garden – humming to herself while she worked. She tilled three neat rows width-ways in the fine, crumbly soil of the raisedbed. Mr Flitwick, their gardener, had generously given the bed over to her and her experiments, along with access to his stash of seeds. She came out here when Mother thought she was resting, reading or writing letters. It was a secret between her and the few trusted staff, and her little winged friends. She scattered the black dots, buried and then sprinkled them with water from the can.

'Hello there,' she said to her usual companion, a robin, who watched her from his favourite spot on the espaliered pear tree that spread its arms out along the wall. 'I see what you see.' She lightly pinched the flailing worm that she'd exposed with her hoeing, scooped a hole with the bare fingers of her other hand and tucked the worm inside, blanketing him with the soft soil. 'I'm afraid you'll have to find your own afternoon tea,' she told the robin. 'My crops need this one.'

The bird whistled back at her, probably an admonishment for not doing as she was bid.

Emily started as Edna, the cook-general, opened the door.

'The mistress is asking where you are,' Edna said. 'She was expecting you to join her and her guests.'

Emily contemplated her boots – John's boots – her mud-lined fingernails, the hem of her skirts that had been steeped in the soil and were now a sepia brown. She would usually dash upstairs, clean, change her clothes and be back down in the sitting room knitting, awaiting Mother's approving nod. But the newspaper article had fired her up, given her dreams a shape, and now she simply couldn't bear to be parked on a sofa cushion while the conversation drifted around like pregnant rain clouds.

'Could you say I have a headache? It's a lot to ask, but I'd let her down if I went in there today.'

And if it was anything but knitting ... Mother's stitches were always perfect and uniform; Emily's always to large and loose. 'The men will have cold feet wearing those,' Mother would say. Always pointing to the spot where Emily had dropped a stitch. And as for the yarn, it went on forever; no matter how many hole-filled pairs of socks she made, no matter how many stitches she dropped, or how unevenly they grew, the yarn kept on coming.

As she wiped her brow with her sleeve the sun came out from behind a cloud, rooting her to the spot. She sighed. How on earth would she ever persuade Mother? When Father was alive he'd wanted nothing more than for the HopBine Estate and its four-hundred-acre farm to be the epicentre of village life. He'd dreamt of the family living the rural idyll that he'd moved them out of London to enjoy.

She'd asked once, when Father was alive, if she could take a course at a horticultural college. Lots of educated women were doing it, and Mother hadn't objected then. She'd even believed it would be good for Emily to follow her dreams. Now, Mother's frown made her shrink inside. Things had changed. A good marriage and being a dutiful daughter – those were the things Mother wanted from her now.

The gate out of the walled kitchen garden led to the lawns. The sitting room, and Mother, overlooked those very same lawns. So, Emily cut around to the front of the house and then raced across the gravel drive, and through the gap in the hedge before the cedar avenue that took her into the paddock that joined HopBine House to its farm. The paddock usually housed Mother's stallion Hawk. The other horses had been requisitioned, but Hawk was old and Mother's dearest companion – though she'd not ridden him since Father had his heart attack.

Today, however, the field had a different guest. She placed her boots carefully now, as if she were sneaking down the hallway again, to keep a safe distance from Lily, a tetchy heifer. Lily had lost her first calf by trampling it, possibly an accident – Mr Tipton the farm's manager wasn't sure – so the cow was being given a

4

second chance and being grafted with a spare twin. Mr Tipton was pleased with how it had gone so far. The new calf had nursed from Lily last night, although Lily had been unsettled and hence she and the calf had been separated from the rest of the herd.

Lily snorted at Emily now, warning her to keep her distance. Emily didn't need to be told twice.

A third of the way down the paddock, she snuck inside the foliage of a low-growing Turkey oak. Its web of trunks close to the ground offered low-hanging, gnarly, twisted arms; the perennial leaves offered a canopy, while the other trees were just warming up for spring. The ground was dotted with scraggy grass tufts like brushes. A crow batted the air as it took off.

She climbed, weaving her way up, until she could peep through the branches to enjoy the view of the HopBine Estate. To think, she might be working by Father's side now, but it wasn't to be. Neither Father, nor his dreams, had survived.

With another sigh, she took in the view of the church tower and Perseverance Place in the dip. Father had built the labourers' cottages there shortly after HopBine House was finished. Beyond them was the crumbling old paper mill down by the orchards next to the stream, and then the villas belonging to the new countrymen, which lit up a previously darkened village enclave, then Hangman's Wood and fields all the way to the coast. There the submarine-infested channel lay, and on the other side of that, France and Belgium being torn apart by the war.

Right in front of her, at the bottom of the enclosure was the farmyard, where the chickens bustled about, clucking. Behind the yard were orchards full of apple, cherry and cob trees, hop gardens and other meadows for the sheep and cows.

Two women she recognised from the village caught her attention. Olive Hughes the wheelwright's wife and Ada Little the blacksmith's wife hurried over a stile to the right of her. Lily's new calf was on its own at the farmyard boundary, while Lily herself was higher up the paddock. The cow stamped a warning hoof at Olive and Ada who were now a wedge between the mother and her adopted baby.

The two women were in such a rush that they hadn't even noticed. What on earth were they thinking, getting in between a cow and her calf?

'Watch out!' Emily called from the tree, causing Olive to start and let out a yelp. Lily turned her head, looking directly at the village women. 'Mad cow on the loose!' The cow snorted. Ada screamed. She tried to smother it with her hand, but it was too late – she had startled Lily.

The cow was slow away, heavy and lolloping, but within a few strides it was clear she was picking up pace. She was running down the hill, her head high as she charged down, homing in on her targets.

Emily dropped from the tree with a thud. 'Stand your ground,' she called to the women. Ada took no notice, turned on her heels and ran like the clappers back towards the stile. Olive, meanwhile, remained rooted to the spot, mouth agape, whimpering.

Lily dropped her chin to her chest, took a deep breath and sprinted. Olive would be trampled if Emily didn't do something. Lily was fast, her size deceptive. Emily's boots thumped down the paddock. She bent to pick up a stick, didn't drop her pace, and then she reached Olive and stood between her and Lily, facing the cow down.

'She's going to flatten us!' Olive cried.

'Run like stink,' Emily yelled, her breath coming thick and fast. 'Don't look back and don't stop until you're over the stile.' Olive hesitated, her eyes darted back and forth, torn between saving her own skin and leaving Emily there. But there wasn't time to think it through – Emily pushed her away. 'Go!' she cried.

As the footsteps and the whimpering receded, it was just the two of them: Emily and Lily. Emily spread her feet wide, waved the stick at the cow, stretching out her other arm to make herself as large as possible.

6

'Now, girl,' she shouted, her heart pounding as violently as Lily's hooves. The thud, thud grew louder; the ground even shook.

Behind her came a scream that carried through the air. Emily ignored the hysterics, and kept on waving the stick.

'Look, you daft beast, the calf is safe. It's just me. You know me. We'll both die if you don't stop.'

She stared into Lily's eyes, willed them to have a better sight than the cow had been born with, that Lily might recognise Emily before it was too late. The beast was a matter of feet away now, thundering closer. She glanced at the stile; she should have run with Olive, she wouldn't make it in time now. She waved the stick, close enough now to make out her spidery eyelashes. She held her other hand aloft and expelled a deep guttural yell that echoed and reverberated through her whole body, making her shake, waiting, waiting for the impact, and to be biffed by Lily's head from here to next Thursday.

As Lily's nuzzle reached Emily's palm, the cow stopped, dead. Emily relaxed her hand and patted the cow's nose as Lily panted. So did Emily, her heart boom, booming in her ears. Lily nudged Emily's hand out of the way, her round gelatinous eyes close to Emily's, then her fleshy tongue dragged itself across her face. Emily giggled.

'That tickles, Lily,' she said, scratching playfully at the sparse fur above the cow's nose. Lily mooed in appreciation.

'It's wonderful to see you look after your new calf, Lily,' she said, backing away now, but still facing the cow. Still holding the stick aloft, she took careful, steady strides back, and back, until finally she gripped the solid surface of the stile, and hopped to safety.

Emily took a deep breath; her heart was just about settling down now.

'Well, that was close.' She leant over the stile to catch her breath. Lily had forgotten all about her charge already, she glanced over at the innocent calf and chewed her cud, watching them with a

7

disinterested gaze. 'Are you both all right?' she asked the women.

Both of them had been struck dumb by the whole event.

'Th-thank you, Miss Cotham,' Olive Hughes said in the end, and Ada then found her voice too.

'How did you do that? How could you be sure that the cow would stop?'

'I couldn't,' Emily confessed. 'Be careful next time. If she can trample her own calf to death, she won't think twice about flattening you.'

Just as she was about to find out what the women had been running from in the first place, dear old Mr Tipton waddled around the edge of the paddock, waving his finger at the women and shouting something that Emily couldn't quite make out.

The two women gawped at one another, thanked Emily again and shot off in the opposite direction to Mr Tipton.

Emily waited, trying to hide her amusement from Mr Tipton at his pink-faced exertion. When he caught her up he tipped his brown felt hat. But as Olive Hughes and Ada Little disappeared over the horizon he put his hands on his hips and kicked a clod of soil with his crusty old boots.

'Whatever is going on, Mr Tipton?' she asked him.

'Those two are skiving off again.'

'Mrs Hughes and Mrs Little?' she asked, confused as to what they might be skipping.

'Aye. Those two are what the Board of Trade calls help. I'm supposed to have the same yields from the farm even though my men are all gone, and in their place, they've sent me two village women who run off whenever my back's turned.'

'You need a supervisor for your new workers, Mr Tipton,' she said.

'Women,' Mr Tipton said with a shake of his head, as if he hadn't heard her. 'No disrespect to you, Miss Cotham, but we're never going to win this war if we have to rely on the likes of those two. The government's lost leave of its senses if it thinks it's so.' He put his hands together in a prayer. 'Please Lord, don't send me any more of your women,' he said, face upturned to the heavens, before he trudged back to the farm.

That was another thing the person who sent her the newspaper notice didn't realise. She could be as highly trained as any man, but Mr Tipton would never view her as anything other than the owner's daughter.

Chapter Two

April 1915

She marched across the lawn on her way back from the farm. She'd start with Mother, simply show her the newspaper notice from the *Standard* and explain how she needed to take the training so that she could help Mr Tipton keep the women in order. They owned the farm, and as the family depended on its profits she might just see it as a solution. It was wildly optimistic. Her pace slowed as she pictured Mother frowning as she read the article.

Once she reached the terrace her courage began to fail her. Mother's knitting-party guests stood at the floor-length sitting room windows. There were two smaller figures – her mother one of them, the other most probably Norah Peters, the village solicitor's wife. And there was a woman with a stout gait, which must belong to Lady Radford from Finch Hall. Members of the titled upper class like the Radfords and the industrial middle class like the Cothams mingled frequently in the countryside, which was a shame because Lady Radford was at their house far too often and always telling Mother how to think.

At the French door, Emily muttered, *oh dear*. The stout hips weren't Lady Radford's at all. Neither was Norah Peters standing beside Mother. Instead, a clean-shaven, smart young man in a suit, and an older woman, wearing one of the widest brimmed and heavily feathered hats Emily had ever seen, waited with smiles on their faces. Mother glared at her daughter's muddy and torn skirts and her brother's large work boots protruding from beneath her soggy hem.

She remembered then: it hadn't been a knitting party at all. It was afternoon tea with Mother's friend's son. It was another of the faceless young men from good families that Mother kept inviting for her to meet – someone who might take care of the both of them. His family were something in construction, middle-class industrialists like them, but he was in banking. Would this one be any more interesting than the others? They were always a little cold, and distant, superior even, and their favourite subject was usually themselves.

'Goodness me, Emily!' Mother exclaimed, as she opened the door, blocking Emily's path. 'Your head is much better then?' Behind her, Daisy bit her lip and pretended to focus on replenishing the teacups. Emily pulled an errant leaf from her hair and straightened her skirt.

'I always said that the expression "being dragged through a hedge backwards" was custom-made for you.' Mother's voice was false, raised with an edge to it that kept up appearances whilst telling Emily she'd be in for it later.

'Use the back entrance, dear,' Mother said with a steel and tightness in her tone that only Emily could detect. 'Smarten up and then you may join us.'

Emily tried to smooth some of her hair back into its chignon, but so much had fallen loose it was hopeless; just like her. What had she been thinking, running off to the farm like that? No wonder Mother was never satisfied with her.

In her bedroom, she made an extra effort to smarten up. She put on a hideously frilly dress that Mother liked best, shook her hair loose and tugged the brush through it again and again until it had the sheen of a sweet chestnut. Then she backcombed and pulled her locks over a pad to create a respectable, curved pompadour. For the finishing touch, she lifted a fuchsia-coloured camellia bloom from the vase on her dresser and tucked it behind her ear.

Downstairs, the man, whose name she couldn't remember despite Mother having talked about him all week, had left the women to talk and was on the terrace admiring the view.

'Lovely day,' he said, as she approached him. He was quite handsome, she supposed. It was his nose that spoiled him; it was too big for the rest of his face, though his ears were in proportion with the nose, which was something.

'Oh, it really is,' Emily said.

He stood so at ease with his hands in his trouser pockets that HopBine could have been his own home. He seemed quite comfortable with the silence. Then he pointed up to the roof.

'You've some tiles missing, and the guttering is in a bad way.'

'Thank you,' she said, sneering at him as he turned away. 'We're aware the house needs some repairs. My brother is away at the Front at present, so our priorities have changed. You work in banking, I understand,' she said. 'Is that interesting? A challenge?' She was talking too fast. It happened when Mother was watching her. The pauses between words evaporated making them all slide together into a chaotic jumble. 'I can't say I know much about money, or investments.' Her mouth really was running away from her. She should be quiet, adopt some of his detached, confident demeanour.

She checked over her shoulder. The women were talking, but Mother's gaze was resolutely on her daughter. She gestured for Emily to remove the bloom from behind her ear.

'No, I don't suppose you do,' he said, not without a hint of superiority. 'It takes a certain level of skill and education to master the markets.'

Her back straightened at his condescension. She twirled the camellia between her thumb and forefinger, before lifting her head and capturing him in her gaze. 'I've always regarded the world of finance to be a little soulless. And you are helping to confirm my theory that people who enjoy the company of numbers are insentient beings themselves.'

'Oh, …' he said, breaking eye contact. 'Well, let me assure you that isn't the case at all.'

'No? Perhaps your remarks don't represent you well.'

He concentrated on the horizon, but she continued to study him fixedly, let him bathe in the discomfort. He found something of interest on the concrete floor of the terrace. His hair flopped forwards to obscure his oversized nose. She paused a while longer, let the silence hang between them and then checked the window. Mother's gaze was still trained on her; probably trying to read her daughter's lips. She shouldn't be picking arguments.

'Do you play tennis often?' She dropped the pink bloom to the ground, slipping into the polite patter expected in these circumstances. But the chap was frowning, he hadn't liked being told off by a young woman.

He told her he didn't, no, he was training to fight a war, and then he excused himself and slipped back in to the safety of the older women's conversation, slamming the French door harder than was necessary, and trampling on the camellia's petals. She hesitated before following him in. Mother's expression was granite-edged. There was nothing she could do about it but limit the damage, which for now meant she would keep her newspaper clipping to herself.

*

When she found Mother in the sitting room after the guests had gone later that evening, she caught her reading a letter, a smile on her face. As Emily crossed the threshold, Mother hastily balled the letter up, stuffed it in her pocket and lifted the knitting from her lap.

'You didn't mention that you'd had some post,' she said wondering which brother it might be from. 'Cecil or John?'

'What?' Mother's cheeks coloured. 'No, no, neither.'

It should have been cosy in the sitting room. Daisy had cleverly used their scant coal supplies to time the fire to perfection for the early evening, but there was a persistent chill in Emily's spine.

'I caught two of Mr Tipton's volunteers in trouble on the farm earlier on,' Emily said before Mother could mention the mess she'd made of the house call. Lawrence, as it turned out he was called, had shown no interest in wanting to hear from her again. No one would ever ask *her* what she thought about him. It didn't matter. All that mattered was the impression *she* made, while the men could be as rude as they liked.

'If I hadn't been there to rescue them, Mrs Hughes and Mrs Little might have been trampled to death by Lily,' she continued.

'I wonder ...' Mother said looking up.

'Yes?'

'If Cecil might be able to come home from Oxford when John is next on leave. Wouldn't it be nice to have the boys back together?'

'I suppose it would, yes,' she replied. 'We could have a Christmas celebration for John – he'd like that, to mark the one he missed.' It would be wonderful to see John again, he always listened when she told him about her adventures on the farm.

'Good idea,' Mother said. Emily paused for a moment to savour the rare praise. She smiled. Mother's eyes glistened, a sure sign she was thinking up ideas of what they could do for John on his next leave. Perhaps this was her moment. She took a deep breath, rummaged inside her pocket for the newspaper article. Just as she was lifting it out, Mother changed the subject.

'Despite what happened today, all is not lost. I told Lawrence's mother that you'd write to him when he gets his first commission.'

'Would Lawrence like that?' Emily asked. He'd hardly said another word to her once he'd been back inside the sitting room.

'Why ever not?' Mother smiled to herself as she began a new row. Emily's stomach tightened; Mother mustn't have false hope. Lawrence had probably already forgotten about her, and she would gladly forget about him.

She may as well get it out of the way. She reached inside her pocket and handed Mother the article, flattening it out for her. Mother reluctantly gave up her knitting, held the piece of paper to the lamplight.

'I suppose if they train up these educated girls they'll soon bring the likes of Olive Hughes and Ada Little under control.'

'Exactly.' So, Mother had been listening to her after all, but Mother handed her back the piece of paper and resumed her knitting. She hadn't understood the relevance of Emily handing her the announcement.

'The thing is, Mother, I wonder, could it be me? I love the outdoors and—'

'You?' Mother said. 'Do you mean go off on a training course? And how much will that cost? We're already paying for your brother's officer commission; his mess fees won't pay themselves.'

'They would pay me,' she said.

Mother pinched her nose. 'I have enough to worry about with your brother away at the Front, and with conscription looming I might end up with both sons fighting.'

The reply would have been the same no matter what she'd said. Many of her old school friends had answered the call for nurses, canteen supervisors, ambulance drivers, tram conductresses, even policewomen. Lady Radford was now the commandant of the hospital she'd set up in her home, Finch Hall, the village's big manor house. Clara Radford, the same age as Emily, was the assistant for goodness' sake. Her ambition was humble in comparison; she only wanted to help out on their family's estate.

'Even if I were to work here on our own farm?'

'Even then.'

Mother glanced up from her knitting. 'Don't look at me like that. It isn't right for you, an educated girl with an Oxford Board School Certificate, to be a labourer. On land we own as well. No, no, no. Not when you're in the market for a decent husband.'

'Lady Clara is of higher standing than us, and she's working,' Emily argued. 'I would be able to live here, and I could work part-time hours so you aren't on your own.'

Mother tossed her knitting to her lap and raised a hand to her head. 'What did I do to deserve such a difficult daughter? I turn a blind eye to you wallowing about in the soil in the kitchen garden. Yes, don't think I don't realise. Climbing trees – I see you doing that, a girl of nearly twenty, of marriageable age, up a tree in her best clothes. Tailing Mr and Mrs Tipton around, making a nuisance of yourself on the farm, when I have other, more important, things to worry about and need a daughter as a companion while she finds a husband and supports me through a difficult time.'

'I only want to do my bit for the war.'

They knitted in silence. The war was choking her, making her life smaller. Emily dropped a stitch and in the act of trying to pick it up a second loop of wool had slid from her needle point.

Emily paused while Mother dug the tip of her needle into a new stitch. 'Is this what you were daydreaming about when you lost your self-control and made inconsiderate and hurtful remarks to Lawrence?' Mother said.

Emily groaned, threw the knitting needles clattering to the floor.

'Emily Cotham,' Mother exclaimed. 'He is a very charming chap, who offers a prospective wife a comfortable life, perhaps with your own garden to tend. The sort of chap who takes care of his mother and would do the same for his mother-in-law. But instead you tried to belittle him.'

'He was rude first,' she began, but stopped herself before she made things worse. Mother was right: she had been trained to show better character than she had today. The newspaper article had fired her up, but she should have shown restraint and not retaliated. Mother was only trying to help and now she was being ungrateful.

'I hope when you write to him you show him more interest, and gratitude for what he's doing for the country.'

'Of course. But would you at least agree to think about me doing some war work?'

'We have pressing issues closer to home to tend to.'

What could be more pressing than putting food on the table, and keeping their own farm productive and running? The movement was growing. The newspaper had spoken of a land army for women; the need for girls like her was growing and she wouldn't give up.

'Please?' she asked. Shouldn't her mother be proud of her?

'Oh dear, your whining is giving me a migraine. I think you overestimate the extent of what you might do. You're not very strong – there's nothing of you and no one will take you seriously if you're smaller than them. Mr Tipton will laugh you off the land.' Mother's withering look and cutting words made her head bow. She couldn't bring herself to say another thing in response to that.

Emily picked up the heel stitches with her needle, a task that could make her distracted by something as benign as the ticking clock, but worse still, she inspected the whole sock; she'd made a mistake when casting off the toes. She couldn't go back and correct it now. She toyed with the idea of throwing the knitting onto the fire and letting it burn. She grabbed the newspaper cutting, folded it back in her pocket and clomped up the stairs. Mother didn't even look up or show that she'd noticed Emily's display of frustration.

In her room, she stopped herself from slamming the door shut. Mother always reduced her to a child, and each time she reciprocated with childish behaviour. She must learn to not yearn for her Mother's approval or affections because it was futile of her to hope for them. She couldn't help herself and slammed the door shut anyway, not caring if she was nearly twenty. If she was going to be treated like a child, why not behave like one?

She slid down the wall and sat with her back to the bedroom door and flicked through the newspaper.

Corporal Williams, fighting for King and country in Flanders, seeks a well-bred country lady for correspondence and conversation and tales from our green and pleasant land.

Well, Corporal Williams. She'd be delighted to write and tell him all about this pleasant land, and it would be jolly nice to correspond with someone who was interested in what she had to say.

Chapter Three

Dearest Emily,

I am so pleased that you decided to write to me. You are quite right that we are in need of good cheer from home. I miss Yorkshire, and the dales more than I can put into words.

Thank you for telling me all about HopBine Estate – it is clear that the place is very dear to you.

I can't say too much because of the censor, but I can tell you that we're stationed up the line, billeted in a barn at the moment. There are no boards so we sleep on the ground, and with no fire it is terribly cold at night.

I admire your desire to work; don't give up on it.

Fondest wishes

Theo Williams

She didn't have to wait long in the evening for Mother to retire to bed. Once the light had disappeared from beneath her bedroom door, Emily crept down the hallway and out through the back door.

There was no moon and a chilly breeze blew across the open fields and straight down her neck. She couldn't go back for a lantern in case she disturbed Mother.

At the edge of the driveway, she stopped to admire her home; cream coloured, and square, it glowed a little in the shade of darkness. It had three pitched gables. Her late father had designed and built the house when he'd moved the family to the country to set up the cement works. Father had built one gable for each of his children. Those gables sheltered each of their bedrooms and protected them from the rain and wind. But the missing tiles and loose guttering that Lawrence had noticed made their situation now an open secret.

She entered the cedar avenue that lined the long drive down to New Lane and then it was a short walk to the farmhouse. All of the lights were hidden behind curtains and blinds and pulled tight in case of a night-time visit from a Zepp. Even the candles on the makeshift shrine at the edge of the village green had been extinguished.

But it didn't matter, she could find the way in the deepest of dark nights.

In the low-ceilinged farmhouse kitchen, she found Mr Tipton stroking Tiger, the tomcat, on his lap. The farm manager was halfway through a story to Mrs Tipton.

'Oh do go on,' Emily urged him, presenting Mrs Tipton with some bluebells that she'd picked in Hangman's Wood earlier that morning. 'You know how I love your stories.' He had a wonderful imagination and his improvised tales of the forest folk had kept Emily entertained for nearly two decades.

'I love the scent of these beauties,' said Mrs Tipton, bending her head into the blooms. Grey tufts escaped from her hair like Old Man's Beard. 'I can't remember the last time the ole man gave me flowers. He was a romantic when we were first courting. Wasn't you, dear? Always bringing me a posy.'

Mr Tipton shook his head and muttered something to Tiger, while Mrs Tipton shook the rafters with an almighty sneeze.

Mr Tipton found his place in his story as Emily took the armchair closer to the fire. Sally the collie dog joined her, rested her head on Emily's feet. The warm weight comforted her toes, as the heat of the flames rose and fell against Mr Tipton's cheeks and stroked the back of her neck.

When he'd finished the story, the conversation moved on to bemoan his dwindling workforce. He'd taken on local schoolboys and a few labourers who'd not yet joined in with the war, but more and more men disappeared every week. Some had volunteered to do their bit, a patriotic answer to the call of duty. John had joined up after the recruitment drive marched through the village. It had encouraged many of the villagers to enlist with him. Then Lady Radford had run a campaign to make their village the bravest in Britain and those who hadn't answered those calls had gone to help build the seaport at Richborough.

'The government are setting up a corps of educated women, to act as gang leaders,' she said, but before she could continue he'd sent Tiger scurrying from his lap. 'Good God and heaven preserve me. Not over my dead body. If women like Olive Hughes who's worked the harvest on this farm since she was a girl can't hack it, how am I supposed to cope with a lady who's never done a day's work in her life?'

Emily stiffened. After all these years of following him around, helping and learning from him, how could he not see that she could be useful?

'What about Mrs Hughes and Mrs Little?' Emily said. 'Lily would have injured them if I hadn't been there.'

'You took a terrible risk to help that undeserving pair. You got lucky, but don't ever think just because a cow knows you that she won't trample you.'

He had a point. Standing her ground like that against Lily had been perilous and she was fortunate Lily had decided to stop, but surely it had shown that she was prepared to put herself forward and be counted.

'Women don't belong on the farm, and I shan't be taking on any more. I'm sorry about that. The Belgians are in need of work, kind souls they are an' all. I'd rather take on a rotten German prisoner o' war than any more work-shy, weak-willed women. No offence.'

'Well I am offended, Mr Tipton.'

He stood, snatched a lantern up from the wall and stomped off into the yard, slamming the door behind him before she could say any more. Emily rose to her feet and watched from the window as he swung his lamp across the farmyard. The shadows stretched and grew to ghoulish heights against the farmhouse and the Kentish ragstone of the stables.

Then as she stoked the fire, she noticed wet newspaper soaking in a bucket, being readied to make into bundles for the fire. Next to that, a pile of old newspapers. The *Standard* sitting on top. She pulled the newspaper cutting from her pocket just as Mrs Tipton emerged from the scullery, wiping her hands on her pinafore.

'You got my hand delivery then.' Mrs Tipton pointed her nose towards the cutting.

It had been Mrs Tipton? She knew more than anyone how much Mr Tipton and Mother would object. What was she thinking of – encouraging Emily to taste ideas and dreams that were out of her reach?

'You shouldn't take any notice of the ole man's bluster. He's ready for his retirement, that's the problem. He wants life nice and easy; he doesn't want the trouble the war is bringing.'

Sally the collie nudged at her with her wet nose.

'It's true, those villagers are a let-down to the farm, your family and the country,' Mrs Tipton said. 'And no one's as surprised as me to learn that Olive Hughes is shirking off. But I think the ole man is wrong to say he won't take on another woman, because a bright, strong girl like you who loves this place and the outdoors and is familiar with the animals is just what he needs. He just doesn't know it yet.'

Chapter Four

June 1915

Dearest Emily,

I expect it is so very quiet with you in Kent. No such luck in Flanders. Fritz called on us twice in the night with his gas shells. I lay in a fitful half-sleep waiting for him to pay us another a visit.

How is your beautiful corner of Blighty? Please fill my head with more tales to take me far away from the goings-on here.

Must dash.

Fondest wishes

Theo

But neither Mr Tipton nor Mother would entertain the idea of Emily working on the farm and even Mrs Tipton's initial enthusiasm for the idea waned. The authorities would be looking for a different sort of girl to her anyway, one with more experience and fewer family commitments.

The whole notion had set her back in the end. Mr Flitwick had taken over much of her kitchen garden work now that Mother had stopped the pretence of turning a blind eye and watched

Emily even more closely so that her opportunities to attend to her herbs and vegetables grew fewer and further between.

Then summer came, and the warmth brought first Cecil, her younger brother, from his studies at Oxford, and then her older brother John, home on leave from the Front.

Cecil took up residence in the library, writing who knew what. He was always writing, or reading, or arguing the case of this and that.

For the first few days John was restless, and never in the house for long before he thought of somewhere he ought to be or something he ought to be doing.

'Wherever is he?' Mother asked her again and again. This time though, Emily knew where he was. Mr Tipton had lost even more men from the farm and asked for John's help to discuss how they might fill the gaps.

'I'll go and tell him you want to see him,' Emily told her mother, desperate for an excuse to leave. She found him mending the broken wain with Alfred, the farm's oldest member of staff.

John had already cast the word out and that morning he'd recruited a couple of Belgian refugees and arranged to move them into one of the cottages at Perseverance Place.

To encourage him back up to the house, that afternoon Emily asked John to help her dig up the rose garden that sat at the edge of the terrace, so she could turn it into a vegetable garden. Mother perched in the window of the sitting room.

'We've got an audience.' John gestured as he thrust his spade into the soil beneath the roots of a stubborn rose bush that she'd not been able to dislodge herself.

Emily lifted herself up. Her breathing was heavy with exertion, her booted feet spread wide in the tilled soil to steady herself. Her skirts were tucked up in themselves and her hair had fallen out of its knot. Cecil sat beside Mother, smirking, while Mother's mouth was gathered in a pinch, her brow furrowed.

'I'm going to make the most of you being here to do as much

24

outdoors as I can,' she said. 'She doesn't belittle me in front of you.'

Emily joined John now to bend the rose bush into submission. 'I'm sure she'll get used to the idea of the Victory Garden.'

Didn't he realise that it wasn't the loss of the rose bushes that had upset Mother? She'd retrieved the newspaper article from her drawer to show him. He'd been the first person, beside Mrs Tipton, not to dismiss the idea.

'Have you asked Mother?' he'd asked.

'I have, and Mr Tipton,' she sighed.

'Like that, is it?'

'Yes, and I suppose …'

'What?'

'Well, I mean they're probably right, aren't they? What do I know about farm work really?'

'What, you mean apart from following Mr Tipton about since you were this high?' He held his hand beside his thigh. 'And growing your own crops and your love of the outdoors, and your natural affinity with the animals?' He shook his head.

'All right, all right,' she said. 'But none of that means I could supervise a bunch of farm workers, not really. Mother probably is right …'

'Would Father have built this place or opened the cement works if he'd questioned himself? You can't give up that easily, Emily. They'll train you, but I'll bet you hardly need it.'

She smiled. He made it all sound so easy. It *was* true; she could do all the things he said, and Edna said she looked forward to her vegetables and herbs because they had the best flavour. Emily always kept quiet about her secret weapons; double digging and the manure she collected from Hawk's stables to enrich the soil. Even Mr Flitwick said she had green fingers. But none of that meant anything if Mr Tipton and Mother wouldn't listen, and even John's golden charm couldn't make light work of the situation.

It was Christmas in July at HopBine House. The last two days of John's leave were a washout; the rain fell with a constant and unrelenting force, while heavy winds whistled around the house.

John said it was too frivolous to take a goose from the farm, but even without any of the trimmings, they lit the fire and hung stockings on the mantelpiece and she began to believe it really was Christmas. Especially being trapped inside the house with her mother, her grandmother – down for the night from London – and Cecil.

After lunch Emily slumped on the sofa, her hand propping up her chin while the rain lashed against the living-room window turning the view to a blurred grey.

'Emily dear,' Grandmother called from the other end of the sitting room. Grandmother had been in mourning since her son, Emily's father, had passed away in 1913. Her hat was alive with twitching black feathers, and she hid behind a nose-length veil and a flowing black dress. 'I'm in need of news of romance. Tell me. Do you have any? An attractive young girl like you, even one with that disconcerting hint of wildness, must have some young suitor in pursuit.'

'Mr Tipton's bullock is the only male interested in my sister.' Cecil smirked.

'Actually,' Emily cut in, 'I'm writing to an officer at the Front.'

As Emily took her seat at the piano, she noticed her mother was holding her breath, waiting. But she couldn't meet her eye; Theo was a lowly corporal, a non-commissioned officer. If she dared to tell Mother the truth she'd say Emily was wasting her time and giving false hope to an unsuitable young man. But lowly or not, he'd been a ray of happiness, and she wouldn't give him up easily.

'He's from Yorkshire, he's very attentive and interested in me and my life,' she said. That seemed to satisfy both Mother and

Grandmother and so she stretched her fingers out across the keys.

'Oh,' Cecil whined. 'Do you have to make that din?' Deftly he turned the attention to himself. He hadn't looked up from his book since he'd sat down. He'd even read it at the dinner table.

'It's a piano, Cecil,' she retorted. 'Not a brass band.'

'Emily won't play if you find it distracting,' Mother said. 'Emily dear, can't you find a less invasive occupation?' Mother's gaze remained trained on her lap.

She sighed and slammed the lid shut. She could do no right. As it was, within a few moments Cecil had lost interest in his books and wandered out of the room in search of something new.

'I would like to hear you play,' said John. 'Cecil?' He called down the hallway. 'Will you come back shortly for a game of charades?'

Cecil returned momentarily to poke his head around the doorway. 'Anything for you, dear brother,' he said.

Emily straightened her back and prepared to play. She hadn't sat on this stool since before the war, before John had joined up, when they all came together in the evenings for piano music, song and laughter. They hadn't done any of these things when it was really Christmastime, and John was away. It would have been wrong to carry on as usual without him. They hadn't sung or played charades, either.

Grandmother and Mother stood beside Emily, while John leant an elbow on the body of the baby grand before them, where Father had done the same when he was alive. He warbled in a silly false tenor, his arms stretched out to accentuate his notes.

John took Mother's hand. Emily had warmed up now, switched to a show tune, and John and Mother glided together to a foxtrot. Emily glanced up every now and then. Mother wasn't hamming it up – she really did have style and grace. She gazed into her dance partner's eyes with unbidden pride. Mother's slim waist and hips meant she could pass for a woman John's age, from behind. Her energy too. She was so often in her armchair these days it was a jolt to see her out of it and dancing and to recall how full of verve Mother had been when Father was alive, especially when she entertained.

Emily smiled to herself in the hallway later that evening. Home really was home when John was there. How did he do it? He was the glue that bound them together. It gave them the confidence and freedom to be and please themselves. To prove the point, Cecil was in his room with his books, while Mother, Grandmother and John talked in the library. On her way upstairs, she passed them, the door open a crack to reveal the light inside.

'I don't think you should ask him for help,' she overheard Grandmother say. 'Too much has passed.'

'But what choice do we have?' Mother said. Emily stopped and held her breath. 'Things can't go on as they are for much longer.'

'I know,' said John. 'We're approaching a point where we'll have to shut HopBine House up.'

'Or sell ...' Mother said. Emily put a hand to her mouth. Sell their home? No wonder Mother was so keen for her to marry someone from a good family; she must be hoping she'd save them.

Why hadn't John said anything when they'd been on their own, digging up the rose garden? He'd had plenty of opportunity to tell her they had problems. Where would they go, and what would happen to the farm? Her legs lost their strength beneath her.

'He's offered help,' John said. 'I suggest we hear what he has to say.'

Emily took a light-footed step back towards the door, straining to hear whether John would reveal who this 'he' was.

'What are you doing lurking about in the hallway?'

She jumped clean into the air and clubbed herself on the chin with the back of her own hand; Cecil had appeared on the stairs out of nowhere. 'I was just getting a glass of water,' she said loudly enough for John and Grandmother to hear her in the library, and then strode purposefully towards the kitchen.

She was about to chastise him for creeping around, but to her surprise he'd joined the others, too. She back-tracked. It must have been a family meeting and she'd not realised. As she reached the door, she caught a glimpse of John. He smiled, but just then Mother came into view, and snapped the door shut in her face.

'Should I come in too?' she called.

'Take yourself off to bed, dear,' Mother said turning the key in the lock. 'It's getting late.'

Chapter Five

July 1915

Dearest Emily,

I am moving up the queue and it will soon be my turn for leave. I ought to go to Yorkshire to see my mother, but I wonder could you meet me at King's Cross station when I break my journey and pick up the train for Wakefield? I keep the photograph you sent me in my pocket, and look at you before I sleep – often you're illuminated by shell light. But I long to see that determined chin for myself, your lively, mischievous eyes alight on me in person, my love.

What do you say?
Fondest wishes
Theo

'You and John have had a lot of clandestine meetings in the library.' She probed Cecil two days later under the shade of the monkey puzzle tree on the lawn, the brim of her sun hat low. Cecil lounged out on the other side of the trunk, reading, as usual. The soporific heat pushed her eyelids shut. 'I waited up for you both last night but in the end I had to go to bed.'

'We were playing chess.' Cecil's tone was falsely flippant. He was no more going to let her in on what was going on than Mother.

'And who won?' she asked.

'I'd like to think I thrashed him, but I think he let me win.'

'He always lets you win.' She chuckled. 'Has he ever beaten you or I at anything?'

Cecil reflected for a moment and then groaned. 'All that effort to try and outwit him and all for nothing,' he said banging his book against his thighs.

She hadn't written back to Theo in the end. It would be difficult for her to travel to London without a chaperone. And after the conversation she'd overheard when Grandmother was visiting, it seemed she might need to a find herself an officer, not a corporal.

Her gardening journal slid from her grasp and her lap, but her hand was too heavy to move and catch the book. The buzzing of the bees and the collared dove in the canopy above all faded away ...

She woke much later with a start, heavy still with sleep. A car door had slammed shut, footsteps on the gravel.

No one had mentioned that they were expecting guests.

Cecil had gone. She carried on where she had left off with her journal for the vegetable garden, planning which new crops she would plant and where. She hated afternoon tea and polite conversation with strangers, but it was nearing the end of John's leave and there was no telling when he might next be back.

Now that the stinging heat of the sun had faded it was safe to emerge from the shade and cross the lawn to the borders she had helped Mr Flitwick to plant. Taking the secateurs from her pocket, she snipped the stems of some cosmos for Mother.

Declining Daisy's offer of help, she placed the blooms into a vase in the kitchen and made her way through to the sitting room so she could casually drop by and determine whether the guest was someone she wanted to stay for.

31

'Hello …' She stopped on the threshold to assess the scene of John and Cecil flanking Mother, who perched on the edge of the sofa, wringing a lace handkerchief with her fingers.

A man with his back to her in the armchair by the door turned to face her. Her hand froze around the vase as she placed it on the bookcase. The man was the ghost of her father yet greyer, sterner, leaner. In a smarter, tailored suit, with neater hair. Altogether more groomed than her father, Baden.

The man held out his manicured hand to Emily.

'I'm your Uncle Wilfred,' he said. 'Your father's brother.'

'How do you do,' she said. Her mother and brothers' faces were a mask of blank politeness, betraying no clue as to what she should think of this unexpected visit.

'I've come to see your family to talk business.'

So, this must be what she'd overheard them talking about. Why had they excluded her from that?

'You didn't speak to my father for years, did you?' she asked. John shook his head at her for being so frank. He was clearly intent on making a good impression.

'No,' Wilfred said. 'Twenty-five years to be precise. And …' he pointed a finger at her '… don't forget – he didn't speak to me either. I regret the whole business terribly.'

It's a little late now, she wanted to say, but the anguished smile pinned to Mother's face stopped her short. 'We used to come to your house in London,' she remembered, 'without Father.'

'A long time ago now. Cecil was just a baby the last time we visited,' Mother said.

'Yes. It was a shame you couldn't come again. Well, if you wouldn't mind excusing us …'

'I'll come too,' Mother said, her hands twisting and turning again.

'It's fine, Mother. Leave it to us,' John said.

Cecil ambled out of the room and down the hallway whistling to himself.

'What have I said to you about wearing those boots indoors!' Mother snapped once the men were out of earshot.

Mother stared at her hands while the conversation took place on the other side of the wall. After a while, Emily realised Mother's hands were trembling and that she was trying to still them. Within ten minutes voices rose in the room next door. Mother joined them then, and then Cecil, and the conversation continued for a while longer. Emily hovered outside the door, hoping to overhear something, but the voices were quiet.

She sat in her bedroom, the door open. She would demand to be told what was going on. It was ridiculous to exclude her in this way as if she was nothing more than a child.

Voices, sharper now they were out of the library, travelled up from the hallway. She scampered down the stairs, but before she could join the others on the front step, Wilfred's car was already approaching the cedar avenue.

Mother marched straight back into the sitting room and poured herself a brandy, which she swallowed down in one.

'Whatever is going on?' Emily asked. 'Is he giving us money?'

Mother set her glass back down on the table as if Emily hadn't spoken.

'Mother.' John appeared in the doorway. 'We need to talk.'

'Of course,' Mother said. She followed John into the library, leaving her once again on the wrong side of the door.

Chapter Six

July 1915

Dearest Emily,

They have delayed my leave – they can't spare us. I've been promised it should be next week now if I am fortunate enough to escape, or there is a shell with my name on it heading my way first.

I can't pretend I'm not disappointed that I won't see you at King's Cross. Your letters have been the only good thing to come my way since I've been here, but I understand the reason why. I'll linger outside the Telegraph Office just in case you change your mind and can meet me there.

Try not to be too hard on your mother – I'm sure she's being truthful when she tells you that she thinks it's for the best if you don't work, even though you may disagree.

Yours
Theo

The chickens scattered to escape the sizeable boots of Mrs Tipton as she stepped out of the farmhouse door and grabbed John by the shoulders. She pulled him close, thumping the air out of him by patting his back with the palm of her hand, even though she'd only seen him the day before. 'Ah, what a sight to see the three of you together again at the farmhouse. In you all come now,' she said as she tugged John over the threshold.

Mrs Tipton poured them each a tea. 'I've been working on him,' she said.

Emily's back straightened. It was the first time Mrs Tipton had mentioned the idea of Emily helping on the farm in weeks. 'The more those women run circles around him, the more his resolve is weakening. Sometimes with men you just have to wear them down – it's the only way.'

Before their tea had cooled enough to drink, Mr Tipton crashed into the kitchen shouting. Mrs Tipton raised her eyebrows at Emily.

'Blasted women, blasted women!'

'Whatever's happened, dear?' Mrs Tipton slid a cup of tea in front of him.

'I thought those cows were temperamental.' He threw his brown felt hat across the room. 'Those beasts have nothing on women. I should never ha' taken them on. They're either jawing ...' he mimicked a busy mouth snapping up and down with his four fingers against his thumb '... or booing ...' he mimed rubbing his eyes with his fists.

'You upset one o' them again, have you?' Mrs Tipton asked, tight-lipped.

'S'not hard, it really isn't,' he said, kicking the table leg with his boot. 'Another one, Annie, I think she called herself, has just packed her bags. They're strong enough to lug their cases to the station when it means they can get out of here. You noticed that too, have you?'

Mrs Tipton nodded in reply. 'What you need is a ganger,' Mrs Tipton said with a wink to Emily. 'And look who the wind has blown in for us, eh?' She gestured with raised eyebrows towards Emily.

Mr Tipton furrowed his brow. 'No disrespect, but what I need is more men. Cecil, you're home for the summer. Couldn't you help us out a bit, lad?'

Cecil's gaze shifted about in the uncomfortable silence that followed. Cecil? Mr Tipton couldn't be that desperate for help, surely to goodness. John caught Emily's eye behind Cecil's back; despite her disappointment at being overlooked again, it was too much to imagine Cecil milking cows and they both crumbled into laughter.

'What?' Cecil straightened his back, and his tie. 'I think I'd command respect rather well amongst the workers.'

'A good farmer leads from the front,' Emily told him, clutching her stomach and grinning. After the drama up at the house, and John's looming departure for the Front, the laughter warmed her insides.

'It's not that ludicrous a prospect, surely?' Cecil asked.

John and Emily nodded at one another and said in unison: 'Oh, it is.'

'I really don't see what's so funny.' Cecil frowned.

'Oh, come on, Cecil,' John said. 'Can you really see yourself muck-spreading, digging, weeding …' Cecil's mouth had wrinkled up. 'My point exactly. You won't have time to loll around with your book, or write a thesis about the land ownership of the upper classes and the plight of the serfs. Whereas Emily here worked alongside me on the vegetable garden and I was tired and ready for a rest long before her.'

'Exactly,' Mrs Tipton agreed.

'I'd like to try,' Emily said. 'Perhaps a trial?'

'I appreciate you wanting to help,' Mr Tipton said. 'And you know I've always enjoyed having you around the place and you have a better understanding of the land than most, but I've had so much trouble. I don't want any more. I can't even risk you, Miss Cotham.'

'It is her farm,' Mrs Tipton reminded him. 'She has every right to take good care of her family's assets.'

She had been bending her husband's ear for months now, and he was beginning to cave in.

'Won't you give me a chance to prove myself?' Emily pressed on. 'If you'd like, I can sign up with the government's scheme and get some training.'

'But she won't need it,' John added. 'She knows these fields and this farm well enough. She's watched you since she was a girl.'

'And I can supervise the girls – you won't need to bother yourself with chasing them about.' It would be wonderful if that was true. Just as John had said, she mustn't listen to the naysayers. She had to believe in herself; that was half the battle.

'This war isn't going to be won any time soon,' said Mrs Tipton. 'You'll have to take on more women. You won't have any choice in the matter.'

Mr Tipton's shoulders sagged at the prospect.

'And Master John is the head of the household,' Mrs Tipton continued. 'His wishes have to be respected.'

Emily was impressed at Mr Tipton's resolve, but he was definitely showing signs of succumbing – all three of them could sense it.

'I know the land and the animals, Mr Tipton. I love this farm. Who better to be by your side?'

'Mmm.' He scratched his chin.

'If it turns out that I'm not any good at it then I'll leave,' she said.

'You'll have lost nothing,' John said. 'But you've everything to gain.'

Mr Tipton narrowed his eyes, suspecting he'd been ambushed. 'And what does your mother say?'

Emily exhaled. He had them there.

'She's coming around to the idea,' John said. Even without the financial problems, Uncle Wilfred storming out and John returning to the Front, Mother wouldn't have given a moment's thought to Emily's desire to become a land girl since she dismissed the idea months ago. But Mr Tipton didn't need to know that.

'If only those new girls had half your stamina, but I can't go against your mother's wishes. If she says no, then the answer's no.'

'Very well, it's a deal then.'

Emily searched John's face for a clue as to what exactly he knew that she didn't. Had John managed to persuade Mother too?

'That's sorted then.' Mrs Tipton rubbed her hands together.

'Don't look so worried,' John whispered. 'We'll win Mother over, you'll see.' He cleared his throat and raised his voice.

'Go on then. Shake the man's hand.' She spat on her hands like she'd seen men do in West Malling on market day, clenched his fleshy palm tight and pumped it for all it was worth.

'She has all the makings of a land girl this one,' said Mrs Tipton.

They were halfway there. Please, oh please, let John be right about Mother.

*

Dearest Emily,

I have been told I go on leave tomorrow. I know what you said, my dear, but I am ever hopeful of an encounter with you, no matter how brief, to brighten my spirits and warm my heart for my return to Blighty. I will be passing through King's Cross between one and two o'clock on Thursday, I shall pin a hankie to my lapel, so that you might recognise me.

Fondest wishes
Theo

'Do you realise what time it is?'

Emily held her breath and froze at the top of the ladder, steadying her brimming basket of cherries. She'd lost track of time. Working did that to her: the whole day flew by and she didn't notice.

'Is it just you?' she called down.

'Of course,' John said with amusement in his voice.

'You aren't going to tell Mother on me, are you?'

'Have I ever yet?' John asked as she steadily clambered down from the canopy of the red-dotted tree and jumped the last few steps, only noticing now that all of the other workers had emptied their baskets and finished up for the day.

'You're running out of time to convince her,' Emily said, lugging her cherries to the large bathtub-shaped bin and tipping them out. 'I might just borrow your old work clothes, register with the Corps, and let her try and stop me.'

'Better I think if you have her blessing,' John said. 'One war is quite enough.'

Emily propped herself on a rung of her ladder. She'd never volunteer without Mother's approval and they both knew it. She didn't have it in her to disappoint or disobey. She might tug and pull at the apron strings and sneak about on the farm when Mother wasn't looking, but she wouldn't cause problems when the family already had enough.

John examined a cherry. 'You do know that Mother needs you more than she lets on. She's never been good at putting these things into words. But I can't see a reason you couldn't work on the farm and go home to her at the end of the day.'

'She says it won't look good to the young men she invites over to meet me. Apparently being outspoken counts against me as it is, I need to at least look the part.' She sighed. 'I suppose if we need the money I will have to assist the search for a husband.'

John popped a cherry into his mouth. She examined his face, waiting for him to say more, but he was checking his watch again. 'John, Mother isn't the only person who can't put things into words. Are you going to tell me what went on with Uncle Wilfred the other day?'

39

'Nothing. A reunion,' he said. 'We ought to go.' For his last night John had invited some guests over for supper at HopBine. 'You know Lady Radford is always the first to arrive. We can't have her steering the conversation.'

He didn't catch her eye. He was too brave to admit it, but it was obvious he would stay on with them if he could.

She put a cherry into her mouth and savoured the burst of sweetness. She contemplated asking him about the conversation she'd overheard, but she didn't want him to know she'd been sneaking around listening in, and her hurt at being excluded from the discussions might seep through and with so little of his leave left there was no place for recriminations.

They walked back across the paddock towards HopBine in silence, but as they approached the cut-through in the hedge by the cedar avenue, she pulled him back.

'If there is anything I can do to help, anything at all … I don't like to think you're carrying a burden, or that I'm being left out because you think I can't cope, because I can.'

John ran his hand through his hair and cast a lingering glance towards the gables of the house their father had built. 'I know. But you mustn't worry, everything has been taken care of. There's no urgency to find a rich husband.' He winked. 'And besides, you're looking after Mother for us, which is a huge weight off my mind, I can tell you,' he said. But there was something else, he was searching her face as if trying to decide whether to say it, and then he blurted out: 'If anything should happen to me … once I've gone …'

'No!' she said. 'Please don't start with that, John. Nothing will happen to you. Do you hear me?' He'd never admitted to his own mortality before now. 'You're to come home safe and sound.'

'I'll do my best. But if I'm injured I need you to promise me that you and Mother will pull together and accept the decisions that have been made. It won't do to have the family divided, and Mother will count on you. I have said much the same to Cecil,

40

and as much as I love my brother, I recognise that he is too caught up in changing the world to ever put the family first – so it will fall to you. You have a good sense of responsibility and the family will depend on that.'

'John,' she said, 'you're scaring me. The way you're talking, it's so final. Please stop.'

'Emily, the war is worse than I'd ever imagined. I believed them when they said it would be over by Christmas, that I'd be home by now, but there really is no sign of it ending, or even easing off.'

Emily had read the Bryce Report about German brutality in the papers and the sinking of the *Lusitania* by a German U-boat, killing more than a thousand people. All the news was so remote though, surely the danger wasn't so great for her capable brother.

He reached inside his suit jacket and removed a small diary. 'In these book pages, I've recorded the name, number and trade of every man I've lost.' He held the small, dog-eared book aloft. 'Their faces come to me in my dreams, memories of a joke they once made, their nickname, a habit. I harbour the knowledge that I censored their letters, read their personal messages, tried to check but not intrude. All are dead or lost now. I'm sorry.' His voice had reduced to a whisper. 'I've shocked you.' He took hold of her hand. 'You shouldn't know any of this, how bad it really is – it's best that you don't, but it's why I have to ask you to promise me to take care of Mother and make the best of the situation that befalls you.'

She levelled her gaze, her own body stiff as if trying to repel the truths John had just shared.

'We're in trouble, aren't we?' she asked, doing her best to match her tone with his own determined and brave one.

'We should have sold up, before the war. I've made mistakes.'

'Well, I'm glad we didn't. This is our home.'

'That's as may be, but we have to be practical now.'

'And is that why Uncle Wilfred came out of the woodwork?'

'He offered to help, yes.'

At least John had told her the truth, and not excluded her again. He saw her as an adult and an equal, even if Mother didn't.

'Was it wise to take from Wilfred, do you think?' Father had feuded with his brother for a reason; surely they couldn't overlook that.

He shook his head. She wouldn't push him. A tear ran down his cheek as he slid his diary back in his pocket, and she was crying too. It was no secret that war was awful. Theo had been more candid in his letters though much of what he wrote was censored. But John had been so cheery, he'd given the impression that he was living the charmed life he so deserved. None of the men should endure what John had just alluded to.

She offered him her handkerchief, swallowed the huge lump of emotion in her throat. 'You mustn't lose hope,' Emily told him. Her voice broke; her bottom lip trembled. 'You're terribly brave. And I want to match that by taking care of things here as best I can. You just concentrate on staying safe, and I'll keep things going until you come home.'

*

The primrose yellow hallway at HopBine was already buzzing with guests when they returned. Emily announced their 'hero' and a round of applause broke out. The guests shrunk to the edges to make way for him.

Emily's mother pinched her arm, and hissed into her ear to get changed. The blood-red cherries had stained the front of her white skirt.

'And put on stays.' Mother shook with rage. 'Do you think nobody can tell?'

When Emily came back down, Lady Radford and her red-haired daughter, Clara, had cornered John. Clara had always been sweet on John, and Mother had always liked the idea of

John marrying into a titled family, but John hadn't felt the same way. He'd said she was too timid and willing to let her Mother speak for her, that a relationship with her would be a marriage with his mother-in-law. Interesting then, that with their financial problems Mother still placed her brother's wishes above the family's need, whilst encouraging Emily to marry anyone who came along.

'Finch Hall is quite transformed. You must visit,' Lady Radford was telling Mother and John. 'The billiard room is a store. The smoking and drawing rooms are wards. I have to remind myself that it was once my home and not always a hospital.'

'It's wonderful to put the house to such good use,' John said, though they didn't need any encouragement and Mother was craning backwards, trying to attract the attention of Norah Peters.

'Lady Clara is responsible for book-keeping,' Lady Radford continued. 'And you're in charge of dispatching packages, aren't you?' she said, addressing Clara.

'Mother has even conceded that I can push the soldiers around the lawn.' Lady Clara raised her eyebrows.

'We're quite a formidable team aren't we, dear?'

Emily forced a smile. 'How wonderful,' she said. Clara was so much more confident now she was a war girl. Even John was looking at her anew as if he didn't recognise this new independent woman before him. He'd better not fall in love with her. She didn't want to spend any more time with Lady Radford.

'Although much smaller, you could volunteer HopBine House as a convalescent home for the men recovering from their treatment up at Finch Hall.' Lady Radford surveyed the hallway and the upstairs. 'You'd be able to offer ten beds here, quite easily.'

'Oh no. I don't think so,' Mother said flatly. 'I think we've done enough for this war – what with John amongst the first to join up. And I'm terribly busy with the knitting and sewing parties and putting together packages.'

John mouthed 'go on' to Emily, but anything she might say

would only antagonise Mother for putting her on the spot in front of Lady Radford.

'Mr Tipton is also cultivating more land for crops,' John reminded Lady Radford. 'He's reducing the land given over to hops and setting more by for important crops like potatoes. For which he will need more manpower.'

Womanpower, was on the tip of Emily's tongue, but Mother was tugging at a brooch that had become enmeshed in her lace trim and the look on her face forced Emily's mouth shut.

'And how is he managing without his labourers?' Lady Radford asked, either oblivious to the tension or because of it. 'You took many men with you when you joined up, did you not?'

Mother's face was set while John explained that Mr Tipton wasn't as young as he was, and they'd not been able to find enough help, how he was struggling to keep up with the demands from the government, and how the village women had proved trouble-some, but that the Board of Trade were training up educated women to lead the volunteers and supervise them on the farmer's behalf.

'Tremendous idea,' Lady Radford said. 'The village women will be an asset, I'm sure, with the right leadership.'

Emily dared to meet her Mother's gaze. Her lips were tightly pursed. She'd been right – it would never be that easy to convince her.

Lady Radford turned towards Emily, the penny finally falling into place with a clunk they could all hear. 'Emily! A young, strong girl like you, who isn't afraid of getting dirty, should be put to work. You shouldn't be knitting, you must leave the lighter, less taxing work to the older women.'

Mother's back straightened, her arms folding across her stomach. 'I couldn't spare her,' Mother said.

'Really?'

'And she has a sweetheart of course,' Mother added. 'A charming young officer, by all accounts, from a good family.'

Ah. Emily's white lie came back to haunt her. Mother thought she was busy solving their problems by finding a respectable husband, rather than corresponding with a corporal.

But Lady Radford wasn't the least bit interested in affairs of the heart, only of war.

'And what about Cecil?' Lady Radford asked, forgetting about Emily now that Mother had sewn her into a pocket of domesticity. Cecil had been talking to Mr and Mrs Peters – the village solicitor and his wife – just next to them, and he turned now.

'And what about Cecil?' he asked.

'Will you volunteer?'

Emily noticed how the crowd around them fell into hush as they waited for this answer. Mother became flustered, asking Lady Radford if she needed another drink, but their neighbour wasn't to be put off, and Cecil wasn't going to give her a fudge of an answer either:

'I just haven't been stirred by the call to fight,' he confessed, as if casually telling them he wasn't all that partial to something as trivial as caviar. The conversation around them died. It was always the sort of thing he might say, just perhaps he might have told the family first rather than announcing it to a room full of people who had loved ones at the Front right then.

Lady Radford's eyes were wide.

'I wish I could stand beside my friends, my brother. But I can't.'

'My dear boy,' she began, 'your country needs you. Now is the time to stand up and be counted, like your brother. Other men will follow your lead.'

'Stand up and be blown to smithereens is more like it,' Cecil retorted. 'This war is for the capitalists, and it's the average man on the street who is paying the price.'

'Louisa,' Lady Radford turned to Mother. Apart from one or two oblivious guests in the far corner, the entire party had abandoned their own exchanges now. 'Like the Radfords, you are in a position to set an example to the rest of the village.'

Mother's grey-blue eyes were wide, the colour completely drained from her face.

John stepped in, when it was clear that Mother was lost for words. 'Cecil isn't nineteen until January.' Emily often forgot there was only a year between them. Cecil behaved as if he were so much younger. 'And he doesn't have to fight if he doesn't wish to. The country needs men like Cecil to challenge points of view and make us think.'

'Yes, well conscription will change all that. And they say it's inevitable. One really can't do enough.' Lady Radford smiled sweetly. 'John and Emily are commendable, but this war calls for *everyone* to do their bit. Everyone.'

The chatter slowly returned to the room and Cecil's revelation, on the surface at least, had been glossed over. But there was no avoiding it. Cecil would go back to university the next morning and he wouldn't be enlisting. Several guests slipped out early without even saying goodbye to John. Mother mingled for the rest of the evening, not once catching Emily's eye. When they'd waved off the last of the guests and her brothers had gone to bed, Mother called her into her room where she sat propped up in bed.

'Oh, my days,' Mother said. 'They will lock Cecil up you know. The way this government is enlisting men they'll make an example of those who refuse. Oh my, two sons to worry about, on top of everything else. I can't cope, I can't breathe. Emily, will you help me up? My chest is quite tight ...'

Mother's skin had a tinge of blue to it. 'Please drop your ideas, for your Mother's sake. Don't leave me, dear,' she said. 'Don't leave me.'

Chapter Seven

July 1915

The morning John was to return to the Front the rain fell in stair rods, and the temperature was so cold they had to light the fires again.

John sat in the chair, biting his nails to the quick while Mother's gaze never left him, trying to store away every detail.

Emily had also woken up earlier than usual, jolted into consciousness at the realisation that John was departing that day. Unlike Mother, she couldn't look at him and instead gazed out the window. Her stomach lurched whenever she returned her attention to the room and saw him shifting about in his seat, checking his watch, his mind already back there, with his men.

No one had mentioned the previous evening's events. Cecil's revelations hadn't been in the script and weren't discussed now. Mother had lines on her face that weren't there the night before. Her usually impeccable appearance was tarnished with unkempt hair and few of her signature finishing touches. She wore no earrings or brooches. Cecil's defiance of convention was brave and he was being true to himself, but he didn't give a single thought to the impact it would have on the rest of the family.

Cecil came into the room, just as Emily was thinking about him. Mother's anguished eyes lifted from John and alighted on her younger brother. Emily avoided his eye, shifted her shoulder away from him as he reached out for her. Perhaps he ought to be made to realise how much this would change their lives too. Hoping and praying that the rumours of a conscription bill for the first time in British history were wrong wasn't much of a position of optimism.

Mother said nothing about the cherry stains on her skirt or the conversation with Lady Radford about the need for land girls. If it had even registered with Mother that everyone else was in support of her working on the farm it had all been swept away by Cecil's shock announcement and John's imminent departure.

Then her heart stopped. The whole world stopped.

Mr Hughes' car crunched across the gravel.

'Time's up then.' John's smile was feeble as he pushed himself out of his chair.

Emily stared at her shoes as Mother clung to him so tight that, in the end, he had to wrench her hands from his arms.

She, Cecil and John travelled to London together largely in silence and at Charing Cross they accompanied him to his train on Platform 5.

'I love you, brother dear,' she said, her voice muffled against his neck.

'I'm sorry I couldn't convince Mother to let you work on the farm, but you mustn't give up,' he said as he slammed his carriage door shut.

'Just come home safe,' she called as his train pulled away.

The two of them stood and waved until the train had disappeared off over Waterloo Bridge and snaked around a bend and into the grey gloom of the day. They remained in silence, a safe distance between them, lost in their own thoughts. John had been ripped away and they were powerless to prevent it.

The crowd on the platform was thinning out when Cecil told

her he'd better be off, if he was going to catch a debate in a pub's back room. Through clenched teeth she declined his offer to escort her back to the platform while she waited for her train back to Chartleigh. He dashed away, his kiss skimming her cheek, as he left her on the platform, awaiting the twenty-eight past twelve. That suited her just fine.

Once he'd disappeared down the staircase to the underground, she checked her watch, left the platform and the station and, on a wet Strand, she joined a taxi rank. If she was quick, she would still make it in time.

*

A wave surged through Emily's stomach every time a man in khaki strode past. She waited by the Telegraph Office entrance with a beating heart, louder than the station clock on the tower outside. She couldn't shift Mother's voice from her mind. She'd be confined to knitting for a month if Mother learnt that Emily had met a man, a stranger no less, unchaperoned, in London. Then her mind flitted to what Theo would be like in the flesh. Would he think she was fast because she'd come without a chaperone?

It was ten past two and her concerns might be for nothing if she'd already missed him.

'Emily?' A voice came, just as she crossed the concourse. She jumped clean into the air, her stomach still twisting and turning as she turned and gasped at him. He was a good-looking young man, as his photo had suggested, better perhaps in the flesh. His sandy hair was parted to one side, and he had warm brown eyes. Nothing within her stirred though. Her knees didn't go weak; butterflies didn't hatch and flap their wings in her stomach. She'd had a silly hope that she'd fall in love and they'd get married and he would take her away from her worries.

She gasped as he lifted her up from the ground and spun her

around, her cheek pressed against his, the sandalwood scent of his cologne wafting by. People stopped to admire the soldier and what they probably thought was his sweetheart. She smiled as if she held some secret knowledge.

He set her back down and now it was her turn to admire him. He was a vision in khaki; stiff cap, brown belt. His shoulders broad, capable and safe.

'I'm glad you could come,' he said. 'Your letters have been a real tonic.'

'I'm glad too,' she said. 'It's been a sad day, and I'm glad of the chance to brighten it up. Now, how long do you have until your train?'

He checked the clock. 'A couple of hours. I was wondering if we might take a stroll beside the Thames, see the Houses of Parliament and Big Ben.'

Together they walked out of the station into the driving rain and joined the taxi rank, the people waiting in front moving aside to let the returning soldier go ahead of them.

The taxi was soon held up in the traffic.

'It's the women's march,' the taxi driver told them. Emily couldn't believe her luck. She'd read in the newspaper about the march for women's right to serve their country, to work in the munitions factories and on the land.

'Gosh, we might see Emmeline Pankhurst,' she said. She suggested they hop out and walk the rest of the way. Theo had on his trench coat to protect him from the rain, and sheltered her with an umbrella, inviting her to steady herself on his outstretched arm.

'I was going to suggest that we change our plans and avoid this part of town,' he said, 'but I can see you're excited by the march.'

'I am,' she said. 'Do you mind?'

He said that he didn't, of course not. She'd never walked out with a man before. She found she couldn't quite keep up with him. His strides were longer than hers and she found herself scurrying to keep under the comfort of his umbrella.

The crowds were thickening up and a brass band moved closer. As they approached Westminster Bridge the spectators were four or five deep, the view obscured by top hats and umbrellas. Emily left Theo's side to thread her way through the crowds, pushed her way to the front. Theo joined her.

'Would you look at them,' she said, pointing at a group of women marching with purpose down the centre of the road, undeterred by a little thing like rain.

'Three cheers for our gallant soldiers,' she read aloud and smiled at Theo. 'Oh, I like that one: mobilise the brains and energy of women,' Emily said, reading the next banner. The word *brain* was underlined. Quite right.

'There's a shortage of ammo,' said Theo. 'That's what's triggered this march, and it's not the lack of women volunteers that's the problem but the unions standing in their way, and the idea of women doing a man's work, I suppose.'

'Do you think women can make shells?' she asked, and then waved at the women who marched by. She was being pulled by an invisible force to burst out of the crowd and walk alongside them.

'I honestly don't know,' Theo said. 'But why not? We won't win this war without shells and with empty stomachs, that much I do know.'

'I still want to work on my farm,' she said.

'Good for you,' he said.

'What do you do for a living?' she asked. 'You've never said.'

'Sorry?' he said. The crowd had cheered and drowned out her voice.

'Your living, what do you do?'

A shadow passed over his face. 'That's all a long time ago now …' He focused on the passing crowds. 'It's as if I've only ever been Corporal Williams.'

51

'But you must have a trade, or a family business?'

He tutted, but he was smiling at her, amused by her persistence. He took her arm and led her back through the crowds to a Lyons' Corner House. Once they were sitting down and had ordered afternoon tea he asked her about her farm.

She told him all about Lily, and how she'd rescued the village women from being trampled. She told him about the cherry harvest, how kind Mr and Mrs Tipton were to her, and how they let her help out on the farm and kept it a secret from Mother.

'And your family own the estate and the farm. Just the one, is it?'

'That's right, my father owned a cement works but my brother John sold that when Father died.'

'So, your Mother has enough to go around then, should you ever need it?'

She smiled and drank her tea. Their predicament was family business. John had trusted her enough to tell her that Uncle Wilfred had come to their rescue and she wouldn't betray that trust with a loose tongue. Besides, Theo had chosen not to tell her about his past, which meant she could opt not to talk about money and spoil a really lovely end to what had promised to be a rotten day.

'Those women were quite a sight today, weren't they?' he said.

She remembered the large float, garlanded with plants and flowers; behind it followed women in white smocks holding their hoes aloft. 'It's clear the country needs educated girls, girls just like you,' he said. 'I feel rather proud to have a girl like you writing to me at the Front.'

'There's nothing I would like more than to be a land girl,' she confessed. She waited for him to snort, or say something to belittle her, but he didn't. He leant in, interested. He beckoned her closer. Her mind raced with the things she could tell him about her ideas and plans for the future.

'There's something I would like more.' His hot, damp breath

blew into her eyes. He held her gaze for a moment longer than was decent. She tried to stare him down, but his eyes were so brimming with desire that it was she who had to break away. And she wasn't comfortable with the way her stomach betrayed her by curling at the edges and threatening to flip right over.

Thankfully the waiter appeared at her shoulder with a tray of tea things. Her cheeks were burning so much that she excused herself and hid in the lavatory until the heat had subsided and her skin had settled back to its normal colour.

He missed his next train, and the next. When the tea rooms were closing and the streets were too wet for walking he suggested they rent a room, spend some time alone together. Her speechlessness was enough for him to promptly come up with another idea.

'What about if I travel back early at the end of my leave? We could have the day together in London,' he said.

She nodded. She'd like that, but she wouldn't be able to come to London without a chaperone. Mother might never let her out again if she caught wind of what she'd been up to today. And that animalistic look in his eyes had made her want to run for the door. He'd been a gentleman in the end, but he might expect more from her next time.

Back at the station he handed his ticket to the guard. He opened the train door and, then, leant in and without warning or reaching out to hold her, he kissed her. His lips pressed against hers while she steadied herself by gripping his arms, sinking into his embrace. His cologne, his skin soft, his shoulders broad and strong. Her eyes were pinned open, close up to his eyelids and the bridge of his nose, until he opened his eyes and his pupils contracted.

'You were watching me?' he said.

Two men whistled and laughed to one another, breaking the spell. Emily gave the soldier looking over his shoulder at them a stern shake of the head that made him turn away, and then trained her gaze fully back to Theo.

'You could marry me,' he said, a huge grin on his face. 'Don't look like that.' He searched her face. 'I'm not that bad, am I?'

'No, of course not,' she said. What was the right thing to say? She didn't want to hurt him or send him away with a bad memory. He had been so sweet and kind to her today, and hadn't complained once about watching the women's march. 'It's just … we have only just met.' Train doors slammed shut on the platform. The atmosphere shifted to one where time was speeding up, running out.

'What about our letters?' he asked. 'I feel I knew you before I'd even met you.'

He was a romantic. It was sweet but one of them had to be sensible.

'Why rush?' she said.

'The war, that's why. I might not get the chance to ask you again.'

'You said I'd see you at the end of your leave,' she said with a wry nod.

'And if you don't become Mrs Williams then, it might be months before we get another chance.'

Goodness. He was right; as with John this morning once they went back to the Front she was left with no idea of when or if she would ever see him again.

She waved as he leant out of the window, his face serious, receding from view as the train glided away from the platform.

'Think about it,' he called. 'I'll write.'

For the second time that day, she waved as a young soldier disappeared from view.

*

HopBine was dark and silent when she returned that night. There was no thin light shining beneath Mother's bedroom door. The tales of her last sight of John would have to wait until the morning.

When the sun came up, Emily raced down to find Mother at breakfast, but Daisy reported that the mistress was sleeping in. Emily assumed it was John's return to the Front that had stirred up her anxiety, but in a hushed voice she told her that Mother had taken a pill from the doctor.

'She slept all day,' she said.

When Mother did eventually surface after lunch, she made slow, careful movements. Her skin was as pale as milk and the skin beneath her eyes purple and bruised. Emily steeled herself for a telling-off for coming home so late. They'd agreed she'd say farewell to John and catch the very next train home. It was the most freedom she'd ever been granted, and she'd violated it terribly. She had prepared her excuses; she was going to say that she'd joined Cecil and his friends for their debate, and would hint at a young officer friend of Cecil's to test the waters, so that Mother couldn't accuse her of becoming unduly politicised.

But she needn't have gone to the trouble of being so creative with the truth. Mother shuffled through to the sitting room, eyes glazed, and sat in an armchair that faced out onto the terrace, and the Victory Garden she and John had begun.

She didn't say another word to Emily; she didn't even notice her, for the rest of the day.

Emily imagined conversations with Theo. She didn't have his address in Yorkshire, so she pictured him rapt when she whispered to his photograph the tale of Mrs Tipton's chickens following her all the way home or when Lily had escaped from the paddock and left a pat on their lawn.

*

August 1915

She'd thought of little else, since she'd decided that she would meet with Theo on his return to the Front and arranged to

55

visit Grandmother in London to coincide with the end of his leave.

'I've asked Norah Peters to come and sit with you. Grandmother says it's urgent,' she lied. She would have to pray that Grandmother didn't call or write to Mother and tell her that the visit had been Emily's idea.

She allowed an hour between her arrival in London and when she would be at Grandmother's to meet with Theo on his way back to the Front. She should perhaps have brought a chaperone; it was clear that he was a passionate man, but she reasoned they were meeting in daylight, and she'd make sure he understood that just because she was deceiving her Mother, it didn't mean she was fast.

She sat on the edge of her seat at the tea rooms, bolt upright. She would raise a hand this time if he tried to kiss her, but despite her anxiety she couldn't keep the smile from her face. She toyed with a stray lock of hair, twirling it around her finger, and laughing at just about everything Theo said, even when it wasn't that funny. She couldn't control it.

He didn't say anything about the proposal this time. His eyes were soft and warm; his gaze wasn't probing. She had rejected him, but it was for the best, and the time at home would have given him the chance to think it through and see that it was madness. It *had* been romantic, and why shouldn't he want to go back to war with a sweetheart waiting for him at home?

Since she'd been at the women's march, she was resolved to do some war work, and just as soon as Mother was stronger she would tackle the subject again, but this time she would have the backing of John and Mr Tipton.

'Grab the opportunity, girl,' he said.

When the hour was up, he walked her to the corner of her Grandmother's mews. He kept a respectable distance this time.

'Don't look so worried,' he said. 'I'm on my best behaviour today. I won't be getting carried away. I got a bit overexcited last time, didn't I? The company of a beautiful, clever girl, well, I was flattered. Can you blame me?' She held out her palm and waved away his concerns. 'But I haven't given up on the idea of marrying you. I admire your spirit,' he said. 'I think it's just the tonic I need.'

He cupped her elbow with his palm, and said, 'May I?'

She nodded, and he pecked her on the cheek, one warm kiss, his breath caressing her skin.

'Don't forget to write,' he said.

She waved, holding her other palm to her cheek.

When she returned in the evening she trod the hallway floor-boards quietly, gauging the atmosphere in the house as to whether Grandmother had telephoned to tell Mother that Emily had arrived for her visit flushed and late. Grandmother had made her views on Emily travelling about London alone very clear, but with more and more young women working now, and so many men away, they couldn't possibly be expected to be accompanied everywhere. The older ones would always cling on to the old way of doing things. It was a sign their ideas were close to being replaced.

The sitting room was empty. The muted fire was dying down without anyone there to tend it. All was quiet and still. She was about to quit while ahead and go straight to bed, when her mother came to life in the chair that faced out towards the window.

Even in the dim light, Mother was paler than usual. Despite the fire she looked frozen. Then Mother blinked, but that was the only movement. 'Where were you?' she asked, her voice thin and choked.

'Some silly cows found their way onto the line near Sidcup,' Emily said. She clenched her fists and waited. She was about to excuse herself, but something stopped her from speaking. Resting on her mother's lap, loosely in her grasp, was a yellow slip of paper.

'What's that?' Emily said.

Her legs were jittery, too weak to move her. Her mother didn't speak. She had to cross that vast space of floorboards to reach her. One. Two. Three. Four. Her boots clipped on the floorboards. Unable to catch her own breath. She slid the piece of paper out of Mother's flimsy grasp.

Her eyes scanned the typed words …

regret to inform …

… *report has been received from the War Office* …

… *Name: Cotham J* …

Her hands shook. The East Kent buffs had been under siege at the Battle of the Hooge near Ypres. Her brother was missing in action. She concentrated on the typed words: *was posted as 'missing' on the … 30th July 1915.*

'He's only been back there a week,' she said. 'It says that missing doesn't necessarily mean …' She couldn't say the last word. She had read about that battle in the newspaper; it was the first time the enemy had used a flamethrower. She read on. 'It says that he may be a prisoner of war, or have become temporarily separated from his regiment.'

The village doctor had received a telegram like this about his eldest son. The son had turned up several months later, in a German prisoner of war camp.

'Yes, all is not lost,' Mother said. A lightning strike of a smile, pained and twisted, flashed onto her face.

'They say if he's been captured that unofficial news is likely to reach us first, and we should notify them at once.'

Emily paused for a moment, tried to imagine John in a prisoner of war camp, or in a front-line hospital unaccounted for; perhaps a nasty blow to the head had caused him to forget who he was.

The letter seemed to be encouraging them to think he'd been captured, and they surely wouldn't give them hope without good reason.

But still, however would they cope with the wait? Mother's

knitting needles and wool were discarded by her feet, her lips tinged blue. Hands trembling, pupils dilated, she wheezed.

'Mother, can you breathe?' Emily asked, her own throat constricting so much she could hardly catch her own breath. After a few moments Mother inhaled, panted, and slumped forwards.

'It's been a terrible shock,' Mother said. 'The letter came in the first post.'

'You're shivering,' Emily said. She stepped out to speak to Daisy, suggested they call out the doctor and give her a sedative.

'I need to lie down,' Mother said when Emily returned.

Emily perched on the end of Mother's dark oak bed. Mother was tucked up and they prayed quietly together for John's return, and silently she wished for Theo's safety too, for good measure. Mother's face glistened with the residue of grease that her cold cream had left behind. Her hands flat on the bedspread, she stared off towards the window and didn't say a word. Mother had managed her regular night-time rituals – that had to be a sign that everything would be all right, didn't it?

'Oh, John,' Emily whispered to herself later in her own room.

The British army had lost her dear, sweet brother. How could she sleep until they found him and returned him safely home?

Chapter Eight

August 1915

Dearest Emily,

What terribly distressing news. My thoughts and prayers are with you and your family, and of course John. We mustn't lose hope that he'll be found and returned to you safe and sound.

Fondest wishes

Theo

The darkness pressed up against each of the window's panes, but she was too alert to think of going back to sleep. She pulled the heavy burgundy damask curtains along their runners anyway, ready for the day that wasn't yet prepared for her.

If she lay down again her mind would whirl and make John's smile merge with Theo's, their voices becoming one, until she couldn't remember whose was whose. Who had said what, who had comforted her, and who had advised her. The tiredness had muddled her mind until she could no longer distinguish one from the other.

She couldn't stay inside and whilst roaming about she found

60

Mr Tipton in the shippon supervising the milking. She told him about John missing in action and without hesitation he embraced her, warm and clammy, his short arms stretching around her shoulders.

'I need to keep busy. I can't sit around up at the house. Can you give me something to do?'

She would worry about Mother later. She had insisted that Emily stayed at the house with her, but she was drugged and drowsy and Emily doubted she'd notice if she was gone.

Out of the corner of her eye, she caught a glimpse of Mr Tipton wiping away the tears with the back of his sleeve.

John was somehow missing like a hoe or a scythe, not a living, breathing person. He had said it could happen and she'd pushed the thought of it aside. He'd asked her to take care of Mother, but their problems were bigger than her – what about the house, the estate, the farm? Would they have to sell up if John didn't come home? If only she'd asked him what it was that he meant, what she would need to accept and how she might be of best help to Mother.

Mid-morning, as she was going into the farmhouse for a cup of tea, she did a double take as Mother, holding her skirts aloft to reveal her heeled boots, stepped around the puddles and shooed away Mrs Tipton's welcoming committee of chickens.

'Emily dear, there you are.'

Mother had aged twenty years in that one night. Puffy pillows had gathered beneath her eyes, new hoods hung over them and shadows lurked beneath her cheekbones.

'Has there been more news?' Emily asked, realising that this was how it would be now: waiting and wondering when news of John would come.

'I'm just so astonished that you deserted me,' Mother continued. 'I think you should come back to the house.'

'Will Cecil come home?' she asked hopefully.

'I've sent him a telegram,' Mother said. 'I insisted he stay in

Oxford. His studies mustn't be interrupted. We must carry on as usual.'

She suggested Mother pay a visit to Hawk; the stallion had grown restless in his stables at Mother's voice. His hooves dragged across the cobbles. It had been so long since Mother had ridden him and yet the faithful old beast was still loyal. He might be the balm, the connection that Mother needed.

'I want to see John, not a horse.'

Emily raised a boot to a too-brave hen. She could never say the right thing.

*

She and Mother spent the afternoon in the conservatory, amongst the potted palms and ferns, Mother with a pristine newspaper folded in half across her blanketed knee. She faced the vegetable garden that Emily had dug with John when he'd been home on leave.

'It makes me sad; my rose garden all ploughed up like it is and then just abandoned to nature. You have desecrated our lawn. Surely it can't make that much difference to food supplies.'

'While there's still a shortage of food, the potato crop …'

'Haven't we given enough to this war?'

It was a funny thing to worry about: the rose garden.

'Can you see to it for me?' Mother continued. 'I want the roses back. Perhaps ask Mr Tipton to send up old Alfred to lend a hand.'

Emily held her tongue. John had asked her not to argue with Mother, to pull together, to accept what had happened. She owed it to him to try her best. But he had also told her not to give up on what she wanted. He'd been certain that she'd find a way; but then he must have known that in the event anything happened to him it would make her escape even harder.

'I'm glad I have you here, dear.' Mother smiled weakly. Her

head slumped in her hands. 'You are quite impossible, but you're all I have.'

*

Bishop warns against spate of hasty marriages

She was under the monkey puzzle tree, the newspaper resting on her knees.

Young people were getting carried away with romantic ideals and marrying when they'd only just met, the Bishop warned. A young man, a gunner with the army, spoke out against the Bishop. The gunner argued that the man of the cloth didn't understand how war made every moment precious. He stated that the marriages weren't hasty at all, but blossomed after couples wrote to one another for many months, becoming better acquainted in pen and ink then they ever would under the watchful eye of a chaperone.

So, Theo wasn't the only one proposing out of the carriage windows. It had seemed so soon, well it *was* soon – she'd only met him that afternoon and he'd asked her to marry him. But they wrote letters often and she discussed things with him she'd never dream of sharing with anyone else. He was interested in her, he believed in her and he'd been such a great comfort to her since John had been reported missing. He was often the only beam of light in an otherwise dark existence.

Her gaze travelled through the jagged branches of the tree. The gunner in the newspaper was right; life was precious. John's disappearance had taught her that. It was important to reach out and grasp whatever the Fates sent you.

*

Emily and Cecil shared a birthday and so Cecil came home from university so they could celebrate as a family. She might have guessed that he'd cause trouble before they'd even got to the main course of their evening meal.

'I'm going to ignore my call-up papers,' he announced. 'I won't be fighting in the war.'

Emily let go of the spoon and it fell into the soup bowl. The Conscription Act had just been passed and all single men between eighteen and forty-one had to join up.

'John's news made up my mind,' he continued. 'I'm not going to fight this government's war for them.'

'Hasn't what's happened to John invigorated you, made you angry and want to fight?' Emily asked. It certainly had fuelled her desire to do everything she could to help them win the war. If the allies lost, John might never come home. And yet Cecil was passing that opportunity up while she was left at home to take care of Mother.

Cecil cut her dead with a withering glance and addressed Mother, who had gone a deathly pale and hadn't moved since Cecil first spoke.

'Asquith has no right to force me to join up,' Cecil continued. 'I'm going to object on the grounds of my conscience.'

Emily shook her head; her brother was to become a conscientious objector. He'd witnessed what sort of response his views elicited at John's leaving party. It was just like him to not worry about the consequences for the rest of the family.

'In that case, perhaps you could stay here with Mother, so that I can go to work and do my duty to King and country.'

'I don't believe that it is my place to run into machine-gun fire so that the upper classes can cling to their position or the capitalists can prosper. That's not duty, that's madness.'

'But what about John?' Emily asked. 'He's a hero, and you will undo that if you bring shame on the family.'

'I don't want to hurt the family. If I could leave you out of it, and just pay the price myself, then of course I would. And I will tell you now, just how sorry I am for the trouble I'll bring to you,' Cecil replied.

'Oh Cecil.' Although it sounded as if she wanted him to go off and risk his life, that wasn't the case at all. Nobody wanted their loved ones to fight, but for both of them to sit the war out was so unpatriotic. 'You will let everyone down.' Mother still hadn't said a word. 'Don't you think our mother has suffered enough?'

Emily pushed her soup away. How would she explain to Theo that her brother was refusing to fight while he risked his life every day in the name of his country?

'What you're talking about is dishonourable, you know?' she said. 'If every man refused to fight then the war would be lost. Mother, you must tell him.'

'If every man refused to fight,' Cecil jumped in, 'then there would be no war and our differences would have to be resolved peacefully.'

She dropped her head. This was just like Cecil. He would be impossible to convince otherwise, but he *would* listen to Mother.

'This war is so unfair,' she said, thinking of Theo out there, still cheerful and doing his best for his country. 'But if we don't fight against the Germans, they might come here and do to us what they did to Belgium. Have you thought of that?'

'Do you want him to go and fight?' Mother said.

Her mouth gaped open. Of course that wasn't what she wanted. Cecil was never meant to be a soldier. He wasn't much older than a boy. His skin was still soft; his face wasn't that of a killer. One brother had been missing for months, what could she possibly gain from losing another?

'That's a terrible accusation,' she replied.

'Cecil, my darling boy.' Mother carried on. 'Are you really certain?'

The rasp of Emily's breathing filled the room.

'My mind is made up.'

'Very well,' Mother replied.

Emily jumped up. Was that it?

'Your family will stand by you ...'

'Mother ...' Emily began.

Mother raised her hand to silence her. 'We must respect Cecil's decision and support him.'

'And does it matter what I think?' she said.

But as usual, Mother didn't answer.

The village would turn against them. The reminders of their patriotic duty were everywhere; Kitchener's finger pointing at them from his poster on the railway station wall. They would lock Cecil up, subject him to hard labour. Would they even accept her on the farm if Cecil brought this disgrace on them?

She wiped her tears away. It was too much: first John and now this.

'I will stand by Cecil's decision.' Mother blotted her lips and then shuffled out of the room and upstairs to bed.

'You are making life impossible for me. Mr Tipton is desperate for help on the farm, and yet Mother insists I'm by her side, day and night.'

'You spoke to me of duty, well Mother is yours.'

'This might well break her, you know. Do you even care?'

'Of course,' he said, his voice breaking. He uncrossed his legs and stood from his seat. Had he even stopped to consider their financial troubles? Did he care that without John at the helm Mother would continue to take handouts and do nothing to resolve the root of the problem?

He was crying now. Huge tears dripping onto the tablecloth. His decision would bring him enough grief – she couldn't add to it. She comforted him, put her arms around him. He was a pitiful sight stooped over with his nose streaming. He was electric to touch as if he exuded the toxic danger that he brought to the family.

He stepped out onto the lawn, towards the monkey puzzle tree, swung back his arm and punched the trunk. He lifted his face to the heavens and opened his mouth, but from inside the dining room his yell was silent.

Chapter Nine

February 1916

Mrs L Cotham
HopBine House
New Lane
Chartleigh
Kent

The envelope sat on the mantelpiece for an entire morning, peeking out from behind the photograph of John in a frame painted with forget-me-nots. Finally, the three of them – Emily, Mother and Cecil – gathered in the sitting room. Emily took the opener and slashed open the envelope.

The War Office had completed its investigations and Officer John Cotham was now *officially regarded as having died.*

Her mother whimpered. Cradled her face with her hands.

'No wonder Kitchener wanted bachelors.' Cecil's bottom lip trembled as he spoke.

Emily tumbled into a long, black tunnel that stretched to eternity; the same tunnel she'd fallen into when her father had died. No matter how far she fell, the dark hole stretched into the shadows. Her legs were filled with a substance as heavy and clogged as the mud Theo described in the trenches. She'd wanted to hide in her bedroom until someone came to tell her it was over, that it wasn't true. But Mother needed them both. She wept uncontrollably as if there was no room in the house for her or Cecil to grieve as well.

When friends and neighbours called on them, Mother put on a show.

'I'm but one of thousands of mothers in the same position.'

Privately, Mother fretted, 'Would I have treated him differently as a baby had I known?' Her food went untouched. She paced about the house in the dead of the night, wept until her throat was sore and winced as she swallowed her tea. Worst of all, she became fixated with John's whereabouts. In a husky voice, she speculated that the War Office had got it wrong. Perhaps they'd confused him with another man.

'It must be difficult to keep track of them all, so many men, scores missing or killed.'

Then one of the sets of John's identity tags was returned to them in the post, along with the diary full of the names of the men he had lost in battle. The officer uniform that they had paid for arrived wrapped in brown paper.

Emily flicked through the pages, pressing her fingers to the inked names, and then at the very last page, at the end of the list she added one last soldier:

John Cotham.

And then she added his service number after his name.

Emily encouraged Mother to write to an old friend of her family. Lady Heath had been widowed when her husband had been killed on the first day of the Somme in 1914. Lady Heath wrote back suggesting that her friend make a remembrance book. Mother pasted in photographs, letters, press cuttings and John's identity tags. Lady Heath shared the poetry she had written about her husband, but Mother said she just didn't have the words.

There was nothing that she could do to reach her.

The letters and bills piled up in the library, but Mother wouldn't allow her to open them.

'We can't ignore our problems forever,' Emily insisted. 'We will have to do something.'

Despite the lack of sleep and loss of appetite, Mother rapped the glass with her fists and yelled that the vegetable garden needed to go. Emily agreed for once. Her hopes of doing any war work had died with John and the plot was a cruel reminder, but even so it was one of the last things she'd done with her brother and she couldn't let it go back to the roses yet.

Desperate to soothe Mother's grief, Emily suggested a memorial service.

'We could hold a service at the church, followed by a wake on the lawn.'

She had to do something to help Mother find her strength. She still couldn't believe it herself, and dear John deserved a fitting tribute. The problem was Cecil. Now that word about his conscientious objection was travelling around the village, they might be alone at the service. The memorial might be for John, but it could end up being about Cecil.

*

March 1916

Emily rushed down to the hallway as the front door slammed shut.

'No good,' Mother said, tossing her gloves onto the hall table, her voice still hoarse. She barged past Emily and Daisy on her way to the kitchen.

'What did they say?' Emily cantered to keep up with Mother.

'They were a bunch of jumped-up old has-beens dizzy on the power bestowed upon them by the Crown. It could hardly be called a hearing, because Cecil wasn't heard at all. They didn't even let him speak. Not once.' She paused to clear her own throat. 'He had written a stirring and powerful speech in defence of his principles.'

Mother searched about her, opening cupboards and slamming them shut. The servants' indicator board behind her was a reminder that they were on the other side of the house now.

'They imprisoned him there and then.'

Emily gripped the kitchen table. First John, and now Cecil, gone within a matter of weeks.

Mother asked Edna for a glass of something stiff. Edna lifted her hands from the butler sink in the scullery, dried them on her apron and took a bottle of cooking sherry out of the cupboard. She set down a thin-waisted glass, but Mother leant over her and took a whisky tumbler down instead.

'Fill her up, please.'

Mother knocked it back and flung open the scullery door, Emily chasing behind her.

Emily was too late to catch her. She was already down at the vegetable garden kicking up the earth.

'Mother! Please! Don't do that. It's John's ...'

'It isn't. It has nothing to do with your poor brother. He didn't ever show an interest in farming and crops in all his twenty-four years. It's just another of your ideas.'

Tears pricked at Emily's eyes. Without a grave to tend, Mother might have found comfort in nurturing this garden and seeing it yield crops. Instead, Mother knocked it all up. Soil and tender shoots flew everywhere.

'And what will Lady Radford say? Her titled relatives are losing sons like a flower surrenders its seeds to the wind. And I suppose you've heard about Lady Clara?'

Emily shook her head.

'She's gone to France to set up a hospital in an abbey near Paris with the French Red Cross. She's taken her car to use as an ambulance.'

That stung Emily. Still Mother refused to see that Emily could and should be doing her bit too.

'Meanwhile, Cecil has been dragged off to prison.' Mother slowed down now. 'I couldn't go on if I was on my own, I really couldn't.' For a moment, she actually stopped and her steel-blue gaze settled on Emily's face, her eyes searching. She steadied her hands on Emily's shoulders and then her body collapsed as she gave into a sob. Emily filled with warmth and reached out to embrace Mother.

'I need a lie-down,' Mother said, straightening up and dusting down her skirt.

'What is going to happen about the house?' Emily blurted out. They couldn't go on not communicating with one another if it was just the two of them. She had to do as John had asked and ensure they pulled together.

But the moment was gone. Mother returned to the house and closed the door behind her.

*

She dug up the seed potatoes herself, and dismantled the frames for the runner beans that had survived Mother's rampage.

Pieter and Stefan, the Belgian refugees, came to help her plant the new rose bushes. The poor Belgians, who had come to England with nothing, were grateful that John had given them a safe home for the war. They would call it John's Rose Garden.

All the while, Mother was in bed. Absent from life in all but body.

The rose bushes were already mature and within a week were budding up. As the green seams of the buds receded, crimson red pushed through.

Chapter Ten

April 1916

The night before the memorial Uncle Wilfred arrived. Mother stayed in her room at first, but eventually she dressed and joined them.

He spread his arms wide and pulled her to him. Mother sobbed into his chest while Emily wished there was something she could do. Supper was subdued. Whenever Mother let out a wail, Wilfred covered her hand on the table with his own and patted it. Later, he raised a hand to her face and she flinched, but he was only wiping a tear from beneath her eye.

Emily was suddenly interested in her rhubarb syllabub. His actions were very familiar for someone who'd had nothing to do with the family for twenty-five years.

He stayed overnight.

News of Cecil's imprisonment had travelled, and the attendance at the memorial service the next day was an insult to John. At the tea, after the church service, it was just Emily, Mother, Wilfred, Daisy, Edna, Mr and Mrs Peters and the Tiptons. Grandmother declined the invitation, on the grounds that it was all too tragic; first a son and now a grandson. She didn't want to dredge up her painful grief.

73

They all stood with customary dry eyes staring at the naked rose bushes as if they'd give them meaning and an explanation for their loss. Emily read 'Remember' by Rossetti but she didn't make it through to the end. She began to sob so hard that at first the words were blurred and then the verse was forgotten and she put up her hand to cover her face, and hung her head to the ground.

A comforting arm around her back pulled her close. She leant on the black-clad shoulder expecting the slight bones of her mother and started when she found it was much fleshier. When she lifted her head, it was kindly Mrs Tipton.

'There, there, my love,' she said.

'I need to rest,' Mother said, her shoulders falling away once the guests had gone home. She remained, hopeless and lost, until Wilfred stepped closer and proffered his arm. He'd hung his head throughout the service, a handkerchief blotting his nose, a show of grief for a nephew he hardly knew. Mother, too frail to carry herself upright, leant into him.

Emily wished someone would support her and let her rest. She'd never been so bone-tired in all her life, but instead it was down to her to thank the others for coming and accept their condolences on behalf of the family, such as it was now.

Mother tilted her face up to Wilfred, basking in his attention; his banal quotations seemingly carried meaning to her. 'But the only way to look now is to the future,' he said.

Mother nodded, her head falling to one side as if straining at the thought of putting John's death behind her.

Her stomach tightened. It was easy for Wilfred to appear out of nowhere and spout meaningless aphorisms, however well intentioned, but it was far harder for those who knew and loved John to move on so soon.

When Emily had said goodbye to the last of the guests, she returned inside the house where she found Uncle Wilfred alone in the sitting room.

74

'I've sent your mother upstairs to change,' Uncle Wilfred explained. It took her a moment to notice what was different. It was bright in the sitting room. He'd asked Daisy to draw the curtains. Light was flooding the room again to make it summer inside as well as out, and glinting the glass of the dark oak sideboard and the china hanging from the rail.

'Mother must have the time and space to grieve,' she warned him, though she wasn't brave enough to meet his eye as she said it.

Daisy came in at that moment with the tea things and set them on the table. Uncle Wilfred eyed Daisy's ankles as she adjusted the vase. She was dressed in her shorter afternoon dress with a white-lace collar and cuffs. Her tiara-like cap was held in place with black velvet ribbon.

'Why don't *you* change?' Uncle Wilfred said to Emily.

'I'm quite all right as I am, thank you.' She raised her gaze this time and smiled at him sweetly, her jaw set in a message of defiance. His support might be welcomed, but she wasn't as helpless or in need as her mother.

'I want you to know that you're not alone. You mustn't feel you have to bear the burden now that the men are all gone.'

'That's kind of you, thank you. But I'm sure we'll manage. One way or another.'

Wilfred laughed at her, his shoulders rising and falling. 'Are you aware that your brother asked me for help?'

The way he was so clinical about it filled her veins with ice. She nodded.

'Inflation is high, as are taxes, and as for death duties, well – something has to pay for this war – so you mustn't think ill of your father.'

'Oh, I really don't,' she said.

'Good. Good. Well your brother also asked that I take care of your mother if anything should happen to him.'

'Really?' John had told her that she and Mother must pull

together, that Mother would need her daughter. But he'd been vague too and said she must accept whatever happened. What had he planned for them all? He'd been so certain he wouldn't return, and he'd been right.

'Don't look so worried,' Wilfred said. 'My goodness they could run trains along those frown lines.' He was clearly amused by her. 'I shan't interfere. The important thing is there's no risk of you losing your home. It's all secure and you don't need to feel burdened either.'

'I'm not,' she said. But it was a lie; of course she was tethered to Mother, unable to follow her own desires.

'Your mother would like to get away from the village. There are too many memories up here and so on. She's to come and stay with me in London for a while.'

Emily narrowed her eyes to search his inscrutable face for a clue as to whether he was telling the truth. He'd been estranged from the family for such a long time, but what motive could he have other than kindness?

'It of course means you'd be free to work on the farm.'

'I'd already thought of that.' Her breath caught, but then reality landed. 'But wouldn't I need to go to London too?' she asked. 'I think I ought to wait and speak to Mother.'

'Very well. Talk it over with Louisa if you wish. It's awfully quiet in the house, isn't it?' He ran his fingertips along the body of the piano. The lid had remained shut since they'd received the letter from the War Office. The gramophone hadn't played a single one of its metallic tunes. 'Your father was fond of music as I recall.'

She nodded, and wished that Cecil was there to help with the small talk. She was far too tired and her mind too foggy to keep up with the events unfolding this afternoon.

Uncle Wilfred pressed the middle C key and its dull reverberation pierced the room and his fingers began to unfold a tune she didn't recognise just as Mother reappeared in a white dress made of linen that accentuated her waist. A wide, white hat perched on the side of her head, obscured a patch where her hair had fallen out.

'Ah.' Uncle Wilfred rose to his feet, casting an admiring glance from Louisa's head to her toe.

Mother let the music pass without comment.

'Uncle Wilfred tells me that you're thinking of staying with him in London.'

Mother nodded.

'That's right. I think it will do me good to have a change. I even thought we might volunteer the house up to the army – they're hunting for a convalescent home.'

She clenched every muscle in her body, and waited for Mother to tell her that she would need her in London with her.

'I thought over what Lady Radford had to say about the need to do all we can for the war, and Cecil has lowered our standing in the community. If you were to take on some war work too it might balance out his damage.' Emily could only have believed it if she'd heard the words coming straight from Mother's mouth. 'Mr Tipton has said you can take a billet in Perseverance Place and start work with him when you're ready.'

Just like that? Every day since Father had died she had told Emily she needed her by her side, that she couldn't cope without her. And now, after months of resistance to her plea to volunteer for war work and outright disapproval of her ambitions to be a land girl, Mother was giving her blessing. Mother didn't need her any longer and so she was letting her go to do the one thing she dreamt of more than anything. So why then didn't it feel like a victory?

'You could park a Zepp in your jaws,' Wilfred said with a chuckle.

'Are you sure?' she asked Mother. 'I mean, will you be all right, without me?'

'Of course,' Mother said, evenly, with a light shrug.

77

Wilfred was some sort of miracle. Instead of a future spent trying to support Mother, and falling short, of trying to stretch across the empty distance between them but finding her still out of reach, she was going to be on a training course, a residential one, and then she was going to work, properly, officially on the farm. She couldn't believe it. She was really going to be a war girl.

Wilfred presented Mother with his arm and suggested a walk down to the village shrine.

'Splendid idea,' Mother said.

They walked away across the driveway towards the cedar avenue. Mother stooped over but there was a lightness to her step that she hadn't seen since John was home on leave. Father, then John and now Cecil. Mother was all that Emily had left, and Emily thought she was all Mother had. She was wrong. For once she wouldn't have minded if Mother had exerted more control over her now and pulled her so close that Emily might suffocate. But grief affected them all in different ways, and perhaps Mother was right and time away from all these memories was exactly what she needed.

It was only just sinking in: a billet, work on the farm. She was free to be a land girl. After all that asking and being met with outright refusal, who could have thought that tragedy and grief would lead to her being granted what she wanted?

She dashed upstairs and wrote with the news to Theo. He would be so delighted for her, she couldn't wait to tell him.

Chapter Eleven

April 1916

Dearest Emily,

I am so saddened by the news of your brother's death. To lose someone so dear to you is a tragedy. I'm afraid I don't understand Cecil's actions, but then I haven't had a brother cruelly snatched away from me, and so perhaps you might know more of what is going through his mind. As time moves on and the grief that clouds his vision lifts, I am certain that he will reconsider and will unite with his fellow countrymen to defeat Fritz.

Quite wonderful that something of good has come out of the whole sorry business. When your eyes lit up at the march in Westminster it was clear that you had a desire to make a difference. Whatever reservations you have about your mother's sudden change towards you, you should put to one side. She is a woman who knows what is best for her, and if she insists that she must be with your uncle then you must take heed and not attempt to sway her because the other path, the challenge ahead of you, daunts you.

This country needs you, and you are keen to do your bit,

so I would urge you not to hesitate, not to look back over your shoulder, questioning whether you have done the right thing, but to train your eyes upon the task in hand – and that is to ensure we win this war.

And finally, my dear, some news of my own: my next leave has been approved. I would love nothing more than to see your beautiful, smiling face. I suppose now you are free to see me, before you begin your work as a land girl? I will wait outside the Telegraph Office at mid-day on Wednesday.

Fondest wishes
Theo

She stood at the top of the church aisle. The third day into Theo's leave. Her stomach turned somersaults when the church organ erupted into a swirling flurry. Whatever happened next, she had to do as John said, and not give up on her dreams.

She'd waited for him by the Telegraph Office. When he strode across the concourse, he was deep in conversation with a friend. His expression was glazed; his gaze didn't settle on her. A tiny whimper escaped from her and the floor fell away from her feet. Then, as he drew level one of his mates elbowed him in the ribs.

'Oh, um … Emily,' he said coming to a halt.

He dropped his kit bag and pulled her close, his chin on top of her head. She burrowed into his chest, shut out the light and there, for the first time since John had died she let the tears flow, the sobs overtaking her body. That evening he proposed again, and this time something told her to say yes. Three days later, here they were.

She searched past the empty rib cage of pews and gawped for a moment at a crooked old dear bent over the organ's keys as her frail fingers conjured up the insistent tone of the Wedding March. Another somersault. This was it. The music would carry her down the aisle.

In front of the altar Theo waited, his shoulders hunched as he rocked back and forth on the balls of his feet. He had his back to her, his face to the heavens, perhaps praying for a happy marriage, or that his bride would get a move on and get things over with before he had to catch his train back to the Front. Beside him, patting the breast pocket which contained the ring, was Theo's best man, who he'd found earlier in The Mitre pub opposite the church.

The vicar, who'd been scanning the pages of his Bible, flashed his gaze up the aisle to Emily, raised his eyebrows and nodded to her. Another somersault. *Believe in yourself,* John's voice said in her head.

She couldn't think about what Mother would say because it might stop her from doing this; but Mother hadn't even replied to her letters. If she had, Emily might not even be there at all. The surprising truth stopped her dead. She pulled back her veil and called: 'I'm sorry about this. I'll be back in a moment.'

The music came to an abrupt halt as she fled from the church and out into the stark morning. She took three of the concrete steps that fanned out to the London street and clung to a pillar, a pensive hand smothering her mouth, her eyes wide and staring off to The Mitre pub over the road.

She should have at least told her Mother what she had planned to do, but there was no getting away from it, Mother had moved on. She had told Mrs Tipton, who'd clucked and said she hoped she knew what she was doing. Theo believed in her; with him by her side she could make anything happen.

A couple of soldiers, home on leave, appraised Emily with a quick up and down as they passed, their eyes drawn to the mid-calf length, scalloped hem of the white-lace dress Theo had bought her in Selfridges. She gave the men a warning glare. They laughed to one another as they moved on. The one on the right, the taller of the two, turned again and winked at her. She shook her head.

'The next couple will be here soon.' Theo was behind her. 'Are you sure you want to do this?' His face glistened with sweat; his soft brown eyes had hardened to black dots. Emily wanted to comfort him. By taking flight she'd clearly given him the jitters too.

On his next leave, he'd promised her they would visit his family, and go to Yorkshire to see the place that they'd call home after the war.

She slipped her hand inside his.

'Let's get married,' she said.

Chapter Twelve

Dearest Emily,

I wonder how you are. Thank you for sending me the photograph of you in your land girl garb. As soon as I saw it, I knew I'd never see you any other way.

Just ten minutes ago Fritz was letting us have it. My good pal Patch and I were lying side by side, barely a movement between us on the ground for nearly half an hour. We didn't strip our eyes away from one another the entire time. It was most strange when the spell broke and we went back to our duties. Captain Robinson brought us all a nip of rum when it was all over.

I am afraid I have little else that I may tell you.

Keep thinking of me.

Fondest wishes

Theo

She skipped over to the farmhouse on her first morning, in her new garb: a wedding ring, a jaunty silk scarf fastened about her head, one of Father's old shirts, and a new knee-length oilskin coat belted around the waist that was the bee's knees, though beneath it she was almost naked with nothing but stockings, knickers and knee-high leather gaiters. The stout boots were rubbing her heels already, but not enough that it would spoil her first day on the job.

'How about starting with collecting the eggs, while we find the ole man?' Mrs Tipton handed her a basket at the farmhouse kitchen door. The chickens crowded Emily's ankles like a cloud of dust as she foraged about in the coop for the little gems they'd left behind. So precious those eggs had become that they had to collect them up quickly in case anyone tramping through stole them away.

'Ah, there you are,' Mr Tipton said when she found him up at the dairy. 'It's muck-spreading today.' He beckoned her towards a hay barn and thrust a pitchfork into her hand and they walked over to the field and a twelve-foot pile of manure.

She copied the other women, sliding the muck down from the wain and fixing as much of it as she could on to the prongs of the pitchfork, then tossing it about, giving a rich texture to the faded clods of earth it covered.

It wasn't as bad as she'd expected – the aroma was quite sweet. For the first half an hour she got stuck in. If only Mother could see her now. She straightened up to enjoy the tease and tickle of a gust of wind on her skin.

After an hour, her mouth was dry and her back was nagging at her to stand up straight. But nothing would make her complain; Cecil's initial sentence was one hundred and twelve days of hard labour, with nothing but bread and water to keep him going.

She outstretched her hand for a glimpse of her golden wedding ring only to find a bare finger. Her mind raced; had she been wearing it that morning? She always wore it. Why would today be any different? She'd not stopped admiring the band since Theo had slipped it on her finger. How had she even managed to let it out of her sight long enough for it to slip off?

She searched about on the soil, crouching down and sweeping her way across where she'd been working, back and forth. What would she tell Theo? She couldn't possibly expect him to buy her another.

'What on earth are you up to?' Mr Tipton asked. She told him about the ring, but he shrugged and checked the position of the sun. 'Time's moving on, you got five minutes more and then you need to get back to work. Have you checked the muck pile?'

She hadn't. There was a chance it had slipped off her finger while she was digging in with her pitchfork.

She turned to her housemate Martha, a girl about her age with raven hair fastened beneath a scarf. Martha had previously worked as a housemaid at a big house the other side of West Malling and had hardly said a word to her since she'd moved in to Perseverance Place, but she had made it clear to Mrs Tipton that she disapproved of Cecil.

'Sorry,' Martha said turning her back on her. 'I prefer to mind my own business.'

Emily gripped the fork and pitched through the muck, but it was shifting in clumps, which was no use. She had no choice but to inspect it closely. She crouched on her haunches again and sieved the muck through her fingers, taking two handfuls at a time, her eyes moving from left to right. She glared at Martha. How could she stand by while she was frantic? It certainly gave new meaning to the search for a needle in a haystack. Halfway through the pile she wiped her brow with the back of her hand. It irritated her throat and made her cough.

'Right then, now,' Mr Tipton said. 'It's time for work. It'll turn up sooner or later – you'll see.'

Her jaw tightened. She'd have to let it go for now. She wouldn't give Martha the satisfaction of seeing her cry.

'You two can follow me.' Mr Tipton walked ahead of them. He was treating her like any of the other girls, which she supposed was how it should be, but she missed the old way he joked with her and always took the time to explain what he was doing.

As they left the lonely muck pile Emily scanned it one last time, but there was just a hundred different shades of brown and nothing golden apart from the sun in the sky and the sheen of her skin.

On the top field, there was a fresh pile of manure already waiting for them. Halfway along the path at the edge of the meadow Mr Tipton stopped and raised a forefinger to his lips. 'Quiet now,' he whispered, and they crept along the path.

At the end of the hedge, Mr Tipton grabbed Emily by the arm, yanked her through a gap and into the top corner of the neighbouring field. He pointed along the base of the foliage. She narrowed her eyes, expecting a flash of a deer's tail to disappear through the hedgerow. Instead, there were two women on the ground, their legs hunched up under their chins, eyes fixed on their novels.

'Ya!' Mr Tipton shouted.

Olive Hughes and Ada Little squawked. They stuffed their books into their knapsacks, dusting down their oilskins as they rose to their feet.

'You puddle ducks ha' been caught red-handed,' Mr Tipton bellowed as he marched along the ploughed edge of the field. Emily traipsed after him, avoiding the large clods that would disturb her footing. 'And not for the first time.'

'We were just having a ten-minute rest,' Olive grunted. 'Miserable ole beggar.'

'You rest and eat when *I* say.'

'We know the men get paid three or four times our one pound a week,' Olive Hughes said. 'You can't expect the same work if you don't pay the same wages.'

'You ducks develop the strength of the men I've lost from here, and I'll pay you the same. Now, you must know Miss Emily. She's been training, and is some sort of farming expert now. She'll be in charge of you lot from now on. I'm washing my hands of you.'

The women switched the focus of their snarling faces from Mr Tipton to Emily.

'Well, these women are quite the cowherds, aren't you?' Emily chuckled.

She had no hope of getting a working party together to search for her wedding ring, if Olive's eye rolling and Ada's muttering were anything to go by. It was most likely that they'd desert her for their beds and she'd be frantically sieving through that muck on her own in the dark.

Once Mr Tipton was out of sight, she puffed up her chest, though they probably could see straight through her. She said, 'Let's get back to work.'

She marched away from the women hoping and praying that they had done as she asked and followed her, because her training course hadn't prepared her for what she was supposed to do next. But they were there, traipsing a short distance behind her. They were moaning and their glares could have toasted muffins, but at least they'd done as she requested. She couldn't have asked for anything more.

When they took a break for lunch, Olive and Ada – who'd had their heads together with non-stop chattering travelling between them like an electrical current – dumped their pitchforks on the ground and started to loll off without a backwards glance. But she had to start now as she meant to go on. She cleared her throat and then called after them: 'Ahem.'

The ladies didn't hear, or ignored her, and Martha also dropped her pitchfork where she stood and stared at her in a way that made her wither like wheat in a drought.

Her cheeks burnt, but if she let them go now they'd never have any respect for her, and then things could only get worse.

'Mrs Hughes. Mrs Little.' She spoke more sharply this time. 'Ladies! Please stop.' Her voice cut through the air – even the birds seemed to hush. Ada and Olive came to a standstill. Her fleeting smile of victory was quickly extinguished. These two women had shown Mr Tipton, the farm's manager, a shocking level of disrespect since they'd come to work on the farm. Did she really stand a chance of making them listen to her?

She let the heels of her boots sink into the mud, her stride wide. Her voice was foggy again; she cleared it.

'You're to work through your lunch today,' she said with a confidence she didn't feel. She held her breath while the two women conferred quietly. 'To make up for the time spent behind the hedge,' she added to make herself quite clear.

She waited what seemed like a day. The two women eyed her up and exchanged mutterings. Her stomach was rumbling so loudly it might startle the crows on the neighbouring field, but if she was in charge she couldn't go and get her lunch either. She would have to stay with them, and try her best not to think about Mrs Tipton's delicious bacon sandwiches.

And then, finally, Olive moved forwards and lifted her pitchfork back up and Ada followed her. Martha kept walking, but two out of three was good enough for her. Emily smiled – she couldn't control it. She had the urge to leap up and down, but a smile would do.

Chapter Thirteen

July 1916

Dearest Emily,

I hope you will accept my apology for not writing before. Patch was hit by shrapnel, not severely but enough to put him out of action. He is back with us now, but it left me queer for a few weeks.

I am hopeful that I will be given some leave soon. It's hard to believe I haven't seen you since our wedding day. It will be wonderful to spend time with you again.

Fondest love

Theo

Emily perched gingerly on her stool, ready to run for it should Lily pull another of her tricks while Mr Tipton led the cows along the straw-dappled cobblestones into their pen. She smiled at Martha, who ignored her. She was almost immune to her animosity by now, but she wouldn't give up, because they might just get along if only Martha would give her a chance.

The cows rumbled past them, eyes peeled wide. They grunted

and stamped backwards, hooves scraping along the cobbles, butting one another.

Martha worked silently, burying her head in Nancy's side-hind and squeezing the teat as the stream of milk pummelled the zinc pail.

'Any word from your mother?' Mr Tipton asked, Sally the collie at his heels.

Emily shook her head at Mr Tipton. She still wrote weekly with her adventures on the farm, inviting Mother to tell her how she was coping in London, and whether she found it helped to be away from the memories of HopBine. But the initial letters had stopped. She checked the post mat and found nothing from Mother, just a slicing draft through the letterbox.

'And Cecil?'

She shook her head again. He'd not written either, which was far worse than a letter telling her he was exhausted, because her imagination was a great artist and could sketch a worse scenario.

She had such mixed feelings about Cecil. The worry about his treatment kept her awake at night; he might be as stubborn as a donkey, but he wasn't as strong physically. He was used to his home comforts, to being pandered to by Mother, and it made her want to scream at the very idea of him locked in a tiny cell with no books and no light, growing more and more feeble on bread and water. That's what they'd heard it was like; the German prisoners of war were treated better. But at the same time, she wanted to hide away from the people he'd hurt and cry for poor desecrated John's memory. How would she ever look at him and not feel a fire burning within her?

She came face to face with Martha and smiled. What else could she do but keep smiling?

She adjusted her girl, Lily, this way and that for a better grip. She'd had another calf. This one had survived, but she was still a tetchy so-and-so and her thin teats didn't help. She butted Martha now with her hind with such a force that she forced her from the stool.

She offered Martha a hand up, but she ignored it.

'Do you think you can control your cow, please?' Martha spat.

Every muscle and sinew tightened. As Martha dusted herself off, something inside snapped. They couldn't possibly go on like this. If she didn't encourage Martha to speak what was on her mind they would have to endure this uncomfortable silence for the rest of the war.

'Do you think you could try to be civil towards me? After all, we have to live together.'

'Just because you own this place, doesn't make you any better than me,' Martha replied.

'I don't for one moment think I'm better than anyone. But I also don't believe I should be held to account for the actions of my brother.'

Emily rubbed Lily's side to warm her hands. She was trembling, giving her away. She focused on the job, willing her hands to stay steady so that she could curl her fingers as tightly as she could. Enjoying the discomfort of her nails biting into her palm, she pushed her hand against the soft udder, pulled the warm teat down in short, decisive tugs and out shot the jet of warm milk.

But Lily wasn't silly; she'd sensed she was in the care of an edgy milkmaid. The cow took another lurch backwards, this time knocking Emily clean from the three-legged stool.

Martha didn't offer to help her up; she just left her lying there. Emily pushed her sore hand into the cobblestones to lever herself up to sitting, just as Lily lifted her rear hoof and set it straight into the pail, sending it clanging to the ground and leaving a creamy puddle.

'What a waste,' Martha said. 'Mr Tipton won't be happy.'

Emily said nothing. It was better that way. Her blood was surging through her veins, and if she said anything else, she'd regret it.

Once they'd finished milking, they took their pails up to the separator and then let the cows out on to the meadow. Emily hung back to see which direction Martha took, and chose the opposite.

*

'Back to it then, my dears,' Mrs Tipton said, as she massaged her calves to stop the cramp.

The farmhouse heat, the low ceiling, the burnt coal, the cats' damp coats and Mrs Tipton's cabbage-soup steam had all made Emily quite sleepy. She pinned opened her eyes. She needed to stay awake so she could do the last of her jobs for the day, and because she'd do anything to avoid sleep these days.

She woke most nights, her chest tight, her skin prickling with cold, gasping for air. In her dreams she drowned in dark, still water, or ran along the bank, John on the other side, but there was no bridge, never a way across.

During the days she was consumed with her work, though the other girls kept their distance. The evenings made up for it; the Tiptons didn't judge, and understood what she'd lost.

After five hours of lifting crates at a neighbouring farm early on and a tramp there and back along a mud-porridge path, her arms, legs and back ached. Even her bones hurt and her heart did too. The shadows loomed in her mind. Mr Tipton had his eye on her, had done all evening, and so she didn't get up when the others did. She was glad. She didn't want to bed the horses down while the girls were engrossed in a conversation that didn't include her, and she didn't want to go back to Perseverance Place and take herself off to bed early, because her blankets were the only comfort and warmth she'd get there.

She shook out her trouser legs – she wore a nice comfy pair of breeches to work now, and she didn't feel quite so naked beneath her oilskin any longer – and adjusted her boots. She would wait as long as it took for Mr Tipton to speak.

'As you're doing well, I want you to take charge of our new

workers,' he said, closing the kitchen door so that it was just the three of them. Mrs Tipton dried her hands on her apron and sucked through her teeth.

Emily waited. Something told her that this wasn't going to be the good news it seemed to be on the surface.

'We've got five German prisoners o' war, coming to work here.'

Mrs Tipton disappeared into the scullery with a shake of her head.

'They'll take one of the spare houses at Perseverance Place.'

Hair prickled at the nape of her neck. 'But no one will want them here.' She shuddered. They might walk in on the girls at night, and do to them what they did to the women in Belgium.

'You'll have to work something out then,' Mr Tipton said.

She didn't understand. Why was she responsible? Hadn't she been taken on to organise the women? And that was hard enough. She implored Mrs Tipton to step in, or to explain, to do something other than clattering about with a crock and refusing to meet her eye.

'But Mr Tipton …' she began, with no idea of how she might finish that sentence.

'The army are also sending two men who aren't fit to fight in the war,' he added. 'One of 'em's deaf, the other's lame. They'll be with me.'

'Wouldn't it be better if those two were with me and the women?' she asked.

Mr Tipton shook his head and explained. 'They're sending us a Fordson tractor and they've trained one of the soldiers how to use it. You women can't be trusted with a great machine like that.'

'But the women will never work with the Germans,' Emily said. This would only make things worse with Martha. She might as well ask her to call her the Kaiser.

*

'Work with the Hun?' Martha said, the rest of the girls crowding behind her. 'No way. No blinking way.' They were up on the top field lifting stones ready for the plough. The deaf soldier had been out on the tractor, ploughing the half that they'd already cleared, but he'd stalled it, claiming it had a mechanical problem that he didn't know how to fix, and it had remained stranded like a relic to the future in the middle of the field.

'You've a brass cheek to even ask. I'm a volunteer, remember? I can go home and put my feet up if I choose,' Olive said.

She didn't need reminding – she'd been thinking the same thing. She'd signed up wanting to make a difference, and to have a wonderful time working the land, not to work alongside the Hun and be treated as if *she* was the enemy by the other workers.

'We can give them the jobs we don't like,' Emily reasoned, letting her heels sink into the ground. There was some marshy land down by the river that needed to be readied for the plough.

'Well that would be all of it then.' Ada sniffed. She staggered under the weight of a boulder. Stone lifting was monotonous, heavy going and for every rock lifted, half a dozen seemed to take their place, but it was better than readying marshland or cleaning out ditches.

Emily dumped a heavy boulder into the cart.

'I'm going to tell Mr Tipton that we must ask the men to stay in their lodgings at night. We won't be mixing with them.'

'What?' Lottie's eyes were wide. 'They'll be living amongst us, too?'

'At Perseverance Place, yes.' Emily trained her eyes to the ground. Mr Tipton hadn't been silly giving her this responsibility, but he'd let her down. It seemed to her that he wanted the German manpower, with none of the aggravation that came with it, and it was unfair that she had to break it to them that the Germans were no longer being held in armed camps. 'We will have to trust them.'

Olive and Ada scoffed, shaking their heads.

'You do read the newspapers?' Martha asked.

'We have safety in numbers,' Emily reasoned. Why did she have to say such silly things? If those men decided to attack them in their beds at night they wouldn't be strong enough to defend themselves, and their only hope would be one deaf and one lame soldier. 'Perhaps we should sleep with pitchforks beneath our beds?' she said.

If only she could take the words back, but it was too late. The women tutted.

'It's as if we've been invaded after all.'

'I won't do it,' said Martha, predictably. 'I'll go and get a job in munitions with better pay and no Germans.' Martha threw her gloves onto the boulders in the wain, and then the others followed, and she was powerless to stop them.

Chapter Fourteen

July 1916

The German voices travelled through the thin walls. Sharp, angular speech that landed like spears against her ears filled her bedroom and made her feel as if she wasn't in her own home any longer, as if they were occupied, which was silly because those men weren't soldiers, they were just trapped in a country that hated them and resented their very presence, that would find satisfaction in seeing them suffer.

Her own home was so quiet. She and Martha mostly stayed in their bedrooms. She even ate in her own room now. They hadn't spoken in days. In Martha's eyes the Germans were just another example of Emily siding with the enemy. And Emily had given up trying to be reasonable with her. She'd sunk to the lows of being just as bad.

The Germans took orders from her, a woman, better than the land girls did. They were friendly and kind and nothing at all like the picture painted by the newspapers. They'd accepted the task of turning over the marshy land, something that would have had her girls complaining every moment, and they worked just as long as the rest of them.

Now in their second week she had them working in the ditches – long days without trouble. Meanwhile, Mr Tipton had already sent back the two men the army had given them.

'Hopeless,' he'd said. 'But I told 'em we'll keep the tractor, thank you very much, but they can have the men.'

'Is the Fordson still up on the top field?' she asked. A broken-down tractor that no one could drive wasn't any use at all.

'Aye. With that machine I'll not need so many workers. And what a blessing that will be.'

She kicked about some dust with her foot. She still couldn't admit that she was having trouble, that the girls refused to work with the men and now journeyed to the lavatory together in pairs, one standing sentry at the door, while the other did their business. All except for her; they left her to brave the darkness on her own.

Could she really make his day worse? Every day his skin was paler and more creased, his necktie hung around an increasingly scrawny neck. And what if she told him and he simply didn't care about morale and only about productivity? Then she really would be on her own.

If Father and John were there, they'd know what to do. Both would use their charm to bring everyone – German and English, men and women – together.

In the dim lamplight her left hand caught her attention. Her wedding band had never turned up. It was all she'd had to remind her of Theo, and she'd lost it. And as if he'd known and was angry with her, he hadn't written to her for a while either.

It struck her then like a stick to the back of the head. Martha was always rushing to the doormat and checking for post too. When Martha got a letter, she sprinted to her room and shut the door, and she didn't knock Emily's shoulder quite so hard when they passed on the landing or slam her dinner plate down with so much force if it was her turn to serve the evening meal.

Only their doormat had been bare every day for over a week

now. They'd collided once or twice in the hallway, both of them empty-handed. The warmth those letters gave when they did arrive couldn't be replaced with anything in the world. The silence in their place left only an aching heart and a desire to run and run until you found them safe, but there was always the knowledge that you might keep running and never find them.

Later, she knocked on Martha's door. But there came only silence. She called, and rapped again. Then Martha sighed. Heavy footsteps grew closer.

'Yes?' Martha opened the door just enough for her nose to poke through. The rims of her eyes were red, the skin around her eyes glistening in the lamplight.

Emily swallowed, straightened her arms and said, 'I just wondered, if you had someone at the Front, someone you missed, and whether it might help you to talk about them?'

'Why would you want to do that?'

'I found it helped to talk about my brother John when he was away fighting.'

'Oh,' Martha said. 'I have, yes, a brother Frank. He's my twin. And he was proud of me for doing this, but how can I write and tell him I'm living with the sister of a traitor and working with the Hun?'

*

The Germans worked so hard and such long hours that the village women had stopped hiding behind hedgerows. They took a short break in the morning and the afternoon together but they were too afraid to wander off alone and too ashamed to be outworked by the Hun.

Now, once the horses were put to bed, instead of everyone going back to their own rooms in Perseverance Place they began to hang around the farmhouse kitchen after they'd bedded down the horses, to play cards on the hearth, warmed by the fire, while

Mr Tipton told them stories or they sang campfire songs. Safety in numbers.

Mother had finally written to her. She congratulated Emily on her marriage to her 'officer chap' and was sorry she hadn't been able to make it. She'd accompanied Wilfred on a business trip to his paper mill and farms in the West Country. She didn't ask about the farm, or comment on anything Emily had told her about her work so far. Mother sounded content enough. She had no desire to lay eyes on Emily and Wilfred appeared to be taking care of her.

Then, Mr Tipton finally succumbed to Mrs Tipton's badgering to take their first day off in years.

'Our girl knows the ropes now. The men listen to her, and the girls respect her enough not to be getting up to any mischief,' Mrs Tipton reasoned, and had harnessed up Bob to the pleasure trap before he could talk her out of it.

'The ole man is taking me shopping and for a pot of tea for two somewhere nice.'

Emily didn't recall a time Mrs Tipton was ever out of her apron and she hardly knew the missus now dressed in a frilly blouse, her hair rolled around pads and filling out the canopy of a wide-brimmed hat trimmed with ribbons.

What would Mr Tipton say if he knew that the women were still refusing to work with the Germans? He might not feel so free to leave, but it would be Mrs Tipton who missed out. It was only one day. She could keep them under control for that long. Couldn't she?

Once they'd waved them off, Emily pulled everyone together in the yard.

'Now then,' she said, standing at the centre of the two respective camps, which had a sizeable gap of farmyard separating them. 'We're going to work together today,' she told them. 'We're going to check the sheep over for foot rot.'

The Germans nodded, but the women shook their heads. Martha stepped forwards, her arms folded.

'First of all,' she said, 'it's not safe working alone with those Huns. Second of all, I refuse to work alongside the brothers of men who at this very moment are trying to shell the very soul out of *my* brother.'

'Very well,' Emily said. It had been coming and she was ready for it. 'You, Olive and Ada can each go and search for the strays. We're missing three.' With no rhyme or reason, the sheep would find their way onto neighbouring land. No matter how many gaps in the hedgerows they filled with spiky blackthorn, those sheep would find a way through. Mr Tipton wouldn't invest in having the hedges made sound, or a fence to keep them in: a sign of his waning interest in the farm and his desire to retire. But they could wander a long way, and always picked the highest spot. 'You can take Sally to give you a helping hand.'

Emily pointed the way, and the three women traipsed off, Sally at their heels wagging her eager tail.

Emily, Heinrich and the others rounded the flock into a corner of the field and they identified those with a limp. Heinrich took the first, grabbing it around the neck and underneath its belly, and with a heave threw it upside down, hooves in the air.

'There you go,' Emily said to Lottie, gesturing that she could work with Heinrich to pare back the hooves and brush them with treacly tar. 'He won't bite,' she whispered in Lottie's ear. The hint of a smile formed on Heinrich's lips. 'Heinrich worked on his family farm as a boy, so he knows all about sheep.'

She paired up Hen with Ernst and the remaining two Germans together. Before she and Otto set to work, she lifted Mr Tipton's toolbox and led him up to the top field where sat the solitary figure of the abandoned Fordson tractor.

'You're a mechanic, I hear?' she said.

'You want me to fix?' he asked with a nod.

'I want you to do one better than that: I want you to show me how.'

It took no more than twenty minutes for Otto to strip the

engine down, and with a series of gestures and explanations – *mutter, schraube und keilriemen* – most of which she followed, he put everything back together again, climbed up onto the tractor and the engine started first time of asking.

'I drive it home?' Otto asked.

She chuckled. It would be a long way home in a Fordson.

'The farmyard will do, thank you,' she said with a smile. Mr Tipton's face would be a picture when he saw the tractor was fixed.

Within five minutes she was back, batting away the metallic green and blue blowflies while she worked. Without Otto, she threw the sheep herself, enjoying the tussle and the struggle and then the sensation when her strength had won out and the animal flipped over.

On the farm, she found time had a habit of passing by quietly like an underground stream. It was so different to time in HopBine House where the clock had marked the dreariness by the second. As she took a breather, Heinrich guided Lottie to grab the sheep by the hooves. The sheep slipped free. Then she lifted him in the air, but couldn't turn the sheep and had to right it again. Heinrich counted her up and with a heave, and an unnoticed helping hand from Heinrich, they set the beast on its back.

Lottie beamed, pushing back her loose hair. She put a hand on Heinrich's arm to thank him, and then quickly pulled it away. But Heinrich had noticed and smiled to himself.

Ernst was the most talkative of all of the Germans. It was his voice that travelled through the walls at Perseverance Place. He was telling Hen how he'd refused to fight in the war.

'I came to England as a boy. I love it here, love the English, and so I said I would not fight.'

Hen's eyes were wide, though it shouldn't be such a shock to learn that not every German supported the war.

The sun had risen high, and sweat gathered around her collar and the folds of her smock. Then came panting, the thud of footsteps, and Martha bent to pass through the half-filled gap in the hedgerow.

'Why are you running in this heat?' Emily asked, wondering if Martha had seen Otto on the tractor and thought he was making a break for freedom.

'We found the strays right up on Sunnyside Orchard.'

Emily tutted and wiped her brow with the back of her tar-stained hand. The sheep always had a habit of finding the highest spot on the warmest days.

'One of them is fine – Olive is herding it back now,' Martha continued. 'But two of them are dead.'

Emily and Heinrich exchanged a grimace. He righted the sheep he was working on and the two of them strode with Martha back up the hill.

'Fly …' Heinrich began as soon as he set eyes on the corpses. Then he muttered in German, his hand twirling circles in the air while he rolled through his mind for the right words. She urged him to spit it out. Come on! Come on! 'Strike! It's flystrike,' he said eventually.

She put her hand to her mouth. Mr Tipton had told her about flystrike. She'd seen him yell at his men as they set about trying to save his flock before it was wiped out in a matter of hours.

They sprinted back to the main field, hastily checking the others over. Heinrich pointed out the telltale signs; three or four had separated from the others, blowflies buzzing in and out of their wool. One rubbed its body along the hedge while another two were biting their own backs. Emily completed her last check, smothered her nose and retched.

'It's flystrike definitely,' Heinrich said. 'Eggs will hatch and eat them from the inside out.' He made a gruesome mime.

A circle of serious faces surrounded her. 'We need to get to work right away,' she said, hoping and praying that Ada, Olive and Martha would work with the men like the other women had that morning. 'There's no time for nonsense. First drag the matted wool away from the horns and their rears. Heinrich can show you how.'

The sweat ran into her eyes; her toes stuck together inside her boots. 'You're all doing a marvellous job,' she said, wiping her brow with the back of her hand and returning straight to the animal in hand.

When she took a breath, she saw that Martha worked away, solemn-faced, taking instructions from Heinrich as he showed her how to cut around the horns.

It was dark by the time they'd finished digging the graves with pick and shovel and burying the dead. They'd lost five sheep in total. It could have been worse, far worse. But they'd acted quickly, worked together as a team.

When they arrived back at the farmhouse as the trap came along New Lane, Emily's stomach turned a somersault. She wouldn't be gloating over the fixed tractor now.

'You did well today,' Heinrich said.

'He's right,' said Martha. 'We could have lost the whole flock if everyone hadn't done their bit, and you hadn't listened to him.' She nodded to Heinrich.

'It was Heinrich who knew what to do,' Emily said. Despite wanting to crash onto her bed, energy still zipped through her veins.

'A good farmer sees a problem and acts quickly. You saved lives today.' Heinrich patted her on the back.

*

That night she awoke from a dream of a field full of sheep corpses and lay awake with her eyes open, preferring exhaustion than returning to that.

She crept downstairs for a glass of water. The moon was up and framed perfectly in the kitchen window, casting a light over the sink. As she sipped the drink, she closed her eyes and jolted as she was met with the image of a dead sheep. She'd nearly fallen asleep standing up. She was just setting the glass back down in the sink when something on the windowsill glinted in the moonlight. Leaning in for a closer view, she gasped. It couldn't be. Her hand wouldn't stay steady enough to pick it up, so she slid it into her palm to measure the weight of it.

It was her wedding ring.

It hadn't been there before – she'd have seen it. She'd fretted about telling Theo it was lost every day. So how did it get there? It fitted her perfectly, as it always had. She gazed up at the ceiling and shook her head. She had a pretty good idea.

Chapter Fifteen

April 1917

Theo's letter finally broke the silence. Nearly a year after they'd married an envelope arrived, postmarked London. It caught her off guard. At first her whole body turned chilled; first John and now it was Theo's turn. Through the mist of panic she recognised his handwriting and her breath flowed freely again. In an instant, she went from preparing herself for her worst hell, to jumping on the spot. Theo was home. He'd been granted a last-minute leave. He was already in London. He had booked them two nights in Dorset. She was sure he'd said they'd visit his family in Yorkshire, but what did it matter where they were, as long as they were together?

He asked her to meet him in London the next day. She found him under the clock at Charing Cross station. He wore his uniform and a khaki trench coat. His nose was red from the cold. She noticed one or two admiring glances from passers-by in awe of the proud returning hero, and it made her puff up her chest as well.

She burst into a run, her suitcase bashing into her shins, and she charged into his chest. His arms cradled her. She sank into his sandalwood scent and the unfaltering beat of his heart.

'Steady on, girl.' He laughed, but she could tell he was flattered.

He had more lines around his eyes. His skin was a sickly grey colour, and his smile didn't last long, fading faster than the sun on a winter's evening. His cheekbones stood out more too, his uniform not so snug across his chest. Those broad shoulders were less substantial.

Before she could take much more in, he kissed her. Not the slow, intense caress they'd shared on their wedding day – this time they were tentative, three or four short pecks, and she still kept her eyes open.

Then they were grinning at each other again, and if she just concentrated on his eyes and ignored everything going on around them, the uncertainty, pain and loneliness had evaporated into the London air.

'You've the look of the outdoors about you,' he said.

That was true. She couldn't scrub the mud out from under her fingernails, no matter how hard she tried. Freckles had dappled her skin during those few warm days at the start of the month when they'd got excited that spring was on the way.

And then there were the dark bruises under her eyes, where she'd cried for John. The skin around her eyes had become soft and sticky with tears and the next day the hoods of her eyes were swollen. She was changed, for both the good and the bad, and the same would be true of Theo.

'You're such a beauty. Such a beauty.' He tilted his head to admire her.

What could she say to that? He said it often enough in his letters but to have him say it to her face just made her cheeks burn.

'I think you're trying to butter me up.'

He gazed at her with a silly, big grin on his face.

'What is it?' she asked.

'Your voice,' he said. 'It's wonderful to hear your voice. Its

106

softness. Its sweetness. The poshn … its Englishness. Divine,' he said. 'Just divine.'

How could something as mundane as the noise coming from her mouth please him so much? Perhaps there weren't many English girls behind the front line.

'And what about me?' he asked her.

'What do you mean?' She fought for time.

'Am I how you remember me?'

She played about; put her forefinger to her smiling lips, tilted her head to one side to get a good view of him. The eyes were as brown and warm as she remembered, but they were flatter now, not as alive and dancing as they had been on their wedding day. As well as the lines he had a shallow scar, like a teardrop, to the right of his eyebrow.

'You don't have to answer if you don't want to.' He sighed and began to walk away.

'Theo.' She dashed after him, grabbing his arm. 'Of course you look every bit as handsome as the man I married.' She was over-compensating and he must know it. 'I was just consigning you to memory …'

He smiled again, and she basked in the warmth of it.

They took a taxi from the station out of Bournemouth, to Durley Chine and their hotel. She got butterflies when they pulled up outside and her gaze rose up to the rows of bedroom windows. Once inside she took a seat beside a baby grand piano, while Theo went to the desk. The crazy, dancing butterflies spiralled out of her stomach and up to her throat.

'Are you all right?' he asked her as he returned with their room key. 'You're pale.'

'It must be all the travelling,' she said. 'Could we go for a walk once we've dropped off our things?'

His head had dipped again, just like in London. 'Don't you want to see our room? I've booked us the bridal suite.'

She swallowed. He'd hardly asked anything about her work on

the land or taken an interest in how she was working with the men and women. Now he wanted her to go straight to the bridal suite.

'Could we get a breath of fresh air first?'

Whatever happened now would set the tone for the rest of their marriage. It was important that he understood that they might be married, but there was more to her than a fast girl with nothing of interest to say for herself.

He sighed, put a hand in the small of her back, and nudged her back out of the reception.

The hotel backed onto the sandstone cliffs that reared up above the golden sands. They descended on a rope-lined, zigzag path through the ochre rock face. He walked a little way ahead of her, running his hands along the rope handle, while she folded her arms to her chest.

At the bottom, as soon as they stepped away from the protection of the cliffs towards the dappled sands, an icy breeze laced with sea spray stung her face. There wasn't another soul on that beach in either direction; it was only them. She pulled her coat close. The churned-up sea loomed dangerous and wild.

'At least it will be romantic to snuggle up with you in our room, Mrs Williams,' he said.

She took a tiny step away from him. Perhaps if she got it over with and went to bed with him, his mind would be clear enough to see her as something other than a girl waiting to be steered under the blankets. She'd been naive to expect anything else from her honeymoon, she supposed.

'I hope we don't have any more snow while we're here,' she said, changing the subject. 'You didn't write to say whether it snowed in France?' she asked, tidying a loose strand of hair behind her ear.

'We had several heavy frosts.' He raised his voice above the waves. 'Don't you remember me saying how ice makes life extra difficult in the trenches?'

She nodded. *Had* he mentioned the frost in his letters? She couldn't remember it.

'Shall we go back to the warm?' He placed an arm around her shoulders. 'Our room has a sea view.'

She stared at the crashing waves, not because she was mesmerised, but rather an idea that she couldn't turn her back on them.

'I'm ever so hungry now after all of that travelling,' she answered. 'Aren't you?'

'I've booked us a table,' he told her. 'For seven o'clock.'

He was a gentleman and waited in the corridor while she changed in their room for dinner.

The room itself was really rather special. Damask curtains and thick pile carpet. As she readied herself and fastened her lace blouse in front of the looking glass, the vast expanse of the double bed loomed in the reflection behind her.

When she was ready and satisfied with her reflection, she waited a moment before calling Theo back a moment to closer inspect the bed with its deep, raspberry pink covers. She pushed her hand down on the mattress. It sunk beneath her fist, to make a dimple in the bedcovers. She let it rise again. She'd a vague idea of what happened on a girl's wedding night. Just things giggled about at her girls' private day school. Her mother would never discuss things like that. Her towels had been left on her bed when her monthlies started, wordlessly waiting for her to fathom it out for herself.

The meal was lovely – especially with the shortages as they were. When he was concentrating on his food, she stole glances at him. There was still so much she didn't know about this husband of hers. And when they were drinking tea, she asked him about his family.

'My mother is wonderful. Kind and fun.' His eyes sparkled. 'She likes to paint – her favourite subjects are men and women at work. Real work: at the forges, the washboard. She likes real life; she's not fanciful or romantic. She captures drudgery so very well.'

'And your father?'

A shadow fell over his face and Emily wished she'd kept him talking about his mother.

'He doesn't see the value in her painting.' He shrugged. 'Father is a self-made businessman.'

'My father too,' she said. 'And my uncle. Father did have a foot up though: a good education and some investments from my grandfather. So, I suppose self-made isn't as true of him as it is of my uncle. He really did start from nothing. My grandmother married twice,' she explained.

'And did you get along with your father?'

'Very much. We both loved the countryside, and shared an enjoyment of being outdoors.'

'My father and I tend not to see eye to eye. He doesn't believe in giving me any hand-outs.'

Theo's father didn't sound like her own had been at all. Baden had wanted the whole village, even the mouse behind the skirting board, to share in his good fortune.

'I wouldn't mind,' Theo continued, 'but he used my mother's dowry to invest and make his money. He's not as self-made as he would have everyone believe. He doesn't respect my mother, either.'

He set his knife and fork together with a clatter. She'd steered the conversation close to the rocks, but she couldn't pull away yet. There were other things she needed to know.

'Is that why you decided we'd come here, instead of Wakefield?'

'You got it in one,' he said, swigging his brandy. 'And last time I was home the pubs were empty. All that was left were old men. It was like a ghost town.'

After the meal they went for a nightcap in the hotel lounge. Emily had a stiff brandy and for ten minutes nurtured nothing more than a small tot. Theo had grown quiet. The more he'd drunk, the further he'd seemed to retreat. The gentle, affable man who'd come to dinner faded away.

'What's it like, out there on the Front?' she asked.

'What's it like?' He bared his teeth at that. 'Not for the ears of girls, that's what it's like,' he snapped. She flattened her back against the chair while he squished his cigarette into his ashtray.

He stood and held out his hand. She hesitated for a moment, her own arms folded.

'I wonder if they have any spare rooms,' she said. 'Perhaps this wasn't such a good idea.'

His hand froze in the air. The hair on the back of her neck stood on end.

'They're fully booked,' he said firmly. How could he know that? He had no way of being sure, but she couldn't pay for another room anyway. She was reliant on him being a gentleman and sensing her unease.

'Come on, *Mrs* Williams,' he said. He jolted his outstretched hand back and forth. The barman polished his glass and wouldn't catch her eye as she tried to catch his.

At the bedroom door, Theo left the key fob to hang in the lock and then he took her face in his hands and kissed her. He was all teeth and brandy fumes. His fingers dug into her jaw bone. She pulled back.

'Just what are you so worried about?' he asked.

'It's your manner, Theo. We have only just met,' she said.

'You didn't say that when you walked down the aisle.'

No, she hadn't, but perhaps if she'd been sensible enough to think this far ahead, she might have done. He opened the door and pulled her in behind him. He had the key in his spare hand. He locked them in. Took the key and put it in his pocket.

As he kissed her again, her eyes flicked towards the keyhole. That small peephole on their room was perfect for spying eyes, which was silly because who would be watching them, and wouldn't there be footsteps in the corridor? His breathing was getting faster, driven by passion, not rage. His grip on her arms was firm, almost too tight. She wasn't sure she could shake him

111

off if she wanted to, and what would happen if she did? Where would she run to if she did break free?

'I'm …' She stretched for something to say, keep him talking. The raspberry-coloured bed covers sat in the room, as brazen as a lady-of-the-night's lips. 'I'm just worn out.' Her mind was blank. It was all she could think to say, but he hadn't cared when she'd said she was tired before. 'Would you mind …'

She held her breath. His brandy haze hot on her face as he brought himself back, focused on her.

'I don't understand what is wrong with you,' he said eventually. He relaxed his clamp on her arms. Her lungs emptied. He fastened his braces. 'But if that's what you want.'

He whistled as he took off his shoes and socks.

'You don't mind, do you?' she said. She stood by the side of the bed, a safe distance now. Was she being foolish? He seemed quite harmless now.

'Of course not,' he said.

She lay on the far side of the double bed, pulled the covers up to her chest and stared into the darkness, willing sleep to suck her in and take her away from all this.

Theo lay on the floor at the foot of the bed. He was beneath his trench coat. He wept, almost silently, but not quite. Her head spun. She'd been too hard on him, had let her imagination run away with her. Should she comfort him? Before she could answer, his muffled sobs faded, his breath lengthened and soon he began to snore.

*

Theo was up from his post on the floor, just at the time that she was stirring and adjusting to the caw of the sea gulls outside and the faint rustle of the waves. She stayed still while he peeled back the curtains to reveal a steel-grey day and rain blowing into the window in gusts. Theo promptly pulled the drapes tight again.

A tremor ran through his hand as it gripped the damask. He started as a door closed down the corridor. His chin bristled with yesterday's growth, uneven across his face it grew in patches and his hair stuck up all over, and had lost its side parting.

She imagined she was pulling the blankets up to her chin in her bed in Perseverance Place, a day's purposeful work ahead of her. He pushed his thumbs into his eyes, and in the next movement lifted his hands into the air above his head and let out a large sigh, expelling something more than the sound itself. She pulled the covers tight. Followed his every movement. He turned, focused on her and smiled. Came towards her. She flinched but his touch was as delicate as being tickled by an ear of grass as he traced the line of her jaw with his forefinger.

'I can't remember much of last night,' he said. 'How much did I have to drink that I ended up on the floor? I suppose that was my idea – insist on doing the gentlemanly thing, did I?'

'Yes,' she said. 'You decided to sleep on the floor.' It was almost the truth. Best not to remind him of the person he'd been the night before. He couldn't feel guilty if he didn't remember, and it was better that he didn't know that she'd rejected him, or that she couldn't bear to be kissed by him.

'Fancy missing out on the chance to sleep in here.' He gestured to the empty side of the bed.

The memory of last night was being bleached away by the daylight. He was so tender now, as kind as he'd been in his letters, and on their wedding day. They'd both been in a state for different reasons; yes that's what had happened. She'd made his behaviour into something it wasn't. The poor thing had cried. But now it was a new day, the first proper day of their honeymoon.

'I can sleep almost anywhere now,' he said.

'I don't think you should drink again, while we're here,' she said, chewing her lip.

'If that's what you want,' he said.

She nodded. She did. She wouldn't stay if that other Theo

came back again. She'd get a train, sleep at the station until the milk train left, anything but stay there. Her arms ached where his fingers had pressed her skin through to her bones. She hadn't imagined that.

'What would you like to do today?' she said. She pushed a cushion up against the brass bedstead railings behind her and slid herself upright. 'We shouldn't let the bad weather hold us back.'

'The sun shines when it r-ains,' he sang in a thin wobbly voice to the tune of 'Tipperary'. 'When you're by my side.'

He stopped singing to soak up her applause. 'Besides,' he continued, 'honeymooners aren't supposed to go outside, are they?'

The bellboy saved her from having to answer that. He brought them breakfast: toast on a rack smothered in marmalade, Earl Grey tea, all on a silver tray.

'Perhaps we should stay inside then, like you say?' She patted the bed. The poor man had spent his wedding night on the floor. Drunk. Weeping. She smiled but her lips twitched, betraying the memory she couldn't shift of last night. He'd said he wouldn't drink though and he deserved another chance.

He sat on the end of the bed. She didn't flinch as he ran his hand through her hair, but she'd wanted to. He leant forwards and kissed her, firmly on the mouth. Much more tenderly than he had in the corridor last night. Less of the urgency. It had been the drink that had done that to him. She didn't pull away this time; she sank into his embrace.

It was just as she'd remembered from their wedding day. Last night was forgotten – a bad start that was all. These were difficult times and they had to muddle through. A match light sparked and glowed within her. Her breath caught. She pulled herself to sit upright from the pillow. What would happen next? Was this *it*?

His hands gently strayed down from her shoulders to her chest.

She was braced to push him away, defend herself from the forceful Theo who'd invaded her space the night before, but it was definitely the drink that had done that to him. Her cheeks burnt and then just as quickly the heat subsided. Energy surged through her veins.

He seemed to have grown an extra pair of hands; no sooner was he stroking her face than he smoothed her hair across her shoulders, straying lower, to her breasts, and then, he shifted his weight and took up the empty space beside her on the bed. Faster, but still not forceful, more like the man she'd met under the clock. He was under the bedcovers, his hand journeying up the soft inside of her thigh. The sensation made her giggle. She closed her eyes and tried to swallow her laughter.

*

After he'd exhaled, he rolled onto the bed beside her and lit a cigarette. She took one too. They lay together, covers up to their armpits, hand in hand. There was so much she wanted to say, only where should she begin? The questions spun through her mind while she quietly contemplated the ceiling.

115

Chapter Sixteen

May 1917

Dear Emily,

    Memories of our brief time together in Bournemouth keep me strong. I'm fuelled by patriotism and honour, and when I do battle, I do so with the thought of protecting you.

    I will write more soon.

    Fondest love and kisses

    Theo

    xxx

Dearest Emily,

    I am sure you are very busy with your war work, but I wonder when we might see you in London. I'd like to know how your mother is getting along, and your uncle still refuses my calls. Have you heard from her? Is she well and settled and content with her decision to stay with him?

    King regards

    Your Grandmother

Mother still hardly wrote back to her, and whilst this was probably a good sign that she was too busy to think of her daughter, Emily decided she would act on her grandmother's suggestion and she proposed afternoon tea.

Mother responded straight away. 'If you only have one day off a week, you mustn't waste it traipsing up to London.' And that had been the end of it. It was so unlike Mother, but nothing surprised her any more. Wilfred was taking care of her, and that was all Mother had ever really wanted. She wasn't meant for widowhood, she needed to be in capable hands, and she'd found them.

Men in bowler hats and suits, holding notebooks, appeared on the farm, mud crusting up the sides of their shoes.

Everyone around the farm paused, leant on their tools, and waited for Emily to explain why there were men huddled around talking in hushed voices, but she was as much in the dark as the rest of them.

'Can I help you?' she asked. They appraised her with a quick up and down, but before they could dismiss her as a rank and file land army girl she added, 'My family owns this estate. Did my mother send you?' But she could answer the question herself: Mother would never initiate anything like this. 'Or my Uncle Wilfred, perhaps?'

'I'm afraid we can only speak directly with the client who engaged us.'

'The client … engaged?'

But the men had shuffled away from her, notebooks secreted in their pockets.

'If you can't identify yourselves, perhaps we ought to ask you to leave,' she called after them, but they took no notice.

They stopped beside the Fordson. The tractor had been in the same place in the farmyard since Otto had driven it back from the field. When Mr Tipton went to market on Wednesdays, Otto had secretly been giving her lessons. The hard metal seat was so high up, the tractor's slender nose so long, the wheels so huge, but before long she hadn't noticed, and drove out of the farmyard, and up to the field where she ploughed a shaky half-moon.

'Did you hear me?' she called after the men. 'You can't just come on to my family's land and start measuring it up.'

She would write to Mother to ask if Uncle Wilfred had sent the men on her behalf.

'Perhaps they're something to do with the army hospital,' Mrs Tipton said, which made no sense at all because the army had only taken over HopBine and had no business on the farm. Two of the men had asked where they might find the old paper mill, by the river. It had once been used to produce handmade paper, but the building was nothing but a ruin now. What interest could that be to anyone?

A couple of the girls had stopped work, curious about the fuss, so she made a show of waving the men farewell and then trudged to the other side of the yard, to inspect the Fordson's engine.

*

There was so much to do that the men's visit was soon forgotten. The War Agriculture Committee was asking more and more of them. Another poor harvest, sustained losses of imports from ships and submarines had led to the food production programme. They had to clear more of the hop gardens and small fruit orchards to urgently cultivate the soil for more cereals and potatoes.

Planes raided London, and Grandmother wrote to say she'd had to spend the night with the mice on an underground platform. Voluntary rations had been introduced, but bread and potatoes had still doubled in price. They had to forgo their daily cheese with bread for lunch, and fuel themselves with margarine on their loaves instead.

While Cecil was trapped in a tiny cell with no human contact,

118

and only the walls to listen to his principles, Emily worked with a sense of purpose that propelled her out of bed in the morning and kept her working after everyone else had gone home, and the pain became impossible to ignore. She often slept in her boots.

Around the farm the hedgerows were untrimmed – efforts were focused on the foods most needed. There were potato boxes everywhere.

Now the Board of Trade was extending its recruitment beyond educated women, to all levels of society.

Across the country, the land army grew in strength, but even Emily who loved to be outdoors whatever the weather, could understand how the better wages of the munitions factories, or the excitement of working as a dispatch driver, could be more alluring than farm work and so she appreciated why they still didn't have the manpower to cultivate the extra land.

One particular night, Mr Tipton had his head in his hands and was asking Tiger, his tomcat, how they were going to manage. She said she had a surprise for him outside.

'If one of us learnt to drive that tractor,' she said, 'it would reduce our ploughing time by two-thirds at least.'

'She's right.' Mrs Tipton's eyes danced with laughter. Mr Tipton had insisted that they keep the tractor, but he was on the one hand seduced by its potential to make his life easier, and on the other he was scared of the machine and too afraid to master it.

'I'm sure it can't be difficult,' she said, with a wink to Mrs Tipton.

'I'll not allow it,' he said. Mrs Tipton shook her head at her husband. But Mr Tipton wasn't finished. 'What would your father say if he knew I was allowing his precious daughter loose on the fields with that beast on the rampage? It takes weeks for a man to master it. You're not strong enough. You'll be flipping the machine over and crushing yourself to death.'

Mrs Tipton was laughing at him now. 'Oh dear,' she said to

her husband. 'You won't learn, will you? This here's a girl that sees talk like that as a challenge.'

She patted Emily on the back as she marched out into the dark to the farmyard.

'I said no, and I mean no.' Mr Tipton took the last word, and she let him have it. She fought to keep a straight face as she strode across the yard, bent double before the radiator grill and began to crank up the engine. The peaceful night was pierced with the alien hum of the motor. Emily hopped on board while the chickens clucked and the cows stirred.

By now she could hardly hide her amusement. Why hadn't Mr Tipton thought to ask the Germans if they knew how to drive the tractor? She put the tractor into gear and with the machine chugging away beneath her she pulled out of the farmyard, into the darkness, navigating the lane she could walk in her sleep, with Mr Tipton chasing behind her.

Dearest Emily,

I am sorry that I haven't written to you sooner. We have been terribly busy with this and that.

Where did Gerald get his posting. Did he make it to Mesopotamia? You must be proud to see your brother off to war. I'll pray he stays safe and warm …

Fondest wishes

Theo

Emily lay in bed staring at the crack in the ceiling. The sinister black damp grew a little more every day, spreading like a new continent.

Her stomach rumbled. She had left her dinner uneaten last night. Flo, their woman from the village, had now worked her way through *Thirty-six Ways to Prepare a Potato* at least three times over. But usually Emily was so hungry she could eat a potato prepared the same way for a week and not mind.

Rolling onto one side, she lifted Theo's letter from the box she kept beneath her bed. It had been the first in a while, and she couldn't make sense of it. Who was Gerald? She didn't even know anyone by that name. Perhaps Theo needed to take some leave and catch up on his sleep, have a rest from it all.

She imagined being propped up in her own broad, comfy bed in her room in HopBine House: the linen sheets, the satin quilt, a never-ending supply of fresh flowers on the dressing table. She pictured a neat breakfast tray with fragrant coffee steaming in a delicate china cup with rose-pink edges and a freshly baked roll that would melt in her mouth. That was all a long time ago. Now, a strange soldier would be sleeping in her room, recuperating after his treatment at the Finch Hall army hospital.

Martha bashed into the wall downstairs while she was tidying. Emily reached out of the side of her bed towards the wooden chair and pulled her dressing gown under the covers and rolled about to put it on. Then she slipped on some warm socks, and slid back the covers, safely shielded from the cold. In front of the full-length looking glass she hesitated. There she stood in her dressing gown, billowing out in pleats from her chest and obscuring her ankles. When had she last even worn a dress? John's memorial. A lifetime ago.

She grabbed the excess material and bunched it together in a fist that she nestled in the small of her back. She pulled it taut around her hips and waist, and then she assessed the snaking meanders of her body's topography. Snatching the material tighter still, she held her breath, pulled in her waist and without intending it, her chin lifted, her small chest thrust forwards, her bottom pushing away. She remained rigid in her invisible stays for a few moments, and then she grew hungry for a breath and let the dressing gown fall, her posture slumping. She began to breathe again.

Before getting dressed, she pulled her sheet and blanket back over the bed, tucked them under the flimsy mattress and plumped the pillow. She'd learnt not long after moving into the billet that, without Daisy to magic everything away, she'd be too tired and hungry to think of caring for herself at the end of the day.

She fetched the broom from the corridor, scratched the dust into a pile, and shook the rug out of the window.

'Are you ready?' Martha called at the door.

'Just a moment.'

Emily continued with her familiar routine. The pyjama trousers dropped to her ankles. She put on some clean knickers, stepped into her breeches and flung the now redundant dressing gown back over the chair. Next, she fastened her tie beneath her shirt collar, pulled her hair out of the way with a handkerchief, belted the oilskin, and slid her cigarettes and matches into a deep pocket.

She contemplated the bowl on the washstand and dipped an outstretched finger. It was cold but at least at this time of year there wasn't a film of ice. Hesitating for a moment, she plunged her hands in, splashed her face with the chilled water and shuddered.

'Morning.' She opened the door to greet Martha as she did every day. 'Was that another letter from your brother yesterday?'

Martha patted her smock pocket with satisfaction; she always carried one of Frank's letters with her.

'There's a rumour that you gave the old man a bit of a shock last night,' Martha said.

The memory of his expression when she mounted the tractor made her smile too. 'I can't believe no one told him about the lessons Otto has given me. When I sailed out of the farmyard it was as if I was walking on water.'

The laughter came then, and Martha – seeing the funny side – joined her. The two of them bent double, laughing so much that tears came. It was an alien feeling to her that set her outside of her own body. She hadn't laughed like this since John had come home on his last leave and they'd shared a joke about Cecil.

122

That memory flooded the laughter now, drowning it and washing it clean away, as if it had never been there.

Outside the lane, she checked the ground, as she did every day. The resentment for Cecil was receding. No one had thrown a blood-stained bandage of protest against the window the night before, which would be the first time since she'd lived at Perseverance Place; perhaps her acceptance amongst the land girls was making a difference.

But her stomach lurched as she caught a glimpse of a scrap of bloodied cloth hanging out of Martha's smock pocket. She'd been wrong. Cecil had been in prison over a year, and still they hated him. She was just fortunate to have finally got Martha on her side, and that now her friend tried to protect her.

Chapter Seventeen

October 1917

Dearest Emily,

I write with a needle, hence I will keep it short. Don't think much of the cook here; only meals = bread and water. The entertainment is limited = breaking stone day after day. Stone surprisingly resilient. Thought it would break me instead. Now in solitary, but feel I am being watched. Made a friend, Bill, a spider, even he is miserable and is a terrible debater.

Yours
Cecil

The Bramleys had fallen ripe exactly on time this year; they'd blossomed in the second week in May, which made them ready right then, the first week in October.

Elsewhere on the land, the ears of corn had been shorn, carted and stacked. With the soft fruit and the hop harvest done, the roots and potatoes cooked for a little longer in the still-warm ground and would need to come up before the first frosts.

The numbers working on the farm had swelled and the tractor relieved them of a lot of ploughing. Mrs Tipton was busier than ever catering for the boys and girls who'd been released from school bringing their mothers with them, more Belgian refugees, prisoners of war, retired farm workers, and of course the land girls were all on hand.

She spent the day up at Sunnyside Orchard, filling her basket with apples, and had earned herself a good night's sleep. Her wrist ached from cupping her palm and twisting the fruit from its bough.

In the darkness, she could distinguish the outline of the small garden she and Martha had planted out on their afternoons off. At the end was the hut, piled to its pitch roof with potato boxes. In the summer, Sweet Williams bloomed and in the autumn Michaelmas daisies shone. She'd added to the herb corner in the autumn, ready to overwinter it while the ground was still warm.

The previous tenants had established pennyroyal, horehound and tansy and Martha had added some lemon balm and rue for physic, while Emily had moved some lavender from the HopBine garden to scent their best clothes, not that they ever had much call to wear them, apart from church on Sundays. But the plants had shrunk back for winter now, except for the rosemary, which she liked to brush with her palm to catch its scent.

Today she was going to take her supper and go straight to bed so that she was strong for the morning. She found the food warming on the range. Boiled onions, creamed potato and a milk pudding.

As she kicked off her faded boots, crusted with barnacles of mud, she started at a pair of men's shoes, also lined up by the back door.

It had been eight months since Cecil was arrested. Could he have been released already? She hesitated by the parlour door, suppressing a yawn. It was quiet in there. She jumped as Martha appeared behind her.

'There's someone waiting inside for you,' she said with a wink.

Emily put her hand on the parlour-room doorknob. She looked

again and realised the shoes were too small for Cecil. Inside, the cramped parlour was dimly illuminated by yellowed candlelight. Martha had already set the fire going with the coal she'd fetched before Emily was even up that morning.

The soot-smudged armchair was tilted towards the fire. The visitor's face was obscured by Emily's copy of the *Landswoman*, feet outstretched towards the flames. Definitely too small to be Cecil's, but she did recognise the socks. She'd knitted them herself. The visitor flicked down the corner of the magazine. She yelled: 'Theo!'

He leapt out of the chair, lifted her up and spun her around.

'You didn't write to tell me you'd had leave approved,' she said. 'What sort of welcome is that?'

'I meant are you wounded?' she added quickly.

'Do I look harmed?' he said, holding his arms aloft and pausing so that she could look him over. 'My leave was granted at the last minute and I thought I'd surprise you.'

He'd done that all right. She had lots to do, and her bones ached. If she didn't go to bed soon she'd never get through the next day.

He was pale and when he blinked his eyes seemed slow and heavy, with no gleam. She imagined much the same could be said of hers. Such a year 1917 had been. There wasn't much call for radiance any more.

She didn't want to dwell on anything bad – she'd had enough of that – but she was aware that Theo hadn't kissed her on the lips when he'd first seen her. He'd simply pecked her perfunctorily on the cheek.

'You look worn out,' he said.

'Yes,' she said. 'Yes. I suppose I am. Would you mind excusing me for a moment, please?' she asked. She shot upstairs to her bedroom and collapsed onto the bed, her pillow muffling her tears. After a while, she sat up, blew her nose and wiped her eyes, straightened herself and went back down to Theo.

'He said to tell you that he's gone for a walk,' Martha called. 'Emily, is everything all right?' Martha said when she caught sight of Emily in the hallway.

'Yes, yes,' she said. She couldn't tell Martha, just as she couldn't tell Theo, that for one silly, mad moment she'd imagined it was John behind that copy of the magazine. She'd once thought the two men were similar, but actually they were nothing alike at all.

*

Theo whistled as he took in HopBine's three gables and the land that sat around it when she took him on a tour after milking.

Some of the convalescing soldiers were being pushed around the lawn in their wheelchairs, blankets over their knees, as the wind swirled autumnal leaves about the lawn. It had been an odd sight at first, these strangers in her home, but they belonged there now. HopBine was a sanctuary, somewhere for the men to regain their strength, to rest before returning to battle. Her father and John would approve too, she was sure of that.

'This is quite some home you have here,' he said. 'Your father did well for himself. What's it worth?'

She was going to tell him. He was her husband and she should be honest with him. If she wanted him to help, he needed to know there was a problem first.

'It's not quite as perfect as it seems,' she said.

'And why is that?'

'When father died he left us in debt. John tried to sell some land to free up some capital. The estranged uncle my mother is staying with has had to clear our debts for us.'

'So what's going to happen?'

'The farm gives us a small income and we don't have to pay to run HopBine while the army are using it.'

'And after the war?'

'I don't like to think about it. We will have to see who wins the war first, but if life returns to normal, I expect we'll have to sell up, although it breaks my heart.'

She petered out. She'd found the courage to tell him the truth and now he wasn't even listening.

'So you're not sitting quite so pretty then.' He didn't look at her; instead he stared straight ahead at the house. 'Don't look like that,' he said tenderly now, stroking her hair. Then he folded his arms and strode off, turning his back on HopBine House.

*

Mrs Tipton had spread out some blankets in the centre of Sunnyside Orchard and set up a picnic of HopBine apple juice, scones and jam with the knife resting in it.

'And who's this handsome chap then?' Mrs Tipton thrust a gypsy tart at Theo, who introduced himself, and stuffed down the treacly pastry in two bites.

Ladders poked out from beneath the branches. They were stairways from the heavens. Had there ever been such a bumper crop? Everywhere the trees were clustered with joyous rosy fruit.

The orchard buzzed, as the pickers filled the boxes littered about the orchard with blushing apples. The wain was over by the path and Bob the horse chomped on an apple a young boy had handed him.

Emily grabbed a ladder before they were all gone, placed a bag over her shoulder and led Theo to an empty tree, some forty-five feet high.

'Please don't say anything to anyone here, about the estate,' she said. 'Nobody knows.'

'I wasn't going to,' Theo said, clearly affronted.

'For all I know Uncle Wilfred might buy the estate and run it for us. He certainly has the money.'

Theo thawed at the mention of the wealthy uncle. Theo mustn't think she expected him to do anything about her family's problems.

'Do you want to have a go at harvesting?' she asked. 'I can show you what to do.'

She told him how he'd bruise the fruit if he held them with his hands, and demonstrated by cupping an apple with her palm and releasing it with a gentle twist.

'You go,' she said. 'That's it.'

He had a gentle touch and the satisfaction ironed out his face as she balanced the pink-hued globe on his flat palm. Emily looped the apple sling over his head. He disappeared up the ladder into the shadows of the canopy, and after a while it became clear that he was in no hurry to come back down. There was still a spare ladder. If it had eyes it would be following her about the orchard, but if she went up, then she'd have to come down, and whenever she did she was always expecting to find John waiting for her, and he never was.

'I thought we'd got the best of the crop yesterday,' Emily said when she met Olive at the crates.

'I thought the same,' Martha said, picking up a stray apple and popping it in to join the rest. 'Perhaps it was a mirage and we were delirious yesterday.'

Hen appeared, gently tipping her yield into the same crate, and chuckled. 'That or Mrs Tipton is fastening the fruit back on to the trees at night so she's got an excuse to keep us company while she drinks that scrumpy of hers.'

Down the orchard at that moment Mrs Tipton took a vessel out of the blanket she'd fashioned into a knapsack and took a discreet swig. The three girls laughed.

'I'm surprised you've the energy to find things funny.' Mr Tipton folded his arms and raised his eyebrows at their empty slings.

'I was just saying that it's a bumper crop,' Emily said. 'I don't think I've ever seen these trees so full.'

'Aye, it's bad news.'

'Is it?' Martha asked.

'Aye. Supply and demand. The more apples nature gives us, the lower the prices, but we still have to harvest the darn things and more fruit means more labour and that means less profit.'

'Oh well,' said Hen, rolling her eyes when he wasn't looking. 'At least it's a nice day. There's always some good to be found in everything, don't you find, Mr Tipton?' she said.

Martha had her hand over her mouth to smother her laughter as one of the ewes lifted her tail beside him and sprayed pellets from its backside onto Mr Tipton's boots. Emily held her breath, and the suppressed mirth pushed out of her belly.

'Oh, come on, you puddle ducks. We're not here to be cheerful – get back to work, for heaven's sake.'

As soon as he was out of earshot Martha pulled the two girls close.

'We're not puddle ducks, we're the Bramley Battalion. I feel like telling him so ...' The sap was rising in Martha, but it wouldn't do her any good if she crossed Mr Tipton.

'He's right about one thing: it's time to get back to work,' Emily echoed the master.

Martha lifted a stray branch from the ground and held it vertically down her chest like a rifle. She and Hen saluted Emily and the three of them marched off back to their work.

Emily checked on Theo. His sling bulging, he emerged from the tree a different person to the one who'd gone up. How quickly he could change. Only then was she aware that she'd been holding her breath. Now he'd ripened like an apple himself. The fresh air and the exertion had reddened his cheeks and his skin glowed with perspiration. He'd forgotten their earlier uncomfortable exchange. Telling him the truth had been the right thing to do; things were how they should be.

But there was still his last letter. Should she mention this chap Gerald he'd asked after? It would just have been a silly

130

mistake at the end of a long day under fire – crossed wires, that was all.

'Farm work suits you,' she said.

'I never would have believed it, but I think you might be right. How long was I up there?' he said. 'I lost track of time.' She caught a glimpse of Mr Tipton shaking his head at her and set back to work.

She snuggled up beside Theo that night, not minding one bit that the bed wasn't big enough for the two of them. She was so worn out from the day's work. A blanket of contentment was pulled over her, and she was sure she could have slept on the cart-shed floor just as long as she was in Theo's arms.

Chapter Eighteen

December 1917

My dearest sister,

I have been released from prison. It will only be a short respite before they come for me again. Could I impose myself upon your humble abode? Uncle Wilfred has declined my offer to visit on the grounds I'm a disreputable house guest. I won't be any trouble; I just want to rest my tired bones and regain some strength before the King's men come for me once more.

Fondest

Cecil

The girls stuck up paper chains with flour and water around the steamy farmhouse kitchen. It was Christmas Eve 1917 and another year had spun around.

Mrs Tipton had been busy in the kitchen for days, knuckle deep in forcemeat, pig trotters constantly simmering on the range.

Emily still hadn't been to London to visit Mother, but then she hadn't been invited. Perhaps she was a disreputable house guest as well. She nearly wrote to suggest she visit for Christmas, but then Cecil had written and if he wasn't going to get a welcome in London, she would have to accommodate him in Kent.

Besides, there wasn't much to celebrate and even less energy with which to do it. The whole country was exhausted, the losses becoming harder and harder to bear. The threat of Zeppelin attacks had shifted from night to day leaving them forever on guard.

Emily hadn't seen Theo since the apple harvest in October. Happy memories as they were she had seen him so infrequently since they'd been married. He'd let slip on his leave that he'd been in England in the summer. His mother's health was failing, but still, he might have thought to tell her that he was home. It followed a pattern though; he often went quiet for a month and then a letter would appear out of the blue with no mention of his silence.

The winter was the hardest time on the farm, but they had to keep their spirits up. No one dared contemplate what sort of country this was now, but one thing was certain: they absolutely couldn't become a hungry nation.

The government had issued more ploughing orders, with never-seen-before guaranteed prices for crops. The district war agricultural committees visited them to check the scheduled land for ploughing. The Tiptons were threatened with ejection if they didn't comply. With the government curtailing beer consumption, they no longer needed the same amount of land for hops. More and more was given over to potatoes, wheat, peas and beans, and it was the land girls and Emily driving the Fordson who ploughed and drilled, sowed and reaped the crops that helped feed the country, and the men at the Front.

She and Martha were on their way back from making a special delivery to the convalescing soldiers at HopBine House. They had used some of their egg supply and saved up their sugar to make the recovering soldiers a proper Christmas pudding. The alternative, as theirs would be, was a pudding sweetened with grated carrot. The matron asked them to sing 'Silent Night'. All those eyes on them had made her cheeks burn.

She might have given up and laughed it off when she reached the high notes, but for a chap right at the front with sea-green eyes who smiled with encouragement. He didn't lift his gaze from her the entire time she sang, but instead of shrinking she bathed in the glow of his spotlight and the misty emotion in his eyes. When his forefinger hastily wiped away a tear, her own jaw tightened. The sensitivity of the man with green eyes reminded her of John. She had to break the spell and focus on the floorboards, otherwise she wouldn't have finished the song.

Once they'd taken a bow she made a point of going over to the man with green eyes and offering him a piece of their home-made Turkish delight.

'Beautiful,' he said, a cube in his left cheek.

She surveyed him while he rolled his eyes and let slip 'mmms'. He didn't have a visible injury, but he moved slowly, smiled rarely. Before she could ask him his name the matron called Martha and her away to visit the men on the ward. Emily left him one last piece of Turkish delight. Their skin touched as she placed the sweet in his palm. His hands were strong and soft at the same time and a jolt of electricity passed between them. She swam in his sea-green eyes one last time.

'Merry Christmas,' she said to him. Then as she walked away she chastised herself for being drawn to an injured and vulnerable man who couldn't be blamed for confusing attention with attraction; but she should know better. She was a married woman.

'I think it's just as well my calling was to be a land girl and not a nurse,' she said to Martha as they reached the ward and her stomach lurched at the sight of the bandaged men lined up in their beds. She'd fall in love with them all, if she were working here. Martha raised a quizzical eyebrow, but Emily kept her eyes forward, took a deep breath and strode into the ward.

In the front room of the farmhouse, stubs of burnt-down candles wedged into empty bottles lit their ballroom for the evening. The candlelight muted the dusty shadows of the sooty room.

'We'll have to imagine that we have high ceilings, polished floors and chandeliers,' she said to the crew sprawled around the edge of the room.

'Most of us have to imagine all that anyway,' Martha said with a wink. It had been Emily's idea for the girls to dress as pirates. Shirts tucked in at the waists of their breeches and teased out to look blouson. Engine grease smeared onto their chins to give the effect of beards. Martha had fashioned an eye patch out of an old stocking and fastened a red scarf over her raven-coloured hair. Emily asked Olive for a dance. She'd thawed towards her now, but it made her shudder to think what Olive would say if she knew Cecil was staying at Perseverance Place.

Martha attended to the fire. They were down to coal dust now. They had all but used up their supplies, even though they'd been careful. They hadn't had enough coal for fires in their bedrooms in Perseverance Place for several weeks.

Martha cut in, raised an eyebrow.

'Care to dance, lady of the manor?' Martha said in a mock deep voice.

'My card is rather full, but I don't like to disappoint. I am sure I can find room for you,' Emily replied. They took to the flickering light of the dance floor, and Emily fought the lurch in her stomach. Theo was miles away and they might all still be doing the same thing next Christmas. How desperate might it all have become by then?

'I'll check on him.' Martha knew exactly what was on her mind. Cecil. He was hiding in their home.

He'd returned from prison gaunt and pinched. His flesh had

fallen away. He hadn't started a single argument, which was the most worrying sign of all.

He had taken a hard decision to refuse to fight but it had a bearing on all of them. If he'd worked on the farm, or been a stretcher-bearer at the Front, people would have been more understanding; but to be an absolutist, and refuse any part of the war, had made it difficult for the whole family. Being tied up, locked up on his own, kept on the brink of starvation, meant it was hardest for him, though. He'd developed the habit of chewing the top of his thumb, as if he was destroying himself, one tiny piece at a time.

She thanked Martha and leant against the piano. It hadn't been so long ago that Martha would have poked Cecil in the eye for being a shirker, but the war had changed them all and forced them to understand decisions and behaviour that was incomprehensible just a short time ago.

Mrs Tipton spilt over the edges of the piano stool, her eyes twinkling with sherry and festive spirit. She warbled 'By the Light of the Silvery Moon' in a surprisingly delicate voice.

Martha came back in what seemed like a matter of moments, breathless, and whispered in her ear. 'You need to come. Now.'

Outside the farmhouse, last week's snow had cleared leaving the tracks around the farm muddy. Her footsteps squelched in the mud. She slipped and slid as she tried to get a grip.

The back door was already open. Cecil ran towards her, panting, his eyes wide. He paused to breathlessly shove his arms into his coat and tug on his hat. His boots weren't even laced, his heels crushing the backs as he started out onto the path.

'Where are you going, Cecil?' she asked, trying to pull him back. 'What's happened?'

'He's not welcome here.' A deep voice from within the dark hallway startled her. 'There are to be no shirkers under this roof.'

She reached for the wall to steady herself.

'Theo!' He emerged into the shadows of the hallway, swaying

unsteadily on his feet. His broad shoulders reached from one wall to the other. As he loomed closer she was smacked in the face by sickly alcohol fumes. 'What are you doing here?'

'Another fine welcome,' he said, sneering to reveal the whites of his teeth. He waved a bandaged hand at her. She stepped back to avoid it.

'A Blighty injury,' he said. 'Shrapnel. A bit of luck. Except of course I come to surprise you and find your ridiculous little brother is squirrelled away, hiding like the coward he is.'

Cecil had taken harbour in the shadow of the shed at the end of the yard, his panting still audible.

'Please, Theo,' she said. 'It's Christmas. And I don't want any fuss.'

She signalled to Martha that she should bring Cecil back inside, and she took Theo back into the front room.

'I have to report back on Boxing Day.' She surveyed him in the candlelight. More lines had etched around his mouth and eyes. The skin about his eyes was puffed up and plum-coloured. The eyes themselves weren't a soft brown any longer; they were a hard black. The man at ease who'd harvested apples with her in October had faded away and all that was left was a brittle core.

'We'll make it a very special Christmas then,' she said, determined that she could thaw him out, bring that other part of him back.

'Not if he's here.' Theo's brow was as heavy as storm clouds.

'I don't want any trouble,' Cecil said, holding up his palms in surrender. 'I'll sleep in the hay barn, Emily.'

'No, you will not.' Emily raised her voice. 'It's the middle of winter and you already look malnourished.'

'I'm prepared to put my differences aside for Christmas.' He held out his hand for Theo, edging into the doorway, his angular knees jutting through his trousers.

'Theo?' Emily framed it in a gentle tone, as if he were a lion in a cage. Cecil folded his arms.

'Suit yourself,' Cecil said. 'Christmas is a time of forgiveness.' At another time, Emily might have respected Cecil's resolve, and determination to stick to his morals, but not now when Theo was simmering like a kettle on the range.

'You want me to forgive you?' Theo let out a bone-shaking laugh. 'France is a stinking cesspit of slaughter and despair. And you want my forgiveness for sitting on the sidelines? Will it make you feel better?' Theo stepped closer to Cecil, leant in towards him, snarled, and then spat in her brother's face.

She was on her feet and moving towards Theo.

'I refuse to breathe the same air as this pathetic excuse for a man.'

Cecil cowered. The foaming spittle sliding down his cheek. 'I only ever wanted the war to end. I couldn't perpetuate it; I just can't be a part of it.'

'Oh, do shut up.' Theo shook his head, his tone low and cutting.

'I think that's enough now,' Emily said, a tremor in her voice. 'Theo, why don't you go upstairs and rest and, Cecil, we'll ask Heinrich next door if you could sleep there tonight.'

'Heinrich!' Theo leant against the wall. 'I'd forgotten we have to sleep cheek by jowl with the ruddy Hun. You Cothams really wouldn't know patriotism if it shelled the living daylights out of you.'

Emily clenched her fists. What right did Theo have to come into her home drunk and hailing such insults at her and Cecil? Her brother had stood by his convictions and one look at him would tell anyone he had paid a high price.

'Perhaps it should be you who sleeps next door,' Emily said. She stared at the floor as she spoke, but she meant it, by God she meant it. She clenched her jaw. 'I want you to leave.'

Theo had been toying with the bandage on his hand. Now he ripped it free and raised a bloodied and scarred hand up to Emily's face. Martha screamed. Cecil stepped forwards, shoved Emily back against the wall, and squared up to Theo; a waif against an ogre. Theo brought the bare hand down, connected with the side of Cecil's head. It rebounded from the hallway wall with a sickening thud.

Emily and Martha charged at Theo, Martha pummelling his back, Emily tugging at his shoulder, desperate to pull him away from Cecil. Theo's fists flew thick and fast. The air filled with the rasp of Cecil's wounded breath. The whole time Cecil kept his arms by his sides, his eyes those of a cadaver.

'Stop,' Emily cried. 'Stop!' She stood wedged between Theo and Cecil to shield her brother as a painful blow rammed into her side, and knocked her to the floor. Martha tried to tug Cecil away, breath expelling in groans, until eventually blood spilled from Cecil's lips. His body grew limper and limper. Still Theo didn't tire.

Back on her feet now, Emily charged at Theo and landed on his back, hitting him and then trying to wrap her arms around his shoulders to prevent him from hitting Cecil, but her brother was on the floor now and Theo shook Emily off and began to kick Cecil in his stomach. She heard a sickening wheeze from Cecil with each blow.

'Help!' Emily screamed, banging on the hallway wall. 'Help!' She threw herself down onto the floor at Theo's boots, shielding Cecil. She held her breath as he retracted his boot behind him, and just before he flicked it forwards towards her head, Heinrich filled the hallway. He was taller, broader, and he was fresh and full of strength. Theo panted, stood his ground. Heinrich shouted at him in German.

Then he was gone, and she had no idea what Heinrich had done with him once he'd lifted him out into the yard.

Martha gasped. Cecil was listless, an outcast fledgling tossed from the nest. She felt his neck for his pulse. It was weak, but it was there.

'I'm all right,' he murmured through a bloodied mouth. 'Just a bit sore.' They helped him up to standing and took him slowly and tentatively up to her bedroom where they laid him on Emily's bed. He gave another wheeze. They fetched him blankets that they would have to forgo that night in the coal-less house, and made a cold compress to put on his swollen eye.

'Would you like me to check on Heinrich, see what's happened to Theo?' Martha asked.

Emily shook her head. Good riddance to him. She applied the compress to Cecil with shaking hands. He was going to be all right. Sensations returned to her own body, and the sharp sting in her side where Theo had struck her. She lifted her pirate shirt to find a purple bruise the size of a dinner plate.

'There, there,' she whispered to Cecil, in a soft voice that broke despite herself. 'Let's be glad that Mother can't see you now,' she said.

'Why didn't he hit him back?' Martha whispered, her face streaked with tears, as they closed the door on him. Martha had offered to share her bed with Emily that night and had prepared her a compress for her bruise.

'Because he'll stand by what he believes to be right, no matter what,' Emily said through her own tears. 'Even if it kills him.' She smiled a wonky, trembling smile. 'It makes him the most infuriating, but admirable brother.'

She collapsed into Martha's arms and they held on to one another with a tight grip while they wept quietly.

*

Sitting in the house, the new marks on the wall, the broken door, were all reminders of Christmas Eve. She started every time the back door opened now, awoken by the badgers and foxes prowling at night. If sleep had been hard before, it was impossible now.

It drove her out of Perseverance Place and back up to the convalescent hospital. She baked a cake. While she clattered about in the kitchen making a terrible mess, Martha popped in and out, amused and curious at what had stirred her into action.

It was a fruit cake, a bit lopsided, and she wasn't convinced it had cooked properly all the way through, but it had turned a lovely golden brown on the top, which was no mean feat with the inconsistent temperature of the range.

She could change out of her trousers and smock, but it was better this way. She didn't want to appear to be making a special effort, which she absolutely wasn't doing. It was nothing like that, she told herself as she fanned the cake, willing it to cool so she could take it up to HopBine before she lost her nerve. She just wanted to see a kindly face.

Christmas had been so distressing. Cecil was so unwell after his fight with Theo that they'd had to call out the doctor, and so the village knew they'd been harbouring him. Then just after New Year's Day he was arrested again and they had no idea of when he'd be released again. Somehow, throughout it all, she was certain that everything would be better if she saw the soldier who'd enjoyed her Turkish delight.

As she stepped into the familiar primrose yellow hallway at HopBine House and her senses were at once assaulted with anti-septic and unfamiliar voices and the scraping of furniture, it was peculiar – as if she'd travelled through time and landed at her home in the distant future.

'Back again!' The matron rested her hands in front of her. Emily craned to look over the matron's shoulder into her old sitting room, but the space was empty. 'So, what can I do for you?' Matron clasped her hands together and rocked slightly on her feet to signal she'd be on the move again in a matter of moments.

Emily cleared her throat. 'There was a chap,' she began, 'when I was here at Christmas. He rather enjoyed the Turkish delight, so, well, I made him a cake. It's sweetened with carrot. He needed feeding up.' She laughed, fiddling with the cake tin.

'And you know this chap's name?'

'Oh, well.' Her cheeks were burning up now. 'I don't, no. He had green eyes, a moustache and a narrow face.' Kind but sad, but she'd keep that to herself.

'I think you must mean the Captain. Shell shock. Rather emotional?'

'Yes, that sounds like him. Might I see him? Say hello and give him the cake?'

The matron tilted her head to one side.

'You might, except Captain Ellery was discharged just yesterday. He'll be on his way back to the trenches, if he isn't already there. He'd better not scream in his sleep as he did here, or his men won't get any rest. Poor chap.'

Emily dropped her head, staring at the frivolous cake tin and wishing she'd gone to the farmhouse. So that was that. It had been a silly idea anyway, fanciful, and the poor man wasn't well. What would he have said if she'd turned up out of the blue? He might have sent her away.

It was for the best that she had missed him; it was a lesson, a message, that she had to face up to what had happened between Theo and Cecil. She could hide in the farmhouse, the farmyard or HopBine House, but it didn't change anything. She had seen a truly terrible side to her husband, and no amount of running was going to change it.

Chapter Nineteen

August 1918

'Is he here again?' Theo stood in the doorway.

She blinked at the sight of him. Since Christmas, since Theo had last been home, they'd prepared the land, planted seeds and watched the crops grow; they'd picked the fruit and the livestock had given birth, but the memory of what he'd done to Cecil hadn't faded. He was capable of hurting a defenceless man. She might never look at him and not remember him kicking her emaciated brother to the floor.

His chest was puffed up now, his black eyes searching the corners of the room. His hand was healed up; just an angry scar ran across the skin.

'Cecil's back in prison.' She pulled her knees up to her chest.

'Good.' He collapsed into the armchair. 'I'm just here for tonight.'

She straightened her back. How could she think that he was welcome? Martha's footsteps travelled down the stairs. Her raven hair appeared around the doorframe.

'Everything all right?' she asked, her eyes wide behind Theo's back.

'I think so,' Emily said, gesturing with her head to keep the back door open in case they needed to call for help.

Theo wiped his eyes with the back of his hand and sniffed. 'I'm sorry,' he said. 'I don't suppose you've got any brandy?'

She shook her head. If she didn't have it here, he would just go out and look for it – it was pointless to think it would be any different. She'd not much to offer him in the way of food either. Since they'd introduced rationing at the beginning of the year, even on the farm they'd had to use what little they had sparingly.

'I passed a public house on my way up from the station.' And there it was. 'Will you come with me?'

She couldn't go to the Queen's Head, even if she'd wanted to. Her family would never drink with the labourers and land girls weren't permitted. She offered to make him a nice cup of tea instead, but as the kettle boiled, he was fidgeting about, his leg twitching, his gaze on the door.

She held her breath whenever he moved close to her. Martha left the room.

'I won't be long,' he said, before heading out.

She waited for him by the fire, too close for comfort, but the intense heat scorching her skin was satisfying somehow. The flames dwindled after a while, and the room grew too cold for her to stay.

A knock came at the parlour door, and she leapt out of her chair. 'Why don't you go up?' It was Martha. 'I've used my secret coal supply to light the fire in your room. Should I stay with the other girls tonight? Leave you two to have some privacy?' she said. 'Or perhaps I should stay, make sure he doesn't get drunk and nasty again.'

Emily chewed her lip. He was her husband. She wanted to give up on him, but she couldn't.

'Does he deserve a second chance?' she asked. 'What he did to Cecil, it was brutal.' Her mind was a blank with no answer of what she should do.

'Has he apologised?'

She shook her head. It might make a difference if he did.

Martha said she'd go next door then with the other girls, leave her bedroom window open, and she'd let Heinrich know Theo was there too. It wasn't exactly the most optimistic of plans for a romantic reconciliation with her husband, but under the circumstances she didn't have much choice. He'd be back, and if he could stand, he'd want his marital rights.

Normally, Emily draped her clothes on the horse in front of the fire. It cost her half a crown a week to get her uniform laundered, and she'd get another few days out of it yet. Tonight, it was just her damp leather gaiters that dried out by the fire, the rest she left in a tired heap on the floor.

The bed was lumpy, the sheets scratchy. Her pillow kept sinking too much in the middle. She tossed and turned, exposing herself to a sly draft that crept beneath the bedcovers, before eventually, she dozed off.

She was certain she'd been sleeping for a week when Theo stumbled into the room.

'Why did you come and visit me?' She kept her voice steady. 'If you were just going to sit in the public house?'

'There's something I need to tell you.' He spoke as loudly as if it were daytime. She jumped as his belt buckle crashed to the floor. 'The reason why I've been home.'

Her eyes stung. She searched out his shape in the darkness. The room was so cold, the draft from Martha's bedroom window seeping in. He tended the fire, but Martha's coal had long since burnt through. She pulled the bedclothes tight, lit a candle beside the bed.

He grew closer, sat in the pool of the light. The mattress dipped and the old springs creaked as he sat on the edge to peel off his socks. He'd taken off his own shirt and his braces hung loose. He tossed down his socks and faced her.

'When I came home at Christmas my mother was very ill. She died, last week. I've been home to go to her funeral.'

His face collapsed and his head flopped forwards as he fought and lost the battle with his tears. He was shivering now and looking at the bed, working out how he would fit in too.

'I'm so sorry for you.' He had his back to her and she tentatively slid an arm around his side. 'Did you get to keep any of your mother's artwork?'

He stiffened. She held her breath.

'Father burnt it all. I shan't see him again. He's as dead to me as my mother is now.'

'Home is wherever you and I are,' she said. She buried her head in his back and closed her eyes while she smoothed his hair.

They could build a marriage out of this rubble, she was sure of it. The war had destroyed so much, but it had brought them together. She'd sensed something about him in those early letters and their day at the women's march, something that was worth fighting for. *In sickness and in health. For better and for worse.* She'd not taken much notice of her vows at the time – she'd still been crying every day for John, and was excited about her training course, but she should have listened more closely to her doubts, waited until she knew him better.

Her fingertips made long sweeping snake-like shapes from the nook of his shoulder blades right down to the small of his back and then up again. He tilted his head back on his neck, his eyes shut. His breath deepened and then seemed to stop altogether.

He rolled over. 'I'm going to London in the morning to visit my pal, Patch,' he whispered.

'How is he?' she asked.

'He had his legs blown off,' Theo said with such defeat it made her heart ache. 'I pulled him from the wire.' He ran his fingers through her tresses. 'I saved his life and he hates me for it, and now I have to face him.' He rested his palm on her loose hair, pinning her head to the pillow.

He pushed himself on top of her and kissed her. It was all teeth and the stench of alcohol again, just like the time in the hotel corridor in Bournemouth. She wanted him to stop, but how could she push him away now after everything he'd told her?

'Theo …'

'I'm sorry about Cecil,' he said, as he edged himself between her legs. 'I wasn't myself.'

The cast-iron bed creaked. She was glad Martha had slept with the other girls after all. She closed her eyes and wished he would move his hand so her head would be free. Her hair pulled at her scalp every now and again. She held on to him tight, until he grunted and the bed sighed. He moved over to the side she'd warmed up. Her hair was free now. But he'd left her with the cold, narrow strip. She clung to the edge.

He sniffed. And sniffed again. The bed was too narrow, the mattress too thin; they'd never get a decent night's sleep like this, and he'd had a terrible day, and another awful one lay ahead of him. She lifted his trench coat and she lay down on the floor.

Chapter Twenty

November 1918

Dearest Emily,

You didn't seem so very pleased to see me when I came on leave, and that has weighed heavily on a mind that is already low from my terribly sad visit to Patch. He told me he wished I'd left him on the wire – what a thing for him to say, and now I have to live with that. I didn't save him at all; I consigned him to a life of misery.

There are times when I'm so close to death that I feel its breath on my collar. I can't close my eyes at night to sleep because a beast awaits me with white eyes and a dark coat and fearsome, yellow teeth.

You most probably don't want to hear all of this from me. The way you looked at me that last night, it was as if you were staring into the eyes of a stranger. You looked so very afraid. Perhaps you expected a husband to look after you and now you're feeling disappointed with your lot.

Yours
Theo

Rumours of peace filtered in from the Front, though the war had gone on long enough now it was hard to fathom an end to it. The allied troops were worn out, and things could just as easily go the other way. One faltering step and the Hun would strike.

Emily was on the Sunnyside Orchard with the Bramley Battalion, armed with their pruning secateurs and spread around the bare-branched apple trees, the sheep resting by the trunks.

An end to the war was what they all wanted, and of course that meant her too, but they were pocketed away here. She was needed, she wore breeches, and played cards, set her own timetable and worked every hour she had the strength to work. Peace meant the end to tragedy and death and the loss of so many, of rationing. But could peace also mean that she could keep on doing all this? Peace meant Mother, it meant moving back to HopBine House, it meant Cecil, it meant being a wife to Theo. She'd cried when she'd read his last letter. He hadn't written to her again.

She finished her tree and moved her ladder along to the other side of Martha. The tune to 'Tipperary' came to her as she propped the ladder so that she could reach a high branch. Martha joined in and the song soon caught like a wave. The trees grew alive with their voices and her jaw loosened. The singing nudged everything else aside.

The women's voices still floated through the air. The branches were bare, the final yellowed leaves thrown to the ground by high winds they'd had three nights previously, before the rain had come. The elegant tree with its wide-open arms had the open centre that would let the light in and allow the crop to blush in the sunshine. Emily imagined throwing a hat through the tree's torso, just like Mr Tipton had shown her; there were a few light-impeding branches that would snag its journey.

At the top, she rested her shins against the highest rung. Canker crusted the joint of a branch that came towards her. She grasped the spear tip, with the young fresh buds of growth from 1918, and slid her hand back along to 1917's darker, thicker wood; then came a short section for 1916, longer again for 1915 and then at 1914's growth the branch crooked like an elbow where the canker had set in.

As one of the girls burst into 'Pack up your Troubles', she unhitched her saw from her belt. The hay-coloured dust rained from the branch. The infected branch dropped to the base of the ladder. She warbled the high notes of the song.

'All gone,' she whispered to the golden scar. The tiny black cankerous dot that ran through the heart of the branch was gone.

The singing had faded. The girls were quiet again. She left Martha to check on them. She slowed to listen in on a couple of girls talking about the munitions workers' marches the night before in London and Glasgow. Hundreds of factory girls had been laid off overnight.

'Do you think they could do the same to us?' Hen said. The others had spotted Emily coming and fell quiet, concentrating on their pruning, as if Hen hadn't asked the question at all. The old order and the pre-war divisions were reappearing before it was even over.

She drifted away from the girls in their trees, and walked towards the stream that ran along the orchard's boundary. A traction engine filled up at the stream next to the old paper mill. Disused for nearly a hundred years, the mill crumbled on the banks on the other side. The horizon was broken by the line of cedar trees that pointed towards HopBine House.

The breeze buffeted her ears. A skylark's reedy whistle. The stream rushed over rocks in the shallows. Saws gnawed through branches in the orchard. Life as usual, but at the same time an ominous sense in the air that they were on the verge of something momentous.

It wasn't just the changes that the end of war would bring. Her life was changing, war or not, and there was nothing she could do to stop it. She'd been sick the last three mornings in a row. Martha was the oldest of six. She'd heard her retching, spied her chamber pot before she'd been able to throw the contents out.

'You need to keep busy,' the disembodied voice of Martha called from behind the branches back in the orchard.

'I'll just check there isn't anyone on their way with news,' Emily replied.

She stood on the toes of her boots in case there was a bicycle on New Lane bringing news from a London train, or a cart coming back from town, but the hedgerow was too high. She'd need to climb the hill for a better view. But then news might not come today. It might be tomorrow. It might not come for weeks, months, years. She might be pushing thirty before Theo came home, and Cecil was released from prison.

She was grateful to the farm for that. The cows' udders still swelled each day; the blossom would frill along the branches each springtime, no matter what the Kaiser, or Fate, had in store.

*

It was nine a.m. and the land girls had gone into the farmhouse for their breakfast.

'I'll wait out in the fresh air,' Emily said.

She didn't have the stomach for bacon and eggs, not even for a cup of tea. She had to take deep breaths when the saliva started to rise, but it didn't always work and she didn't want anyone else to know.

A flock of hungry fieldfares and redwings clouded over and descended onto the low hawthorn hedgerow that formed a wall between the field and the farmhouse. Three birds, with grey-crested heads, blue-grey backs and speckled chests hopped along the base of the hedge, stabbing haw berries from low-lying branchesThe rest, perhaps as many as twenty, dissolved in amongst the thorns to feast, chuckling and chattering away as they did.

The farmhouse door opened. Like a cork from a bottle the musty air was set free. Breakfast was over. Mrs Tipton, hair escaping from its knot, hands fisted on her hips, emerged onto the yard. The birds flapped their wings in unison and took off. Emily's stomach cramped as she made her way down the last of the field towards the stile, while the other girls filed their way out of the cramped kitchen.

Lifting a leg over the stile, Mrs Tipton pointed up towards her and she waved back, but they all continued to point up the paddock.

It was Mr Flitwick, the gardener at HopBine, stumbling across the field towards them. He lost his footing on the ground, spatless boots gathering mud, scattering a small murder of rooks feasting on the grass, as he staggered forwards, his palm in front of him ready to land first. She joined the others.

His furrowed brow was intense and determined, and he was panting. He took his cloth cap from his head and waved it at them. 'What is it, Mr Flitwick?' Mrs Tipton called. They all waited for Mr Flitwick to answer. There wasn't any sign of anguish in his expression, but it wasn't joy either, it was something in between.

'I've come to tell you.' He wiped his forehead with his cap and rested his hands on his thighs to catch his breath.

'Come on, come on,' said Mrs Tipton. 'Out with it, out with it.'

'The war,' he panted. Emily leant in. 'They've signed the Armistice. The Germans are defeated. Peace,' he panted. 'Peace!' He threw his hat high into the air and let it fly.

She put her hand to her mouth, retched and ran across the yard, into the hay barn. The retching wouldn't stop. Her stomach contracted, and up came the water she'd had for breakfast. Three chickens arrived, pecking about in the hay at her feet, scavenging for goodies. Again and again, she retched until there was nothing more to give.

When she left the barn, Mrs Tipton was waiting for her. 'It's over.' She flung her arms around her. 'It'll all change now,' Mrs Tipton said. 'This way of doing things had almost begun to feel like normal. Even the ole man has stopped complaining about all the women.'

Emily stiffened. 'Just because the war is over doesn't mean I can give all this up,' she said. 'This is where I'm meant to be, and this is where I'll stay.'

Chapter Twenty-One

December 1918

Dearest Emily,

Did I tell you that Asquith has made a journalist of me? You're looking at a lead reporter for the Canterbury Clinker. *We write on toilet paper mostly, and the news is mostly ficti-tious. The irony eh? A reporter, with no education and a criminal record.*

Fondest wishes
Cecil

Martha was the dealer. She'd just won the hand and now collected up the cards.

'Has your Theo written?' Hen asked.

Emily paused. 'They sent him to Germany,' she replied, with what was just a white lie. He hadn't written once since the war had ended, which meant he could be anywhere: hospital, a demob camp or Germany. Or, he might be home here in England, and he hadn't visited.

'Germany, isn't that were Olive's son's gone?' Lottie asked.

Emily nodded. It was just like Olive's son. Of course! That was where she'd got the idea to say it. She would have to be more careful if she didn't want to get caught out.

She raised a hand to her stomach as the baby fluttered about. Martha had spied where she'd positioned her hand and winked. No one else knew and she wanted to keep it that way. The morning sickness had let her be by the end of November, around the same time as the doctor had confirmed she was pregnant. She would have a summertime baby, born in a time of peace and long, warm nights. And perhaps the baby would have a father too, if only he could come home a changed man.

She yawned as Martha dealt out another hand.

'Are you in?' Martha asked.

Emily hesitated. She'd had an early start and would love to turn in, but these nights with the girls wouldn't last forever. The prisoners of war and the refugees had gone home, but no men had yet returned to work on the farm.

'I'm in,' she said.

She was to the left of Martha and so it was her turn to lay her first card.

'And have you decided if you'll all live at HopBine when he comes back?' Lottie asked.

They didn't mean any harm; they were just being friendly. A circle of expectant faces waited for her answer. The army had already moved out of HopBine. Mother might know whether they would return to their home, but she still didn't write. She'd not even written to her friend Norah Peters.

'Do you know, I'm much more tired than I realised.' She gave a big yawn, stretched her arms, and then pulled down her smock to prevent it from rising up. Her smock was baggy enough to not give the slight thickening of her waistline away, though she had loosened the belt by a notch.

She threw in her hand.

'Any news from the family?' Mrs Tipton, drying her hands on

155

her apron, intercepted Emily just before she could escape out of the kitchen door.

'Cecil will be in prison until the spring.'

Olive flinched at the very mention of her brother's name.

'They're only letting the very ill out first.'

'If you need help, just say. I'm sure your mother will see things differently now the war is over.' Mrs Tipton whispered, 'You've proven what we all knew you were capable of.' She lifted the back of her skirts to warm her behind on the stove.

'I hope so,' Emily said. She'd been too engrossed in farm life to stop to think about Mother and her long silence. It had been convenient and suited her needs, but she would write to her again, and make enquiries about taking over the farm. She gave Sally a farewell rub and pulled the latch.

'He's back late, isn't he?' Mrs Tipton nodded at the clock on the mantelpiece. As she opened the door, Emily checked the clock. On Wednesdays, Mr Tipton went into West Malling to the market. He always went to The Swan and he was always back late, and Mrs Tipton always complained about it.

'Stay 'til he's back, will you?'

Emily eyed the girls. The conversation had moved on. The girls were playing a new game whilst Martha had abandoned them and now knelt over a tub where she lifted out the sheets of soaked newspaper she was preparing for the fire. The conversation about the Cothams appeared to be forgotten. She sat at the table with Mrs Tipton.

'How did Mr Tipton enjoy his first vote in the elections?' Martha asked.

'It was quite a thing,' Mrs Tipton said.

Her mother would have had her first vote too, though she'd never had an interest in politics and most likely wouldn't have even gone at all.

'I don't know what I'd do if they ever let me in a polling station. I suppose, I'd put an X next to the man Mr Tipton was voting for. I don't know whether I think it's right that some women are being asked to make decisions like this. Who are we to say who should be running the country?'

'We're as capable of making the decision as anyone else,' said Martha. 'We've shown our worth with our war effort.'

Yes, and while some women over thirty had been rewarded with the vote, Cecil had been disenfranchised for five years.

'House!' Hen called from the settee.

The kitchen door rattled, and in with a draft of chilled and foggy air came the scrape of hobnail boots, and claws on the flagstones. Sally jumped to her paws, her ears pricked, baring her teeth and growling.

'Here, girl,' Emily said.

In came a dog, twice Sally's size with a two-tone coat: thick, dark hair on top and golden strands beneath. It peeled back its black, filmy gums to reveal fangs that would tear a good chunk out of Sally's hide with one bite and a bark that cut right through her.

The dog stepped away from the shadowy legs of his master, still in the shadows, encroaching on Sally's territory. Undeterred, Sally yapped back, with a vicious snarl.

Lottie and Hen put their hands over their ears.

Mrs Tipton was up and out of her chair. She slapped Sally on the back. 'You be quiet!' She hit the dog again and tugged her by the scruff of the neck.

The collie glared over her haunches, her speckled eyes brimming with aggression. She whimpered as Mrs Tipton booted her up the behind and she scampered under the table. Emily put a discreet hand beneath the tabletop, reaching out for Sally's fur, and then massaged the poor dog's head.

'Percy Greenacre! Look what we have here. Clear some room.' Mrs Tipton gestured at Lottie and Hen on the settee to move themselves onto the floor with the others to make way for Percy.

'Girls. Make way for HopBine Farm's very own war hero.'

He sat with his hat in his hands. His broad thighs almost filled the space taken by the girls. The dog, superior now it was victorious, positioned itself facing into the room between Percy's legs. Percy reeked of tobacco and something unfamiliar that Emily couldn't quite pin down.

The dog was panting, his pink tongue lolling, and the grooved gums all out on display. Sniffing around the shadows of the table, his fishy breath pumped into the room. Emily nudged him away, careful not to get too close.

'Who's your new friend? Has he a name?' Mrs Tipton called the beast over, and rubbed his back.

'Rover,' Percy said. 'I picked him up from a German prisoner of war in France and brought him back with me. Loyal creatures are Alsatians. Not like their masters.'

He teased his fingers around the dog's ears. Rover responded by tilting his head backwards. Sally's head now rested on Emily's thigh. She gave a long, steady blink and disappeared back into the shadows.

'The war has really turned things upside down on the farm, Percy. This here is Emily. Williams now, but she's one of the Cothams who own this place. She has been working here with us, she has. Haven't you, dear?'

They shook hands. He had only given the girls a cursory glance as he'd stepped over and around them to reach his seat, but now he appraised her afresh.

'I can see it now,' he said nodding. Emily was certain she'd never laid eyes on him before, but that happened a lot. The villagers knew her, but she didn't know them. 'You're the young girl who always followed the ole man around the farm.'

She nodded. If she was going to run this place, she'd have to become acquainted with these men.

He had heavy lines on his face, his brow folding down over his eyes. His hair, smarmed down to one side, stuck up in places where his hat had worked it free. His shoulders were broad. His frame suggested strength and capability, but he was shrunken, as if his body wasn't reaching the potential that his structure offered. He definitely wasn't the sort to take orders from a woman.

'Another hand?' Lottie asked the girls. Emily joined them. Mrs Tipton and Percy slipped into their own conversation, catching up, talking about people from the farm and village Emily didn't know. Once or twice she would break away from the game only to find his eyes on her.

Mrs Tipton was still talking. Percy stroked his dog. Emily laid out the cards, edging forwards away from Rover's fishy breath hot on her collar. She laid down a seven of hearts and won the hand. Percy mumbled in a monotone voice about railway coupons, an allowance for clothing, pension, thirty-eight shillings a week.

'How many men are still out there?' Emily asked.

'How many?' he repeated. 'Hard to say. It's chaos. They said it'd take just a few weeks, but it'll be months more like it.'

'She's waiting for her sweetheart,' Mrs Tipton explained.

'What was his work? Those with jobs to go to are being let home soonest.'

She took a deep breath; here she went again. 'He's gone to Germany though.' She was getting better at lying, just as long as she didn't catch Martha's eye. Her friend still kneaded wet newspaper, but had barely taken her gaze from Percy since he'd arrived.

'They let you go because you had work, did they?' Mrs Tipton steered the conversation back to Percy before Emily could ask if there were many men in the hospitals.

The drip, drip of the damp newspaper being wrung out by Martha came into focus. Her friend wouldn't take kindly to the threat to her livelihood.

'Aye, well if the master will have me back.' Percy fiddled with the trouser fabric on his knee. After all he'd seen and done for his country, it wasn't right he had to beg for his job, but the girls had worked hard too, kept his job open for him.

'The little 'uns eat so much,' he continued. 'The missus says it's been a right struggle.' His smile was feeble. He picked at his trousers with increased urgency.

Martha had said that the tighter the newspaper was squeezed, the longer it burnt, but never usually that much. Her knuckles shouldn't be turning white or her mouth pinching to a knot with the force of her effort.

'Of course the ole man'll want you back,' said Mrs Tipton. 'It's market day today. He has important meetings to attend, as you might remember. But come back in the morning. He'll be so pleased to see your strong arms. We've lost the war men now and Alfred can't lift a shovel these days without wheezing like his lungs are about to burst.'

Percy's shoulders relaxed and he smiled widely, but Emily clenched her jaw and blurted out: 'We girls have proven that we can do the heavy work too, Mrs Tipton.'

'I know you have, girl. Heavens, I didn't mean to go upsetting you.'

She might not have intended to, but she had. It was as if everything they'd done was forgotten already.

Martha took a lump of soggy newspaper and tossed it at the hearth. It landed with a sulky thud. The dog jumped up, but Martha snatched it away just in time.

'And what are you boiling up about?' Mrs Tipton straightened her back.

'Nothing,' Martha snarled, daring the dog to come closer with her no-nonsense gaze. Percy told the dog to sit down and he obeyed his master.

'Out with it,' Mrs Tipton barked.

Martha was shaking too much to have a clear enough head for a proper argument.

'I think Martha's just wondering,' Emily began, 'we're all wondering, where we might fit in with all this.' She sat on the edge of her seat, leaning forwards to address them both. 'We've

160

kept the home fires burning and we've really found a purpose, and enjoyed the work. We don't want to stop just because the war's over.'

Mrs Tipton frowned. 'You've a husband now, dear. It'll be up to him whether or not you can work as you hope, not me or the ole man, and as you know, girls like you don't normally work so you'll be asking a lot of him.'

Emily slapped the table with her palm. 'But, Mrs Tipton, the war has changed things. Married women have worked for the last four years.'

'Aye, because the men were away fighting. What choice did they have but to call on every soul this country had?'

Who was this woman sitting in front of her? Was it really the same person who'd cut out the newspaper article, planted the very seed in her mind, who had sent her on her journey to where she was now. Only now she said it was over, and time to go back to the sewing.

'You know how much this has meant to me,' Emily said. 'It isn't over for us. It isn't.'

'Maybe it won't be how you think. You could keep working on that kitchen garden o' yours, you'll get your horses back from the Front and then you'll be able to take up riding again.'

Emily shook her head. Martha was on her feet now, her composure growing. 'And I suppose I'll just go back to scrubbing floors, and working all hours for a pittance, shall I?'

'Now you look here.' Mrs Tipton was on her feet too, hands on hips. 'Work is work and you're lucky those ladies in their big houses have need of your services. Lloyd George says this is a land fit for heroes and that's never truer than on HopBine Farm.'

'It's all right.' Percy was on his feet now.

'You come back in the morning,' Mrs Tipton said. 'I'm dreadfully sorry about this kerfuffle. The war's given young girls big ideas I'm afraid.'

'I'll do that,' said Percy. 'Thank you, Mrs Tipton. It's a relief to learn there's work – I can't lie.'

'Good to have you back, lad. Take no notice o' the girls. Welcome home.'

'And what about us?' Martha's knuckles were white where she gripped the wet ball of newspaper.

Percy and Rover had barely closed the kitchen door behind him when Martha erupted.

'Which one of us doesn't come to work tomorrow, then, if he's to take our place?'

Emily darted outside. She'd said enough and if she stayed she'd only make things worse. There must be a way for the women to work alongside the men. They just had to find a compromise.

'Mr Greenacre,' she called after Percy's silhouette on the far side of the yard. They met in the middle of the yard, in the midst of the inky darkness, the raised voices from the farmhouse floating around them. He had taken off his cap to speak to her, and now scrunched it in his hand.

'Over in France and Belgium. Are there many men still in hospital?'

'The influenza has caught up with many,' he said. 'They say the war has ground them down. The flu will finish them off – not all though. Many are getting better, so they say,' he added. 'The nurses know what they're doing and take good care of the soldiers.'

'Did you ever come across a man by the name of Theodore Williams?' she asked. 'He's my husband. He fought in the Wakefield regiment.'

'You said he was in Germany?' Percy said.

She circled her head, not quite committing to the nod. He would understand the state Theo was in by the end, but if she told him the truth, that she had no idea where he was, and he didn't respect her confidence then it might spread to the whole village by tomorrow lunchtime.

'He didn't sound himself in his last few letters,' she blurted out. 'He hadn't been right for a while.'

He didn't flinch, or even raise an eyebrow. Theo wouldn't be the only man to have changed because of the war.

'I'm sorry, I never came across him.'

'Was it very bad, the war?' she asked.

'Aye. It was indeed.'

Dearest Theo,

Still no news from you – at least I can rest easy knowing that the fighting has ceased, but it would put my mind at rest to hear from you. I'm sure you're busy clearing up from the war and by all accounts the fighting went on until the last and now the authorities must catch up with Armistice. There are some men home, but many more still to come.

Perhaps you will write soon.

Fondest wishes

Emily

'Please don't let Martha go just yet,' Emily said to Mr Tipton when she caught him in the farmyard.

As the other girls returned to their old lives they'd urged Martha to do the same while she had the chance. The war had cost the country and there'd be a scramble for jobs. There were the women in the munitions factories all out of work, and the men coming home. Martha had refused to return to service.

'She's headstrong that one,' he said.

'But an excellent worker. Loyal too.'

Once Martha gave up on working the farm and returned to her old life, that would be it. The only way out of service would be another war and not even she was desperate enough to wish for that. This was a time to take what they had gained from the war and forge forwards, not to throw it all up in the air and retreat back to where they were before.

'Oh, all right then, but only while I can afford to, and only for as long as it's me in charge.'

She pumped her fists, and scampered to catch up with him. She hadn't finished with him yet; the most important question was still to come.

'I want to take over from you when you retire at the end of next season. What do you think?'

He frowned. 'What do I think?' He glanced at her sideways. 'I think it's not my farm; it's your mother's.'

He trudged away again.

'But would you put in a good word for me, tell her you think I'd make an excellent manager?'

'I'll do no such thing,' he snapped, coming to a standstill and turning to her with a tired, sagging face. 'You've shown as you're able, a hard worker. I'd go so far as to say it's in your bones, and with a man at the helm I dare say you'd be fine, but the future of this place is not my business; it's family business. I'm sorry.'

Chapter Twenty-Two

December 1918

'It's been so long I nearly forgot the look of you.' Grandmother, still wearing her mourning clothes, held out a gloved hand as Emily arrived in the dingy sitting room of her mansion flat in Belgravia.

She'd called on her mother at her uncle's house in De Vere Gardens but the footman, Henderson, had told her she was unwell, a migraine attack, and he'd pass on the message since she'd called. Then the door had been shut firmly in her face, leaving her no option but to call on Grandmother.

'My goodness you've quite changed. Stand here, in the light. Yes, your complexion is really quite improved, though you ought to acquaint yourself with a nailbrush, my dear.' She dropped Emily's hand.

Once tea was served Grandmother launched straight in.

'Emily my dear, now that this war is over you need to concentrate on your duty to your mother.'

'She seems to be doing perfectly well without me,' Emily said without a pause. Grandmother had no idea of the freedoms she'd enjoyed as a land girl. There was no way she could return to how things were before, even with a baby on the way.

'That's how it might appear. She was knocked low by John's death and Wilfred was a port in a storm, but it's time now, don't you think, that your family pulled itself back together? And you, with your husband, should be the ones to do it.'

Emily blinked quickly. She hadn't told the family about the baby yet. She'd wanted Theo to be the first to know, but whether or not Theo would feature in her future, she'd come to London with other ideas; and that didn't include being Mother's lap dog again.

'The war has changed everything. We can't go back to how it was before.'

'Well, you might think differently. It's only what I hear … Call on her again and see for yourself.'

This wasn't how her trip to London was supposed to pan out. A baby on the way and an absent husband was complication enough without Mother being in need. Emily sighed and tossed herself back into her armchair. She'd had enough of all this. She too had lost her father and a brother. Cecil had brought shame on her as much as Mother.

Grandmother slammed her cup onto its saucer. 'Oh, pull your bottom lip in and go to her for heaven's sake. See if you can encourage her to stand on her own two feet. That has always been your mother's problem.'

*

She stood outside of De Vere Gardens, her uncle's home, and surveyed the blank white veneer, the pillared entrance, and gasped. Someone was spying on her. A face at the window, now gone.

Then the black front door opened, and from behind Henderson in his livery, a woman appeared, a cloak draped around her shoulders, fastened with a decorative brooch, her hair pulled back into an elaborate roll with curls ironed into the back.

Could it be? She craned forwards. Heavens, it was.

'Mother!' she called.

Mother charged towards her with a blank expression. It had been such a long time. Emily opened her arms to embrace her, wanting to tell her all about her war work. But then Mother swept past her, her cloak billowing in her wake. She grabbed Emily's arm.

'Why are you intent on making such a fuss?' Mother hissed. 'What are you doing here?' Mother's gaze didn't settle on her; instead her eyes darted around her, scrutinising the pedestrians that went by. She wasn't how Emily had imagined she'd be. The contentedness that had emanated from her scant letters had caused Emily to imagine the departure of Mother's shadows beneath her cheekbones, the raw patch of hair at the front, and grey streaks running through her chestnut hair; but it was all just the same. The beauty of her slender nose, her delicate-as-porcelain jaw remained, but the grey-blue sharp eyes were as faded as the day she last saw her.

'I'm visiting you, that's all. Our house is empty and the war is over. And I wanted to tell you that you're going to be a grandmother.'

Mother's eyes widened. 'Goodness! Well you always did like to shock, didn't you?'

Emily put her hand across the small bump that was growing; she would make up for any love that might be lacking.

'Has this officer chap of yours got somewhere for you to live?'

She'd forgotten that Mother still thought Theo was an officer – not that her fib mattered any longer because she had an even bigger disappointment for her mother now. It was a wonder Cecil hadn't written and told Mother what sort of a man she'd hitched herself to.

'I want to move to the farm,' she said. 'Mr Tipton is going to retire and I want to take over.'

Mother searched her daughter's face. 'With a baby? I suppose your husband will do the work. It's hardly the life of a gentleman, is it?' Mother checked over her shoulder. 'I need to get back.'

'But what about HopBine House? It's empty now. And the farm. Mr Tipton is going to retire after the next harvest. There won't be a manager soon. We need to plan for the future.'

'You'll need to speak to Wilfred,' Mother said.

Emily opened her mouth to ask more, but the cloak flapped back up the stairs, and Mother was gone.

Chapter Twenty-Three

Christmas 1918

Emily held out her arms, but when Mother didn't moved towards her, Emily hid her discomfort by retrieving the brace of rabbits from the back seat and handed them to her uncle.

'Can you take them to the cook?' Wilfred said. As he glanced behind him she snatched a look at Mother. 'She'll know what to do with them.' He handed back the animals to Emily.

'Mr Tipton sent you some butter as well.'

Mother reached for the pat, but Wilfred's hand shot out and snatched it and smoothed the greaseproof paper with his thumbs. 'I'm having to hide my sugar ration from her.' He rolled his eyes in mock amusement. 'She has a terrible sweet tooth.'

Emily's meagre selection of luggage, three suitcases and an old Gladstone bag, were stacked in the dusty road and the porter lifted it in.

'It was a surprise to receive a letter from you,' Uncle Wilfred said. 'What with your new life taking shape, but I couldn't put a war girl out on the street at Christmas.'

Which was just as well; a farm labourer and his family had moved in to her old cottage in Perseverance Place. Martha was in a spare room at the Tiptons' and until she could persuade Mother to reopen HopBine, she had nowhere else to go.

Emily's footsteps echoed back at her as she entered the hallway, which on its own was wider than Perseverance Place. She crossed the gleaming black-and-white-tiled floor and passed beneath the looming shadow of the crystal chandelier that framed the base of the staircase.

'You don't have a Christmas tree?' she asked.

'I don't like a fuss,' he said. 'Or noise. I'm used to the quiet.'

Two maids with their hands clasped in front of them bobbed their heads. Wilfred introduced them, Bassett and Green. Sullen-faced Bassett had been there forever – Emily remembered her from those days long ago when they'd visited Uncle Wilfred without Father.

'Once your bags are up, why don't you change out of your travelling clothes?' said Mother.

Emily poked her head through the doorway of each of the three pristine, high-ceilinged rooms that led off the hallway. 'Why isn't there a photograph of John on the mantelpiece?'

Her Mother cowered, pushed Emily into the room and shut the door, checking over her shoulder. 'Wilfred has rules. Dwelling on the past won't help me over my grief.'

'I see.'

Mother rubbed her daughter's hand, as if to push away any discussion on how they might feel.

'Well, I must be off.' Wilfred appeared behind them making them both jump. 'I have a drinks party.' He rolled his eyes as if it was a terrible chore, but someone had to do it.

'It's always business with Wilfred,' Mother said, with a frothy little chuckle. 'Even at Christmas.'

The footman, Henderson, came back down the stairs empty-handed.

'I'll show you to your room.' Mother had been jumpy when

Uncle Wilfred was there. Now her arms swept around her as she walked, and she had more colour in her cheeks.

She led Emily around in squares, hands smoothing the bannisters until they reached what was to be Emily's bedroom on the fourth floor. A sickly pink affair, with a blushing carpet and roses on the wallpaper and curtains, a coral upholstered velvet stool in front of the dresser, and bedspread.

'Here you are. I suppose it's cheery,' Mother said. 'If that's your cup of tea. I'm directly beneath you in the yellow room.'

At least that was something. Mother fawned so much over Wilfred that it wouldn't have been a surprise to find them sharing a room.

'Maid will be up shortly,' Mother said. 'To dress you for dinner.'

Emily said she could dress herself, but apparently that wasn't an option.

Her window overlooked a small back garden, a tiny patch of lawn with some sorry-looking shrubs, diseased and dying, along the borders. The brick wall either side was piled high with ivy, which crept its way around the fruit tree at the foot of the garden.

'Maid is on her way,' Mother announced, standing rigidly as the footsteps grew closer.

'Perhaps we could make some garlands, decorate the hallway. Isn't that a holly bush?' She pointed to the far corner of the garden. Entwined with the ivy it would jolly up the hallway. Just as she had done at HopBine.

'They won't like the fuss. Have a rest after your journey,' Mother interrupted. She glanced first at the wedding band and then at Emily's stomach.

'Perhaps you can find me some secateurs. I will get to work. There isn't even a wreath on the front door, Mother.'

Inside the wardrobe, her clothes were already hung up. She'd hardly worn any of them since she'd been working on the farm. They greeted her now with the silent judgement of abandoned friends who expressed their dissatisfaction with blank stares.

Outfits she'd owned in another life. She pulled each dress, blouse and skirt out in turn and examined it. Then she let them go. Let them swing. One of them would have to do for the rest of the evening, and she didn't much care which threadbare, out-of-mode outfit it would be.

Just as she began to unbutton a blouse there came a knock at the door. She swung around.

'I have come to help you change, Madame.' It was Bassett. 'I am to be your maid, if that's all well and good with you.' Bassett didn't exactly sing her announcement.

'Of course,' Emily said, her hands falling from her buttons. 'I remember you, I think, from when I came here as a child?' Emily made conversation while Bassett removed a heavily boned camisole embroidered with blue ribbon from a drawer.

'Most probably,' she said. 'I've been here over twenty years, stayed on during the war, too.'

'You must remember me and my brothers John and Cecil then – we visited once when we were young?'

Bassett's cheeks coloured. She pulled the blue laces tight, forcing the breath out of Emily's chest. Emily glanced down at her stomach. 'Leave it loose at the bottom,' she said. 'I haven't worn these since before the war. I ought to get measured for new ones while I'm in town.'

Bassett yanked the laces again. Emily hoped the baby didn't mind being pulled about. 'John always enjoyed visiting here. He liked to feed the ducks in Hyde Park.'

'Miss Emily, I'm afraid the master doesn't permit talk of Masters John or Cecil in the house.'

'Either of them?'

'Yes, ma'am,' she said. 'The master says it doesn't do to dwell.'

'Very well. I'll do my best to remember that,' she said, stepping into her skirt and pressing her hands on the material that covered her up.

Once she was dressed and Bassett had brushed and waved her

hair with curling irons she left Emily alone in the pink room. In the mirror was an alien in a starch-heavy chemise, ruched up under the stays.

'Who are you?' she asked the reflection, but it didn't answer. It was too busy wondering how Mother could tolerate this place.

'Are you happy here?' Emily said outright when she found Mother perched on the edge of an armchair in the drawing room.

She'd had to find the secateurs for herself, tucked away in a glass-fronted lean-to that ran along one wall, outside the French door in the library.

Mother must have heard her banging about in the hallway, as she wound the ivy around the staircase and threaded in the holly berries, but she hadn't left the drawing room to help her, or to ask if there was anything she needed.

Emily had made a base for the ivy itself by twining the two fronds together into a circle and then added adornments of holly and some scarlet berries she'd found on a bush in the public gardens opposite.

Then she joined Mother in the immaculate drawing room. The silverware in the cabinet behind her gleamed in the candle-light. Emily snapped the door tight.

She repeated her question.

'Is this really the best place for you?' Grandmother had been right, things weren't as they should be. Wilfred was her son – she knew him far better than Emily did – and her advice echoed in Emily's ears.

'Of course. I'm taken care of here. Wilfred does everything. I have no concerns at all.'

That hadn't been Emily's question at all.

'What about HopBine?' Emily said. 'It's empty. You could move back there.'

'Why would I want to live there alone? No, no. It's out of the question. HopBine is in the past. I'm settled here. And what about you – you didn't tell me where you and this chap ...'

'Theo,' she reminded her.

'Theo and you are going to live.'

She took a deep breath. She couldn't keep avoiding the truth. She told her that Theo hadn't written to her since the war had ended.

Mother's gaze settled on Emily's stomach. She continued to be a disappointment to her; first a bad marriage, then a career on a farm, and now she was having a baby without a father. Mother asked all the questions Emily had asked herself: had he abandoned her, was he still at a demob camp, was he injured and in hospital?

'I don't know, so I must forge on with plans for me and the baby. As I mentioned, I want to run the farm.' She jumped around, avoiding her lies: he wasn't even an officer; he'd been a working-class man. That hadn't mattered to her because he'd been kind and supportive at a time when she'd needed it, but it had been a mistake, a terrible error of judgement and she hadn't known him at all.

Mother shook her head, wrinkling her nose. Emily couldn't tell her all of that.

'You've been quite irresponsible. You'll have to look for him, contact his family. You'll have to stay here until you find him. Wilfred will allow you to remain here.'

Emily sighed. What else had she expected? 'I can provide for us if I need to.' She put a protective hand over her stomach. 'And what about you?' She took the conversation back. 'Surely you can't want to stay here.'

'It's not a case of what I want,' she said.

'But we could all live together, at HopBine. You could ride Hawk out on the gallops.'

Now Mother scoffed. 'I've been here almost three years. It's not perfect, but it's tolerable.'

Mother fiddled with her outstretched fingers. Her ring finger was bare, the wedding ring gone, along with the eternity ring she wore on her right hand.

'So what will happen to HopBine?' she asked.

'You'll need to speak to your uncle. John thought it best if anything happened to him that Wilfred take control of the family affairs.' Mother fiddled with the skin where her wedding ring had been.

'What! Why would John do that? Is it because he gave us money?'

Mother nodded. 'That and the fact I made it clear that I was never raised to deal with finances, land management, running an estate and dealing with staff. I could never count on Cecil, and you wouldn't be any more able than me.'

Emily sprung out of her chair. 'That's simply not true,' she said. 'Of course, I can manage the estate.'

Mother shook her head and gave an irritating mocking laugh. 'No, you will not.'

'Well then, I'm going to go home and open up HopBine, and when Mr Tipton retires I'll take over there, and you can sit around here and do whatever it is you do all day that doesn't tax you or cause you to worry.'

Emily strode to the door. As she flung it open, Mother called her back.

'Sit down,' Mother ordered. Emily folded her arms. They were back exactly where they had been before she became a land girl. 'Sit,' she said. Emily flung herself back on the sofa and buried her face in her hands.

'Wilfred owns half of HopBine. John had no choice but to offer him the property when Wilfred cleared our debts.'

So, he hadn't been the munificent uncle swooping in, in their hour of need. He had seen an opportunity to own half of their estate and steer it too if anything were to happen to John.

'You'd need his permission and his money to reopen HopBine. He would be your employer on the farm. He could appoint you as a manager. But frankly that's such a ludicrous idea I wouldn't even raise it with him. He'll simply laugh you down.'

Before she could say any more, Uncle Wilfred burst through the door, spic and span in a double-breasted frock coat unbuttoned to reveal his waistcoat, stiff high-winged collar and narrow, striped trousers.

He pecked her mother on the cheek, as if it were a nightly routine.

He addressed Emily by pointing his silver-topped walking stick at her. 'You're pale, my dear niece. You need a pick-me-up.'

He leant heavily against the doorframe to remove his gold watch from his waistcoat, then pressed the call button for Henderson.

'My niece doesn't have a drink,' he said. 'And what about you, Louisa? Have you been taken care of?'

Her mother's hand rose to the nape of her neck to tame imaginary loose hairs. 'I'm quite all right, thank you.' The way she fawned turned Emily's stomach.

'How about a glass of port wine?' Wilfred suggested.

Mother agreed. Emily wanted brandy but kept that to herself. Wilfred's mood had a troubling edge to it.

'Didn't Cook bake another batch of mince pies?' he asked Louisa with a tut.

'I'm still hungry – the meal at the club wasn't up to much. May I have a mince pie?' Henderson poured him a large whisky on ice, handed him the cut crystal tumbler, set a coaster on the table and left the room in search of mince pies.

'It's been a sad day one way or another,' Wilfred said.

'Whatever happened?' Mother asked.

'Some blasted young girl: a clerk. She asked me for a pay rise.'

'And?' Mother prompted.

'I had to let her go.' He shook his head, took another swig of his whisky.

'On Christmas Eve?' Emily said.

'Yes. You see why I've been drinking now, don't you? I should point out that she's married so she has no concerns over keeping a roof over her head. She's earning pin money, that's all,' he slurred. 'But I had to let her go – it's the example it sets to the other girls. I already have more females on the payroll than I need. She was being greedy. What would she do with the extra other than buy herself some fancy clothes? And this, a time of sacrifice.'

He had rested his walking stick by his leg and he raised it now towards Emily. 'You've been a dutiful girl. Very admirable, your war effort.' A mincemeat-stained drool escaped from the side of his mouth. 'And it was right that I should step in and take care of your mother to allow you to do so. But you saw, didn't you? You were bright enough to see that your time was over.' He raised his voice. 'Why didn't that girl today see things the same way?' His eyelids drooped, and then his face clouded. 'If she had, I wouldn't have had to put her out of a job at Christmas.'

His words turned her stomach. Mother was already watching her, waiting for her, so she could glare at her with raised eyebrows. *See?* the look said. *You really think he will hand the estate back to you? You really think he'll employ you on the farm?*

'We fought to maintain our way of life,' Emily countered, 'but at the same time the war has changed things, and life won't ever go back to how it was before.'

He mocked her by rolling his eyes at Mother. It was a noble hope. But now her father's estranged brother owned half of everything, and Mother was too weak to do anything other than cling to him. The past was rather inviting.

Mother kept her head down and played again with the spot where her wedding ring had been. What had happened to her rings? Had she sold them, or had Wilfred taken those from her too as part of his deal?

Emily closed her eyes and shook her head, trying to shake it all away. When she opened them again Wilfred's head had fallen awkwardly to one side, his mouth gaped open, and the half-eaten

177

mince pie sat in the flat of one palm, while his walking stick slid forwards and landed onto the rug.

She eyed her uncle as he slept in his chair. Unless she could persuade Mother to stand up to him, she was stuck living in De Vere Gardens. She'd really rather be homeless.

Upstairs later, she knocked on her mother's door. It opened a crack.

'I shan't stay here. And I don't think you should either,' she whispered. 'He's horrid. I'm only sorry that you've been here so long.'

'I hope you have some money then,' Mother replied. 'He is in charge of the bank accounts, too.'

Emily had some savings, but her wages as a land girl had only just covered her living expenses. Rent she had thought had been going to Mother had been paying her uncle.

She returned to her room, sat at the dresser. The alien in the chemise reappeared in the mirror. The first tear squeezed its way out, and fled down her cheek. She wiped it away with the flat of her hand, but there was another already taking its place. She swiped at that too. She hadn't stopped to think about the life Mother was living here, should have guessed that Mother would settle for anyone who would take the strain and prevent her from standing on her own two feet.

More tears came than she could fight off, those ones for John. She had trusted him, and he had surrendered half their home and put an uncle they hardly knew in charge of their estate. He'd told her to accept what was to come. But she wouldn't. Her cheeks soaked, her face creased up, she turned away from the mirror and dived headlong on to the bed, face down, a fleeting care for the waves that Bassett had ironed into the front.

But the only way she could defy John, and ask him why he had made such a terrible decision was if he were to walk through the door at that moment, and that could never happen.

Chapter Twenty-Four

January 1919

Dearest Theo,
 Wherever are you? It is January now and we are to stay
on in London, but only for a short while, I hope, until we can
return to Kent.
 Please write soon, Theo.
 Fondest wishes
 Emily

As soon as Wilfred closed the front door behind him the morning he returned to work, she shot out of her room and down the stairs to find Mother. Her uncle had gone back to the office. The festive celebrations, such as they were in De Vere Gardens, were over. Mother was in the morning room being served her second breakfast course.

'I'll take my porridge now,' Emily said to the maid.

She noted the headlines on the front page of *The Times* and then pushed it away. Uncle Wilfred's newspapers tainted the morning room, bringing a heavy cloud of unrelenting mourning and international unrest into the house.

More trouble brewed in Germany. There had been another revolt, the uprising crushed within four days and the leaders killed.

'Grandmother said she'd like to see you,' Emily said once Bassett was out of earshot. Mother speared a burgundy nugget of kidney with her fork and didn't reply.

Concentrating her efforts on pouring the tea, Emily continued: 'Did you sleep well?'

The door to the yellow room had creaked open and then shut shortly after she'd gone to bed herself. Her relief that the two of them had separate rooms had been short-lived. She'd been in the house for several nights and each night she'd been stirred from her own sleep by footsteps on the landing below.

'Quite well,' Mother said.

Emily stirred her tea, but eyed her Mother discreetly, as a bowl of porridge was slid under nose. She preferred it as sweet as possible. The cook added too much salt for her liking, but she'd have to be content with a light dusting of sugar. She blew on her porridge. Gosh, she was hungry. She ate, not minding the saltiness or that it burnt her mouth.

Once finished, Emily pushed away the empty bowl. It was swept up from the table and a plate of kipper fillets appeared. Morning sickness might be behind her, but her stomach flinched at the pungent salty aroma. The porridge sat heavily, too. But the butter melted on the top kipper and cascaded onto the plate in a way that she couldn't resist.

The room was silent but for the clink of the cutlery against the china and then Mother sliced a fried egg in two and the yolk oozed and merged with the bloodied kidneys. Even without Wilfred there, the staff were ever present, whispering in one another's ears.

Emily stabbed right through a chunk of kipper, making her fork screech across the china while Mother popped in the slice of fried egg.

'We should go today,' Emily whispered. 'To see Grandmother.'

'Wilfred won't allow me,' Mother said.

Emily couldn't eat any more. Her plate was removed with a remaining kipper on it. Tiger the tomcat at the farmhouse would have been first in line for that.

*

In the end, Emily went to Grandmother's flat by herself. She'd had enough of De Vere Gardens. When she arrived at the Belgravia mansion flat, her Grandmother was just winding up a small meeting in the drawing room with a group of men she introduced as ex-officers – sons and nephews of Grandmother's friends that she had rounded up to tackle the cause of the ex-soldiers in East London with lung damage. Thousands had perished from tuberculosis since the war's end courtesy of London's dirty air.

'The thought of it keeps me awake at night,' Grandmother concluded, the black feathers on her hat twitching. 'We must act, and quickly, to save lives.' And the men all nodded in agreement. She'd been quick to dismiss Grandmother's fundraising as unimportant, but it was clear that she was making the most of her position in society to make positive changes for the less fortunate. 'These men may live a matter of miles from where we sit today, but it is a very different world, a place where one won't survive without robust health. These men need and deserve clean air, and we must see that they get it.'

'So, what's to be done?' she blurted out.

All heads turned to face her. She had only meant to wait quietly at the back of the room until Grandmother had finished. The faces of the men turned her way shone as if they'd been polished with beeswax, all except one, who looked like it was a great effort for him to be there.

Grandmother introduced each man by name. She nodded and

repeated, 'Pleased to meet you,' until she got to the tired-looking chap. He was familiar, but she couldn't think …

'… And Captain Ellery.' Of course! Her smile garnered a quizzical frown from Grandmother. She was about to point out that they'd actually already met, but his green eyes were flat, and uninterested. She tidied away her loose hair, glancing up furtively once Grandmother spoke again. It was definitely him – the same sea-green eyes. The man who'd convalesced at HopBine, who'd liked her Turkish delight.

While Grandmother continued with her rallying speech she took in his long legs, how he wrung his hands. His green-eyed gaze suggested he was far away. Somewhere else altogether. He appeared to have more lines on his face than the others, but it was tiredness not age that had faded him. His shoes wore a lustrous sheen that wasn't in keeping with the rest of his appearance.

'What do you think, Captain Ellery?' Grandmother asked in a way that suggested he was another of her pet projects. 'Could some visits to the seaside possibly be enough to stem all of these deaths, or do we need to look at something more drastic such as rehousing the men?'

'We could consult with a doctor …' Captain Ellery had a soft voice, gentle, little more than a whisper. It was familiar to her too. 'Beautiful,' he'd said as her Turkish delight had melted in his mouth.

'It's such an expensive business though,' said one of the other men. Emily involuntarily sneered at him, for interrupting Ellery.

'You are resourceful men and men of means too,' Grandmother said. 'That's why you are here. You can find a way, I'm quite sure. I intend to ask my son for a donation, but there can be no guarantees there I'm afraid.' She flattened out her curled lip with a beaming smile and pushed herself to standing with her stick to bring the meeting to its end.

Emily met Captain Ellery's gaze. It was the perfect opportunity to remind him they'd met before, but he turned away as soon as their eyes met and faced the front after that.

The meeting finished shortly afterwards. Emily noted when they would convene again; perhaps she could come along too. Energised now, with Grandmother to herself, she raced through her account of the situation at De Vere Gardens.

'He is controlling her, and she's letting him.'

Grandmother nodded with a heavy head. It was as she'd suspected.

'And, John put him in control of the estate. He cleared the debts and now Wilfred owns half of it, and he doesn't believe women should work now the war is over.'

'Well, I'm in agreement with him there,' she said. 'You only have one choice, and that is to persuade your mother to leave.'

Dearest Theo,

I shall go on writing, because what else can I do? Shouldn't you be back with us by now?

Fondest wishes

Emily

Dear Sirs,

I write in connection with my husband, Officer Williams of the Wakefield Regiment. I am writing for news of his whereabouts. I'm afraid he might be in hospital, or worse, as he has not written since the Armistice was signed. He doesn't yet know that he's going to become a father later this year and I wish to tell him the news as soon as is possible.

Any information would be most gratefully received.

Yours sincerely

Emily Williams (Mrs)

Dearest Martha,

I wonder how you all are on the farm? Have you begun to plough the fields yet? Will Mr Tipton use the Fordson, or is he determined to let it rust now I'm gone? How many sheep are with lamb? I often imagine you walking Bob up and down with the plough. It might sound strange to anyone else, but I know that you will understand when I say that I envy you your aches and pains from lifting stones, and the sensation after standing up from thistle weeding. Please write to me with every detail to colour this grey and brown world with a vibrant Kentish green.

Your friend
Emily

'Families are such complicated beasts, dear,' came Grandmother's unhelpful reply when Emily telephoned her again after Mother had been in bed with a migraine for two days. 'But in the long term she'll thank you for encouraging her to leave. She doesn't love him at all.'

Staying another moment with her uncle was unbearable, and she couldn't allow Mother to remain either.

'While I have you …' Grandmother continued, 'I'm friends with Captain Ellery's mother. She's terribly worried about him. He won't return to work and he sits in his room all day with the curtains closed. We thought some company his age might lift his spirits.'

Emily agreed – of course she could help. The doctor had advised the baby needed regular fresh air. It would be the perfect excuse to get her out of De Vere Gardens.

'And don't worry. I'll make it very clear that you're married and expecting.'

Emily swallowed her laughter. Of course she would.

*

She and Ellery strolled in silence to the end of the road. There was so much she wanted to know about this quiet man that she didn't know where to begin. But it didn't matter – she just enjoyed the rhythm of his stride, the clip of his boots, fresh air and leaving the problems in De Vere Gardens behind her.

They crossed Kensington High Street at the corner of De Vere Gardens to join Hyde Park near the Round Pond and her mind began to settle. They wove in and out between the nannies pushing baby carriages until they came to the Serpentine and the grass fell away towards the water.

A lone fieldfare, driven to the city by the cold snap, jumped from branch to branch. It had a delightfully plump, speckled belly.

'He's a long way from home,' she said. 'I used to work alongside those birds all the time when I was a land girl.'

'The birdsong reminds me of the trenches now,' Ellery said.

Oh dear. So much for encouraging him to talk about his time in Kent; instead she'd managed to remind him of the war.

'So, your family are from London, I understand,' she said.

'Your grandmother mentioned that your husband is missing,' he said by way of reply in a soft voice that invited her to lean closer.

Her cheeks began to burn. So he'd heard about that. 'Oh, did she?'

'She meant well. Enquired whether I could offer some advice, help you track him down.'

Of course she had. She bit her lip. Grandmother was so much more than a gossip. She'd proven that already with her charity to help the men with lung troubles. Her concerns for her daughter-in-law had alerted Emily to the difficulties at De Vere Gardens.

'I've written to the War Office,' she told him. 'I hope they might know where he is.'

The Captain nodded slowly, his hands buried deep in his trench coat pockets. A boy in long shorts righted a toy yacht that had capsized in the shallows. The Captain gazed at him too.

'You could write to his CO. Write to his friends and family perhaps.'

She sighed. 'Thank you. I will try that.'

'Do you think he wants to be found?' Ellery asked.

She smarted at the directness of his question. He was staring straight at her making her skin tingle. His eyes weren't as green in this light; they had a deeper, hazel hue around the centre if the light caught them in the right way.

'I really don't know. And, if I am perfectly honest, I don't even know if I want to find him. That probably makes me a terrible person, given my condition. But if things were different ...' She tailed off. If it wasn't for the baby or the problems at home she would have given up on Theo by now, but he deserved to know he was going to become a father, deserved a second chance at being the husband he'd promised to be, all that time ago.

'The war did strange things to us all,' Ellery said. 'Our challenge is to accept who we were then, and not blame ourselves for the things we did.'

Her hand was reaching out towards his arm, before she caught herself and pulled it back. He understood her predicament and didn't judge her, or Theo, but he had problems of his own and she mustn't expect too much from him.

He sighed, frowning heavily. His pained eyes were trained on the water, but seeing something else altogether, she suspected. The things he had done, actions he fought now not to blame himself for, would be very hard to accept.

She let her back settle into the bench, stretched her legs out in front of her, her thighs brushing his with an electrical charge, while the winter sun soothed her bones, and warmed up the baby.

'I've somewhere I ought to be,' Captain Ellery said, his heels dragging across the ground as he pulled himself up.

'So soon?' she said, kicking herself for sounding too keen. 'Grandmother hoped I might cheer you up.'

He gave a wry smile at that, flipped up his collar. He sunk his head down as if the sun wasn't shining at all. She must keep her behaviour seemly. She was expecting a child, searching for a missing husband. What if he responded to her? She wouldn't think him much of a gentleman if he did offer her lingering looks or touched her arm.

'Cheerio,' he said, and with that he left her sitting on the bench alone. She gathered a handful of snowdrops from beneath the tree trunk to take back to De Vere Gardens and put in a vase, a reminder of those that grew beneath the monkey puzzle tree at home.

*

Dearest Emily,

I have to tell you that we're missing you at the farm. It really isn't the same around here without you. I am now the worst at milking time for one thing!

Mrs Tipton misses you too. It was her that urged me to write to you. When I last saw you, you spoke of taking the place over? I had hoped it might be true, that I might be your assistant and this wouldn't all come to an end. It all seems quite fanciful now. Mr Tipton wants to retire and yet he says HopBine still lies empty. I suppose London has much to keep you there and you've forgotten about us here already.

They are not far from being back up to strength at the farm now. The ole man longs to retire more with every passing day, but says he won't leave your mother in the lurch. The Land Army haven't demobilised us yet. They say it might be as late as the end of the season, what with demob in France still taking so long.

We're back up to eleven labourers now, only four shy of a full set, and there are men appearing over the horizon every day, out on the tramp searching high and low for work. It means us girls are on our bicycles and travelling to farms far and wide around the parish. The ole man says I ought to think of finding more work afore the harvest even.

Yours in the field
Martha
First Corporal – Bramley Battalion

Her pace quickened; Captain Ellery was waiting for her at the bench at the far end of the Serpentine.

'I was rude to you the other day, especially going off like that.' He stood as she approached. 'I apologise.' He spoke quietly, but as if he really meant it.

'Did you come of your own accord, or did my grandmother send you?' she asked, tilting her head to one side playfully and raising her eyebrows.

He smiled. 'You've found me out. She does make me feel as if I'm a small boy again. She's doing a good thing with this project to help the East End soldiers though. Men like me never have to worry about money and that makes it easy to forget what privileges and freedoms wealth can give you.'

She nodded. How true that was – and power too. Prosperity gave you the sort of power that allowed you to buy out your own family and leave them beholden to you.

'At least you're doing something useful with your capital; that has to count for something. I brought some bread for the ducks,' she said. 'Will you feed them with me?'

She edged away from him as he sat down to keep a decent distance between them, but her gaze still strayed towards him while she broke up the bread and scattered it on the pond.

'My uncle keeps talking about retribution,' she said when the bread was all gone and she sat next to him again. 'It's surely time to rebuild, don't you think?'

And then there was Cecil. He would be released soon. What sort of future did he have now? Who would lead the rest of them into the daylight?

'Perhaps it falls to the women to save us this time,' the Captain said.

'Do you think we're capable then?'

'Of course. The men made a mess of things. The women couldn't do any worse.'

Emily chuckled. 'It's not a glowing endorsement, Captain Ellery. I would love dearly to take on my own little world, but I've got more immediate concerns than rescuing mankind.' She rubbed a hand on her pert belly. She chose her words carefully so as not to mention HopBine; the moment had passed for them to remember that shared experience. If he'd wanted to talk about it, he would have done by now. 'I need to persuade my mother that it's time to accept what's happened, to go home and live this new life that's been foisted upon us.'

He remained quiet, his hands buried in his pockets, his eyes on the horizon and the rails at the edge of the park as if he were waiting for his enemy to arrive. He never judged her or told her what to do, or inflicted his opinion on her, but he always listened and paid attention.

'I have a lot to learn about that myself,' he said. 'But on the subject of saving mankind, your grandmother might yet rescue us all.'

'Really?' Did he know that she had no money of her own, that her home was paid for by a son to whom she didn't speak, and that her charity work was all funded by the wealthy people she brought together?

'Well. All right, not exactly – I'm to supervise a trip to Brighton that the charity is funding. The men are to breathe in the clean sea air, back to the Victorian way of doing things. She's organised the whole thing.'

'Well, it might just work.'

'I fear it's going to take more than a walk on the pier,' he said. 'For all concerned.' He unfolded his long legs, tipped his hat, raised his collar. The earlier apology forgotten.

She let him go this time without insisting he stay. His figure receded across the park. He left her alone again, but it didn't matter – those five minutes had been the brightest of the entire day.

Chapter Twenty-Five

February 1919

Dear Mrs Williams,

I am a secretary here at the War Office, and I am writing to you in response to your inquiry about your husband, Theodore Williams.

The above-named officer was demobilised in France, on 20th December 1918 after a short stay in hospital for shell shock. We don't have an onward address on record.

I trust this information is of some use to you.

Yours sincerely

Ruth Farthinglow (Miss)

She'd found the letter in the evening when Uncle Wilfred was in his room, singing to himself as he got ready for dinner guests. She'd crumpled onto the stairs, and scoured it again. He'd been home for over a month, and could have been with her for Christmas, only he'd not tried to find her. It wasn't a shock, and even worse she had no desire to cry or wish he was there, but there were practicalities: a baby to provide for, a need to wrench her mother away from London and to face up to her responsibilities, and now Emily knew that she would have to tackle it all on her own. To think, she'd been deserted by a man who was once her saviour.

She had so many unanswered questions. Had he gone barmy? Was he a drunk? Wasn't he drinking on his last leave in August? He must regret marrying her. He might never have loved her at all. The war, his mother's illness, Patch's injury – might all have been part of a madness that had driven him to beat up Cecil and abandon her.

Mother let her into her room. Her latest migraine had improved, but she still held a hand out to steady herself when she walked. Her complexion was sickly. Before Emily could tell her about the War Office letter, Wilfred knocked and barged straight in. Her silent exchange with Mother was like that of two oppressed internees in a camp.

'Our guests will be here in five minutes.' He regularly used Mother's good looks to his advantage when entertaining business guests. 'Perhaps you could stay out of things,' Wilfred said to Emily, a pointed glance at her bump. 'Your predicament might cause a fuss, and distract from the purpose of the evening.'

That was fine with her. She could hide away, abandoned and pregnant. She didn't even have an appetite.

'Why don't you say you have a headache?' she said to her mother, when he left the room. She was applying powder to the tops of her arms to conceal the fingerprint marks his grip had left behind.

'I don't mind. It makes me feel as though I'm earning my keep.'

Emily resisted the urge to point out that she was already doing more than that.

*

Back upstairs in the pink room, she unthreaded her boots and climbed into bed with her clothes on, bathing in the room's overpowering rosy infusion, her mind racing. There was more than just Mother to contend with; a letter had arrived from Cecil that morning. The conscientious objectors were being released in batches. He would be free soon, and Wilfred had made it clear his nephew wasn't welcome.

They'd all be much safer at home.

Closing her eyes, she imagined pushing the baby down the cedar avenue, New Lane. He'd learn to crawl in the paddock, paddle in the stream, chase the rooks off the lawn. Would Theo be with her? She sensed a shadow by her side, but Theo's face didn't emerge. But it didn't mean anything. He could be anywhere. He could be wending his way to her right that moment. What would she say to him if he walked through that door now? Would she be so relieved that she'd simply run into his arms, or would she tell him to leave?

She crept down the stairs to the study, the muffled whisperings of Wilfred holding court coming from the dining room. She tried the door to his study, and then moved to the desk.

The pen in her hand hovered over the page. If she spoke to Mother first she'd simply talk her out of it. An insidious puddle of ink stained the clean page of the blotter. If Wilfred found out, he'd exert his authority and tell them they had to stay.

She put the nib to the page, and the ink flowed freely.

Daisy,
I am writing to ask if you could open up HopBine, air the house and lay the fires. I will write again when I have an exact date, but expect us all very soon.
Yours truly
Emily

The next morning she posted the letter and then whipped down the road to catch Captain Ellery at the Hyde Park bench.

But as the seat came into focus, the shape of Ellery morphed into an elderly man in a top hat. Emily walked on by. Ellery wasn't at the next one either. By the time she'd crossed the Serpentine Bridge, the lightness in her stride had deserted her. She ventured into Kensington Gardens, and checked the Round Pond, but he was nowhere to be found.

Why *would* Ellery be there? What interest would he have in an abandoned, pregnant fool who'd rushed down the aisle to marry a man she'd never really loved?

Dearest Emily,

I have left HopBine Farm! I am filled with sadness, not just for the work that has been such a surprising joy to me – something you understand yourself – but for the dear people too. Mr Tipton continues to groan and gripe, but Mrs Tipton says his heart isn't strong and it makes him tetchy.

As you'll see from the address, I'm in London, staying with my mother again. I've become one of the country's six hundred thousand registered unemployed women. I suppose that if they counted girls like you, who wouldn't register for benefit, then there must be many more.

I've been offered my old service job back. Mother says I should take it, but the wages and conditions on offer are the same as before the war, and I have to provide my own uniform too. My war work has shown me how badly they treated me, how little freedom I had, or how little worth they placed in me. I'm sure there's something better out there for me. I've not had so much as an interview and Mother says she can't support me much longer and that I'll have to pay my way again.

My unemployment benefit had already gone down. If I refuse my old post in service they'll stop it altogether. So, I suppose before long I'll have to do as they say and take something, simply because it's better than nothing.

That's enough of my troubles. Have you any news? Is the baby sickness improving? Is your Theo home yet?

    Best wishes
    Martha

*

April 1919

Mother's thin but defiant voice penetrated the walls. Emily froze, holding the nightdress she'd been folding for the suitcase she'd been steadily packing and hiding beneath her bed. Mother shouted again. Wilfred was entertaining, and she'd been asked to stay in her room, but she dashed out of her door to the top of the stairs. The bruises on Mother's arms were occurring more frequently. He yelled at her almost every day, and yet she still refused to leave.

Emily put her hand to her mouth, but the gasp had already escaped.

'Please won't you stop it. How can you be so cruel?' Mother shrieked. 'Look at him. My poor boy – what have they done to you? Please, Wilfred. You must let him in.'

Emily took the stairs two at a time, gripping the handrail in case she should trip. Cecil stood in the hallway. The guests, curious about the commotion, had filed out, but when confronted with the scene that was unfolding, they all did the honourable thing and retreated into the dining room, leaving Cecil, her mother, Wilfred and the awkward footman, Henderson.

'Cecil!' Emily ran to her brother and threw her arms around him. The flesh had fallen away leaving him leaner and more lightweight than ever.

'You're a hypocrite to say that Cecil did nothing for the war. Your war effort involved buying your Eau de Cologne from Boots the Chemist.' Her mother had readied herself for a fight. She

195

stood tall and her hands made delicate fists beside her as she spoke.

Emily couldn't help but gawp at her mother speaking out finally. But Wilfred was unruffled.

'The thing is, my dear, I am a businessman.' His tone was perfectly reasonable, and hard to disagree with. 'People will stop dealing with me if it gets out that I'm harbouring a shirker.'

Cecil's thick, dark hair had grown longer and more unkempt. His face was drawn; his dark eyes bigger, hungrier.

'I don't want to cause you any trouble,' Cecil said.

'I know you don't, son,' Wilfred replied.

'I'm not your son,' Cecil said. 'And I'm not a shirker either.'

Wilfred shrugged. 'That might not be how you see it, but others will, and I rely on trading with those people to put a roof over our heads. It's not a question of throwing you out.' He reached for his inside pocket and pulled out his wallet.

Emily waited for Cecil to rise to the bait and charge at his uncle as he would have done once, but instead he buried his hands deeper into his pockets.

'I don't want your money.'

'Suit yourself. I'll put this outburst down to hysterics if you control yourself immediately,' Wilfred said to Mother who was no longer standing tall and ready for battle, but was crumpled and cowering.

'Take the money, Cecil,' Emily said. 'We'll talk in the morning.'

With the notes folded and pocketed, Wilfred turned on his heels and steered Mother back to their guests.

Emily grabbed a cloak and joined Cecil out on the top step so that they could talk out of the earshot of Henderson.

'Why are you both still staying here for goodness' sake?' Cecil said. 'Father would be so mad if he were here to see this.'

'You knew about him buying us out. Well this is the consequence of that and I'm now trying to find a way to move back to HopBine.' She glanced at the pavement. Bassett's lodgings were in the basement, hopefully she wasn't in there listening but Emily didn't want to take any chances. 'I'll explain everything tomorrow. Where will you sleep tonight? Grandmother likes a good charity case.'

'I can stay with friends nearby. Alice, a suffragette who supported us conchies during the war, offered me a place to stay if ever I was desperate.'

She left him to slip back inside for paper and pencil in the drawing room so that she could take down the address.

'We need to pull together now, Cecil. This isn't the time to try to save the world. Your family needs you,' she told him as he jotted down the address.

He rolled his eyes. 'Always so dramatic, Emily.'

She told him that she was pregnant with Theo's child, but that her husband had been demobilised and hadn't come home to her.

'He did apologise though, for what he did to you.' Cecil chuckled. 'But I'm not sure it counts for much.'

*

Once Wilfred had left for work, they took a cab over to the address that Cecil had handed her the night before.

The door sprung open, and the frame was filled by a handsome girl whose face was flawed only by two oversized front teeth that drifted away from one another to leave a gap.

'Alice Turner-Wood, delighted to meet you – are you here for the meeting?'

'Erm, no.' Mother pulled her hand away. 'I'm here to visit my son, Cecil. I believe …'

'There is a resemblance. Yes, by all means, do come in.'

Alice bustled down the hallway. Raised voices filled the first room they came to. She craned her neck. It was full of women, not the black-clad, moribund older women who called on Grandmother; these were all much younger, far more animated and vying to make their voices heard.

'Cecil is avoiding the women,' Alice explained, as she led them down to the back of the house, where a humid solarium was attached to a music room, overlooking a lusciously green back garden.

'We're quite a force to be reckoned with, as you can imagine. Men who aren't used to it can feel intimidated with all of the ideas. Not that that's the case with Cecil …'

They paused on the threshold of the music room. The white-framed glass doors to the solarium were shut and Cecil, unaware of their arrival, was hunched over a desk, intently writing.

'He has so many ideas, doesn't he?' Alice said.

The gaps in the chair's spindles exposed Cecil's untucked shirt and crumpled tails. He wore a cravat around his neck.

'Whatever do you find to discuss?' her Mother asked with a hint of incredulity.

'There is so much, Mrs Cotham, so much that we wish to change that I fear we will only ever achieve a fraction of it.'

Mother widened her eyes discreetly at Emily. An expression that said, 'Oh dear, they're that sort.' Her mother had had little time for the women's movement before the war, claimed they were raising trouble in her name and she hadn't asked for it.

'But now you've won the vote, haven't you blue stockings done enough?'

Alice laughed at that idea, a big hearty guffaw that exposed her wayward teeth and set her bust in motion.

'We don't stop until we get our way.' As if she'd let herself into Emily's mind and read her very dreams she said: 'I understand you were a land girl?'

Emily told her that she had worked on the farm, but the heat of Mother's frown stopped her from sharing with Alice her unmistakable calling to return to it all.

'And I'm betting you don't want to give that up now, do you?'

Emily smiled. She hadn't needed to explain to Alice – she understood perfectly.

'She's married now,' Mother said. 'A baby on the way, and other … family commitments.'

'Well,' Alice said, her gaze flicking between them as she tried to fathom what battleground she'd strayed onto. 'Wonderful.' She rubbed her hands together. 'Life is full of surprises. And who's to say a woman can't have a career, and a family, eh Emily?'

Mother broke away to call Cecil. He started at his desk.

In the solarium, the floor beside Cecil was littered with scrunched balls of paper. A sheaf of notepaper, thickened with his ink, piled beside him.

Cecil quickly covered up his writing with a blotter, but he hadn't hidden the title in capital letters, or the word, 'Bolsheviks'.

His night's sleep, and its obvious discomfort, made his eyes bleary and crumpled his brow. He'd grown an untidy beard that stuck to his face in tufts, but it wasn't high or dense enough to hide the dents beneath his cheekbones.

Her words the night before hadn't got through to him. He would be quite happy to live on Alice's goodwill while he wrote and indulged his interests. He wouldn't help them at all.

Mother lifted a pile of books to free up the cushions of a wicker seat. 'Cecil,' Mother said. 'I mean really, how have you ended up in the midst of this rowdy mob of troublemakers?'

Cecil showed Mother his discharge letter, shaking his head as he read aloud the red notice informing him he'd be imprisoned for two years if he tried to enlist with the army, as if he'd been a disobedient soldier this whole time. She left the two of them to talk and caught up with Alice.

Cecil said she'd been a great help to him while he'd been in prison. She'd apprised herself of his legal rights and ensured he was represented fairly. Things might have been worse for him without Alice by his side. And if she knew about the rights of conscientious objectors, she might have advice about the rights of the families left behind.

Chapter Twenty-Six

April 1919

Fresh from another visit to Alice's house, Emily passed Uncle Wilfred in the library, bent over his accounts and lit by a small pool of lamplight. She crept up to Mother and cleared her throat.

'May I have a word?' she asked.

Mother was lying down in her nightgown on top of the bedcovers. She exhaled and lifted a corner of the mask from her eyes.

'Mother.' She swallowed. 'I need your help.'

Mother lifted the mask clean from her face and checked it was Emily before her.

'The baby is due in a matter of weeks. It can't possibly be born here.' Wilfred would never stand for a screaming newborn in the house. Neither would Bassett.

'We can't afford to go back to Kent.'

'That's where I have news. Wilfred has given me permission to reopen HopBine,' she said. Mother's eyes widened, and rightly so.

He'd called Emily in because Bassett had complained about the petals dropping from all of the flowers she brought into the

200

house, and she took the opportunity to confront him with the information Alice had given her: Mother should have been receiving a pension for John. He'd flinched, enough to tell her that Alice had been right and he'd been keeping their self-sufficiency from them. Unlocking his bottom desk drawer, he produced a folder and said, 'Please don't tell your mother.'

It turned out that they had the means to support themselves until HopBine was sold, and they had Alice to thank for the revelation. In return for Emily's silence he was letting them go back to Kent, for now at least.

'I can't go to HopBine and have the baby on my own. And Wilfred is happy for you to come with me.'

'And Theo?'

'Who knows.'

Mother pulled the mask back over her eyes and sighed.

'If we could just go home until the baby is born.'

'You realise it's going to have to be sold.'

That had been inevitable from the moment John had asked Wilfred for his help; but John couldn't have known that Wilfred would view it as a business transaction rather than a call for help from his family. But her dream wasn't over; with the proceeds of the sale Mother could buy a place of her own, and if there was enough left over she could buy the farm from Uncle Wilfred.

'Our stay will be temporary. But it offers a haven for Cecil, too.' Emily took a heavy blink.

The eye pillow came down from her mother's face again and she stared at the ceiling.

'Mother, you aren't happy here. You cry at night. Some time away from Wilfred might show you how life could be.'

Mother hadn't moved the whole time, but now she cleared her throat.

'You've made a terrible mess of things, and this baby coming along is an added complication. Now you expect me to help you,' Mother said.

Emily's hands clenched. It was true in part – for the first time in a long time, she did need Mother, and was that really so much to ask? Frankly, she didn't much care how Mother saw it, just as long as it got them away from Wilfred.

She took a deep breath. 'You're right, Mother, which was why I requested your help. And so, I ask: will you do this for me?'

*

Emily tried to control her own pace as she walked from De Vere Gardens with one hand beneath the bump, her coat gaping.

Alice's house was just three streets and a small square away, but the pregnancy had shortened Emily's gait and the muscles in her stomach twinged and pulled. In such a short distance she drew attention and passers-by stopped to ask if she needed an escort.

'The information you gave me was a great help,' she panted. Cecil was out at a meeting, but she lingered a moment on the doorstep, peering over Alice's shoulder for signs of activity.

'I suppose you're having a meeting about your cause, are you?' Emily asked.

Alice shook her head. 'You've caught us at a quiet time.'

Emily sagged. The seeds of change fell from the very plants that grew in that house.

'But I do have something for you to read actually.'

Emily perked up, and followed her into the library. Alice retrieved a book from the shelves and slid a newspaper cutting out and into Emily's palm.

The Desire to Work

I can drive cars. I can repair them too, and I can plough the fields and milk the cows, but no one will employ me in either capacity. I am patted on the back for having been a 'war girl' and told to stand aside for the returning soldiers and 'working girls' all because I hadn't needed to work before the war.

What does my future offer? Isn't there a way that I can live my life without idleness and loneliness?

College courses for captains and corporals, schemes for sergeants, benefits and bureaux for munitioneers, but what about me and my hundred thousand sisters?

'I should imagine that's how you felt when you had to give it all up?' Alice said.

'Yes. I miss it so much,' she confessed. 'It was the most wonderful time of my life.'

'You're not alone,' Alice said. 'The war gave us freedoms, and it's difficult to accept that it's over, isn't it?'

Emily nodded. 'Only, despite everything …' Emily's gaze fell to the ever-growing mound that protruded from her stomach. 'Despite everything standing in my way, it isn't over, not by a long stretch.'

Alice slapped her thighs. 'Wonderful,' she guffawed. 'That's the spirit!'

'When we return to Kent,' Emily told her, 'I intend to take over the farm on my family's estate.'

'Good for you. Good for you.'

'And I'll take on some women too, I hope.'

Alice believed she could do it – that much was clear. Emily told her about Martha. She'd promised her a job and she intended to keep that promise. Even with Uncle Wilfred threatening to control them, and Theo missing, Emily still had more options open to her than Martha and she intended to give her friend a helping hand.

'Some of the suffragettes are campaigning for colonies for ex-land girls,' Alice told her. 'Have you considered that?'

Could HopBine Farm really be a colony? She could imagine it: the old girls – well not Ada Little and Olive Hughes, but Lottie and Hen, and Martha of course. She could rent out Perseverance Place, perhaps divide out the plots and let the women earn their own income from their bit of land. Cecil would approve of that idea, so would Father. Her mind raced away with the notion.

'How do I find out more?' she asked.

Alice offered to arrange a meeting with the right people, but Emily was only in London until Friday, and then they were going back to Kent. They simply couldn't delay their escape, for risk of Mother losing her nerve or Wilfred tightening his grip. Perhaps he'd decide to come clean to Mother and not release the pension money to them after all.

'Isn't there another way I can find out?' she asked.

At the door, Alice raised her palm to her forehead. 'Oh, how foolish of me. Thursday night! Eleanor Kirby will be here for a meeting.' Emily waited for a clue. 'She's organising a deputation to the Board of Trade. Bring your friend.'

She was wary of introducing a hardworking girl like Martha to a privileged suffragette. Martha might biff her on her well-to-do nose, but if they could help them turn HopBine Farm into a colony for ex-land girls then it was worth the risk.

*

Alice welcomed Emily and Martha in with one hand cupped around the flat champagne glass in her hand. 'Grab yourselves a drink,' she said, raising her voice above the music and chatter. 'And then I'll introduce you both to Eleanor. Do you need a seat?' she asked Emily.

'I can stand for now, thank you,' she said, a protective hand over her ever-growing stomach as they backed towards a corner out of the way. The baby shifted about. They were close to the gramophone, so they sidled their way down towards the window where it was quieter.

'You didn't tell me it was a party.' Martha, her nose crisp with powder, straightened her suit jacket, and smoothed her freshly shingled hair. Emily hadn't known.

'Shouldn't you be at home in your condition?' Cecil cut through the crowd to ask what half the room was probably thinking.

'Yes. If I was doing things the right way, I suppose I should,' Emily huffed.

'Who'd have thought the war could bring out the rebels in us both?'

'I'm not staging an uprising, Cecil,' she said loudly.

He gestured towards his ear and shrugged. 'I can't hear you.'

'No.' Martha nudged him in the ribs. 'She's put others first the whole war long. You could learn a thing or two.'

'How dare you!' Cecil said.

'Now, now, children.' Alice reappeared and Cecil delivered a slow, dismissive blink to his sister and disappeared into the crowd before she could say any more.

They followed Alice to meet Eleanor, who was secreted away from the commotion, along with a few splayed-out guests in the more sedate music room.

'Here are the land girls I mentioned. Martha just told me about the fines her friend's factory had been threatened with if they didn't let the women go.'

'Twenty-five pounds.' Martha addressed the room as if she was at a hustings. 'Twenty-five! And the rumour is that it's going up to one hundred. Seems they'll do anything to keep the trade unions satisfied.'

'It's called exploitation and we won't stand for it,' Alice trumpeted. 'Now meet Eleanor Kirby, an agriculture suffragette.'

Eleanor cradled Emily's hand, squeezing the knuckles tight enough for them to pop whilst shaking it, as if she were cranking an engine.

'I know what you're thinking,' she said to Martha. 'But I'm on your side.'

Martha folded her arms and took a step back. It would take more than that to convince her.

'Let's hear what Eleanor has to say,' Emily said. She blurted out her ambition for HopBine Farm. She was talking too quickly, but she couldn't slow down. She wanted more than just a farm; she wanted to own a place where women like them could keep working, and be self-sufficient.

'Now.' Eleanor tilted her head. 'The women we speak to have lost husbands and need to provide for their families. They deserve to work, but …' She raised her forefinger and made eye contact with each of them in the room before continuing. 'We mustn't view women as being in competition with the men. Cooperation – that's the aim.'

Percy Greenacre and the others hadn't thought about the women when they took back their jobs. None of them would ever take orders from a woman. It wouldn't be as simple as Eleanor might think; the women wouldn't be in control if they did it her way.

'What you're suggesting will mean that women will still be taking orders from the men. They'll get the jobs the men don't want and they'll be paid less,' she told Eleanor, who wrote down what Emily said in a notebook.

'Interesting, yes. I suppose you're right. And would the men take orders from a woman?'

Martha sniggered. Emily didn't need to add anything else. Eleanor scribbled again. Emily hadn't expected this, for the suffragette to be learning from them.

She'd read about the government's plans to rush through a bill to legalise the pre-war injustice to women. They intended to make it illegal for a woman to work in a post she wouldn't have held before the war.

'We aren't equals any more, not now the war is over,' Emily said.

'Quite. Many women, from clerical girls to those in the factories and on the land, are disgruntled. They feel pushed aside. If we come together, then united we're a powerful force. But I still feel there's a need for cooperation. A move away from them and us.'

Emily shuffled in her seat. She wouldn't mind working alongside a man, but only if he took her seriously.

'I have a fund to help establish cooperatives,' Eleanor went on. 'Women would be responsible for and work their own land, but they'd toil alongside veteran soldiers.'

Martha raised an eyebrow at Emily. Could this work? These women had money, and good intentions, but they were idealists and didn't have enough hands-on experience to know the realities of breaking into a workplace where they weren't welcome. Perhaps she and Martha would be better off tackling this on their own.

Chapter Twenty-Seven

April 1919

The driver dropped them in Oxford Street, right outside Hitching's Baby Store. Wilfred told them they had twenty minutes and then the car would take them home again.

'Is there anything in particular we can help you with today, Madame?' The assistant addressed Emily's mother.

Emily shed her gloves, flattened them into her right hand. She adjusted the ribbons on her hat with the ring finger of her left hand. The wedding ring basked in the glory of the bright shop lights.

Mother asked if they might start with the bassinets up on the first floor. They both agreed to stretch the budget as soon as they clapped eyes on the hooded white wicker cradle on wheels, sweet little bows on the side and a delicate, pink silk lining.

On the way downstairs to the clothing, Emily lingered at the baby carriage showroom.

'Do you have an appointment?' asked a clean-shaven shop assistant, hands fastened behind his back.

She shook her head. They hadn't. But she had ordered a Hitching's baby carriage booklet and had been reading it before she went to sleep at night.

'My eleven o'clock hasn't arrived yet. If you'd like to know anything, please feel free to ask.'

She went straight to the Hitching's Empire carriage and ran her fingers along the elegant handlebar. It was the most popular pram at Hyde Park. It had ball bearings in the wheels, which would give the baby a smooth ride, an important asset on the countryside's uneven tracks. The assistant pointed at the diagonal line of three carriages.

'Take it for a run,' he said.

She backed it out of its space. It was marvellously light, nothing like as heavy as she'd expected. One hand on the bar, she pressed her finger pads into the lined base. A bit of give for the baby's back. She glided down the runway in the middle of the rows of baby carriages. It bounced on its suspension. Its wheels purred. It exuded a factory scent.

'There are three colours to choose from,' the assistant called. 'Brown, grey or blue.'

As she turned to glide, the eleven o'clocks arrived. A fawning couple, husband and wife, arm in arm. The woman, who hardly looked to be with child at all, and was accentuating her baby bump by smoothing it with her hand went straight to the brown Empire model.

'The grey, don't you think, Mother?' Emily said.

'We give a special discount to war widows,' he added with a gentle tone.

'Oh … no.' Emily was trying to find the words to explain. She'd rehearsed them before they'd come shopping; she was going to say he was still away, home soon, but it all deserted her now.

The assistant excused himself, and suggested they make an appointment to come back. He began to run through the features of the Empire to the eleven o'clock couple. Mother lifted the price tag entwined around the handles. She raised her eyebrows and discreetly let it fall.

'That's very thoughtful,' Mother cut in and then asked the assistant: 'How much is the war widow discount?'

Emily stepped away. 'We'll leave it, thank you,' she called and fled down the stairs to the counters with the gowns and napkins.

When Mother caught her up, she hissed. 'What an *embarrassment*. You are a widow – that's the story. Nothing else will do.'

Emily pretended to be fascinated by the towel napkins, rubbing them with her fingers. What was so wrong with the truth?

*

'This place is really not bad at all.' Grandmother spoke as if she were on safari in Africa, not a Lyons' Corner House. She wore a grey-coloured dress and a discreet black band on her upper arm. 'Very modern of you to suggest such a place.' Emily took an unnatural interest in the tablecloth, certain that she'd giggle if she made eye contact with Captain Ellery. 'The atmosphere here is quite jolly, don't you think, Louisa?'

Mother nodded. 'It's rather noisy for me, actually.'

Emily gave the tablecloth her full attention again.

'Although, yes, you're right, Louisa, the tables *are* rather close together. I shouldn't want to come here for a private conversation. But to come and say bon voyage … What's the matter with you?' she asked Emily, who hid a snigger behind her glove. 'Are you coming down with a cold? You should be careful in your condition. Confinement might seem old-fashioned to you, but it serves its purpose. Far be it for me to interfere.'

'I'm very well. It's the excitement,' Emily said.

'Well enjoy it, because I don't suppose you will find vanilla slices back in Kent.' Grandmother took a sip of her tea and spread a thick layer of cream on her scone. 'How's Cecil?' she asked, in a flippant tone.

When she'd told Cecil they were leaving for Kent, he'd wanted to talk about the Russian revolt and workers' rights. She wanted him to think about returning to Oxford, pursuing his career in journalism. But he'd argued that the newspapers were just part of the establishment in the end. The government controlled them during the war; they ended up a part of the propaganda machine. The reporters didn't spread a word of truth about the war.

'Cecil, you're a grown man now,' she'd reasoned. 'Ideals are commendable, but it will be a tight fit in the farmhouse. You need to plan for your own future.'

But it was as hopeless as it always had been, no doubt always would be. Employers didn't want him; job advertisements stated: no conscientious objectors need apply. He'd been let down by the system in his eyes and he was too young for responsibility. Perhaps he was right. But the same could be said of her and she would have to juggle the care of Mother, along with a baby, while she chased down her own dreams.

'He's a free spirit,' Mother said. 'He must do as he feels right.'

Some things would never change. Cecil was a free spirit; Emily was a nuisance.

'And has Captain Ellery told you his news?' Grandmother asked.

'The trip to the coast?' Emily answered.

The day to Brighton had been a great success, spirits raised and a lovely day had by all, but it had proven ineffective when one of the men had died a week later.

'Days out are just not enough; we need something more permanent for those men,' he said. All three of them were silent, hands on laps, waiting for him to go on. 'And it will happen. The charity has a new investor,' Ellery announced. His eyes sparkled, and a rare smile lit his lips. 'A relative of one of the other chaps – it means we can find somewhere permanent for the men to live. Start to make a real difference.'

211

'That's wonderful, Thomas.' Emily rested a hand on his arm, and then quickly snatched it away.

'Captain Ellery.' Grandmother frowned.

'Yes. Yes.' She dipped her head. What a fool she must look being so over familiar, and in front of Mother too.

But the important thing was that he would head up the search for a residence for the East End men. He might not have accepted his past quite yet, but he could channel his energies into something worthwhile.

When he excused himself to go to the W.C. Grandmother leant across the table and behind a discreet hand, but at an indiscreet volume, she told them that Ellery's mother was cock-a-hoop. He'd fallen for a girl.

'That's wonderful,' Emily said in a high pitch, a huge beam pinned to her face.

Once the taxi had dropped Grandmother and Mother back in Belgravia, Emily asked Ellery if they might take one last stroll in the park. Her mind had been buzzing with possibilities for the farm, and what ideas to take from the suffragettes to use as her own, and which to leave out, and he was so attentive. But she went and spoiled it all by asking the one question guaranteed to clear the smile from his face.

'You must come and visit,' she said to him. This couldn't be how it would end between them. His friendship was too valuable to let it go. But as soon as the words were out she knew that she shouldn't have suggested it.

'I don't think that would be a good idea.'

She jumped, her breath snagging in her throat. It was too painful for him to revisit that part of his past and it was wrong of her to push him. Unsurprisingly, the frown didn't fade to a smile, nor did he nudge her in the ribs and say that of course he'd be delighted to keep their friendship alive and know her in the place she loved best.

He lifted his collar, and before she could tell him how much of a tonic he'd been to her in London, or to thank him for listening and offering his advice without judgement, he had said goodbye, buried his hands in his pockets and walked away.

She didn't move from the bench. The park was fuller than ever with nannies pushing perambulators along, smaller children scurrying about picking up treasures from the edge of the path. Down by the Serpentine there was a line of them along the water's edge tossing bread to a mob of ducks.

He was doing perfectly well now. He didn't need her, or to be reminded of the man he'd been at HopBine House.

*

She shut the door on the pink room without a backward glance. Downstairs, Mother was already waiting for her.

'He's back,' she said to Mother. 'Are you ready?'

In the hallway, they retrieved their things from the cloakroom, slipped into their cloaks and buttoned their gloves. Bassett was smiling despite herself, her arms folded across her chest. She would have her master all to herself again now. They declined the offer of a driver, preferring instead to take a cab to the station.

The commotion roused Uncle Wilfred from his study. The door handle rattled, and the two of them swallowed, moving closer to one another as they waited for him to appear.

'I'd like to make a suggestion,' he said. He would never let them leave without flexing his muscles. 'We should sell HopBine.' He put his hands in his pockets. 'After the baby is born, if Louisa returns here, the free capital would enable you, Emily, to buy your own home.'

Emily didn't like the way her mother was hesitating, as if he was the victim in all of this.

'We'll think your offer over,' Emily said. 'But I won't be needing anywhere to live. I'm going to take over the farm.'

'Well, no.' He frowned. 'I own half of the farm, too.' He paused, examined her face. 'You didn't know?' He smirked at her now, but she nodded with assurance as though she'd been aware all along, and her plans for the farm and a colony hadn't just grown wings and flown out of the door right before her eyes. She should have thought to check what sort of bargain he'd struck with Mother. Why had she assumed the debts only applied to the house, not the whole estate?

Well it wouldn't stop her. She had influential friends now, with their own wealth, who wanted to set up a land colony. He might have half a stake and half a say, but he couldn't force them to sell. Let him think it was over if he liked, let him think he had won and held all the best cards, because it wasn't true, not by a long way.

He insisted that Henderson arrange for a driver to take them to the station.

The three of them hesitated, trapped in the moment. Was his lip trembling as he gazed across the hallway at Mother? He was certainly dewy-eyed. He tried to speak but he was choked, and he obscured his mouth with his fist. If he did really care for Mother, he had a terrible way of showing it.

'We ought to go,' Emily said, and ushered Mother out of the door before she changed her mind.

*

The drive to Victoria station was a short one from De Vere Gardens. It had been so easy in the end. All she'd needed to do was to stand up to him, and he'd released his hold on Mother without any resistance, for now at least. Until the baby was born.

They swung into Pall Mall, but now they headed away from Buckingham Palace, which was behind them, St James's Park to their right.

'Excuse me. Are we headed in the right direction for Victoria station?' Emily called to the driver.

'I'm to take you all the way to Kent, ma'am,' the driver called over his shoulder. 'The master said to say he insisted you got home safe and sound.'

She instinctively checked the rear window. With a bit of luck that was the last they'd see of her uncle for a very long time.

Chapter Twenty-Eight

May 1919

Once they'd left behind the city and hit the narrow high-sided lanes, Emily let down her window so the breeze could tickle her face.

The driver whizzed alongside the land from Cob Tree Farm, the neighbour to HopBine. The tall wooden poles were adorned in the fur of the green hop bines. The drowsy white-green cones drooped, ready for the influx of the hop-pickers come the harvest.

The car turned sharply, the driver asking Mother questions about the village all the while. Who had gone to war and who had come back. He was undeterred by her one-word, clipped responses, oblivious to how, as they grew increasingly closer to their home, her gaze grew blanker, her eyes wider.

They were now running alongside Sunnyside Orchard; then they approached the estate and tucked into the cedar avenue. Hop Hill on which their house sat. It had been bare when she'd left in midwinter. Now the grass had charred, the leaves were heavy as if the summer's party was just getting going.

At the end of the cedar avenue HopBine House popped up to greet them. A cheery cream facade, the protective three-gabled windows. The missing roof tiles and peeling paintwork.

Out on the lawn were some stray bags of cement, a delivery of timber, and the area over by the monkey puzzle tree was staked and roped off. Her heart pulled her towards the paddock. She could be at the farmhouse in five minutes, but Mother cowered in front of the house as if facing the jaws of a tiger. She'd go later. Daisy flung open the door and called out a welcome to them, pointing and covering her mouth at the sight of Emily all bloated up like a Zepp.

The primrose yellow hallway walls were scarred with signs of scrapes from its time as a convalescent home. Antiseptic still hung in the air. A glass was abandoned on the hall table, next to the silver post tray with a pile of letters, some addressed to the Cothams, others to people they didn't know.

'It's a bit shoddy of the army, don't you think? All that stuff dumped outside. It's as if they haven't really gone.'

When a response didn't come she turned around, but Mother wasn't there.

'Will you come with me?' Mother called from the sitting room. 'Let's look around together. Reacquaint ourselves.'

Together, silently, they visited each room of the house, one by one.

'Remember how I used to sit on Father's knee while you played the piano?' Emily said. 'I remember when John captured a badger and wanted it as a pet. Father said he had to let it go, but the two boys kept it hidden from us for nearly a week. Until it scratched Cecil and he had red marks down his face.'

'He was a good son,' she said.

In some rooms, the ghostly dust sheets covered the furniture; others were set, in anticipation of their arrival. All were still. All were empty.

'Coo-ee.' Breathless and red-cheeked, Norah Peters was in the hallway. 'I wanted to be the first to welcome you back. I was just at the post office and they said that you were here.'

'I'm tired after the journey.' Emily excused herself to take a nap and let Mother catch up with her friend.

She paused in the library, in front of the floor-to-ceiling glass windows that opened out on to the terrace. John's rose garden was overgrown. Some of the bushes hadn't survived the winter, but one or two were in full leaf now. There were signs of buds, keeping the crimson blooms locked up tight.

She'd played battles out there with her brothers, not so far from the spot where Cecil had told them he would become a conscientious objector.

It was different now, as if the house wasn't embracing her any longer, no warmth, no comfort, but they were only just home. It would come – she had to give it time.

The familiar twinges pulled the side of her belly. The doctor had told her it wasn't the baby coming. The muscles were just practising, preparing for the birth. She took herself up to her bedroom. Daisy had made up her bed. She climbed under the covers.

'At least we're safe here,' she told the baby, 'away from your horrible Great Uncle Wilfred. You wouldn't like him.'

They were home. Away from Wilfred. Mother could rebuild, learn she did have the strength to face her responsibilities, and then Emily could chase after the life she wanted for herself.

She lay on her bed, with the curtains and windows opened. A fresh start. Somehow. With her head propped on the pillow, she listened to the bleating of the sheep, until she was dreaming of them.

*

Mother was in and out of the room like a jack-in-the-box to ask Emily's opinion on where she should put furniture and where they might put the bassinet in the room they were to use as the nursery. Emily pulled the pillow over her head. She'd overdone it, and she'd never be well enough to visit the farm if she didn't get any peace.

On the second day, Emily flung back the blankets. The baby had settled down; her legs were steady. She'd left Mother taking morning tea with Norah Peters and Mrs Woods the new doctor's wife. The old doctor had been killed in the war. The three of them were knitting for the baby's layette.

'It's all right,' Mother had said. 'You don't need to look so petrified. You don't have to join us if you don't want to.'

Emily nearly pointed out what a delight it was to hear her say that, but it was better that it passed unspoken. Mother would never admit that Emily had been right to bring them home, or that she was changing for the better, she just had to let it happen.

She went out the front door, straight in the direction of the paddock. She waddled more like a duck every day, but it didn't matter here, where the long golden grass was laden with cricket song, wild daisies and poppies that threaded themselves through the jungle of it. By the time she reached the bottom she had a colourful posy for Mrs Tipton.

A labourer was at work in the yard. He'd returned to the farm from the Front just about the time she had left for London. She waved, and he tipped his cap in reply. As she crossed the yard, she sensed the heat of his gaze tracing her progress towards the farmhouse. She'd had no idea that a pregnancy could draw so much attention, but she was growing used to it, which was just as well because the baby would bring even more.

The labourer had stopped what he was doing and strayed forwards, his arms folded. As she rapped on the kitchen door, he was still behind her. The door opened and Mrs Tipton, her hair wild and free, and her cheeks apple-red, pulled Emily into a tight hug.

'You're still here then,' she joked.

'We're waiting for you to take over from us, girl. What's taken you so long?'

'Complications,' she said. She hated to tell them that her plans to run the farm had become all the more unattainable. Being allowed to skip a knitting party was the first tiny step of many to where she needed to be.

Mrs Tipton asked after the baby's father. Emily hesitated, nearly told her mother's lie that he was dead; but no, she couldn't do that.

'I don't know where he is,' she confessed. 'But can you keep that to yourself?'

Mrs Tipton clucked and invited her into the farmhouse's steamy kitchen. She sat back, soaked up the crashing and clattering and the old familiar aromas while Mrs Tipton fussed about, preparing the lunch for the labourers, and asked after Cecil. She told her how she'd had the idea of running the farm as a land colony for ex-war girls with Martha.

'But ... come on, what's the but?' Mrs Tipton said. 'If you were ready to take over this place, baby coming or not, you'd be upstairs packing my bags for me.'

She told her everything.

'At the moment, Wilfred thinks I'm a noble ex-war girl, who should know her place. But it looks as though he's going to force us to sell up. At first I thought we could stop him, but we can't afford to keep it all running. My best hope is that the new owner will appoint me, because Wilfred will never agree to it.'

Mrs Tipton sucked air through her teeth. 'And if the new owner won't take you on?'

Emily couldn't think about that. Even without a baby to take care of it would be almost impossible to convince anyone to take her on as a manager. And even if she could convince the new farm owner she was up to the job, the male labourers would never take orders from her. Her only real hope was if one of the suffragettes set up a colony, otherwise she'd have to live with Mother.

Mrs Tipton dumped the teapot back on the table.

'Sometimes, my dear, you have to accept when you're beat. That baby will change everything.'

Emily's head drooped.

'Oh, I've upset you. I always speak as I find. The ole man always says I should button up.'

Mr Tipton. What would he say? He'd been holding out for retirement and would have gone by now if it wasn't that he'd promised to wait and hand the reins over to her.

'Would you tell him that we'll be selling up? Explain that Wilfred will leave us with no choice.' Emily asked. Mrs Tipton nodded.

'Don't worry about him. He'll survive.'

One hand rested on the chair behind Emily, the other she lowered so that the palm curved around Emily's belly.

'I'm sure you'll do whatever's best for you and your family.'

The baby was resting. He'd been quiet today, and then just as Mrs Tipton lifted her hand a tiny foot pushed up at her.

'Oh my, another determined one in the family, eh? A true Cotham.'

*

'Come this way first.' Mother sashayed in front of her, smiling to herself. 'There's a surprise in here for you.'

A delivery had come while she'd been out. Boxes were stacked on top of one another in the hallway. Her mother stood in the midst of it all, hands clasped. She'd been waiting for her.

They paused outside the sitting-room door. Emily put her hand to her chest. Surely not, it couldn't be Theo, here in time for the baby's arrival. She swallowed. Her mother's hands were on the door handle. She adjusted a strand of hair that had strayed across her face, pressed her lips together, and straightened her skirt. Gosh, she was such a size and she had mud on her boots.

Mother pushed back the sitting-room door with gusto. Emily blinked fast.

'Surprise!' Mother called.

The smile froze to her face. The sofas were empty. The room creaked with its own emptiness. Mother was beaming, pleased with herself. It all appeared to be the same.

'It is the one that you wanted, isn't it?'

She checked again. Ah. She nodded. There it was. The glint of the brass handlebar, the crocodile jaw of the collapsible hood.

'Elephant grey,' Mother said. 'Don't tell me I remembered it wrong. I was sure you hadn't liked the brown, and the blue would be no good for a boy, and you're so sure it's a boy. I thought it would be useful if you wanted to get the baby out in the fresh air.'

Emily moved towards it. She kept her arms by her sides though she longed to curl her palms around and make the wheels click-click as she rocked it back and forth.

'Did you …'

'Ask for the war widow's discount?' Mother said.

Emily nodded, and swallowed. She couldn't accept it if she had.

'I decided if you wanted to be forthright about the truth then we should do it your way. But I would add that I ran through our household expenditure last night and that discount would have come in rather useful.'

Chapter Twenty-Nine

May 1919

They placed the bassinet closest to the wall between her own room and the nursery.

The baby's room wasn't going to be on the unheated top floor like it had been for her and her brothers. She wanted the baby to be nearby. There wouldn't be a nanny either; she was firm on that. Even if they could have afforded one, she wanted her family to be as close together as possible, to make up for lost time, with no interferences from anyone outside of their small circle.

There was an adjoining door to her own room. The nursery was smaller, cosier, had a small hand basin in one corner and the same aspect as her bedroom – the view of the rose garden, the terrace and beyond the orchard, the sheep, and the spire poking up from the valley.

Mother hadn't called her a nuisance for several days now, and emptied out a chest of drawers from a guest room. They borrowed Joe from the farm to move it into the nursery. It would have been far easier to take the set of drawers from John's room, but it was still full of the clothes that were pressed and folded and innocently awaiting his return. They would have to deal with it soon, but for now there wasn't a rush. They would take a step at a time, and deal with the more difficult tasks when they were ready, and not before.

Emily shook out the gowns. It was hard to imagine a person so small that they would fit. The mixture of terry and muslin napkins were piled into the top of the drawers. Emily hugged the teddy bear close.

When it was all complete and everything was away they both stepped back to admire their work. It was the bassinet that made the difference, a small change, but everything pointed towards it. If she was right and the baby was a boy, she would call him John.

She sent Joe off for a slice of Daisy's Victoria sponge cake and reminded him to take a piece back in a napkin for Mrs Tipton too. And while he was at it, remind her to come up for tea.

'Thank you,' Emily said to Mother.

Mother wrinkled her nose and rolled the bassinet back and forth. 'I'm quite looking forward to becoming a grandmother to a little ray of sunshine.'

'And how about London? Are you missing it?'

'Don't gloat – it's unseemly …'

A twinge stabbed her side. She put her hand to it. Then it came again. A lightning strike of pain flashed across her belly, forcing her forwards. The teddy bear slumped to the floor.

'I'm fine,' she wheezed. Her mother surveyed her from a safe distance.

'It won't be long now,' Mother said.

*

Mrs Tipton cooed as she stepped into the nursery room.

'Very cosy, very cosy indeed.'

'I think it's the perfect start for him, for all of us,' Emily agreed.

'It'll not be long now,' Mrs Tipton said. That was all anyone said to her now.

224

'I hope so,' Emily said, rolling the bassinet back and forth.

As she held the door open for Mrs Tipton a heavy splat of water hit the floorboards. Then a hot pain shot through her, a sudden tightening sensation that snatched her breath away and made her shut her eyes tight and scream. There was a great darkness, a tunnel that pulled her downwards.

Mrs Tipton called for Mother, for Daisy, for the doctor, for Jesus and the Lord himself.

Emily opened her eyes, got her fingers to the call button. The pain fell away but the air still reverberated from the force of the screams.

Mrs Tipton shook her hand now that it was free again. 'My goodness you've a grip on you.'

Mrs Tipton called again for Mother, while steering Emily down the corridor.

'In here.' Emily pointed to her room. Mrs Tipton directed Emily towards the bed, and apologised before taking a peek up Emily's under skirts.

'Goodness me, baby's on its way.'

Before Emily could cry out 'no', the pain came again and threw her back against the bed's rails.

Mrs Tipton gripped her hand this time.

'I'm here now.' Mother arrived. The pain had subsided and Emily slumped back in the bed. It was softer behind her back.

Mrs Tipton went off to fetch hot towels, fresh linen. Everything was blurry; the room danced. Emily's legs couldn't hold her up.

The tide of the pain rose and fell. She couldn't say for how long it went on. Her bedroom curtains were drawn, but the glint that pushed through faded after a while. The sun had passed over the top of the house.

'The baby's in a rush,' Mrs Tipton said. Emily gasped for breath. Fought the pain. She must stay strong to see this through.

'Where's Theo?' she asked.

Neither said anything.

'We're here for you now,' Mother said.

'Things have slowed down.'

'Maybe it's changed its mind,' Emily panted. She must keep going. Resist the urge to close her eyes and sink.

'You're doing very well.' She fought against it as she slid down the dark tunnel again. She pulled at her own skin, slapped herself. She opened her eyes, saw the doctor, the new one, the old one hadn't come back from the war. She slumped forward again. The pain came.

Ether. Morphine. Episiotomy. Alien words.

'No ether,' she called. 'No. I want to do this. No ether,' she yelled as pain ripped through her, smothered her like a hungry flame. Then darkness came.

*

She awoke to a rattling cry coming through the wall and the urge to do something, though she wasn't sure what. The room was dark. Her head thumped so badly she had to lower her head straight back to the pillow. When she moved her legs and put her feet to the floor, down below burnt like hellfire.

The crying stopped. Her head was too full of wool for her to work it all through, her legs too watery to take her own weight. But the baby was crying.

The door between her own room and the nursery was locked so instead she hobbled, clutching her stomach, down the hallway.

'Emily darling. You were right – it's a boy.' Shards of light haloed Mother's body.

'Is he all right?' Her voice came from the other side of the room. In the candlelit nursery, Mother sat in the nursing chair, the baby in her arms. His mouth was pushed wide by a rubber nipple.

'You're unsteady on your feet. Come and sit down.'

Mother stood. Emily lowered herself with a wince into the

nursery chair and then Mother slotted the floppy bundle into her arms, warm and heavy. Mother unplugged the bottle from his lips. His little face creased, his lip quivered, his eyes tightly shut while he bleated.

'The doctor said you should rest. You were terribly unwell. He advised us to make up an emergency formula – cow's milk, sugar and honey – until you were strong enough to give him the nourishment he needs from these small little feeds, until your milk comes in.'

Emily held the bottle aloft, wondering if the milk came from Lily, her troublesome cow. Mother admired the baby over Emily's shoulder. 'He's full now.' Mother's voice was soft. 'You can try and feed him later.'

'You should have woken me,' Emily said. 'When he was first hungry.'

Mother leant forwards to kiss his creased-up, red forehead.

'Emily, I'm not sure you appreciate how very ill you were. Your baby needs a mother who is well enough to take good care of him. And look, isn't he the most beautiful thing you've ever seen?'

Mother left her. She weighed him in her arms, a warm little bundle. Lifting the blanket to better see him, she traced her finger around the shape of his velvet face. The candlelight flickered and she mistook it for her own heart flowing with gold.

*

When the baby awoke for the next feed she was there, beside him, waiting for him. She wouldn't let him down, not ever again. She'd always be there for him. She stroked the tip of his nose, dipped close to drink in the scent of his new skin. He had a mop of dark curls like his Uncle Cecil.

She leant over his bassinet all night. She ached and stung. Her eyelids drooped. Once or twice she dropped off and awoke with a start, but she couldn't leave in case he needed her.

'Did the baby nearly die?' she asked the doctor when he made his call.

'You had a difficult labour,' he told her, 'but you've both made it through. You're both fighters.'

'Did I nearly die?'

The look on his face, the second he took to answer, told her that she had come close. She had nearly perished, and left her baby without a mother. She'd almost abandoned him before he'd even opened his eyes, taken his first breath.

'He is doing well. You just need to see that he gains in weight and keeps growing.'

She could do that. She could feed him and keep him alive. She would watch him grow. He had to keep getting heavier. And she would be strong for her baby.

'You should rest. Sleep when baby sleeps. You won't benefit from watching him sleep.'

She nodded. But she wouldn't go to bed – not yet, not when he might need her.

'Make sure she eats,' he muttered to Mother as he left the room.

*

'There's something I need to tell you.' Mother sat beside her, resting her clasped hands on her lap. 'And I want to tell you now, get it out in the open and then I want us to move forwards. Without any arguments.'

Emily's eyes were still heavy, flitting open and closed.

'You were right to bring me back here. I can make decisions for the family. And I have begun by accepting Wilfred's suggestion to sell. And he's making it easy, he is going to buy us out.'

'Right.' Through the fog she tried to concentrate on Mother's words. Mother had conceded that Emily was right about something; either that or the morphine was making her hallucinate.

She'd taken a decision. They would sell their share of the house to Wilfred, and with the proceeds set up a new life. It was perfect, what she'd hoped would happen, and yet there was something in Mother's tone that told her it wasn't.

'The problem is the farm; there won't be one any more. He's going to close it down.' She pushed herself upright. 'Now don't start carrying on about how you're going to live in that farmhouse. You've no husband and a baby. It simply wouldn't work.'

'It would if Martha was with me. We could run it together.'

'And who's Martha? You don't mean the ex-housemaid? Oh for goodness' sake. You had your time; now you need to be responsible.'

'Don't sell the farm to him,' Emily said. 'Exclude the farm from the sale.'

'It's too late,' Mother said. 'I've accepted his offer. It's time for a fresh start. Now everyone in the village thinks you're a widow it makes sense that we would want to move away.'

Emily pulled her hand away. It was her mother of old, knitting socks for soldiers by the fire, ashamed of a daughter who would never follow the script Mother had written for her.

The fog in her mind had burnt away now. It was all very clear, but she was pinned to the bed by an invisible hand, while a fire burnt inside her.

'If you go through with this, I won't ever forgive you,' Emily said.

'You will,' Mother said. 'The idea of an educated girl like you living in that damp old farmhouse, with a baby, was simply preposterous and you'll thank me for saving you from it one day. Now' – she pulled the cover back up over Emily's chest – 'you get some rest. You need your strength.'

Chapter Thirty

May 1919

A letter had arrived for her. Daisy had brought it up with her morning tea.

'Will we see you up today?' Daisy asked. Emily hadn't been downstairs for three days, wasn't sure she wanted to ever again be in her Mother's company. Once she re-entered Mother's sphere she'd be surrendering to afternoon teas and house calls and there'd be no more crops and weekly trips to the market.

'A Yorkshire postmark,' Daisy commented.

She handed the tea tray, the letter and the miniature dagger-like opener to Emily and left. Emily set the tea tray down on the dressing table catching a glimpse of herself. Her hair was lank; free of pins it hung down by her face.

'Mrs Tipton has called twice now,' Daisy said. 'She'd love to see the baby. And she asked me to tell you, you're not to worry about the ole man. He knows everything, and he doesn't blame you.'

He'd forgiven her, but he'd be leaving the farm at the end of the season, and he wouldn't be handing the reins over to her.

The letter stayed unopened on the dresser, the tea un-drunk, while Emily leant over the bassinet as the baby opened and closed his mouth in his sleep as if he was dreaming about milk.

The letter still lay on the dresser. It could be from Theo. He might have returned after all, and he might take her and the baby far away from here. The stationery was familiar, but the handwriting wasn't Theo's. It was fatter, more curvaceous, and the tail of the y in her name curled around on itself like a pig's. She sliced the envelope along its ridge, gutting it, and pulled out the entrails. Perhaps Theo was staying with his father. She unfolded the letter and her gaze skittered across the inked words.

To Emily,

    I am writing to tell you something that I hope is a terrible mistake, a mix-up of some sort, but I fear the worst. I found a letter from you in Theodore's trouser pocket. I don't know what might have passed between you in the war; I must assume that there was some sort of a romance, but I must ask you not to write to him again.

    He wasn't a well man after the war. He wandered off and ended up in New Zealand. He's home again now and his boys need their father. I don't suppose you meant to cause us any harm. He might not even have told you about us, but it would be the kinder thing to leave him be and to let us be a family again.

    Mabel Williams

She ran to her basin and was sick. It splashed the porcelain and the wall with a brown-flecked bile. How could he have done a thing like that? She retched again, but she was empty, her head hanging low beneath the hand and arms that rested on the basin. How could *she* have done a thing like that? Marry a man who was capable of becoming angry and violent, who dropped in and out of her life when it suited him.

She dropped to her knees by the bassinet, her mind spinning.

When she did find the strength to push herself to her feet, white shapes swirled in front of her eyes. She swayed and waited for the images to disappear. She was observing herself from above. She wasn't inside any more; she'd been pushed out of her own body. She'd married a criminal. What would Mother say to that?

She lifted John, opened the nursery door, descended the stairs. She kept going straight, straight through the door, out of the house, down the path. Straight. Straight. Straight.

*

She ended up at the rose garden with the baby in her arms. She just arrived there, with no memory of leaving the house, even. She pulled John close to her chest, tilted him away from the glaring sun.

One hand pulled at a stubborn rose bloom that leant forwards into the garden. The woody stem creased but the flower stayed in place. Her thumb caught on a thorn and dragged across the pad to leave a slit that oozed her blood. Still one-handed, she tore off the crimson petals, one by one, tossed them to the ground behind her.

'Whatever are you doing out here …'

Mother's strides slowed. She edged towards Emily now. 'Emily, my dear. The baby – he'll feel the cold, even on a sunny day like this.'

The bloom was stripped bare now. Just its yellow, fertile centre remained bare. As Mother moved towards the baby, Emily pulled him tighter.

'Why don't you come inside, dear …'

Why did she sound as if she were coaxing a cat from a tree? She held John close. What was wrong with being outside? John had on his gown. It was warm. Surely better out here than hemmed in within four walls.

Norah Peters arrived carrying a posy of Sweet Williams. She

stopped a little way short, surveying mother, daughter and baby surrounded by a confetti of crimson petals.

'Louisa? Emily?' Norah's searching gaze travelled from one to the other.

'We ought to get the baby inside,' Mother said. 'Or at least wrap him up in his carriage.'

'I've got him,' she said as Mother bent to kiss the baby on the head. She shook off Mother's arm and strode back towards the house. The baby *did* need to be warm, but she didn't want to go back in there. The glass cabinets, the windows and the looking glasses would reflect back at her exactly what a fool she was.

But then outside, none of this was hers any more. It would soon all be Wilfred's. That staked area by the monkey puzzle tree was probably something to do with him. He had plans, and their return here had only ever been temporary. First John had put him in charge and now Mother was going to sign it all away. She just wanted to run. Mother was right about that: she needed to start afresh.

'Won't you come inside?' Mother asked. 'Could you go ahead, Norah? Ask Daisy to light a fire in Emily's bedroom.'

It was a warm day. The sun was shining, but she couldn't feel its warmth, just its hard, unflinching glare.

'I don't want to go inside with you,' Emily said.

Mother laughed, but she was checking Norah's reaction. 'Of course you do,' she said in a high-pitched voice. She pulled closer to Emily's ear. 'Not in front of Norah, for heaven's sake,' she hissed.

But Emily didn't care if it would be all around the village. She was used to being on the outside. 'I don't want to live with you any more,' she said.

'She's as cold as ice,' Mother said to Norah by way of explanation. 'A bad case of the baby blues I'd say. The little one isn't wrapped very tightly either.'

Norah eyed her as if she were a specimen in a case at the Natural History Museum.

'It might be for the best if you leave us,' Mother said.

Norah hesitated. 'Are you sure?'

'It's fine. Both of you,' Emily said.

Upstairs, in her bedroom, she sat in front of her dressing-table mirror and her foolish reflection while Daisy fussed about laying the fire. Bashing and clattering, in and out with coal and kindling, poking about, and then tutting when the kindling smoked and the flames didn't come, until finally a small flame licked at the back of the grate.

Emily's hair was tangled. Tiredness distorted her face with little hillocks. She had shrivelled onto her own bones since her baby was born.

Mother clucked at the mess in the basin, and then read the crumpled letter and closed her eyes. Her lips flattened into a line. 'It's just as well that everyone thinks he is dead,' she said.

'I don't need him,' Emily said. 'Neither does John. The two of us will be fine on our own.'

Emily lifted the heavy wooden hairbrush and pulled it down through her hair. It snagged and refused to go through, tumbled to the floor and stayed there.

'Now, you mustn't think that I take any pleasure from this,' Mother said. 'That man took advantage of your innocence. If I saw him now ...'

Emily managed a feeble smile. 'You drove me into his arms,' she said.

Mother gawped like a fish. 'But ... what ... you ... you blame *me*, for *your* mistakes?'

'No,' Emily said. The mistake was hers and she could admit to that, but if Mother had trusted her to live her own life, if she'd allowed her freedom to be herself, if she hadn't pulled her close one minute, rejected her the next, Theo would never have been so appealing.

The fog in her head had thickened and the muscles in her face wouldn't do anything she asked of them. The fire was catching now. Its warmth hadn't reached her yet. Her mother pulled a chair close and angled it so that it faced the flames.

'Baby John will be ready for his lunch soon,' Mother said. The letter was folded, Mother's finger sharpened the crease, then she buried it deep in her skirt pocket. 'I know it won't be easy, but the thing is to try and carry on. Why don't you sit yourself in front of the fire and feed the baby? It will warm you both.'

Mother encased Emily's hands with her own warm ones. 'That formula …'

'Please, stop telling me what to do, and leave me alone.'

She wouldn't go; she'd never let go. For a while everything might seem fine, but Mother would never approve of her, always be disappointed by her and there was nothing she could do about it. If Emily didn't do something drastic she'd be tied to her for the rest of her life.

'Go!' Her hands shook.

The wedding ring slipped off her shrunken cold fingers, and sang as it hit the floorboards. She slipped it into her stocking drawer, buried it deep beneath the wool. Emily pushed the drawer shut, fed John and then sought refuge in her bed, pulling the covers up and over her. Where the ring had been there was a slight indentation. The skin beneath was softer, paler, a sliver of innocence.

She closed her eyes and swam towards the fringes of darkness. When she woke, she asked Daisy to run her a hot bath.

'Of course, of course. I'll put the copper on.' Daisy fetched buckets of water.

'Don't tell Mother,' she pre-empted her.

Daisy put a fresh towel over the rail and hung a clean dressing gown on the inside of the door.

Steam rose off the water. It stung her skin, leaving a vivid red tideline. Tears fell with so little pomp or ceremony like water from a dripping tap and she soon grew used to them and just wiped them away every now and again.

The bath water was clear and exposed her scarred, swollen, empty and yet laden body. She sank down into the bath, submerged her head. Her hair softened and floated. She closed her eyes, and held her breath.

Back in her bedroom, she opened her wardrobe door, pulled out a tango corset. She could wear it loosely, very loosely. She slipped her foot into her stockings, rolled them up to her thighs, clipped them to her girdle. Took out a skirt, a lace-collared blouse. Brushed the tangles out of her hair until it was smooth. Found the hairpins in her drawer and then paused. Slid open the drawer next to it, took out a pair of scissors and snip-snipped through the curtain of hair, in a straight line beneath her chin.

The wet tendrils fell away from her. She had a bob now, like the girls in London. The hairline caressed her jaw. She shook her head. It would be dry in no time. The hairpins were shut away, back in the drawer.

She painted two cheery red circles on her cheeks that stood out against her ashen face. Tears instantly ran through them turning them into cracked hearts.

Downstairs, she followed the chattering to the library where she found her mother, one hand on the baby carriage pushing it back and forth. Norah Peters was visiting again; stooped over the elephant-grey Empire pram, cooing.

'Emily!' Mother said. 'Would you like a cup of tea?'

'It was time I was off.' Norah clattered her teacup into its saucer and didn't wait to be shown out of the house.

'He's awake,' Mother said. 'He's just like you were at that age; he doesn't like to sleep during the day in case he misses out. Perhaps you might be able to get him off to The Land of Nod.' Mother lifted her hand from the pram. She passed her what had been Emily's own *Book of Garden Verses*. Emily set it down on top of the piano.

'I've reached a decision.' Emily adjusted the grey hood of the baby carriage. 'I'm going to join Cecil's suffragette friends and work on a land colony.'

'Those blue stockings won't want you with a babe in arms.'

The hood was up now, the nasty grey plastic stretched to its limit by the frame.

'They're very amenable, and they don't give up.'

'We could take care of the baby between us.'

She lifted the hood, up and down, up and down. She was trembling.

'Well.' Mother straightened up. 'I'll just have to go back to London, won't I?'

'If that's what you want. There are things I want to do with my life and you can't stop me, not in the end.'

'I can't, but this baby might. He needs you,' Mother said. 'You can't be a mother *and* a farm labourer. Good grief, child.'

Mother stepped away now, her arms folded.

Emily hid her trembling hand in her sleeve. Mother's concern wasn't what she wanted, despite what she might say. In the end she was taking care of herself. Emily might have lost HopBine Farm, but the country was full of farms, and resourceful women like Alice and Eleanor, and somehow she'd find a way.

The baby's crinkly mouth had drifted open. His head set to one side. He made tiny sniffles in his sleep.

'We're going out,' she said. Mrs Tipton hadn't met the baby yet and it was about time she did. She pushed the pram into the hallway. The baby needed fresh air, not to be cooped up in the sitting room all day long.

Chapter Thirty-One

July 1919

She pulled the pamphlet from the envelope first:

A right to work. A right to live.
Women have the right to suitable work for a living wage.
A right to leisure.

Dearest Emily,

I thought you'd like to see the pamphlet we delivered to Downing Street. Can you imagine me, in Downing Street? I can hardly believe we did it. The number of us, women from all over. The NUWSS, WFGA, the LSWS. I don't know what most of the letters mean, but they all represent women who are disgruntled and feel they've been discarded.

They wanted me to come to the deputation. It was so plush inside the house at Number 10. Alice and Eleanor and some of the other educated girls really gave the government official what for. They said there'll be no forcing women back into the home. Eleanor said to the official, shaking her fist: 'You think you can enfranchise us with one bill and cut our throats

*industrially with another?' She had me scared. I think the
minister would have made a run for it if he could!*

*She was talking about the bill, the pre-war work practices
one that has upset her so much. She's some nerve, I tell you.
If it had been me I'd have put her in charge of the Treasury.
He didn't budge at all, mind. Just sat there nodding away. He
gave away nothing and I thought it was a waste of time and
I said as much when we were back outside and walking down
past the spot that they're going to build a national war memorial.*

*Alice said that these things took time, but two days later
they wrote to say the government wouldn't fund the colony.
So that's that I suppose, but Eleanor said we mustn't give up
hope. She has funds and we'll still find a way.*

Fondest wishes
Martha

'John's sacrifice will be acknowledged and remembered for gener-
ations to come. For this little one to remember,' Mother said,
tickling the baby's chin on her return from her meeting with the
village war memorial committee, bringing a bag of cherries from
Mrs Tipton, with a spring in her step. Funds were to be raised
for a small, stone statue on a patch of land opposite the green
donated by the Cothams. On it, they'd engrave the names of all
the village men, and one of Lady Radford's maids who'd been
killed in a field hospital near the front line.

It was Peace Day and the King had sent a message of gratitude
to wounded soldiers, while riots took place all over the country.
At HopBine, more stakes had gone in the ground on the lawns
that ran alongside the cedar avenue, and down to New Lane. A
huge stack of bricks had been delivered too, and sat down by the
old paper mill. Their time there was running out, and if she didn't
act soon Emily would have no choice but to move with Mother,
wherever she went.

The problem was baby John. The baby blues had lifted, but John hardly slept at night, and he was hungry all the time. Mother was right: it wouldn't be easy being a mother and getting what she wanted.

Dear Mabel,

I am sure you can imagine your letter came as quite a shock, but I am glad to you for writing to me because at least now I know the truth and everything makes sense. I married Theo in 1916, in what I think of now as haste, but at the time, in the midst of war and turmoil and following the death of my dear brother, John, it seemed a perfectly sensible thing to do.

In hindsight, the signs were there but I chose to ignore them. I didn't want to believe that I had made a mistake and I'm sorry not for myself but for you, his first wife, and your children, that you have been hurt by my error of judgement. I am writing to tell you how deeply, deeply sorry I am for marrying Theo, for not finding out about him first, for not noticing the signs that his mind wasn't as it should be.

But I am also writing to tell you that I too have a son, Theo's son. A bonny young baby boy, named John after my brother killed in the war. He was born in May this year. Whether you tell Theo is a decision that I will leave with you – I'm torn. Part of me believes that he must learn that he has another son, and that John too should know his father. The other part of me feels we should leave you be, to live your life and the terrible things that the war has done to Theo. I feel it isn't my decision to make, but yours.

Kind wishes
Emily Cotham

Cecil filled the doorway. He'd put back on the weight he'd lost in prison, and he'd remembered how to put a comb through his hair.

'You called,' he said, waving the letter that she'd sent to him. 'Am I needed to prise you and Mother apart?'

'It's not quite that bad,' she said, her body sagging. 'She's just difficult, and controlling, and vulnerable and caring all at the same time.' The best thing, in the end, was simply not to talk to her.

Cecil waited, admiring John in the bassinet. 'And?' he said. 'You always save the bad news until last. Out with it.'

Very well, he'd asked for it. She took a deep breath. 'As soon as I feel strong enough, I'm going,' she said. 'You can take care of Mother for a change.'

'And where are you going to go?' he asked.

'I don't know yet,' she admitted. Eleanor had viewed land near Lingfield. She had the funds to lease it outright, and she intended to gift it to the war workers. Martha had checked it and declared it perfect, but things were moving slowly. There wouldn't be a colony for her to work on for a while, but Wilfred's solicitor was apparently in a hurry to complete the sale and begin with Wilfred's plans for the estate.

'Who do you think he resembles?' Cecil asked. He pulled the blanket away from John's chin. He wasn't the likeness of anyone in their family, or Theo. She supposed he was just himself.

'He has your hair,' Emily said. 'I've always envied you.' She sighed. 'You can be whoever you want to be, and no one will stand in your way. At least the baby has been born a boy and I won't have to watch him endure the same frustrations as me.'

His face fell, and in an instant his head was buried in his hand and he sobbed. That was insensitive of her. It hadn't been easy being who he wanted to be at all, and coming back to Chartleigh would be difficult. Last time he'd been here, he'd been almost beaten to death and no one except the prisoners of war or the doctor had looked him in the eye.

'It's a very brave thing to come back,' she said, handing him a handkerchief. John, meanwhile, was warming up, his face

241

scrunching, tight and red, giving little grunts, each one a bit longer than the last.

She asked Cecil if he was ready to face the village.

'Yes,' he said, wiping away the tears. 'Better to get it over with.'

John stopped grizzling and began to suck on his own fist as soon as they were outside with a view of the sky and within hearing of the birdsong. The bees were busy; everything was golden.

They pushed the pram down New Lane and she asked Cecil to tell her what was going on in the world. She'd lost track since they'd been back in Kent.

A lot, it transpired. Over two million people out on strike across the country: bakers, miners, even the police. The Riot Act had been read in Liverpool, the troops sent in to deal with the looting.

'And meanwhile in sleepy Kent life goes on. Untouched by Zepps, far from the battle cry of strikes and riots. Joe's let the sheep into the orchard, the village children are aiming their arrows at the squirrels, Mrs Tipton is throwing corn at the chickens. My goodness, I'll miss it all so much if I have to leave.'

'I can't do what you want of me,' he said as they approached the house. 'I'm sorry, Emily, but I can't live with Mother. Life is so exciting at the moment … The suffragettes' campaign against the trade unions has been successful,' he began. 'The Bolsheviks are forming a society in England. The likes of Lady Radford are on the way out. And we're leading the way, handing the land back to the workers …' He trailed away.

'But?' she asked.

'But' – he sighed – 'I can't go back to university – it would be too claustrophobic – though I can change things, change the world.'

She couldn't ask Cecil to be anything less than Cecil. He would make a difference, and she wouldn't try to stop him.

'Mother might run back to Wilfred,' she said. 'He's a bully, utterly controlling her life. She was diminished there.'

'I'm sorry, Emily, but if I promised you that I'd try, in the end, I'd fail. It's better I am honest from the beginning.' He left her unable to climb the front steps, and he disappeared into the house.

*

It was time for Cecil to heal old wounds. His first stop was the farmhouse. Mr and Mrs Tipton welcomed them in and told Cecil he'd not let anyone down. Then he went door to door around Chartleigh. One or two turned away from him, one widow shouted at him, hoped he was satisfied, but Olive Hughes caught him passing and invited him in, told him the German prisoners got a better treatment than him.

On his way back up he bumped into Ada. She told him all about the wonders Emily had worked on the farm, and said she respected him for following his calling. When he returned to the house his eyes were red, his hankie scrunched up in his hand, and he kept repeating over and over, 'wonderful people, wonderful people', and she couldn't disagree.

*

On the Thursday in the sweltering heat, as they walked along the New Lane, cart loads of labourers down for the harvest trundled past on their way to their lodgings at Perseverance Place.

August had faded into September. She talked things over with Cecil. There had been no news from Martha about the land colony. If Martha didn't write soon she would have to scour the papers for vacancies for farm managers, but no one would ever take her on: a woman, on her own, with a baby.

The next morning, she woke at six o'clock, before John had even stirred. She fumbled for a blanket to cover her icy toes. She'd kicked it off in the night because it had been too warm for anything other than a sheet, but now her breath blew clouds into the room.

She checked on John, put the back of her hand to his cheek. His skin was cold. She slotted a hand beneath his back and without waking him slipped him under the blanket into bed with her. After twenty minutes or so she warmed her toes with bed socks and put on a layer over her nightdress.

John woke, raa-raaing for his morning feed. While he fed, she listened to a blackbird's song. It was quieter than normal outside, the bird's song flatter. John had dozed off at her breast. She lowered him back to the silk insides of the bassinet. Pink for a boy, pale red for the war god Mars – she had got that right.

How could the house be so cold? She pulled back the curtains and gasped. The sky was so blue she could slice it in two, but the landscape was still; a heavy haw frost coated the land and froze it rigid. Each blade of grass distinguished itself from the other, standing to attention.

The blackbird was quiet, without much to sing about.

Her hand flew to her mouth. The harvest would be ruined.

She scampered to her wardrobe and lifted out her old land army uniform. Boots, still crusted in mud, sat in the depths on a newspaper spread. She dressed in her breeches, half-brushed her teeth at the basin and splashed her face with water from the bowl. Emily pulled on her thick overcoat, woke Cecil to ask him to take care of John, and dashed out of the house.

The farmhouse door was open. Men she didn't recognise darted in and out like ants from a kicked nest. Mr Tipton wasn't anywhere, neither was Mrs Tipton. A labourer from the village doffed his cap at her as he fled past.

'Can I help?' she called after him.

'Nothing doing, ma'am,' he said. 'It's too late.'

She paused in the doorway. Its whining creak echoed around the empty room. The air was sharp and clear – no steam or cabbage-soup fumes. The black-leaded range had gone out. She took a deep breath and stepped inside. Mrs Tipton sat on the worn-out settee, her head in her hands, sobbing.

'Can I help?'

'It's done, isn't it? A whole year's work. Gone.' She mimed a handful of nothing going up into the air.

'Surely something. The apple crop?'

'S'all ruined.'

'What does Mr Tipton say?'

'He's in a proper pickle. It's the shock. The shock! He's scared of that uncle of yours. He knows what he'll say when he tells him there's no profit this year.'

Emily fetched the coal in and got the range going. Filled the kettle and got out the leaves, and the teapot. She rummaged about in the depths of the dresser cupboard until she found the little tin, in which Mrs Tipton hid her sugar. This cup of tea was going to need to be as sweet and as warming as she could make it.

*

Percy Greenacre's head hung low. His hands perched on his hips and he stood in a circle with the other labourers up on the Sunnyside Orchard.

It didn't need to be spoken out loud; the apple crop would thaw on the bough and go soft and rot. The trees would be damaged too. Percy plucked a low-lying apple and kicked it into the hedgerow.

The labourers, hired help, who now wouldn't get paid, hovered around the cart smoking and talking in low voices. Some of the villagers' children, innocent to what this all meant, chased one another around the trunks.

'Where's Mr Tipton?' Emily asked.

Percy was talking to one of the seasonal workers. He walked past her, so close he brushed her arm, but he didn't answer. It was as if she were a ghost.

She should go. Leave them be. There was nothing she could do to help. She'd be better placed trying to keep Uncle Wilfred under control once he found out his profits would be down. She might be able to stop him from bullying Mr Tipton. It wasn't his fault that the harvest had failed. She crossed over to the ridge, kept far away from the others. She'd walk down to the old paper mill and trace the stream back towards HopBine.

At the edge of the orchard, her gaze trained on a shape on the ground. A brown heap. A pile of abandoned sacks? But then, she raised a hand to her mouth. The brown felt hat. She sprinted towards Mr Tipton, supine on the ground, staring up to the heavens. She called for the doctor. She lifted his floppy arm and put two fingers to his wrist. But she was too late.

Chapter Thirty-Two

September 1919

The day after Mr Tipton's funeral, Wilfred arrived. He asked Mrs Tipton up to the house. More grey hair hung loose than was in the knot itself, and the rims of her eyes were scorched red. Emily wanted to run from the room.

'It's important to squeeze every last profit out of the farm,' Wilfred explained to the grieving widow. 'One last push until the end of the season.'

If it wasn't for Percy Greenacre, and to everyone's surprise Cecil, stepping in then the farm would have ground to a halt.

'It's rather a lot to ask,' Emily pointed out. 'Given what's happened.'

'The Tiptons are still employed to work for us until the end of the season. There are three more weeks' work owing, or I shan't be paying any wages and I certainly won't be allowing Mrs Tipton to stay on in the farmhouse.'

'Can I help her then?' said Emily. Mrs Tipton had her head on the table and wept. She was in no state to run the farm on her own. 'I'll step into Mr Tipton's boots,' she said.

Wilfred cast his eyes heavenwards and then levelled his gaze at her, shaking his head. 'You can't possibly run a farm.'

'Why not?' she asked. 'I've done it before, when Mr Tipton wasn't here.' She didn't add that it had been only for a day at a time, or that she was only giving her orders to women and prisoners. 'I had some drama then.' She still dreamt about those poor sheep.

'You have a baby,' Mother reminded her.

'Cecil can babysit,' she said. 'So could you.'

'Those days are behind you. There are plenty of men who could step up. What about that tall chap with the Alsatian?'

It was hopeless. She couldn't even persuade her own family to let her take over the farm in a crisis. How ever would she induce a landowner to give her a job as a bailiff or a supervisor?

'Let her do it.' Cecil entered the room. 'She knows the ropes and you won't have to pay her. If you ask Percy Greenacre, or bring in another manager you'll have to pay the wages, and you've already made a loss because of the frost.'

Wilfred was nodding; it always came down to money with him.

'It's just for three weeks,' Cecil continued. 'Let her recoup our losses until the end of the season, and the sale is completed.'

Mrs Tipton lifted her head from the table, her handkerchief soaked through. She put an arm around Emily's shoulder.

'It's what the ole man would have wanted.'

*

Her return to the farm had galvanised Mother into finding a place to live in London. She was ready to buy once the sale went through at the end of the season.

Wilfred still lingered about the place, his visits frequent. There were more deliveries of building materials, and more men in suits came. His plans to own the estate and to invest in the farm had been in the making for years. All the while she'd been dreaming, he'd been putting his plans into action.

Their first market day loomed ahead of them. Mr Tipton had always taken charge of this important weekly event. It all just happened by magic; no one else on the farm had any idea at all of the details.

Mrs Tipton had chewed her nails so low she'd reached the skin. So Emily called the men together around the farmhouse table to decide on a course of action.

'Joe and I will herd the sheep down to the station.' Percy spoke first, before she'd even sat down. 'Mrs Tipton should come. It'll take four of us to load the sheep. I'll help Mrs Tipton with negotiations – and before you say anything else, it needs to be a man because of the meetings after in the public house.'

The others all nodded in agreement. Before she could ask what she should do, Percy had called the meeting to a close with a heavy palm on the table. Mrs Tipton had stopped chewing her nails, and that was the main thing.

On the morning of market day, Emily came down whether she was wanted or not, to see them off. The sheep rumbled into the lamplit yard, bumping and bleating, as she arrived.

Percy bared his teeth and whistled at Sally. Her tail fell between her legs, her ears pinned back to her head. Two sheep had already strayed away from the flock and were in the entrance to the cart shed.

'Yur! Yur!' Percy called, just as Mr Tipton used to command the collie. Only instead of jumping to her paws and circling her herd, keeping it as one, Sally twitched her brow and with lazy defiance lowered herself to the cobbles. 'Sally!' he called. 'Come on, you stupid mutt. Yur! Yur!' He put his teeth together and whistled. Still nothing.

'Sally!' Mrs Tipton cried. 'Come on, girl.' She took the dog by the scruff of her neck and pulled her to standing. 'It's market day. We can't do this without you.'

Percy whistled again. Sally stood. Her tail lolled about. He instructed Joe to run around, keeping the sheep together as one pack. It was a delicate operation. If Joe ran too close to the flock he spooked them and they would all clatter into one another, then scatter, and his job was even harder. The force of the lamplight was fading now as the daylight grew in strength.

'Joe!' Percy called the boy over and sent him off at a sprint in the direction of Perseverance Place. Meanwhile, the sheep were scattering about the farmyard.

Mrs Tipton raised her eyes to the heavens and called, 'Oh dear. I hope the ole man isn't watching this.'

Emily widened her arms and tried to keep them all as one. Sally made it look easier than it was. She had an idea, and dashed into the farmhouse to fetch Mr Tipton's brown felt hat, which she handed to Percy. But he shook his head.

'That's the ole man's,' he said. 'It's not for any of us to wear.'

'Yes, and he needs us to get those sheep rounded up so that Mrs Tipton gets paid this month.'

Percy refused so she dumped the hat on her own head. Sally splayed her front legs, barked. The poor girl was confused. Emily whistled. And yur, yurred. Sally barked. Bared her sharp teeth. Closing in on her, Emily tried again. A couple of sheep were already trotting off down the lane. If they missed the train for market, the week's profits would be down, Wilfred wouldn't pay Mrs Tipton and he'd sack Emily before she'd even started. Sally stood her ground and yapped.

Percy went towards her with a stick raised above his head.

'I'll teach her to work,' he said.

'No you won't.' Emily stepped in his way. How could he think of beating the collie when she was clearly missing her master? The poor dog cowered, her back legs all hunched under, waiting for the blow. Emily stroked the dog's head.

'It's all right, girl.'

Percy threw the stick down. 'You're too soft,' he said, just as Joe came wheezing back down the lane with a black wolf lolloping behind him. It was Rover, Percy's Alsatian, who responded instantly to his master's whistle and went to his side.

She peered at Sally, urging her to do her bit. 'Give her one last chance,' Emily said.

Even Mrs Tipton had lost patience with the dog, and she shook her head. 'Let's just get the sheep to market.'

It was no using pressing it further. Sally wasn't going to be of any help today. She gestured for Percy to carry on, while Sally rubbed herself against Emily's shins, her warm coat comforting.

'Never mind.' She tickled Sally's ears. 'Everyone's entitled to an off day.'

'Off we go.' Percy signalled to Joe, who opened the gate to the lane and the sheep poured out. Rover came up at the rear, growling at any strays.

As they left the yard, bow-legged Alfred, with his big scraggy beard, hobbled up the track towards Percy. There was a problem. Five cows had wandered further than ever and were in Hangman's Wood feasting on young boughs.

'Emily, you'll have to deal with it,' Percy said to her.

'But I want to make sure you get on the train.'

'We need the cow's milk more than we need you watching us doing our jobs. And if those beasts wander on to Finch Hall land, we'll have to pay for any damages they do.' Percy didn't stop his pace.

'Lily's there, I suppose,' Emily called.

Alfred nodded to the top of her head; she was still wearing Mr Tipton's hat. She would keep it on. Percy might not be so rude to her if he was reminded of who was supposed to be in charge.

'Afraid so,' he said. 'She's in a terrible mood. And there's a calf with them. You know her history with calves if she's in a bad mood. We can't afford another loss.'

'Just bring them back,' Percy called as they reached the crook in the lane.

251

'You watch that Lily,' Mrs Tipton called.

Emily went on ahead of Alfred, striding across the uneven ground, until she came to the stream. The cows liked a paddle. On a hot day she'd often been amused by them cooling their hooves. Her boots wouldn't take kindly to a soaking, but she didn't have much choice. She ran along until she reached the old paper mill and then paddled through the shallows, her boots squelching, feet damp, her soggy breeches flapping around her ankles.

Hangman's Wood sat at the edge of a cornfield, a dense copse, thigh-high in bracken and obstacles of trunks and logs carpeted in lichen. She found three cows, not too far in. Rosie was amongst them. She was a sensible cow, and could be trusted to lead them all back to the farm without needing to herd them. She clapped her hands at them, widened her arms. Spooked, they ran to the edge of the copse and in the direction of home.

A little further in she found Lolly. Her sides were wide and she moved slowly. She was due any day now.

'How did you get out?' she asked Lolly. She couldn't leave her to make her own way back. She'd better find the fifth cow and quick. Pushing her way through the bushes and skipping over logs, twigs snapped underfoot, leaf mould rustled and kicked up a filthy dust. She slowed to a stop. Oh dear. A cow lifted its head, chewing on a branch.

'Lily,' she said, sweat on her brow. 'I might have known that this was your work.'

The cow beat her hoof again. Emily clumped her leather boot in return.

'None of your nonsense today.' But Lily was in no mood. She snorted and started towards her. Emily backed off, but in slow, steady steps. That cow was capable of trampling her own calf; she'd not hesitate to flatten her if the mood took her.

'Come on now, Lily,' she said. 'You're late for milking.'

Lily stopped. Emily breathed out and widened her arms,

signalled a path for Lily to take. And continued to walk backwards towards Lolly, who was slowly working her way to the stubbled cornfield. Lily stopped again. She stamped her hoof and with a startling acceleration she took off, stampeding straight at Emily.

Emily had nothing to wave at the cow, and even if she did she'd seen her and recognised her and still she was charging. Of course, it must be the hat – she'd confused Lily. She could try to stand her ground – it had worked before – but something told her today might be different. She had no choice but to turn her back on the cow and run like stink. Hurdling a log, hands up to her face, twigs scratched her skin, she pulled the hat from her hair. The hooves hammered behind her.

'Lily,' she called over her shoulder. 'Please, girl.'

Perhaps she should have dug in, but her instincts told her no, and it was too late for regrets now.

She was nearing the edge of the copse. Out on the open ground Lily might tire, or she might gain pace.

'Yap. Yap.'

Emily scanned the ground. The woof came again.

'Sally!' she called. Sally at the edge of the stubble ran at Emily, jumped up at her in greeting, her paws to her thighs. And then Sally spread her paws wide and barked at Lily. Emily glanced over her shoulder. Lily rumbled to a stop. Emily slowed too, panting. She held on to an oak's trunk just in case. Sally growled, sidled around the edge of the cow and snarled at her. Lily started. Swished her tail. Her coat steamed. Lolly emerged now and came alongside Lily.

'Good girl,' Emily said to Sally, brushing her coat. Sally panted and tilted her head to Emily's thigh. 'Good teamwork,' she said.

Lily and Lolly swayed out of the copse with Sally at their heels, through the stubble, across the stream, the orchard and the dairy. When Lily was locked back inside the dairy, Emily fell to her knees and buried her hands in Sally's fur, her head resting on the dog's.

Alfred sauntered down chewing an ear of grass, checking up on her. It would all make its way back to Percy later, and thankfully the report would be a good one.

'Would you look at that,' he said. 'Our Sally has found herself a new master.'

Chapter Thirty-Three

September 1919

Her blood still thumping in her ears, she ran all the way home. Sally followed her the whole way. She couldn't wait until Mrs Tipton was back from the market and she could tell her how Sally had run down to help her bring in the cows.

She went in through the back door, peeling off her soggy boots. The dip in the river had cleaned the mud off. She'd forgotten that the leather could shine. Edna smiled at the sight of Sally, and filled her a bowl of water.

But when she passed the conservatory, she stopped in her tracks. Mother sat on a chair, blanket on her lap. Wilfred, opposite, was bouncing John up and down on his knee. Cecil was in front of them both with his arms folded.

'Thank goodness,' he said, when she approached him. 'Someone with some sense. You need to come in and hear this.'

Mother eyed the straw stuck to her breeches with mud, but Emily stepped into the room anyway. She was in no mood for Wilfred, or her mother. She lifted John away from Wilfred. She'd take him with her to the farm tomorrow. No matter if he grizzled and stopped her working every now and then, he'd be happier outside. The last person she wanted him around was Wilfred.

'Ask him,' Cecil said. 'You'll want to hear this before the rest of the village gets wind. Ask him what he plans to do with the land once the sale has gone through.'

Emily cupped John's tiny feet in her palm, waiting for an explanation.

Uncle Wilfred appraised her with a quick up and down, his eyebrows raised. She put a hand to the fringes of her bob. He was trying too hard again, and although he was in full country regalia he was completely out of place in his Norfolk jacket, tweed cap, knickerbockers and long woollen socks.

'It's of no concern to Emily, or to any of us what happens here after we've left,' Mother said with a sternness Emily had never before heard directed towards her youngest son.

'Very well. I'll tell her,' Cecil continued. 'Oh, Emily,' he faltered, his face drawn taut. She steadied herself by leaning on the door-frame in readiness. 'He's going to have the estate turned into a new paper mill.' She took a step back. 'It's going to be the biggest of its kind in the country, with tennis courts and a community centre. Finch Hall is up for sale as well, and he's buying up that land. He's going to destroy the village.'

It couldn't be true, but then the building materials had been piling up – she'd just never thought … She waited for Wilfred to explain.

'I had to come up with something to give me a return on buying this decaying old pile and an unprofitable farm.' He shrugged. 'What did you expect?'

Her legs were losing their strength beneath her.

'You can't do this,' Emily said. 'Mother, you can't let him do this. What would Father say?'

'Your father isn't here,' Mother reminded her.

'And what will happen to the farm?'

'The land provides vital access to the river, which is essential for paper making,' Wilfred explained.

So the staked-out pieces of land, the piles of building materials and those men measuring everything up, testing the ground – it had all been going on beneath her nose, and she hadn't questioned it.

'Does anyone else know?' She removed her clammy palms from John's back one at a time and rubbed them on her breeches. If now Cecil knew, then the talk of the plans would have spread through the village like sprouts from a taproot. In a village like theirs, people just got to know things without you even trying. They'd be outcasts all over again.

'On the bright side, you'll have moved out,' Wilfred said. 'The sale's completion will coincide with the end of the season, and my men will start work; this place will be demolished within a month. I was under the impression that business was slow in the countryside. Now that I'm here I can see that it never stands still. It's all very industrious.'

Emily's insides bubbled and rocked away like a kettle on the range about to whistle for all its worth. Mother was looking anywhere but at her; at least she had the decency to be ashamed. Mother had the power to stop this. If she refused to sign those papers, the sale wouldn't go through and Wilfred couldn't pave over their village.

Dearest Emily,

I'm sorry to learn about Theo, but if you want the truth I don't think you ever needed him anyway.

I have some news to cheer you up; Eleanor has secured the land. It's the plot near Lingfield in Sussex, not so far from you in Kent. She says the government can go whistle – she's putting her own money in.

The accommodation isn't much, but there are four cottages for us to live in. It will be just women; they took our advice on that in the end. We'll work on the land and make a living from our own smallholdings. Market gardening, livestock etc ... They want a supervisor and Eleanor has only gone and asked yours truly to take the position.

There's so much to plan and do, and think about. Mother thinks it's a risk, but it's what I know and love and if Eleanor can put in her money to advance our cause then I think I owe it to her to do the very best for the colony and the other land girls.

There's a plot of land with your name on it, Emily, literally a little board on which I've painted 'Property of Emily. Keep out.' It's next to mine. Won't you come and see it, bring the baby? I'd like to meet him. Come, you'll never look back.

Best wishes
Martha

The next day she tried to fix the old Fordson, get it going again and sold off before Wilfred took control over everything. The American tractors were fetching as much as two hundred pounds now. She snapped a bolt and couldn't say how she'd done it, or what she was even doing loosening the thing in the first place. She couldn't remember any of Otto's German names for the engine parts. It was such a long time ago.

She'd been right: word of Wilfred's plans had spread quickly. Percy had returned from market and when Alfred had told him about her work with the cows he had apparently said he might have misjudged her, and she might be all right after all. But that was all undone now. This morning both Percy and Rover had snarled at her. Joe had thrown a stone in her direction. She'd been working alone all day, with only Sally for company.

Mrs Tipton emerged from the farmhouse with a steaming cup of tea. Good old Mrs Tipton, she could always rely on her. The chickens crowded at her feet. She kicked them away. Her entire energy drained away as Mrs Tipton came closer and Emily registered the frown.

'You don't have to say it.' She spoke before Mrs Tipton had

the chance. 'Don't worry. It's not your fault – it was bound to happen.'

'I'm sorry, my love,' she said. 'Percy's the worst. He's refusing to work at all while you're still here. He's riled the others up and they're talking as if it's all your fault now. No matter what I say. And after market day he admitted you were a good worker, and had all the others agreeing. Rotten timing.'

She held up her palm and left the tea in Mrs Tipton's clasp. She'd feel the same way. 'I'm sorry,' Emily said. Wilfred had said he wouldn't pay her if Emily had to be replaced.

'Think about your other options,' Mrs Tipton called after her. 'Don't give up.'

Could she really move to the idyllic Lingfield colony when the steam engines would be thudding in and flattening their village?

The farmyard came to a standstill, as Wilfred's car created a cloud of smoke, followed by another car that sent the chickens scurrying for the cart shed. Two men in suits climbed out. They all shook hands, admired the old Fordson and headed off towards the old paper mill.

Chapter Thirty-Four

October 1919

Out on the church path, John's wailing hammered at her head. A red cheek, agitated by a new tooth, contrasted against his pure white christening gown.

Reverend Winters waited for them at the entrance, his wife notably absent from his side. At least with no one accepting their invitation to the christening there would be no awkward silences or platitudes of sadness about the poor boy's father.

She wrenched her mouth out of its grimace and into a smile. She hadn't wanted to go ahead with this. It was unfair on John that so few from the community would come to see him blessed by God, all because of the mistakes made by the adults around him. What an example they all were to him.

A hat travelled along the hedgerow on the path the other side of the church. Martha.

'Snap,' she said, lifting her hat and pointing to her own dark, bobbed hair.

She flung her arms around her friend and squeezed her tight. 'Thank you for having me as John's godmother.'

As they passed under the church's wooden arch, Emily peered

back towards the gate, but still no Mrs Tipton. What would Fate make of it if John's other godmother wasn't there to bless him? Perhaps they shouldn't go ahead.

'Come on, dear.' Mother quashed her hesitation.

At least Wilfred had left them in peace to pack up, while he got back to his blueprints, and concrete, but without him there the village's anger had been channelled at them. Even the war memorial was under debate – the proposed site was on an access road to the mill. Little wonder that Mother had been excluded from the committee meetings.

Emily had tried to persuade Mother to reconsider selling to Wilfred. 'Call off the sale. I'll find us another buyer for the estate myself. I'll do everything.'

They had a duty to the village; they simply couldn't let this happen.

But mother was resolute. 'The decision is made. You wanted me to take responsibility, and so don't complain now I am.'

She had wanted that, but she didn't want this. Why would Mother let Wilfred do this to their village when she had the power to stop him?

The church was empty. Just the family and Martha. Emily lifted John out of the Empire, his left cheek blotchy and red. His furious cries filled the church, right the way up to the wooden rafters. Mrs Tipton would suggest gripe water and a drop of whisky, if she'd come.

The Reverend emptied handfuls of water onto John's forehead. The baby kicked back, his legs cycling the air. Poor thing.

'There, there,' Emily hushed. 'Nearly done.'

Had Mabel told Theo about John in the end? Perhaps he knew he had another son and yet he still hadn't come to see him. The embers of hope that John should have a father he knew were reduced to a trail of smoke now. The orange glow had died; the coals were black and grey and crumbling with barely any heat to hold a hand over.

She'd tried to imagine taking her revenge on Theo. At times she bubbled inside to think how easy it was for him to hide away safe with his wife and family while she had to battle on alone. But no matter how many mistakes he'd made, and how much he'd humiliated her, he had given her the most precious gift of all.

'Will you bring my new godson to visit me in Lingfield?' Martha said after they'd walked her back to the station. As the supervisor she couldn't be gone all day, and had to get back. 'It's just one change at the village of Gatwick, easy as pie,' Martha said. 'You'll love it there, Emily. It's paradise.'

'I'll come and visit,' she said. It was the most she could agree to, though she risked falling in love with the place and wanting it even more.

'I'll hold you to that,' Martha said as she kissed John on the forehead.

*

A week later, after a morning of packing she'd taken John out for some fresh air. She could walk all day long with John in the Empire; it made him so happy.

As she rounded the corner to reach the wooden arched gate that led to the churchyard she came across Olive Hughes and Mrs Tipton with Sally. They were re-fastening the gate on their way out and they must have spotted one another at the same time because the two women stopped talking. Mrs Tipton gawked at her feet. Olive kept her head high, her chin jutting out, and her nose set in a sneer.

'Afternoon!' Emily chirped, gripping the pram's handle. Sally crossed the path to her, tail wagging, and lifted her head for a pat. Mrs Tipton whistled her back. Sally cowed back with her ears flat, fading into her owner's skirts.

'That lot're still here then,' Olive said, timing her comment to the exact moment that Emily walked by.

'Now, now,' hushed Mrs Tipton. 'She's going to visit her father's grave.'

Emily unclipped the gate and opened it wide. The pram was a squeeze. She tried to push it through but it wouldn't go. She'd always left him outside on the path before, but today she'd wanted him to come too. The Empire was stuck. Whichever way she pushed or pulled at it, she would scrape its elephant-grey side, or risk twisting the hood's metal jaws.

'Oh dear,' said Mrs Tipton but Olive held her back from crossing the path to help.

'You just think of all that cultivated land that your ole man worked for many a year. The toil killed him, so her lot could pave over it.'

Emily gave the carriage a heaving shove right through the gate. The posy she'd picked for her father's grave scattered on to the higgledy brick path. The post scraped against the Empire's sides. She couldn't look.

'Let me help you, dear.' Mrs Tipton came rushing forward towards the scattered stems, but Olive caught her arm.

'Ivy Tipton, you'll offer no help to a family that's left you short of money when you've been widowed and won't rest until they've spoiled our village. Let her pick up her own mess.'

'It's all right,' Emily said. 'But thank you anyway.'

She gathered in the posy and still down on her haunches she forced her eyes upwards, and faced up to the damage the post had done to the pram.

*

Cecil was hunched over the library desk, making notes. Books splayed opened, bending their spines. Flat moons of candlelight spilled onto the desk. A musky, musty aroma flooded out into the hallway.

The baby was of more use to them than Cecil. But none of

this was his fault. He was the youngest and they'd wanted him to be the eldest, the head of the household, and he didn't have it in him.

He'd tried to organise a protest with the villagers, but they'd sent him away, told him they wouldn't be told what to do by a shirker. Wilfred's money gave him a voice and power, and it made people listen to him. Deeds counted for something when you had cash in the bank. They had none. No one in the village could match Wilfred's clout – even Lady Radford was on the way out. All they could do was wait for the sale to go through, and once they had some capital again, start over, somewhere new.

Cecil crumpled a sheet into a paper snowball and dropped it with the others onto the library floor. They had brought Uncle Wilfred and his plans for redevelopment to the village, and they would have to accept their blame for that.

'Are you going to tell me what you're doing?' she asked.

*

London was the last place she wanted to be when she only had two more weeks at HopBine, but she needed to see Grandmother.

'I need you to tell me why Wilfred has such a hold over Mother.'

She came right out with it. 'He gets his own way,' Grandmother said. 'You've seen what he's like.'

'But it makes no sense now. Mother had begun to find her independence back in Kent. She'd lengthened the apron strings and even conceded to my being right on several things. She has the pension, and with her proceeds from her half of the estate she'll be financially independent. But now she's letting him ride roughshod over the village, when we could just sell to someone else.'

Grandmother shifted out of her seat and walked over to the window. 'It's family business,' she said.

What was that supposed to mean? She was family, so why

didn't she know what was going on? But Grandmother didn't have the time. She was hosting a charity meeting. Emily was ushered out onto the street.

Instead of going back to the train station, she called by Hyde Park. Her eyes searched the benches for a man in a trench coat with the collar flipped up, but there were only nannies and children, and couples out for a stroll. If Ellery sat by her side on her bench by the water, she could tell him everything, and he'd listen and he'd gently offer her some advice, or steer her towards her own answers. It was a good thing for him that he was no longer there but off living his life with the girl he loved.

As the afternoon light began to fade she straightened up and returned to Grandmother. Doors had been closed in her face before, but not any more; too much was at stake.

'I need to know,' Emily said. 'I'm not a child. I'm a mother now, and I need to know why Wilfred is choking my family, and our village, to death.' Emily took a long slow blink, drumming her fingers against the polished wood of the table. Grandmother was amused. 'You have a responsibility here. Wilfred is your son,' she pressed on.

'Oh, you Cothams are such a stubborn lot.' Grandmother tossed her lace handkerchief onto the side table. 'Very well. Though knowledge won't change anything like action will. Wilfred likes to have his own way and on one occasion he didn't and he's never really recovered from it.'

'Mother?' Emily asked.

'Quite. Louisa broke his heart when he was young, and he's never loved anyone again.'

Emily frowned. 'But what about Father?'

'Your mother courted your uncle first and he was really ever so in love, the happiest I've known him. Then Wilfred brought her home to meet the family, and that transpired to be quite catastrophic. Once she met your father, Baden, she found she loved him more, despite herself. It was all very ugly. She was torn out of loyalty to Wilfred, and a deep yearning to be with your father.'

Emily couldn't imagine how Mother could ever have loved Wilfred. He was as unlovable as Percy Greenacre.

'The whole business changed him quite terribly, and money became the only thing that didn't let him down.'

It made sense that Wilfred would bear a grudge. To be rejected would of course change him, and he would be angry with his brother, but why was he still trying to control Mother now?

'Is there more?'

Grandmother closed her eyes, her mouth shrivelling as if the words in her mouth were as sharp as lemons.

'Your mother was never certain which brother was John's father, and Baden loved your mother so much that he was prepared to play the cuckold ...'

'But Wilfred was denied the chance of being a father to his son.'

'Quite.'

That explained the clandestine visits to London, the attention Wilfred lavished on John, and why he had appeared to grieve for John at the funeral. John had known, that day Wilfred had come. That was why he'd allowed him control of the estate. He was trying to compensate for those lost years by taking Wilfred into his confidence.

'And then you encouraged your Mother to leave him, and he was rejected for a second time, and now he is going to hurt her the only way he can, and she probably thinks she deserves it.'

266

Chapter Thirty-Five

October 1919

'You can't let Wilfred win.'

Mr Hughes had collected her from the station and now Emily marched straight into the sitting room where Mother was attending to her embroidery. 'You might have hurt him in the past, but that doesn't mean he can bully and control you.'

Mother sighed, and set down the embroidery, a hand to her head. 'Please don't barge in here and talk to me of things that don't concern you.'

Emily came to a standstill, shrinking into her shoes at Mother's tone.

'It is beyond your understanding.'

Emily moved forwards again, growing taller, until she loomed over Mother. 'But that's just it, Mother. I do understand, perfectly. I have made my own mistakes too, but I won't punish myself, or be held to ransom by my past.'

She took a seat on the sofa beside Mother, perching on the edge, her knees towards her.

'But I deserve it.' Mother put her head in her hands. 'I told him I loved him, and then I married his brother. And then when

I couldn't cope with life, I let him take care of me, only to reject him again. Little wonder he hates me so much.'

'But, Mother …' She took Mother's hand in hers. 'It isn't hatred he holds for you, it's love, a terribly twisted-up and mangled love.'

Mother's eyes lifted from her lap, and she stared at Emily now as if seeing her for the very first time.

'And what's more,' Emily continued, 'you made a mistake for which you must apologise and then call a stop to this.'

She called Cecil from the library. His dark hair was all ruffled and on end. He blinked in the face of the daylight.

'Mother, there's something you should know. Alice has heard some rumours about Wilfred, and I've conducted some research into his activities during the war.'

'Activities?' Mother said. 'He ran his businesses during the war.'

'He did that all right. Wilfred invested in munitions and clothing factories that made uniforms. He owns farms in the West Country and they formed a cartel to fix prices during the war. He has the audacity to challenge me over my matters of conscience whilst profiting from the war.'

'I had no idea …' Mother said. She cast her eyes about the room, before her gaze settled upon Emily. 'Very well. I will apologise and then stand up to him. It's the decent thing to do.'

*

Mother steered Wilfred into the library and shut the door. Sometime later she emerged alone, and nodded to them – it was done. She wouldn't sign over the rest of the estate to him. It would go on the open market. Emily would arrange for an agent to come the next day.

Unfortunately, it wasn't quite over. Uncle Wilfred had travelled to them by train and a rail strike had been called. The whole country's network had ground to a halt. Emily wanted to call his driver to collect him, but they agreed he was an unexploded shell in their midst; they must handle him carefully.

'Did you make it clear that he has no hold over you any longer? That we could make his war effort public knowledge?'

'Yes. Yes. He understood that all right. He never likes anything that's bad for business. We must leave the past behind us. Those were his exact words.' Mother shuffled upstairs and locked her bedroom door behind her.

Perhaps it hadn't sunk in yet. It would be different when he had finally left them. For now, the weight still depressed Emily's shoulders.

*

Wilfred stayed well away from them all the following day. He slept late, dressed in the same ridiculous country garb, and then after making some more calls, he went out for a long ramble by himself.

The three of them took an early evening supper, jumping at every bang in case it was him returning.

'And what are you going to do now?' Mother set down her soup spoon and glared at Cecil. 'You've said you can't go back to university. And you dislike living in the countryside.'

'There are lots of causes I can get behind ...' he began to explain but Mother spoke to cut him down.

'You need to do *something* with your life. Look at your research into Wilfred, and what it uncovered – that was useful, Cecil. You can't protest about life for the rest of your life; you have the intelligence to change it by *doing* something.'

He put his hands on his lap beneath the table, reminding Emily of when they were children and he'd been in trouble with Father for setting the sheep free or refusing to eat his lamb chop. Mother had never admonished him before.

'Why don't you enquire to the local newspapers and ask for

an apprenticeship? Liverpool is rioting. Why don't you go and report on it? The miners are out at Tilmanstone – that's where you should be, not here, moping about the house.'

'What about the family? I'm the eldest male now …'

'Why don't you go and write to the newspapers?' Mother said gently.

*

The gravel rustled outside, announcing the arrival of a car.

'I sent for my driver.' Wilfred appeared in the dining-room doorway. 'There's no telling how much longer those militants on the railway will hold out. Don't make a fuss,' he said. His eyes lingered on Mother for a moment, willing her to look up and tell him that she'd changed her mind, while Emily silently implored her to hold her ground.

A brief flicker to acknowledge his departure. And then the front door thudded to a close, the car engine roared, and the gravel danced at the car's departure.

'I'm going to bed,' announced Mother.

Later that night Emily knocked on Mother's door and asked her what was troubling her.

'I'm on my own now, aren't I.' She shrugged. 'For the first time in my life. I feel as though my toes are level with a cliff edge.'

*

Martha met her at the station with a huge heart-warming hug. Her friend had been right: the train journey to Lingfield was easy. John had been soothed to sleep by the swing and sway of the train travelling along the tracks, giving her a chance to rest as open fields flew past the window.

She and Martha took it in turns to push the carriage all the way along Windmill Lane. At the pond, they stopped so John could watch the ducks, and then finally they arrived at the colony.

A day away from the village should be long enough for word to travel, and for everyone to learn that Wilfred's plans for the mill were finished. Tomorrow she might be able to walk down the lane without being jeered or cat-called from a neighbouring field or a passing cart.

'We've had teething problems,' Martha said. 'Somewhere like HopBine Farm depends on the unpaid labour of a housewife. None of us have a Mrs Tipton working for us for free and that's proving to be a challenge.'

John was quite a weight now and too heavy to carry so she pushed the baby carriage through the gate and onto the plot, waking him up. She lifted him out so he could inspect his new surroundings with his serious face.

'There will be thirteen holdings in the end,' Martha said. 'Poultry, fruit, market gardens, a horse girl ... I'll be doing fruit.'

'Of course you'll be growing fruit. I wouldn't expect anything else from a Private from the Bramley Battalion.'

'Corporal, thank you. And I'll have you know I'm Officer status now.'

Together they pushed John along a nobbled, narrow track that ran alongside Martha's plot. Number three, sloping down the hill.

'And your lodgings?' Emily paused to catch her breath.

'Not as roomy as Perseverance Place.' Emily would never have described their old home as roomy. 'Not as cheap either.' Nor that. 'My board and lodging is thirty-five shillings a week.' Martha raised her eyebrows.

'Do you think it will work?' she asked. 'Will you make enough money to live?'

'It all depends on the goodwill of the suffragettes. Eleanor's money is paying for it all and she's brought in Miss Wilkes, whose expertise has got things up and running. If we don't earn, we don't pay back the ladies' loans. All it takes is a bad harvest or a fall in demand, and it's back to the pre-war ways of importing. I'm not optimistic, but I'm going to make hay while the sun shines.'

Martha waved a hand at a churned-up plot, overgrown with weeds and thistles. A diseased dwarf apple tree was halfway down. 'And here's yours. It's not much now, but plenty of potential.'

It did have – she could do so much with that land. 'Think how many men would have died in Ypres for a piece of land this size,' she said. 'It's so precious, isn't it, such a gift.'

Martha nodded. 'Have you thought about crops? You must have livestock,' she said, 'the way you have with the animals. What about a goat to keep the grass trimmed?'

Emily put John back in his pram, fiddling with the blanket, adjusting it this way and that. Martha came over and then narrowed her eyes. 'What's going on, Emily?'

Emily closed her eyes. She was going to have to tell her the truth sooner or later. 'I can't take it,' she said. 'The plot.'

'What? Why ever not, Emily? Working your own land, it's all you ever dreamt of.'

It was, and it would still be, but it would be selfish of her to come here now.

'Mother has been through a lot,' she said. 'I need to know she is settled and can cope with being on her own before I can move here.' Mother had let her down badly over the farm sale, but she'd never forgive herself if Mother ended up back in the arms of Wilfred simply because Emily had left her when she needed her most. She'd done it once; she couldn't do it again. 'It won't be forever,' she added. 'Just not now.'

'There's a waiting list, you know. A dozen women will take this plot if you're not on here when the new season starts.'

She nodded. She understood, but that plot of land simply didn't have her name on it.

They walked to the boundary of Martha's rectangle, before they took up their spades and dug over the pasture. She'd wedged two large stones under the Empire's front wheels. John was kicking his legs about, blowing wet raspberries – his latest trick.

'We're off to London, next week.' Emily forced her spade into the ground with her foot and cleaved the turf apart. 'To view a small apartment that's come up in Grandmother's mansion block. It will suit Mother.'

They worked on together, side by side, until John grew irritable and she took him for a stroll towards the sheep.

Later on, after a ploughman's lunch at the Wheatsheaf, they walked back to the station and they got to reminiscing about the old days with the land girls.

'I nearly forgot to say. Hen is to be wed,' Martha said.

'Hen? She wanted to go to agricultural college, but then she did miss her tennis parties.'

They hugged up close to the hedgerow as the bus chugged down the lane. 'It's easy to slip back into the old way of things,' Martha said.

'Well, I'm glad you didn't,' Emily said.

Once they were at the station, the guard helped John and the pram onto the carriage.

'Come and see us again soon,' Martha called as the train pulled away. 'My plot is yours too.'

Before long, John dozed off again. The afternoon began to draw in and instead of the fields, her own reflection grew stronger in the window.

A gentleman in a morning suit and top hat read *The Times* in the seat opposite her. Discreetly she snatched glances of herself. Her hair had worked free of its coil. She had tufts reminiscent of Mrs Tipton's. She inspected her blouse; it was covered in soil. Mud had lodged itself under her fingernails. Her skin had that same radiant glow that she would have at the end of the day as a land girl.

It wouldn't be long, and she'd be by Martha's side.

Emily had lost the thread of the conversation. She was too busy keeping an eye on John, as he was passed around Grandmother's sitting room like a prize marrow at the Chartleigh vegetable competition.

The Welfare for the Poor Committee meeting had come to the end of its business and Mother was at the heart of the discussion, boasting about how soundly John slept and Emily's war effort. The sale to Wilfred had been called off. HopBine was back on the market.

Grandmother wore the largest hat in the room, piled high with glossy fruits. Under the hooped rim, she had the largest hair roll too. Her skirts were the fullest. Her boot heels the sharpest. The tips the pointiest. Her voice the loudest, most forceful. But since she'd discovered that she lived on the spoils of a war profiteer, she planned to move somewhere smaller, more modest, less desirable.

Nothing had changed in the months since they'd first come to London. They were coming towards the end of the year, and the end of the decade and yet everyone was stuck in the past. The women still complained about the lack of servants and still hadn't caught on to the idea that they would have to start to do things for themselves. They'd soon learn how easy it could be to dress oneself, or put the kettle on the range but how tiring it was to black that range or shine the brass, and what caged birds their servants had been for all these years.

'Such a terrible shame, isn't it?' said one of the ladies quietly to her neighbour while passing the baby on. Both ladies glanced at Emily. She fiddled with her wedding band. She was wearing it today as an outward show of respectability as the widow they all thought her to be. To her it was nothing more than a gleaming reminder of her mistakes.

It was unlikely anyone believed she'd really been widowed, but she'd rather not talk about what had happened. If it ever got out Mabel might lose Theo too, if he was sent to prison.

John complained at being held up to the light by yet another lady with raven-like feathers on her hat. Grandmother asked her companion to take him outside for a breath of fresh air.

'We've heard what your mother thought of the apartment, but what about you, Emily dear?' Grandmother said.

'Yes. It was ... comfortable,' Emily answered.

'Well appointed,' Grandmother countered. 'Near to your mother's friends. Cecil can conduct his journalism from here, and it's also very convenient for the parks for young John. And available straight away.'

'Yes.' It was true. The apartment offered all of those things. Mother was happier here in London, around a variety of friends. It suited her. She'd done her best to meld with the doctors, solicitors and clergy in rural life, but it was amongst these people in the salons where Mother really belonged. It wouldn't take long before she'd be enjoying her London social life, and Emily would be left at home all day with John.

But while the battered Empire's wheels ran more smoothly on the neat paths of the park, it was a poor substitute for the countryside. It wasn't the life she wanted for John, or herself. Mrs Tipton had all but packed up. Percy Greenacre was to take over the farm until a buyer was found and a new manager appointed.

'We might view a few more places while we're here,' Emily said. A garden mews was out of their reach but to be near a park would be something.

'The windows let in so much light, and there's a view of Hyde Park all along one side.' Mother broke away from her conversation to chip in. 'But if you want to keep searching ...'

'We'll have to wait, until we have a firm buyer, before we make a final decision,' Emily said, which reminded her – she checked her watch. Her escort for the evening was due any time now.

Emily left Grandmother's flat wrapped in a silk shawl, eyes trained on the fourth-floor window, as the cab pulled away.

'I'm sure the baby is in good hands,' Captain Ellery said. She'd been lucky to catch him in town. His work with the committee for East End soldiers occupied most of his time. 'Now, first things first, no more of this Captain Ellery nonsense. We're friends – please call me Thomas.'

He was leaning in towards her, but she kept her eyes forward towards the front seat.

'Do you remember the silence in the teahouse when you called me Thomas?'

Their laughter filled the car, but the memory of the way he'd behaved towards her when they'd last met still stung her.

'Very well, Thomas. But you still haven't told me what we're going to see,' she said. Was he still in love? Grandmother hadn't said any more about it.

'*Monsieur Beaucaire* at the Palace Theatre. I think you'll like it.'

His voice was stronger, more certain now, and he was right: she should enjoy herself. When had she last done that?

'Grandmother mentioned you were still on the hunt for a property,' she said.

They sat in the stalls, five rows back, right in the centre. She crossed her legs so that they couldn't touch Ellery's.

In the front row was a young man, not very high in his seat. Her view of him was obscured, but his smoothed-down sandy-coloured hair and his handsome nose, made him the spit of Theo. Just as the play was about to begin a tall gentleman sat right in front of Emily, and kept his hat on, which blocked her view of the centre of the stage. As it happened this was where most of the action took place, and also concealed the front row and the man sitting there.

At the interval Thomas had noticed she'd been craning and offered to swap seats. She took up her new spot, one seat along. The man from the front row had left his seat in the interval. She scanned the queue behind the usherette, but he wasn't there.

The theatre was a bit too bright and garish: the golden cherubs, the red velvet curtains. It struck her as rather like being inside the devil's belly.

'What do you think about the play?' Thomas asked on his return from the usherette.

'I'm enjoying it.' She'd read Tarkington's novel when she worked on the farm. The barber that Lady Mary was in love with would turn out to really be the King of France. 'Thomas?' She trained her eyes on the stage. If she didn't come right out with it the whole evening would pass and she wouldn't have asked what she'd come here to say. 'Would you consider coming to Kent to view our estate? The house would be perfect for your ex-soldiers. There are eight bedrooms and the cottages down on Perseverance Place would house the same again.'

'No,' Thomas said, ruffling his moustache. 'It's not the area I've been concentrating my search. I've seen a property that would suit the men in Hertfordshire.'

'So, there's nothing wrong with the property itself. HopBine,' she said waiting for his response.

As she suspected he flinched at the name.

'Are you afraid to face it?' she said.

'I don't know what you mean,' he said. 'From what you've told me, there's more land there than we need, or could afford to run.'

'That's not the case, Thomas – you've been there. It made a ten-bed convalescent home during the war – you were there. Why won't you talk about it?'

His expression hardened. 'What are you insinuating? You're too late that's all. As I say we've got surveyors going out to Hertfordshire. It wouldn't be right to muddy the waters with another property, no matter how suitable you think it might be.'

'Or how desperate we are for it to fall into the right hands.'

Thomas closed his eyes. Breathed deeply.

'You've nothing to be afraid of,' she said, holding his arm. 'You're so much more alive than the broken man I first met. You won't become him if you go back.'

'The funds we have to rehabilitate the men would be drained by maintenance costs on a place like that.'

She folded her arms. Her father had dreamt of HopBine being a home that would provide for his family and the community; it would be simply the perfect place for those men.

'Emily, you've put up a worthy fight for your family home,' Thomas said. 'But you will find an interested party, someone prepared to make it sound.'

'Or raze it to the ground.'

'Perhaps. But it just doesn't sound practical for our needs. I am sorry.'

The man from the front row was back. He had his head turned away from her while he spoke with a woman. The embers ignited. Could it really be Theo? She sat forwards in her chair. Waiting, waiting. His head faced forwards now, as he contemplated the path back to his seat. He did have brown eyes. A kind face, a handsome nose. But it wasn't Theo. A bucket of water drenched her. She must be losing her mind if her best hope was to be reunited with her bigamist husband.

'The barber character makes a good comic.' Thomas returned to the operetta.

'He's a bit silly if you ask me,' she snapped. 'The whole play was a bad choice.' He was being stubborn beyond measure, and he wouldn't even try to help when she needed him most. She folded her arms tight.

Thomas shifted about in his seat. He was pretending his ice cream was fascinating. Licking it into a round. Admiring it as it glistened against the backdrop of the velvet curtains. What was there left to say? If she asked him again to come to Kent, the answer would still be no.

She didn't want to be in London. Stuck in these stalls watching this frivolous play. Life as she knew it and wanted it was coming to a close and here she was hiding, drinking tea, viewing apartments, finding that her friend wasn't such a good one after all, and accepting that John would never meet his father.

The bell rang, two insistent drills: ten minutes until the show began again.

'I'm very sorry, Thomas,' she said. 'I feel I ought to check on John. I haven't left him this long before.' They pushed their knees to one side to let a train of people squeeze past and go back to their seats. 'I'm afraid I'm going to worry during the second half.'

He was on his feet and had her back at Grandmother's apartment without another word passing between them.

Chapter Thirty-Six

October 1919

The agent had shown some prospective buyers around the house, but they had relayed that the need for repairs was too great. The house would need to be pulled down. Emily persuaded Mother not to write and tell Uncle Wilfred, thankful she was there to intercept her. They would just have to hold an auction, which was a risk but one that guaranteed them a sale and an end to the waiting.

She edged the pram towards the ditch at the rattling approach of a car. The vehicle slowed as it passed her, and the driver wound down the window.

'Hello there!' the driver said, the green of his eyes shining in the sunlight. 'I found you.'

'Thomas!'

He had a map open on the passenger seat.

Her delight faded. She'd been so irritable and rude towards him at the theatre. She didn't deserve his forgiveness or his friendship. When he'd dropped her off at Grandmother's flat she hadn't even thanked him for taking her out, or apologised for cutting the evening short.

'You we were right,' he called through the window. 'I ought to at least consider your property. Especially if you think it might have potential.'

Her heart started to thump in her chest, not just at the possibility of what this might mean for HopBine's future, but what it meant for Thomas. He was back, facing down his demons and that had to be a good thing.

'The agent is already up at the house with an elderly couple who will no doubt complain that the roof needs fixing.'

'I'd like it if you could you show me around,' he said. 'I saw that the big house – Finch Hall – is sold?'

'To my uncle, but he can't put his plans into action without our farmland that offers access to the river.'

'And what of the family there?'

'Lady Radford is staying with friends; Lady Clara is to be married to her French sweetheart. They met in the war, while she was running a hospital near to Paris. They've been separated all this time, and then a chance meeting reunited them.'

'How romantic,' he said. And then his footsteps slowed. He took her hands. His were soft and warm, his green eyes twinkling in the sunshine. She pulled her hands away.

'You really do make the most delicious Turkish delight. Did I mention that before?'

'So you did remember me?'

He grinned. 'I was difficult with you. I'm sorry. I just wanted to forget everything about my time here. I wanted to hide from what a terrible wreck I was, and I thought if you remembered me as that man, slumped and listless and afraid of the door slamming shut, then you wouldn't look at me in the same way.'

'Of course I knew it was you, I understand.'

'But you got me thinking, after I dropped you back at your grandmother's. It was here that I began to recover. I left here with hope in my heart; partly put there by you and in part by whatever healing magic is in the air here.'

She was close enough to kiss him. She'd helped to make him better and well enough so that he could fall in love with another girl.

'What's the matter?' he said.

'Grandmother mentioned you'd fallen in love.'

'Ah. Yes. I told my mother about this girl I'd met in London, but she was already married, expecting a baby, and living with an unpleasant uncle. She had enough on her mind.'

If she closed her eyes, and let her face drift closer … no. Not yet. It could wait. She held his hand now, stroked the skin with her thumb.

'I can't stop myself from smiling,' she said.

'Me neither,' he replied. 'Let's not.'

Hand in hand they walked on.

'So were you treated at the Finch Hall hospital?' She eventually found some words and settled in to find out what he'd held back from her all this time.

'That's right. A shrapnel injury to my thigh, but I had shell shock too, though my CO wouldn't have it – they wanted me back at the Front. I wasn't here long enough. My favourite spot was there.' He pointed to the monkey puzzle tree. 'The nurse would wheel me out for a quick shot of winter daylight.'

'Oh dear,' she said, putting a hand to her mouth. 'I've just remembered. I sang, didn't I? "Silent Night".'

'I was going to be a gentleman and not bring that up. But I will say I still think your Turkish delight is very good.'

She rolled her eyes at him.

'The funny thing is, in my mind, this place was exactly what I wanted for the soldiers we're going to help through the charity. It was so restorative here, a much-needed pause. I'm not sure I would have made it through that last stretch without being here, and my all-too-brief encounter with an out-of-tune young woman, with straw in her hair, mud on her face and a blissful contentment I'd never seen before, or since.'

He pulled her closer, rested his hands on her waist. 'Thank you,' he said, 'for storming out of the theatre.'

'That's all right,' she joked.

'Emily, before you get your hopes up, I should tell you that we're still short of investment. We can't commit to buy anywhere until we have more funds in place.'

'It's still worth you viewing it though.'

'Of course; if we need more capital then we'll simply have to get it.'

They strolled up the driveway together.

'So. I'm trying frantically to recall everything you told me about the house and apply it here. Your father designed the place?' he prompted.

'He pulled the last house to the ground and had this built,' she began. She parked John by the front door and then took Thomas around the other side to the lawn, the rose garden and once there she scrambled up on to the boundary wall. 'He changed the entrance so we had more privacy and closed the lane down there so that New Lane was built and then he added the cedars. He wanted us to feel as though he'd sewn us our own little pocket.'

'It is a safe haven from all of that.' He gestured towards the horizon.

'Father's biggest project was the farm. He had no idea on the day-to-day running of it and left that to the Tiptons. But he redeveloped it – new buildings, new orchards, everything a gentleman farmer could aspire to own – and had ideas about retiring it and running it, but knowing what I know now, he wouldn't have lasted five minutes.'

She wanted to take him down to the farmhouse to meet Mrs Tipton, Lily and Sally and the Fordson lurking in the cart shed. She jumped down from the wall and approached the rose garden.

When she glanced up, Thomas smiled at her.

'It seems like a lifetime ago that I made Turkish delight,' she said.

'Well I'm glad you shook me out of myself and brought me back here. You …'

'What is it?'

'A raincloud followed you around when you were last in London.'

'It did,' she replied.

'Then you shouldn't be there,' he said.

'I can't leave Mother, yet. I will, eventually, but only when I'm sure she's ready.'

She put her hands in her pockets, began to walk back to the front of the house. John would be stirring soon, but she stopped at the corner.

'Do you remember that I told you about Martha and her women's colony over at Lingfield? I can't get out of my head how something similar could work here at HopBine to give the soldiers a trade. You could turn the lawn and the paddock into plots for the men to work. Eleanor and Miss Wilkes could advise us. Your ex-officer committee could roll up their sleeves and make the repairs to the house.'

Thomas was nodding, surveying the land around him.

'You could employ some ex-land girls,' she continued, 'to work alongside the men, learn a trade from the women in the fresh air they need so much.' She was talking too quickly, and he was smiling at her, shielding his eyes from the sun. 'The profits could be shared between the soldiers themselves for their families, and the rest could go towards running the place.'

She stopped to catch her breath. What would he say? Another outright no? But he was here, wasn't he?

'And the farm?' he asked.

'The farm needs a new manager and the ex-soldiers and land girls could work for him.'

A collared dove waddled along the bridge of the wall. Its mate flew overhead.

He didn't say anything, but she'd expected that. Thomas was

284

cautious, the sort to weigh things up before jumping in, but she had got him thinking, and that was enough for now. Back at the front of the house, Mother had already lifted John out of the carriage and hugged him close to her chest.

'What do you think of the place?' Mother asked.

'I stayed here for a short while, during the war,' Thomas told her. 'When I emerged from those trees I had the overwhelming sense that I was coming home.'

*

Dear Uncle Wilfred

You can never make amends for your decision to prioritise profits during the war, but I have a suggestion that might help you to at least redress the balance. As you know, Grandmother began a committee to help soldiers in the East End whose lives are at risk because of injuries sustained during the war. The ex-officers she rounded up would like to buy the HopBine Estate and the men will now call this place their home.

More investment is needed to turn the land over so that the men can not just live, but work at HopBine too. There would be no return on your investment, other than perhaps to show your mother and mine that there is some good in you after all.

Your niece

Emily

Chapter Thirty-Seven

November 1919

There was still so much to do in their last remaining days at HopBine. They returned from a shopping trip to London for curtains and new furniture for the Belgravia flat, to be welcomed by an empty echo in the hallway. Few of their belongings were there any longer to absorb their footsteps and voices, many of the rooms were shut up, and much of the furniture had been taken to auction while they'd been in London.

At the end of the week they would move to London permanently so that the team of ex-officers could begin their repairs.

They cleared out cupboard after cupboard, unearthing treasures long forgotten. But no matter what they put into boxes, they couldn't take it all with them. The stories, the family folktales were everywhere, and nowhere. Their walls didn't so much talk, they breathed; inhaling the memories, exhaling them in fragments of golden dust. What would happen without the four walls of HopBine to keep them safe? Would they simply drift away?

They left her brother John's room until last. They emptied it together; the three of them. His jumpers were folded for the Salvation Army, just as Mother had done for Father. They reduced

John's life down to a small box. Photographs, dog-eared and browned *Boy's Own* magazines, a mouth organ, his spotter's guides to birds and trees. His diary from the war.

'Why are you keeping those?' she asked Mother, pointing at a frayed box of toy soldiers.

'I thought your John might like to play with them, when he's older.'

'No,' she said. 'Let's not.' She would bury them in the garden, and she had just the spot.

*

Visitors called to say their goodbyes. Told them they would be missed, thanked them for not selling to the highest bidder, saving the village from Uncle Wilfred's vision, and opening the estate and the village up to ex-war heroes.

Norah Peters called by with news.

'So, have you heard about the Radfords then?' Norah said. The news that Finch Hall had been mortgaged in the depression before the war was commonplace now. Tax, interest rates and death duties had crippled the Radfords too. Uncle Wilfred had quickly sold it on to an educational consortium who were to convert it to a private school. 'About Lady Clara?'

Emily shook her head.

'It's terribly sad. Clara Radford's French sweetheart suffered from some complications to his war injury, and he died. Lady Clara has cried for a week. She's home with Mother, except she's not home of course. The poor things no longer have one. They're living at a hotel, and then Clara is to take up the duty of her mother's travelling companion on a trip to Pompeii. Such a shame when you consider all that family did for the war.'

Norah shook her head. Emily shuddered for poor Clara. The war had given her so much opportunity, and now she would be carrying her mother's bags around the streets of Italy.

By the end of the week, Emily's throat and eyes were sore with dust. Her knees ached from kneeling and just when she wanted to sleep for a week, they were finished.

Mother's skirt bounced as she strode around. Her laughter filled the house; her skin had the sheen of a younger woman. Emily often came across her humming to herself.

Thomas had taken on board her suggestion; he'd enlisted the help of Cecil's suffragettes and he was going to turn the farm into a colony. All the key people had come together at HopBine. The dining room buzzed with the chatter and ideas. Thomas had wanted her there, but she'd found a buyer for the Fordson and needed to help Mrs Tipton to sell it.

*

The tractor's interested party was from a neighbouring farm, the other side of West Malling. He wanted a demonstration. While John slept in his pram, Emily cranked up the engine and then climbed astride it, the motor chugging away. While Mrs Tipton gave the farmer the patter about the drastic improvements it would make to productivity she steered it around the farmyard.

'It's a dream to drive,' she yelled over the engine. She was so busy, craning the wrong way that she had to swerve as a horse trotted into the yard. It was the velvet-brown coat of Hawk. Such an elegant stallion, his head always high, he headed straight for the barn.

'Mother!'

Mother sat astride Hawk. She clicked her heels and brought the horse to a stop outside the stables and waved to Emily as the tractor took another lap, and then another. The buyer was convinced, a roll of notes pulled from his rear pocket, which would set Mrs Tipton up nicely for her retirement. Emily killed the engine.

Mother applauded her. 'Masterful,' she said. 'Quite masterful!'

'He remembered me,' Mother said, stroking Hawk's mane as she clipped over. How could Mother have thought it would be any other way? 'And now I'm in love with him all over again. I'm going to ask Thomas if they could afford to keep him on so the soldiers can ride him and perhaps we can visit from time to time. I neglected you, didn't I, boy.'

*

Emily parked the Empire outside the farmhouse. Male laughter escaped the kitchen window. It was probably Percy Greenacre. He was the most likely to be appointed the new manager, and was probably visiting to fit his furniture for size.

She'd come back later. She was just wheeling the pram away when Mrs Tipton called from the window: 'Coo-ee. Where are you off to without saying hello? I've someone here to meet you. Says he was a seasonal worker on the farm one summer, but I'm damned if I can place him.'

Inside, Mrs Tipton was on the sofa warming her toes in front of the crackling fire. Emily peeled off her coat, hung it behind the door and was about to greet the chap with a cheery beam, when she stopped short. It wasn't an old labourer at all. She yelped and leapt backwards, standing on Sally's tail and making her shriek too.

'You remember him then?' Mrs Tipton asked.

'I would say.' She held on to the table for stability. 'He's my husband.'

'Theo?' The colour drained from Mrs Tipton's face. 'You, you rotten little weasel. I'd have never made you a tea if I'd known.'

'I came to speak to Emily – I owe her an explanation,' Theo said.

'It's a bit late for that, Theo. Your wife already wrote to me and told me what sort of a man you are. How could you? It was all lies from the very beginning.'

'You deserve better.' He hung his head. Yes. She did. 'I wasn't a well man for a long while. It's no excuse, for what I did,' he continued. 'I woke up every day thinking it could be my last, or the end for some poor sod over the other side of the battlefield, who I had to kill. Or not knowin' if I was going to witness another friend blown to bits. It wasn't easy finding a way to live with all that. And then a bright girl like you wrote to me, filled with all the romance of your life in the country, and I got caught up in it all. Ended up living two lives at once, but neither could save me from the trenches.'

'I ought to call the police,' Emily said, gripping the table now. 'You could go to prison.'

'Shall I leave you two to talk?' asked Mrs Tipton. Emily nodded. 'I'll just be next door in the parlour.'

'It's been more than a year, Theo,' Emily said once the door was shut. 'Cecil still has a scar.'

'If he's here, I'd like to say sorry to him.'

She froze for a moment. Was it really Theo? His handsome nose and melting eyes. His eyebrows edging forwards, the etched line between them deepening. He was shabbier now he wasn't in his uniform. His jacket frayed around the lapels.

She snapped to attention. 'I need to get on,' she said. 'We're leaving for London tomorrow.'

'I don't blame you if you can't forgive me. But I'd like to hold my son.'

'Perhaps he's better off without you,' she said.

'I understand if you can't forgive me. But I can't leave without seeing the baby. Now, Emily, you wouldn't keep a man from his son, would you?'

It was tempting, but she couldn't do it. Although he'd been the one who'd kept himself from John. He'd been the one who'd deserted her, not the other way around.

'I can send you a photograph.'

'I'd like that, but it's not the same, is it? Come on, Emily. I've come all this way. Where is he?'

She must have jerked her head, or twitched her eyes, because Theo had sidestepped her and pushed the kitchen door open.

'Just let me hold him,' he whispered, 'and then, I promise you if it's what you want, I'll be gone. I won't bother you if you don't want bothering. I owe you that.'

'Wait,' she called, but he shrugged her hand from his arm.

The chickens rushed over to them as they approached the Empire in the yard. His arm brushed hers as they leant in. Their hands connected as she slid the baby into his arms.

'Be careful with him.'

Theo whimpered. 'Christ,' he said. 'Christ alive.' The tears poured down his cheeks. His face crumpled. His nose ran.

'What? Theo? What is it?'

'He's the spitting image of my mother. I'm sorry,' Theo said. He held the baby close; his hands wrung the blanket. 'I'm sorry for everything. I did want to marry you, and I did love you. That was all real. It was all such a tangle up here.' He tapped the side of his head. She believed him, but there had been other lies too.

'You asked when we first met if Mother had enough money to go around. You asked me questions about the estate; how much it was worth. Was that part of the attraction?'

He didn't answer.

He reached out a hand from John and stroked her face. She shut her eyes. 'I missed you,' he whispered. 'My wife, Mabel, we married so young. We don't love each other and that's as true as I'm standing here. We married because she was expecting, the war was coming, and I did the right thing in case I didn't come back, so she could get my pension. We've two beautiful children to show for our trouble, but not much else. We never were happy together, properly, not like when we first met. Do you remember that? As soon as you wrote to me, I knew you were something special, that I couldn't let you go. And look at this beauty.'

He rocked John in his arms. Mrs Tipton spied on them from the window.

'If you'd told me the truth at the beginning ...' Even then she wouldn't have taken another woman's husband, or children's father.

'I had to go back,' he said. 'Face up to what I'd done. And then you wrote and told Mabel about the boy and I knew then what a shambles I'd made of everything.'

She nodded. She couldn't argue with that.

'He's a beautiful baby. I'd like him to know me, to be part of his life.' Tears ran down his face again. She took John from him while he pulled out a hankie.

'I slept last night in the farmhouse barn,' he said. Her spine tingled; he'd been lurking around the village all day. 'Can I see you and the baby again?'

'We leave tomorrow,' she said.

'Mrs Tipton said that there's not been a decision on who will take over here. It was always your dream for us, wasn't it? It still could be – we could manage it together.'

'Percy Greenacre is a capable pair of hands. If you'll excuse me, I've got things to do,' she said.

'Sleep on it,' he said. 'You might feel different in the morning.'

He took her hand and rubbed the skin where her wedding ring had been. The indentation had all but gone now. She would hardly know it had been there at all.

'Bring your ring tomorrow, meet me by the river, and I'll know that you're mine again,' he said.

She went to bed amongst a shadow city of boxes. In the morning, vans would arrive ready to ferry them to London and Theo would be waiting for her.

*

Emily was the first to wake on their last day at HopBine, if she'd even been asleep at all. Thomas had called her before she went to bed, so animated with his plans for the estate, so many questions for her.

She dressed quietly so as not to wake the baby, and then gently pushed the bassinet into Mother's room. Theo might be already down by the old mill, but he'd kept her waiting and now it was her turn.

She clambered up the old oak tree, until Joe came out the kitchen door after breakfast, and then she crossed the field and the stile down to the farmyard. Sally barked in greeting when she knocked on the kitchen door.

Mrs Tipton beckoned her into the farmhouse. The range was already going and the windows were coated in steam. Sally rested her head on her paws on the hearthrug. The two of them sat across from one another at the kitchen table.

'What will you do with your retirement?' Emily asked.

'I don't know.' Mrs Tipton shrugged. 'I'll stay with my cousin for a while, down near Lenham. She says I'm to come for a rest. Something'll turn up. Life usually works that way.'

Mrs Tipton would never ease up – she'd go mad with boredom.

'This place is all we've known really,' Mrs Tipton continued. 'Been here since we were first wed. Lord Radford took us on back when they owned the land.'

Emily swallowed hard, trying to force the tightness in her throat away. 'Now come on. You've lots to look forward to.'

Did she?

'In time, your mother won't need you.'

The question was, how much time? How long would it take before Mother would let her go? Mother had made tiny steps since they'd returned to HopBine and then Uncle Wilfred's reappearance had knocked her back to where they'd started.

Mrs Tipton reached her hand across the table and squeezed Emily's. 'It comforts me to think that Mr Tipton might have clapped eyes on you up on the orchard before he was taken away. And that he wasn't alone when he passed.'

'I'm glad too,' Emily said, dragging in a breath.

She searched for Theo in the cart shed behind the wain.

'Are you there?' she said one last time. She tutted. Why did her encounters with Theo always leave her sure that she'd dreamt him up? So much for waiting for her. He'd most likely run out on her again.

It was there, hidden in the hay, behind the wooden wheel. She ducked into the shadows, down on her haunches, cleared the straw away. Theo's knapsack. She wasn't too late. She pulled it out; worn, limp and insubstantial. Hardly much to show for a lifetime, nothing like the volume of belongings they'd waved goodbye to that morning. But what did any of that count for in the end? Their things weren't what made them rich, or poor.

As she left the shed she nearly collided with him in the yard, where he cradled John in his arms.

They walked in silence, the three of them, Theo still holding on to John. Across the yard, through the orchard until they reached Sunnyside. On a few of the trees the pure-white apple blossom had been tricked into coming out early, but now the weather had turned colder again and it was caught on the branches. They cut down the track to the old paper mill and the stream.

'I'm sorry,' Theo said. He was unshaven. Had grime on his face. His mouth was all puckered up with regret and despair. He was nothing like the man in his photograph, the man she'd married.

'Don't be. It's over with now.'

'I've made some stupid mistakes. The biggest of all was lying to you. But I don't want to keep moving, running away. I want to put things right.'

Emily smoothed her skirt beneath her and sat on a fallen trunk. This was where the water grew shallow and you could cross to the other side. They'd paddled in it as children. Feet anchored on algae-smooth stones, eyes trained on the green-hued water waiting to spear fish with sharpened branches. It's where she'd chased after Lily, Rosie and Lolly and where Sally had saved her.

Just around the bend the sudden change was dangerous. The water deepened, picked up its pace. The babbling gave way to a gush, a slight decline in the level, and the water was sent down, past the old mill and on to the main river.

'We could run this place together,' Theo said, spinning to his feet and grabbing her left hand. He snatched her hands and smoothed them with his own fingertips. She was on her feet. Fell into his arms. His embrace was warm and comforting. She sunk into it and back in to Bournemouth on that cold day on the beach, when he'd slept on the floor of their hotel room.

'I love you, Emily,' he said. She hadn't dreamt it. It had all been real, and those embers had kept their heat because he needed to meet John.

She dipped her head to the ground. And then she pulled inside her pocket and took out the gold band that the stranger who'd been Theo's best man had guarded for him on their wedding day. It had passed from the stranger to Theo and Theo had given it to her. They'd been a chain of strangers who'd all since scattered to the wind.

He took the ring from her palm and held it between his fore-finger and thumb. He splayed her left hand. She was trembling like she'd been on that day in the church. Her ring finger stayed flat. She didn't raise it taller than the others, so the ring would slip on. He wanted her help. But her hand fell out of his grip, and her fingertips closed to her palm.

He didn't know her, he didn't know what she'd been through, or what her family had lost.

She took the ring, put it on his palm and curled his fingers around it and then stood up from the trunk, bent to kiss him on the cheek. 'I don't blame you,' she said. She lifted John from his arms and rested him on her hip. 'But your family need you more than I do. And at least now you know where to find your boy.'

Theo kissed John on the forehead, smoothed his son's hair. Emily shrank back as he leant in towards her. He stayed on the trunk, knees high, and lit his pipe. Puffs of the sweet aroma sickened the clean air.

As she walked back up the hill, a golden hum filled the air, and then the most delicate of splashes. The wedding ring had left barely a ripple in the stream.

*

It was so quiet, just John gurgling and birds singing in the trees. The front door was closed tight behind her and Mother sat on the front step, bouncing John on her knee. Three suitcases by her boots. One for each of them.

The delivery vans, packed with the boxes, had left to go ahead of them up to London. All that was left was the Empire and the dinner plates from which they'd eaten a cheese and ham sandwich ahead of their train.

'There you are,' Mother said. 'I was beginning to worry.'

'I've laid a posy of dahlias and lit a candle at the shrine,' she told her. 'Theo is here.'

'I know,' Mother said. 'He just saw Cecil before he caught his train to Cardiff.' There was an uprising in Wales and Cecil had been recruited by an activist group to report on it for their pamphlet. 'Theo apologised to him. But the man's no less a criminal because he said sorry.'

Emily tugged her suit jacket tight around her.

The hum of a car engine came along New Lane, took a breath and then continued to grow louder before it emerged at the top of the cedar avenue.

Sally had been following her around all morning. How was

she ever going to say goodbye to the collie? The poor unsuspecting thing would lose two masters in quick succession.

'I called Mr Hughes to ask for a lift,' Mother said.

Emily stared at the Empire. It wouldn't fit in the car. The elephant grey was scratched to white on the pram's sides and the hood's metal jaw was so stiff it needed greasing, but it was the only place that John would sleep or play and pushing him about the London parks had been about the only thing she was looking forward to.

'Thomas called late last night,' Emily told Mother as Mr Hughes leapt out of his car. She still hadn't got used to not calling him Captain Ellery. Mr Hughes lifted Mother's case. 'Mother, he asked me to manage the farm and the colony for him. There is so much he needs to learn.'

'I'm sure there is. It's a big undertaking. Ambitious too.' Mother handed her the baby and nodded to Mr Hughes. He slid the suitcase into the boot. Then returned and lifted Emily's and John's cases. 'And what did you say to Thomas?' Mother asked.

'I said that I would love nothing more than to be the manager.' She swallowed. 'But as long as it was a joint position with Martha, so we can share our duties and care of this one, and of course only if you were to say that you could cope in your new flat alone.'

She laid John in the pram and he grumbled at being abandoned.

Mother called to Mr Hughes. 'Leave those two here,' she said pointing to the suitcases. And then to Emily: 'You've always been impossible – I hope Thomas knows what he's in for.'

Before Emily could check whether Mother would be all right without her she pulled Emily to her, squeezing her tight. Emily buried her nose in the sweet-pea scent of Mother's shoulders and closed her eyes while Mother rubbed her back.

Mr Hughes was back in the driving seat. The engine was running now.

Mother let her go, kissed baby John softly and patted Sally. Then she climbed into the car, and was gone.

'I don't know,' Emily said to Sally. 'It's just as well that I had accepted the job. Hadn't it occurred to Mother that we would never get the pram in Mr Hughes' car?'

Chapter Thirty-Eight

December 1919

The weather was icy cold, and up on the ladder it blew across the orchard and tickled her face.

'Now let's look at you.' She took in the top of the apple tree. They were late with the pruning this year. She had to move fast before the trees fell into their deep winter slumber.

A letter from Mother had arrived that morning; she'd fallen in with a circle of war widows who accompanied one another on trips to the theatre and concerts. There were parties all over town. As they stood on the eve of a new decade, the silence that had roared in their ears now stood aside for music and laughter. That was how Mother told it anyway.

Nothing much ever changed in the countryside. The birds still sang, the grass still rattled and the leaves still rustled.

She tapped her secateurs back along the branch to the growth from 1918, slotted them around it and snipped. A single fieldfare landed on a branch just beneath her. She didn't move. There were individual speckled feathers on the bird's chest where the wind lifted through them. It was a mute-coloured female, her head darting to and fro. The rest of her flock chattered at the bases of the trees eating the windfall fruit that no one else wanted that year.

John sat up in the Empire. A chubby prince surveying his kingdom, Sally by the wheels, his guard dog. Emily had given him some branches to wave about. He flapped an arm, pleased with himself, and disturbed the bird. It chack-chacked down to the others who in turn alighted together and swept across the paddock.

She snipped at another branch, and then another. Her pruning bundle was building up nicely, alongside Martha's from the adjacent tree.

A familiar figure came across the orchard towards her, stopping to coo at John before carrying on. She clipped off the tip of one last branch, but the pruning could wait. She hooked her secateurs back on her belt, and descended the ladder. Tucked her hair behind her ears. Smoothed the ends. Straightened out her breeches.

'How's it going?' she asked.

'The men are settling in well to the house.' Thomas greeted her with a peck to the cheek. Her eyes closed. His skin on hers was so soft. 'They're having lunch. Would you and John come up and say hello? We don't want to overwhelm them, but I'd like to introduce your ideas for the plots as soon as possible. The sooner they're thinking about what they want to grow and how they'll make their mark, the sooner this will start to feel like home.'

He'd been so busy since he'd moved in to HopBine and taken over as the centre's manager. He had lists pinned to every wall, and so many friends visiting and contributing: ideas, funds and equipment. All of it welcomed and all of it received into Thomas's opened arms.

'I'll be up there with my seed potatoes and plot plans as soon as they've unpacked the suitcases. While they're unpacking if you like?'

300

They'd ensure those soldiers settled and loved the place as much as they did. Leaving Martha to work, Thomas pushed John down the aisle of fruit trees towards the village. Sally gave a superior glance at Rover and followed Emily.

When they turned into Forge Lane, they followed the track that led to the centre of the village.

The war memorial had been built in a month so it was ready for Armistice Day. It was more personal than the Cenotaph in London – the huge white coffin of the unknown soldier, which had become the national monument to grief and loss.

There's was simple: a stone with the name of every villager lost etched into it. Including John Cotham. A fitting memorial at the end of a quiet track. A place where the people who had known, loved and respected their boys passed by every day.

Further down the lane was a holly bush. She threaded her hand amongst the violently red berries. Mrs Tipton would say this meant a cold, hard winter, which would mean a wonderful blossom on the apple trees come the spring.

She pinched a stem between thumb and forefinger and walked at a slow steady pace back down the lane. She laid the sprig, with its barbed leaves and scarlet berries, at the foot of the memorial and then gazed up at the sky. Thomas had closed his eyes. She shut hers too. And, when she opened them again, Thomas was there, waiting.

Historical Note

The women's movement really sprang into action at the end of World War I. Positive steps forward in the workplace made by wartime women began to move backwards. In recognition of their war effort, pockets of land were given over to women who had worked the land. A colony for ex-land girls was set up in Lingfield in Sussex, funded by a suffragette, although it was established later than I have written it here. Sadly, mainly due to issues around housing, by the 1930s these projects had largely disappeared.

Acknowledgements

The first round of thanks go to Hannah Smith for her invaluable editorial input and support, and to both Hannah and Victoria Oundjian for seeing the potential in my idea in the first place. Also, to the team behind the novel, with notable thanks to Anna and Helena.

Next thanks to my writing group. Tanya Gupta for suggesting I went back in time from the thirties, and for sharing your knitting expertise. Sue Wilsher for help with the decision on whether to include *that* word in the finished novel, and to you both for your moral and practical support, as well as being there for the highs, lows and the gin.

During my research for this novel Hadlow College, The Women's Library Reading Room at London School of Economics were particularly helpful.

Ralph Ruge for checking the German language and to my early readers; Jane Everett, Kerry Postle, Freda Burnside and Sian Pullen. And to my fellow land girls from Hadlow College – Jo, Sophie and Nancy – for listening to my ideas while we pruned, dug and planted.

Thanks to my mum, for being my mum.

To Evie and Dylan for feeding themselves when I approached my deadline, and Andy for checking locations of battles and regiments, and because without your support I couldn't have written this story.

Read on for a sneak peek of

The Lido Girls …

Chapter One

The naughty boy

*After gambolling to the edge of the board,
the diver bounces from it in a seated position, using her
behind to propel her into the air.*

Natalie turned the key in her bedroom door, once for the latch, twice for the deadbolt. She tugged at the depressed handle, and only when the door was clearly locked tight did she drop to her knees and pull out a package from beneath her narrow bed.

Inside the cardboard box, cradled in crinkly tissue paper, was a white V-necked blouse adorned with the black silhouette of a lady mid leap, and beneath it a pair of black satin shorts. The uniform of the Women's League of Health and Beauty. This morning's special delivery.

She held the shorts in front of her. *Gosh, there's nothing of them, but …* She smoothed her fingertips across the fabric and in one swift movement she was standing and unfastening the buttons on the shoulder of her gymslip. Her navy pleated one-piece, a uniform she wore every day, made her who she was and had done for more than ten years as both student, teacher and now Vice Principal. She couldn't help but see her gymslip as a relic of the past compared to these glossy upstarts, harbingers of a new era, masquerading as a pair of shorts.

Is that what she was becoming herself: a relic?

The curtains! Before undressing any further, she reached across her bed to pull them shut and as she did she saw Margaret Wilkins cutting through the fir trees at the edge of the empty playing field. She had a book under her arm. Now there was a young lady who wasn't living in the past.

In Natalie's many years of physical training she'd not yet come across a young lady so dedicated to following her own fancies, wherever they may take her. Margaret Wilkins was a dreamer who thought nothing of skipping anatomy class because it was irrelevant, in her eyes, choosing instead to sit by the river and read a good romance novel. She was a girl who obfuscated her sporting talent with devilry.

But it wouldn't end well. The college didn't reward individuality; the system didn't want change. You either met the expected standard or you were sent packing, and when it happened to Margaret Wilkins, which seemed more and more likely, Natalie feared that she wouldn't be able to save her.

Natalie considered the gymslip hanging around her waist. She was one to talk about breaking the rules. She should be in her office dictating her weekly letters to parents. But how could she be expected to concentrate on her work when the insistent call of that package had been whispering, no yelling, to her from under her bed since it had been delivered that morning? *You'd better be quick then, before someone notices you're gone.*

In the muted daylight she let the heavy tunic drop to her ankles, peeled off her thick woollen stockings, slipped on the blouse and then stepped, barefoot, into the shorts.

She splayed her hands over her exposed legs, redeployed her fingertips to read the zigzagged Braille of the elasticated seams that pinched against the tops of her thighs. Then she twisted her torso to get a good view of the shorts across her behind. She smoothed them again and then lifted her knees to skip lightly on the spot. The fabric glided across her skin with an elegance that spread to her state of mind, her movements, and she added a light bounce at the top of each skip.

Wonderful. But not meant for the likes of her, not really. They were as likely to introduce a uniform like this here at Linshatch College of Physical Education as they were to have a beauty contest; and if she got caught wearing these clothes, well she'd be in more trouble than Margaret Wilkins.

Angling her hand mirror this way and that, she inspected her legs in the shorts. Athletic, sturdy and of course, dove white. She hadn't embraced the new fad for sunbathing; she much preferred to be on the move.

There was a knock at the door and the hand mirror fell to the linoleum floor with a clatter, but she hadn't the time to flip it over and see if it had survived. She dived into bed instead, eyeing the keyhole, with nowhere to hide in her room but under the bedclothes.

'Miss Flacker, are you there?' It was her secretary, Miss Bull. 'Miss Lott wants to see you in her office.'

'Very good. I'll be there right away,' she called back, hoping Miss Bull wouldn't think it odd that she hadn't opened the door to her. 'I was just er ...' There was no explanation to be had. 'I'll be with Miss Lott right away.'

*

The sight of *Olympia* in tram-sized lettering made the hairs on Natalie's arms stand on end. She'd seen pictures in the newspaper last year; Mosley's British Fascist party rally had filled every inch under that hall's giant glass roof. Now it was the turn of the Women's League of Health and Beauty.

311

Tributaries of the League's members jostled into her as they left the station in one giggling river, and were lured across the busy London street to the exhibition hall.

She paused at the top of the underground station's steps. *It's not too late to make a run for it.* She wasn't sure what she feared the most: Miss Lott finding out she'd come here today or her friend Delphi's disappointment if she let her down. She curled her hand into her satchel, felt around for the satin shorts and rubbed them between her thumb and forefinger.

Delphi waited for her by the station entrance. She faced the imposing red-bricked Olympia across the road. Keen to make a good impression today, her friend wore an asymmetrical red felt hat and the feathery tendrils of her hatpin danced in the breeze. Natalie watched as she blotted the bridge of her nose with a puff, then lowered her hand to steady herself on the wall.

Natalie shook her head. Perhaps she should have done more to discourage Delphi from pursuing her idea of becoming a teacher for this increasingly popular movement. Delphi's health made training for a career in physical education difficult, but many years ago they'd made a pact to support one another in their professional life, and she'd be true to her word. Today she would see just what this group was really like, and whether they were a suitable target for her friend's ambitions.

The compact clicked shut. Delphi turned her head; her poppy-red lips spread to a smile.

'There you are, Natty.' She untangled herself from a group of younger girls in her path. 'You look as though you've just arrived at your own funeral.'

'Well, there *is* a risk that you bringing me here has murdered my career.' As she saw Delphi bite her bottom lip, she winked to let her know that she'd been teasing. They linked arms, and joined the stream of women to cross the road.

'This is going to be an education for you. The old establishment is being shaken up, Natty. Imagine if you led that change.'

'I don't think the Board of Education would listen to my ideas.' Natalie sighed as they reached a standstill at the back of the queue. 'They'll argue that their way of doing things has worked very nicely for decades, and it will continue to do so for many more. And they're probably right.'

'Well, today you'll see a different way of doing things.' Delphi steadied her hat as she tilted her head around the older ladies in front of them, searching for acquaintances further up the queue.

They would see and experience enough today to feed the volley of correspondence between the two of them for at least a month.

'And,' Delphi continued, 'I think you'll be impressed. You've always been bothered by the way the Phys Ed colleges exclude girls like the ones here today. The League is for everyone.'

It was true; they were, in the main, privileged girls who trained at her physical education college, and with only five establishments in the whole country places were in demand.

'Do you know what else, Natty?' Delphi poked her in the ribs. 'You're going to see how much *fun* exercise can be.'

'But we get enjoyment from playing lacrosse or cricket, or diving, and you know that.' Natalie thought of the students' ruddy faces out on the playing field on a frosty February morning. *How could Delphi say that they didn't have fun?* She wrote to her often enough to report on the exhilaration she'd felt in the heat of competition, how the bond between the team became as present in the air as the steam from their mouths.

'You did promise to give this a go today.' Delphi looked at her closely.

'Of course, if you're serious about training with these people then I want to see what they're all about.' But Natalie's approval was the least of Delphi's worries. Her ill health put her under her mother's control, and Natalie couldn't imagine Delphi's mother would ever agree to her latest idea. 'I just hope it isn't frivolous.' She'd been taught that exercise *developed good character in testing circumstances* in the words of Madame Forsberg, her college's founder. 'I am worried about the lack of science in their work.'

'Yes, I was a little as well, but times are changing, Natty. You said it yourself, the Board is too wedded to its way of doing things.'

'I didn't exactly say that.' Natalie back-tracked on whatever she might have said in her letters after a bad day at Linshatch. The Board thought the Women's League a bunch of cranks, and called their work unscientific and dangerous. It would take an event as major as another war to persuade them to consider another approach. 'Let's just see whether I think this is right for you.'

'Just don't be too sensible.' She waved, spotting a friend from her training class, and left Natalie alone in the queue.

'There's nothing wrong with being sensible,' Natalie called after her. The woman in front, a good deal older than Natalie, but with curls as luscious as Ginger Rogers', turned to look her up and down.

Natalie was glad she had a moment alone to let the sting of Delphi's remark fade. Yes, she had been prudent when she'd invested her father's inheritance in her teacher training. It had meant she could support herself, but being responsible wasn't always easy, or much fun.

'Quick! The hall is nearly full,' Delphi said as she returned. 'They're expecting two and a half thousand. That's double last year's rally.'

Delphi hooked her by the arm and swept her past the snaking queue. 'My friend Francine is saving us a place near the front.'

Adorned with black kohl, stem-thin eyebrows, Francine took Natalie by surprise with a forceful hug more appropriate for a long-lost friend. Just as they passed through the arched doorway, a man edged by with a sign: *house full*; then his arm formed a barrier just behind Natalie. The whines and tuts of disappointed women faded behind them. Francine's affections, Natalie realised, were short-lived. She'd already run on ahead, leaving the two of them to descend into the bowels of Olympia together.

The open hall teemed with women changing into their Women's League of Health and Beauty uniform. Too late, she realised if she'd put the shorts on under her clothes she wouldn't have needed to reveal her underwear.

'Did you remember to shave your armpits?' Delphi asked.

Natalie nodded.

'Did you apply deodorant?'

'Could you be a little more discreet?' she hissed. But there was such a din that only those changing right next to them would hear anyway. She could hardly make out her own voice. 'I'm sorry,' she said, regretting the tone she'd taken and seeing the funny side to it now. 'My armpits are in perfect order.' The laughter at Delphi's fastidiousness loosened her muscles. The tension she felt from stripping off in a busy room lifted.

An older woman, with flesh spilling over the top of her worn girdle, shunted away from them. *Did she come home from a hard day's work to soak flower petals with baking soda and soap flakes, too? Had her family dined on bread so she could spend her housekeeping on two and six for her annual League membership?*

'Do you think the deodorant matters?' Natalie asked, looking about to check no one was looking at her legs in the shorts. 'The League's instructions for appearance could put undue pressure on the members, don't you think?'

'Not at all,' the older woman butted in. 'How often do you think I get to think about myself and how I look? Not very, I can tell you!'

None of her college students gave a hoot about how their hair was fixed, or whether their gymslip showed their legs in the right manner – well except Margaret Wilkins perhaps. The rest were focused on the victory, on building character.

She looked about her while she waited for Delphi. Compared to these ladies her reputation at the college for being concerned

315

with her appearance was nothing. Her waved jaw-length hair, gripped back from her face at the crown, looked really as dour as a schoolmarm's bun.

Delphi was blotting her nose again. Her hairdo seemed so impractical, with her blond locks fastened in a complicated twist at the nape of her neck. But that wasn't what concerned Natalie. For some inexplicable reason her friend's nose always bubbled with tiny beads of sweat just before one of her sleeping fits. Extremes of emotion, including excitement, were just the things that caused her to black out.

At the sight of the sweat on her friend's nose, apprehension descended on Natalie. *What if Delphi does have a sleeping fit in the midst of all these women?*

'Are you sure this is a good idea?' she whispered in her ear.

'Please don't,' Delphi said with her usual soft defiance, powdering her nose to blot away the perspiration. 'I'm tired of my health holding me back.' She had slipped off her dress and was smoothing down the white V-necked blouse beneath. 'What about your hankie?'

'Blast.'

Natalie had forgotten the handkerchief. The League had been very clear that it must be pressed and placed in the left leg of her elasticated satin shorts. Not that there was much room for anything inside those shorts.

'You'll have to borrow mine if you get upset. They're going to pay tribute to Prunella's mother.'

Prunella Stack, the founder's recently bereaved daughter, was now in charge of the League.

They followed the chattering girls through to the Grand Hall. The hairs on her arms stood tall again. The sweeping latticed glass ceiling, way above them in the heavens, was both a hothouse that at once amplified the chatter of two and a half thousand excited women, while also bringing them closer to the serenity of the clouds above on this grey April day.

She threaded an arm through Delphi's and they smiled at one another, sharing the thrill of the moment, the tingle in the air.

A troop of women brushed past them as they marched up and down behind banners from their home towns or counties; first Portsmouth went by, then Yorkshire was followed by a rowdy group from Yeovil. On either side of the central concourse – the same dimensions as a swimming pool, though broader and longer than anything she'd ever seen – were steep-sided seats for the spectators: the children, sisters, brothers and husbands of the women demonstrating today.

'I want to be near the front,' Delphi said, 'as close to Prunella as possible.'

Natalie held back, noticing the flashbulbs coming from the front. Prunella had been the main topic of many of Delphi's letters, but they had to be practical and not get too close. They'd both told lies so they could be there today. It would do neither of them any good to find themselves pictured in the press, nor would it help Delphi's career prospects if she had a sleeping fit right at the foot of the stage.

Delphi gave up on pushing through when an instruction came for them to sit down. They noisily lowered to the cool concrete floor and sat cross-legged. Delphi and Natalie squeezed into a row in the midst of a group of Scots wearing tartan ribbons on their shoulders, about half a dozen lines from the very front. They had an excellent view of the stage and the three-piece jazz band, but were safe from the photographers, and hidden from view should Delphi take a turn.

Natalie lifted her head and looked all the way behind her at the rows and rows of ladies, all in matching white shirts and black shorts. All with their hair set in waves.

For all their uniformity, the women inside the outfits were much more of a mixture than she'd expected. At her college there was a definite sort of girl who thrived there – she'd been one herself — usually wealthy, or as in her case, with a father in a respectable profession.

These ladies weren't of one sort at all. Some were their age – *surplus women* as the press liked to label them, women like she and Delphi, in their thirties, still single and not much hope of that ever changing. The loss of so many men in the war had seen to that. Not that she'd ever give up the hope of finding a husband. Others around them wore more lines about the eyes, and had rounder hips. *War widows, no doubt.*

All of them, whatever their age or circumstance, had come more out of the need for company than exercise and so for that reason she should fit right in, but still she couldn't shake the feeling that she was wrong to have come.

Prunella, with glowing skin, nape-length bouncy curls and a radiant smile, welcomed them all to this special memorial rally. The rumour in the Phys Ed corridors was that first the Women's League founder, Mary Bagot Stack, and now her daughter, Prunella, the so-called *Perfect Woman*, had made themselves rich on a system of exercise with no grounding in science and no discipline whatsoever. They were simply profiting from lonely women like her and Delphi.

Prunella cocked a hip and bent a long leg as if she were chatting to a friend, not addressing a packed hall. As she spoke she maintained a smile at all times. Even as she wrapped her lips around an 'o', the rest of her face pulled the other way.

It was the newspapers that had given her the moniker the *Perfect Woman*. Natalie and Delphi had discussed in their letters what constituted perfect. The journalists who'd come up with the name were undoubtedly male but even so, Natalie had expected Prunella to be much more athletic. She showed good leadership though and she had charisma too. Perfect or not, she had captivated the Grand Hall.

Wherever she moved at least one photographer crouched in front of her, the flashbulb illuminating her every few moments.

Delphi swooned, her red lips stretched to their limits by her smile. She was so happy and that had to be a good thing. Her illness had a habit of ruling her life.

Prunella's voice echoed about the hall as she told them of her mother's dying wish. How she'd hoped her work with the Women's League of Health and Beauty, and her aims for spreading peace and cooperation, would continue.

A bugle blew behind Prunella. The resounding cheers faded as the lights dimmed, and their collective heads bowed. Delphi had warned her this display would be sad and yet still a tingle travelled along her spine. The tribute to Prunella's mother was to be the Representation of War that she'd helped choreograph for the previous year's rally.

First came the deathly rattle of the drum. Next the women erupted into the shrill whistle of 'Tipperary'. Then the drums retaliated with a rat-a-tat-tat, before the assault of the bugles and then the women won the battle with the unity of their voices. The hairs on her arms betrayed her for the third time that day as a slow procession of women criss-crossed the stage; some bandaged, one a white strip bound around her eyes, feeling the air in front of her.

The sight of one woman as she propped up another, drunk with pain, clogged her throat with a fist-sized lump. She'd imagined her two brothers had been there for each other at the end in that same way. The idea that they hadn't died alone had been a story she'd had to believe. One small island of consolation in an ocean of grief.

She wished she'd remembered to bring that damned handkerchief to tuck in her left short leg now. Delphi stroked the back of Natalie's arm and then opened her palm to proffer her own crumpled hankie. The two of them held hands while Natalie blotted her eyes.

'Isn't it wonderful?' Delphi whispered.

*

The dance demonstration came to an end and they all began to march in formation. Each large group of them made up the spokes of a wheel. It put her in mind of the photograph she'd seen in *The Times* of last year's Nazi rally in Nuremberg where they'd formed a human swastika.

'What do you think?' Delphi asked as they marched, knees high.

'It's more ordered than I expected, but it does feel rather that they've plucked their ideas out of the air.'

'Just look how happy everyone is.' They both checked along the line as they rotated.

They often came to blows on this matter. Delphi's ideas were a little more abstract when it came to the benefits of physical exercise.

Delphi had stopped a few times to catch her breath during the dance and now as they marched she didn't look too well. She smiled and opened her eyes wide each time Natalie caught her gaze, as if to say, *there's nothing to see here.* But her nose was beading in sweat; her forget-me-not blue eyes had clouded over. All was clearly not well.

As the hall full of women sat to watch the choreographed cabaret on the stage, Natalie saw Delphi's knees buckle. She made up her mind in that instant to take advantage of the pause.

'What on earth are you doing?' Delphi asked as Natalie took her hand and led her down a covered walkway that stretched from the stage area and through to a dark corridor lined with doors. 'Peggy St Lo choreographed that routine,' she slurred. 'I want to see it.'

'You don't look well.' Natalie swung open the first door that she came to. She had just enough time to flick the electric light switch and illuminate the drab clothes hanging from a hat stand and the horizontal mirror edged with light bulbs, before Delphi's legs buckled again. Like a puppet with its strings cut, sleep triumphed and she piled to the floor. Natalie slowed her fall as much as she could and then crouched beside her. There was a tatty knitted polo-neck on the back of the dressing-table chair, which she smoothed over her.

Natalie watched and waited. She was still the same beautiful Delphi in every way except her jaw was clenched, and she was asleep on the floor. Natalie didn't touch her. Sometimes in these fits she was actually still awake, but trapped by the paralysis of her own body. Natalie's touch would be leaden to her.

She looked at her watch. So much for the quick escape after the rally. She'd promised Miss Lott that she'd check on the girls at the college's ten o'clock curfew, but Delphi would be in no fit state to get the tram home by herself. The changing room had its own telephone on a stand, next to a vase of carnations. That was their first bit of luck because she was going to have to call up Delphi's younger brother, Jack.

*

'Oh, I'm terribly sorry.' Prunella Stack twitched her head and backed out of the room, checking the name plaque on the door. 'I thought I was in my changing room.'

'No, no, it is. That's to say ...' Natalie found herself unusually tongue-tied.

'I was feeling a bit light-headed ...' Delphi explained. Her voice still groggy with sleep.

'... So I brought her inside for a rest.'

Delphi had come around twenty minutes ago and she'd grown cold and was now wearing the polo-neck jumper while they waited for her brother, Jack, to arrive and drive them home.

'Oh, you poor dear,' Prunella cooed as Delphi and Natalie introduced themselves and shook hands. There was a kerfuffle at the door. A photographer tried to push his way in; the flashbulb went, and a woman with dark hair sent him packing.

'These newspaper photographers become a nuisance after a

while,' Prunella explained. 'You were taken ill during the demonstration, I recall? I saw you leave; you looked terribly pale.'

'Oh it was nothing.' Delphi flushed red. 'I was giddy with excitement. I want to train with you, you see.'

Natalie made for the door. They would wait for Jack in the corridor. She regretted sneaking out of the college to come here as it was; to now be meeting Prunella Stack was one dance with the devil too many. But Delphi hadn't even let go of the woman's hand. She was under her spell, and at close quarters Natalie could see why.

'Well I hope we didn't make you overexert yourself with the demonstration.' Prunella wore a look of concern as she asked her Aunt Norah to fetch both of the visitors a glass of water and told Natalie to sit down. 'Our teachers are a lot fitter than they might look. It's all too easy to expect too much of our members.'

Natalie laughed at Prunella's suggestion; she couldn't help herself. Delphi nudged her in the ribs and she stopped, but it was too late. She had piqued Prunella's interest. The other woman leant against the dressing table, her long slender legs and bare feet stretching out in front of her, her face upturned and serious, inviting Natalie to explain her mirth.

'I'm a physical training teacher, that's all,' Natalie explained, but the sharp gaze coming from Delphi told her that her tone was a little too heavy with pomposity. 'Actually I'm the Vice Principal at Linshatch College of Physical Education. I suppose, I just wouldn't say …' She stopped herself before she said too much and offended Prunella.

'What wouldn't you say?' Prunella enquired after a moment's silence.

'Well …no …it's nothing.'

'I'm interested,' Prunella said. 'You don't have to worry about offending us.'

She thought of her promise to Delphi to *give it a go*, and *keep an open mind*, and she had done that. Besides, Prunella's smile

322

was warm and friendly and made her feel there was nothing to fear in being honest.

'Very well then.' She cleared her throat. 'I was surprised at what you said about your instructors, that's all. Your activities – I just didn't find them terribly invigorating.'

'I see,' Prunella said with a sniff. The smile had evaporated. Delphi delivered another nudge in her side.

Aunt Norah, whose jet-black hair rose up from her forehead like the fat end of a cream horn, had returned with two glasses of water and had overheard Natalie's credentials. 'You probably know that we're trying to gain national recognition for the League,' she said, addressing Natalie, 'but we're finding the Board of Education is rather a closed shop and wedded to the methods employed by the colleges.'

'I'm sure Natty could help …'

'I'm sorry, but I really couldn't.' Natalie clasped her hands in front of her. Their pact to support one another's ambitions didn't extend to sabotaging one career for the advancement of the other.

'Could you offer any advice?' Norah pressed her.

Natalie looked to Delphi. She was just smiling and encouraging her to say something charming, but if these women deserved anything, then it was the truth.

'The problem is that the establishment puts a lot of faith in science and it's because of that scientific grounding that we know that our methods work, you see.' She paused. Aunt Norah had folded her arms at that last remark. 'I was curious to come along today. I must admit I have heard some suspicious rumours about you, but Delphi is quite taken with her classes and wants to train as an instructor. And I did have a lovely day out …' She paused again, hoping the conversation might take a different turn, but they both still looked at her with expectation. 'At the end of it all, I am left wondering whether without rigour and discipline, is this really educational?'

Prunella's smile had grown over-ripe and was beginning to sour.

'The ladies have had fun today.' Prunella almost punched out the words. 'You said it yourself. Our classes lift spirits and let women express themselves through movement ...'

'Absolutely,' Delphi murmured.

'Mmm.' Natalie scratched her neck. 'But none of that is ...' Stalled by the fear of making things worse she came back to the same word '... educational. I mean what has anybody actually learnt today?'

'Oh, Natty!' Delphi shook her head. 'You were moved to tears today.'

'Yes but that's not exercise as I know it ... Miss Stack, in my view it's bordering on artistic poppycock.'

She saw Prunella's eyes widen.

'What she means to say is ...'

'It's all right.' Prunella held up a hand. 'We come from different worlds. And we've heard worse, much worse. Our methods are based on exercises used in India for many hundreds of years. What's more, the number of women here today means more to us than the support of the Board of Education. Now, if you think you're feeling quite well,' she said to Delphi, 'perhaps you and your friend wouldn't mind ...'

Keen to comply with Prunella's request, and mindful that she'd spoiled what should have been Delphi's moment to create a good impression, Natalie rushed to the door and opened it while looking behind for Delphi to follow, and in doing so she collided with the chest of a man in the corridor.

'Steady on, Natty!' The man held her in his arms. It took her a moment to realise it was Delphi's brother, Jack, come to take them home. 'Knight in shining armour at your service.' He winked.

She pulled herself free, stepping back to take him in. This was the first time she'd seen him since he'd returned from living in America, and what a difference those seven years had made. His hair – more of a white blond than she'd remembered – flopped forwards over the side of his forehead and lightly fringed his lively eyes. She appeared to be frozen to the spot by the blue of them.

'Hello, Jack,' Delphi said with a sigh. 'Are you here to take Cinderella back to her scullery?'

'Keep the jumper.' Prunella addressed Delphi, and then as Natalie reached the door, she said, 'Discipline or not, we run the League on good intentions and a rather frayed shoestring. In regards to the things you've heard, I'd be grateful if you could quash any rumours you hear about us profiteering. We actually barely turn a profit at all.'

They walked down the corridor shrouded in an uncomfortable silence, Jack looking from one of them to the other as if trying to guess who would speak first.

'Mother's snake venom didn't work then?' He tried a joke, a reference to Mrs Mulberry's attempt at finding a cure for Delphi's illness with a tonic she had purchased from the reptile curator at London Zoo. Neither of them found it funny.

'That was just the foot up my career needed,' Delphi said eventually, once they were far enough away to be out of earshot. 'I can't possibly apply for a place on their instructor training course now.'

'I'll put it right,' Natalie called after her as Delphi stomped on ahead and then slowed again as her tiredness caught a hold of her.

'And how will you do that, exactly?' Delphi shook her head in exasperation and took Jack's arm to steady her.

Natalie had no idea, but she was going to have to think of something.

Dear Reader,

Thank you so much for reading *The Land Girl*. I really loved researching and creating this story and if you enjoyed reading it I would very much appreciate it if you left a review online.

Reviews really help a new book, and the author, and are so useful for helping prospective readers to see whether a book might appeal to them. It need only take a moment and be a word or two.

If you have any questions about the book or you're interested to hear what I'm working on next, please find me on my Facebook author page. The link is below.

Thank you!

Allie x

https://www.facebook.com/AllieBurnsAuthor

Dear Reader,

Thank you so much for taking the time to read this book – we hope you enjoyed it! If you did, we'd be so appreciative if you left a review.

Here at HQ Digital we are dedicated to publishing fiction that will keep you turning the pages into the early hours. We publish a variety of genres, from heartwarming romance, to thrilling crime and sweeping historical fiction.

To find out more about our books, enter competitions and discover exclusive content, please join our community of readers by following us at:

🐦 *@HQDigitalUK*

🔲 *facebook.com/HQDigitalUK*

Are you a budding writer? We're also looking for authors to join the HQ Digital family! Please submit your manuscript to:

HQDigital@harpercollins.co.uk.

Hope to hear from you soon!

ONE PLACE. MANY STORIES

ONE PLACE. MANY STORIES

If you enjoyed *The Land Girl*, then why not try another sweeping historical from HQ?